Mother of Serpents

John R Gordon

Published February 2025 by Team Angelica Publishing,
an imprint of Angelica Entertainments Ltd

Team Angelica Publishing
51 Coningham Road
London W12 8BS

TEAM
ANGELICA

www.teamangelica.com

A CIP catalogue record for this book is available from
the British Library

ISBN 978-1-7397739-3-9

Cover image by Boris Mitkov
Model: Urbain Hayo

Rikki Beadle-Blair, Diriye Osman, Patrik-Ian Polk,
Larry Duplechan, Mark Foster & Kate Farquharson

Thank you

"The function, the very serious function of racism is distraction."

– Toni Morrison

Kita, kita, kita
Bind and bind and bind
This lady, this madahôdo
To this hunting ground

Prologue: Eight Documents

1.

Excerpted from Folkloric Curiosities of Kwawidokawa County *by J. Wentworth Walker, © Collington-Osprey County Library Press, 1914, 77pp, stapled mimeographed booklet. From Chapter Three, "A Hamlet Without a Name and a Snake Charmer" (p24):*

[]...the aforementioned series of violent incidents and unnatural acts reaching the ears of the authorities, the remaining inhabitants, by then reduced to no more than eight families, were removed from the vicinity, both for their own safety and for the safety of others, by State Troopers on May 17, 1892. Several of the children alleged to be missing remained, and as of this writing remain, unaccounted for. However, in the absence of proper record-keeping – baptisms and even births being noted only irregularly following the retirement through ill health of the resident pastor around 1870 – it is possible they did not in fact exist, one child perhaps being confused with another by a mentally failing parent *in extremis*.

The tiny hamlet, which was thereafter wholly abandoned, has since been suffered to fall down entirely, a process accelerated by those hardy souls from nearby, newly-established Gauge Village, who, after several years had elapsed, found the courage to approach and carry off whatever they thought useful. This included stoves and hoes, forks and shovels, boards, shingles and timbers, but not pots, kettles or pans, through fear that such items had been tainted by some substance in the well-water, lead or some other heavy metal – science by then having to a large extent supplanted the Puritan superstitions of those earlier times in which the hamlet was first established, though never, either then or later, graced with a name.

Because they were built of lathe and plaster rather than brick, by the turn of the century little trace of the buildings remained, and the wilderness soon reclaimed entirely that small and nameless place where men had flickeringly established a fleeting toe-hold. This the writer of these words himself confirmed when, from scholarly duty, he reconnoitered the area. It is to be noted that none of the original inhabitants – those few, that is, who could be rehabilitated sufficiently to reënter society – chose to return there subsequently to the events of 1892, most preferring to move altogether away and start over.

An odd tale that some recall concerns the appearance, sometime in the late 1880s, it seems by invitation, though the circumstances are likely to remain unclear, in the community of the itinerant preacher Nehemiah Light. A Southerner who brought with him the then novel practice of snake handling, Light avowed that the pure of heart could, without being harmed, drink what was bled from the serpents' fangs, and, quoting from the Gospel of Mark, 16:17-18, declared,

"And these signs shall follow them that believe: in my name shall they cast out devils; they shall speak with new tongues. They shall take up serpents; and if they drink any deadly thing it shall not hurt them. They shall lay hands on the sick, and they shall recover."

Though he achieved a measure of popularity in a community by then inbred, poverty-stricken and despairing, the preacher's convictions did not prevent him sickening from the consumption of contaminated wellwater as had the others. By the time he was removed in the intervention of 1892, owing to incipient cretinism he was unable to remember his own name, and only a basket of starved and mummified rattlesnakes found under his bed, along with a handful of personal letters from a distant cousin, testified as to his identity.

(The foregoing was transcribed from several loose pages purchased for 25¢ at a yard sale in Gaugeville, ME. The rest

of the pamphlet is lost – excepting the copyright page, the contents page [on which chapter titles are listed], and the cover, which is of pale blue card, and on its front features, in addition to title and author, an outline map of Kwawi-dokawa County in black ink.)

2.

Transcript of an incident, 09/09/86.

Collington-Osprey PD

Case number: #1002323
Reporting officer: Edward Cutler
Report entered: 09/10/86, 08:45 a.m.
Prepared by: [omitted]
Report date: 09/09/86   Report time: 11:58 p.m.

Incident type(s):

Code 187 -- murder
Code 192(a) -- manslaughter
Code 245 -- assault with a deadly weapon (ax)
Code 11350 -- possession narcotic controlled substances
Code 11550 -- under influence/controlled substances
Code 273 -- assault on child/spouse/cohabitant
Code 273(a) -- child endangerment

Occurrence address:

13. Cottonwood Way, Gaugeville Bounds, Gaugeville, Kwawidokawa County, Maine M.E.

Offender(s):

Nancy Mary HANCOCK -- address residence as above -- d.o.b. 03/06/63 age 23 years

Victim(s):

Richard hereafter "Rick" <u>DYER</u> -- address as above -- d.o.b. 01/05/63 age 23 years

Thomas Richard hereafter "Tommy" <u>HANCOCK DYER</u> -- address as above -- age approx. 5 years

Narrative of events

Telephone calls were made by several callers commencing shortly before 12 midnight through 12:30 a.m. morning 09/10/86 complaining of domestic disturbance at residence <u>13 COTTONWOOD WAY</u> Gaugeville Bounds, Gaugeville. This was followed approx. 10 mins later by reports of yelling and screaming in the woods back of the property. Callers identified themselves as 1) <u>MEHITABEL PORTER</u>, living directly opposite, 2) <u>ANN MILLER</u>, resident 3 doors away at no. 7. Callers 3), 4) and 5) declined ID, citing fear of reprisals from the inhabitants of 13 Cottonwood Way or their associates.

The address is known to the police and has several times been under observation due to suspected traffic in controlled substances (see attached reports #1000301--3, filed 05/08/84, 10/11/84, 09/03/85; no charges entered). Owing to the stated presence of a minor in the residence (<u>THOMAS RICHARD</u>), officers <u>E. CUTLER</u> (lead) and <u>J. WYMAN</u> were priority dispatched to 13 Cottonwood Way at 12:07 a.m. 09/10/86. Calls from nearby residents continued to come in after this time that the disturbances were continuing (see attached list)* though added no new information.

(*list missing)

Narrative of responding officer EDWARD CUTLER

Officer Wyman and myself, responding to the initial noise complaint of yelling, screaming and smashing up, reached the above address approx. 12:45 a.m. The residence, a two story house, is one of the oldest in Gaugeville Bounds, a generally quiet, rundown area two miles to the west of the town of Gaugeville, which is somewhat of a tourist "hotspot" due to the lake, trails and recreational amenities. Vacationers visiting the lake area have brought increased drug traffic to the locality in recent years. The house, which is spacious with 4 bedrooms including a nursery, appears somewhat neglected, is the last on the right and backs onto the deep woods.

Despite the late hour, the lights were all on and the front door stood open. A white Chevrolet Corvette was parked at an angle in the driveway, suggesting possible intoxication on part of the driver (vehicle property of <u>RICK DYER</u>: license plate/reg. details appended. No wants). There was no sight or sound of activity within the house. Several neighbors in nightclothes were standing on porches or looking from windows with the drapes pulled back. For reasons of safety I gestured them to go back inside/step back from windows.

Drawing our weapons and announcing our presence, Officer Wyman and myself entered the residence through the open front door and made a brief search of all rooms, first downstairs, then the upper story. No one was present, including the known child. The residence seemed generally well-maintained and in good order, with no narcotics or narcotics paraphernalia in evidence, however the kitchen had apparently been the site of a recent violent event, with furniture overturned, plates and glassware smashed, blinds torn down and the kitchen door broken in in a way indicative of a possible home invasion (the kitchen is to the rear of the house, the kitchen door is to the side, with steps down to a small yard with clothes lines, a tall hedge screens it from neighbors). This evidence of forced entry strengthened our suspicion that a drug transaction gone wrong could be at bottom of it, with the residents and their child maybe abducted from the location by (most likely) rival drug dealers or (possibly) dissatisfied (but still potentially violent) customers into the woods for purposes of intimidation or worse.

Exiting the residence by the route we had entered through, we crossed to the residence of MEHITABEL DYER, [error in transcript, corrected by hand: "should read PORTER"] opposite. Opening the door to us, she indicated she had seen no vehicles arrive at or depart from the residence that evening ("Even when I was off my porch I would have heard," she stated), and that she had seen no one exit from the front of the house at any point, but further stated that after the initial disturbance she had heard screaming and yelling from out back. Ms. Porter used the words "way back" to indicate she meant the woods, rather than the backyard. I asked were the raised voices male or female and she said both. She said several times "it's a bad house." I asked did she mean drugs and she said "No--unlucky." She affirmed that living there were <u>RICK DYER</u>, his common-law wife <u>NANCY</u> and their son <u>TOMMY</u>, age uncertain, she thought 4 or 5 years, and that the car in the driveway belonged to Dyer.

With weapons drawn we made our way to the rear of the residence by the right-hand side (facing). The backyard was deserted. We crossed to a gap in the back fence where pickets had been knocked down from the outer side and entered the woods. In front of us was a trail with when we examined it by flashlight brush recently trodden down. A short way along, in the middle of the trail we came upon a discarded child's shoe. With this indicating the likely abduction of the child or at least the mother fleeing in fear we proceeded with renewed urgency.

The sky was clear and the moon was full and up so we could follow the trail without use of our flashlights. Unsure what we might be going to come across, which could include armed rival drug dealers intent on beating and even murdering those they had taken away, for so long as we could we kept our flashlights turned off. We heard no sounds of any sort but continued to follow the trail, in the absence of other information on which to base a decision taking the larger of any divide we came to. The woods there are dense so we could not see far ahead, maybe ten feet, though we would have seen a light source ex. a flashlight or lamp at a greater distance. I indicated to Off. Wyman that we turn our radios to silent so as not to alert anyone concealed in the darkness close by to our presence. After going on this way for approx. 15 minutes

Officer Wyman and myself paused briefly to discuss with quiet voices radioing for more officers, because with more manpower we could carry out a faster and more wide-ranging search--our motive at that point being concern for the missing/possibly abducted child. However we decided to "give it 10 minutes more" and went on along the main trail. Approx. 5 mins later we entered a clearing, at which point we encountered both offender NANCY MARY HANCOCK (age 23 years) and victims RICHARD "RICK" DYER (age 23 years) and THOMAS "TOMMY" RICHARD (age approx. 5/6 years).

Rick Dyer and Thomas Richard were laying on the ground and did not appear to be moving. With only moonlight to see by, the extent or seriousness of their wounds was initially impossible to ascertain, and also because they were 20 feet away from where we were stood.

Nancy was faced towards us, holding a large ax in both hands as if ready for use, and standing between the bodies and myself and Officer Wyman. I observed the blade of the ax appeared stained with something dark. Nancy's expression was vacant, it appeared she was in some sort of narcotic stupor or possibly shock. She is of slender build with small hands and appeared to struggle with the weight of the ax. Keeping his weapon trained on her, Officer Wyman instructed her to lower the ax to the ground. As if relieved of a burden, she complied with his order, then stood with her arms loose at her sides, her hands open with the palms turned towards us. She wore a pale blue floral pattern nightdress to mid calf, had on no makeup, her feet were bare and she did not meet our eyes, instead staring off into space.

With Officer Wyman keeping Nancy securely at gunpoint, I came forward to assist the adult male Rick Dyer and the child Thomas Richard ("Tommy"), turning on my flashlight in order to do so. I now saw the adult male had serious ax-wounds to the head and had sustained significant blood loss. He wore blue denim jeans, white tennis shoes and a pink tank top. I cannot comment on what style his hair may have been, owing to the injuries. The wounds were to a level I did not check for a pulse. Around his lips was a greenish foam mixed in with what appeared to be clots of blood, suggesting a possible internal hemorrhage due to ingesting a corrosive substance.

I next examined the boy. He wore blue pajamas with elephants on them and had a "bowl" haircut. He had not been struck by the ax but was also non-responsive and appeared to me to have been overdosed and had some sort of violent fatal seizure. I observed on his neck a large syringe-type puncture wound through which the drugs had likely been introduced into his system. Black lines spread out from the puncture under his skin in all directions to about 4" circumference. I have seen OD's (overdoses) before but this was somewhat different owing to the black threads, which more followed nerves than blood vessels. Tommy's lips were coated with foam and vomit and I concluded from my cursory examination that his father had been attempting CPR/mouth-to-mouth resuscitation when he had been struck by the ax from behind. I felt for a pulse but could not discover one. Bar the fact of his sudden violent death he appeared well cared for.

I informed Officer Wyman that both victims were deceased and radioed the situation in, calling for R.N., ambulance etc., giving our location in the woods as well as I could.*

[*Appended to the report is a handwritten note by Officer Wyman: "Laying nearby as if thrown aside was a large leather suitcase/sack/steamer trunk of a size to contain an adult or child's body, torn or burst open from inside. It was odd shaped, without hinges or catches, making me think of what fishermen call a "mermaids purse" (dogfish egg) but was empty so I left it. JW"]

Officer Wyman and myself then turned our attention to Nancy Hancock. She is a pretty girl, and I remembered she had been Homecoming Queen of her year. Though stuporous she did not have the usual signs of drug addiction in terms of self-neglect, poor skin, excessive skinniness, bad teeth or the addict's "twitch." In fact her hair was in a fashionable "poodle cut" style, though wrapped in a headscarf for the night as if she had gotten out of bed and gone in the woods without stopping to dress.

I first asked her what she had taken, but she was non-responsive, as she was when I asked if she knew where she was or what had happened. Deciding she needed a jolt to "bring her out of it" I took her by the arm and led her over to the bodies of her common law husband and child. [Note: I was not 100%

certain at this point that he was her son and not another child, though this was confirmed later by photographs in the house, pinned to the refrigerator.]

On being confronted by the bodies Nancy appeared confused and somewhat upset and muttered something about her mother and that it was her mother's fault. Suspect then stated that her mother had come out of the woods, "risen up," and told her that she (Nancy) must "do it." Due to the unlikeliness of this statement I assumed it to be a hallucination induced by drugs. I asked what was her mother's name and she replied, "Mother Poison." I then asked "Do what?" and she said "kill him," indicating Rick Dyer.

I then asked her "what about the child." She appeared to "come to" as if seeing her son for the first time and commenced to scream in a piercing register which seemed to me more of an animal noise than expressive of true emotion, until after some minutes I had to slap her to quiet her down.

Suspect then said "I didn't do it. It was her. Mother Poison. She wanted to ~~take her away~~." [corrected by hand: "take him away."] She said this several times. I took Mother Poison to be a drug slang which I did not know. I asked was it her or Rick who injected Tommy, or some other person not present. She repeated "It was her" but I remained convinced she was not referring to an actual person but to a delusion in her head. When I asked her what drugs had been taken/used and where obtained, she once more became non-responsive. I judged that she had "wised up" that she was in a lot of trouble. Other officers/R.N. reached us approx. 40 mins after my initial calling it in. Nancy kept singing a nursery rhyme to herself but I do not recall the words.

3.

From North Maine weekly The Collington-Osprey Sentinel, *10/12/86**

"'It's drugs is what it is' – a local tragedy"
by T. E. Pierce

The quiet, normally staid community of Gauge-ville Bounds, Kwawidokawa County, has been rocked by a family tragedy that left a young father and his five-year-old son dead, a mother institu-tionalized. Rick Dyer, 23, was a former star quar-terback, Nancy Hancock, 23, a cheerleader and homecoming beauty queen. Both popular young people, they attracted many signatures for their high school yearbooks and are fondly remem-bered by fellow students, who called the college sweethearts "bright," "nice" and "attractive." Rick "loved cars," Nancy was "a natural home maker." But somehow, something went wrong.

Setting up house together straight out of high school, Nancy quickly bore the young couple a son, Tommy. After a promising start, Rick, who had acquired a reputation for being quick-tem-pered, struggled to hold down a job, and financial difficulties for the young family soon led to an in-volvement with narcotics – first using, then deal-ing – alongside noisy domestic disputes that led to the police being called to the old-fashioned home on Cottonwood Way on more than one oc-casion. "It was quiet until they moved in," said a neighbor, who asked not to be identified. "They had people over at all hours."

Nancy's mother, Denise Flint Hancock, 44, told *The Sentinel* that Nancy was "a good girl but fragile, easily upset. Rick was on drugs and he got her into drugs too. They were always short of money, and they fought over everything. In my mind I think she was planning to leave Rick and take Tommy with her, and that led him to lethally inject Tommy, to punish her. I think she struck him with the axe to try and save her son."

Nancy is currently in a catatonic state and is undergoing medical evaluation at the Dorothea Dix Psychiatric Center in Bangor.

When asked about the remark Nancy was reported to have made, "Mother told me to do it," Denise replied strongly, "It's drugs is what it is. Drug madness. Certainly I wanted her to leave Rick, he was nothing but bad for her, but no way would I ever even say anything like that. No way," she repeated for emphasis, adding, "I just want my little girl to get well."

A curiosity of the case is the statement in the coroner's report that no evidence of proscribed substances was found in the bloodstreams of either mother or child, though the report goes on to state that Tommy's death was the result of an injection of "a lethal mixture" of mercury and a combination of neurotoxins and cardiotoxins, "suggesting perhaps some new, as yet unfamiliar recreational high." Rick Dyer was found to have ingested substantial quantities of cannabis and methamphetamine in the hours prior to his death by axe-blow to the head. Peculiarly, given the mildness of the weather for the time of year, all three were found to be in the preliminary stages of frostbite, Nancy later losing her right little toe to the condition.

Nancy Hancock currently faces multiple charges of manslaughter, malicious wounding and child endangerment. Due to her mental state it is unclear whether she will ever be found fit to stand trial. **

(*The Collington-Osprey Sentinel, *later just* The Sentinel, *ceased publication in 1992. Archives are available online at* *www.collingtonospreysentinel.org.net.*

**Subsequently appended, top righthand corner, by an unknown hand, prior to digital scanning: "Nancy M. Hancock dob 3.6.63 died renal failure May 3 2007 DDPC"*)*

4.

An article from The New England Journal of Genetics and Genomics, *Volume 36, Issue IV, Winter 1986:*

Rapid-Onset Dyschromosomal Mongoloidism: A Case Study in Kwawidokawa County, Maine by A. L. Sullavan, MD

Child A was first brought to my office by his concerned mother on June 5, 1986. I had been the family physician since his birth and had previously found him a very normal boy with an IQ perhaps a little better than average, who hit developmental milestones at very much the expected times. However, aged 5 years and 3 months, he presented at my office with a highly unusual set of abnormalities that I have provisionally labeled Rapid-Onset Dyschromosomal Mongoloidism (RODM). Not only had Child A become markedly less mentally responsive and physically dynamic in the preceding week, the mother informed me that the features of his face had noticeably softened, becoming rounder, less distinct, in appearance similar to a child suffering from severe Mongoloidism (Down's Syndrome, DS). In all my previous interactions with Child A, his appearance, bone structure and general muscle tone (which is usually lacking in DS) had been entirely normal.

Over the three months following the initial presentation, Child A's mother brought him in biweekly, during which the effect became increasingly pronounced, the reduction of "personality" more apparent, and the mother increasingly distressed. I ran all standard screening tests to ensure no drugs, whether illegal or prescribed, or toxins were present in Child A's system. Results for these were entirely negative. Consequently, I arranged for a CAT scan and EEG. These both yielded results within the normal range, and evidenced no brain trauma or defect that could plausibly account for the sudden mental degradation. Since there were no prior scans with which to compare them, I arranged for further scans to be made in order to establish a baseline from which to track the progression of the RODM, however the mother, perhaps disappointed by my reluctance to prescribe any course of treatment ahead of a clear diagnosis, failed to attend these appointments.

On my last contact with the mother, which was in late September of that year, I was informed that she had withdrawn Child A from kindergarten, as she said the other children were making fun of, or scared of him; also that other parents had begun to warn her off, afraid of what might be a previously unknown, possibly infectious and clearly extremely serious childhood disease. Consequently, I approached the kindergarten and, with the support of a concerned administration, was able to ascertain there were no other cases of RODM present, nor have any similar cases been brought to my attention subsequently.

(Appended is a handwritten note in blue ballpoint on lined paper, undated and by an unknown author, apparently a journalist: "Rather disheartening to find Down's Syndrome referred to as 'Mongoloidism' & those with Down's as 'suffering' from it in a reputable medical journal as late as 1986. Since DS is caused by the presence of a 3rd copy of chromosome 21 the term 'dyschromosomal' is nonsense here. I contacted Dr. Sullivan *[sic; passim]* through the editor & he wrote me he had photographic evidence of the rapid change in Child A's physiognomy but said he didn't want to send copies through the mails, he claimed out of concern for the privacy of the family & the child, who he also said had since died. Attempted to arrange to meet up with Sullivan & see the photos but my follow-up letters (to a box number not a residential address) went unanswered. Used internet to do some digging & found a possibly similar case in Kanata, a suburb of Ottawa, Ontario, c. 1919, but too poorly documented to confirm the existence of the condition (never mind support [or contradict] any of S's analysis of its etiology). Forwarded copies of what I found to Sullivan but he didn't reply to that either."*)*

5.

Here is presented the only extant letter written by Nehemiah Light, likely to his sister Eleanor, undated, c. 1890.

Dearest E.,

I know I have Offended many in our Congregation through the Sudden Manner of my Departure, but when a man hath a Calling it means he is Called; & being a man of God, as I hope & believe I am, & alert to the Siren song of that Old Serpent Satan as any other such, he cannot refuse the Summons when it comes to him both Loud and Clear; though Others, doubting, may confuse a Divine Vision with a Mere Dream and rest content, thereby Excused, or so they tell theirselfs, until that Final Day when no excuses shall suffice. For it seems to me truth that Men are more often possessed of a forked Tongue than was the Serpent in the Garden; and that the Serpent may be a Woman also; and Slanders spread like brush fire in a Dry Summer while the toiling Godly are bent to Prayer, and True Faith calumnied as Madness, as I have been, but I know what Madness is, and What it is Not.

The Journey here hath taxed my sparse reserves 'til none remains. Please Send On such money as you are able to support this Inspired Endeavor post haste and Post Restante to the Address writ on Back of this envelope, which is the General Store and Trustworthy. The plowshare & mule may be sold, Excepting not to Joseph Brown by reason of Things Known which I shall not write here.

Yr. Brother in Christ,

Nem

(Source: archives of the Ophitic Church of Christ To Come, www.occtc.org.net)

6.

From Dying Dreams Caught in Glass: a Deconstruction of C17ᵗʰ North Maine Witch Trial Transcripts, *unpublished doctoral thesis, Paloma K. Osterberger, 2015. While the bulk of the thesis is a fairly unrewarding mass of then-fashionable psychoanalytic and postmodern talking points mostly derived from Deleuze, Lacan, Foucault, Baudrillard and Pollock, an endnote to* Chapter 3: To Sleep, Perchance To Dream, *cites text from, and incorporates a photocopy of, what appears to be a page from an unknown C17ᵗʰ manuscript. Both title and author are unattributed – part of the somewhat slapdash approach to correct citation that mars and devalues the thesis throughout. However, internal evidence suggests the manuscript is authentic to the – probably later – C17ᵗʰ. Without context, little more can be said.*

[]...elderly and without anny living relations and besides illiterate, her name was given variously in the Record as Jane, at times Janet Barre, or Barry, or Barray, or Bar, & it was said of her most curiously that she had Bewitched certain persons to walk up & down at night, just that & nothing more, yet so fatigued did they become that it was to them a great burthen. Where they walk'd they did not afterwards recall, but the trails they left could be seen by all, from door to door and Elsewhere, and at nights end, where the pathways circled back all ways it was from the Left that they departed, and returning Right, which is called by the Common People widdershins, the Meaning and Significance of which is widely known.

Matters came to light in this fashion. Discomposed by the many of his congregants Slumb'ring thro' his Sermons, after some time the vex'd pastor of the District, on hearing the claim'd reason for their Inattention and seeking guidance, writ too a Man of Knowledge and Expertise. This person, upon visiting the Hamlet, in his turn confirm'd the Worthy Divine's suspicions anent the presence of a witch amidst his parishioners, with Jane Bar, by reason of her age and habits of Seclusion and Uncleanliness, a most Likely Candidate.

When brought before the ad hoc Court for Examination by the Magistrate, for it is but a small hamlet of an dozen families or so, Jane, though considered by many deficient in wits, spoke readily and it appears loquaciously, if not in truth with Overmuch sense or clarity, of a coven or conclave that gathered in the woods when the Moon was full, whose fellow members she averred were to her strangers, with at its head a Tall Lady, forbidding in manner, cloak'd and hooded in grey.

When pressed concerning this Lady, Jane insisted she did not know her; that she, the Lady, had first come to her in a dream and taught her words to say, foodstuffs to abjure, and Heavenly Conjunctions to follow. Jane offer'd no explanation as to the Lady's purpose, nor remembered any of the strange words in which she had been instructed; nor could she say (the which claim her inquisitors struggled to believe) whether this personage was, in the manner of her speech, ill- or well-bred.

Asked at the last when it was she had pledged her Soul to Satan, the Account I have read gives it that Jane answered ramblingly and grossly, in summary, as put down by the clerk, saying of the Evil One that he had a member like a serpent, and in his knowing of her it was cold as an icicle, and that Hell was in no ways an Inferno, but entirely cold, and not below as all believe but up in the sky. When I sought to enquire as to *[page ends]*

(Though the phrase "at the last" suggests condemnation following confession [however that confession was obtained: the disjunction between the first part of Jane's account and the summarized – and theologically conventional – second is striking] and consquently, we might therefore plausibly presume, execution, no charge of witchcraft is recorded against any person with any variant of the names given in the above account in any extant court document in New England.

Side-note: Osterberger, who had a history of mental health difficulties, took her own life in 2022.)

7.

An anonymous letter to the Lakeside Times, *a free weekly newspaper serving the Gaugeville district of Kwawidokawa County, dated 03.10.88 and printed the following week under the headline* "Stories of Giant Eels: an Old Timer writes."

Sir:

In your story of Feb. 25, "Decapitated body of monster eel caught in propellor of pleasure boat" – telling of a great lamprey or hagfish swept downriver from the old Charles tungsten mine, following its closure by dynamiting and flooding the day before – your correspondent claims the size of the beast was "unprecedented." Yet I recall a story my father told me of something similar from the early part of the century, when logs were still largely transported by river rather than as now by truck or lorry. His father, my grandfather, was lead log driver on the Flume River, a very dangerous job. Around 1905, after a period of heavy rains swole the river into a rapid, while attempting to clear a log jam by dynamiting, as was common practice in those days, he and his fellow drivers found an eel or perhaps a gray snake nine feet long crushed between the rolling logs. When they prized the logs apart it sunk as if it were very heavy, but my grandfather told my father that everyone had been very scared as it had a human face. It's certainly a shame the recent specimen was decapitated, as it might have confirmed my grandfather's strange story!

Sincerely,

"an old-timer"

(Source: Collington-Osprey Public Library microfiche records. Digitization paused 2015 due to funding being withdrawn.)

8.

From Folksongs of Upper Maine *by Abigail P. Clutter, (Bird-song Press Editions, 1922), an example of a Kwawidokawan skipping song:*

> There was an old lady called Skog Madoo
> She had one tooth and she wore no shoes
> She was so hungry, she was so cold
> She looked up at the moon and swallowed it whole
>
> Skog Madoo had a silver hen
> She kept it in the cattle pen
> The poor little hen, it had no legs
> 'Twas Skog Madoo had to lay the eggs!

(Miss Clutter offers the following gloss: "Skipping song, trad. Origins unknown, 'Madoo' poss. a corruption of Abenaki 'madahôdo,' a word signifying an evil or malign spirit. A variant of the name, 'Skog Nannybo,' is also known of. 'Skog' is perhaps of Scandinavian origin." (p27))

One

Brooklyn, New York, 7:05 a.m. A Sunday morning in late October.

Keys jingling, DuVone Mapley-Stevenson made a quick final idiot check of the Fort Greene apartment that had been his and his husband Jack's home for the past seven years, and the only home their now five-year-old son Jay-Jay had ever known. With everything cleared out but the larger pieces of furniture, which they were leaving behind, its shabbiness was laid bare, the ghost rectangles on the dingy walls evidence of how effectively the pictures that used to hang there had masked off the grimy air – air Jay-Jay was breathing 24/7; grime that, however moment-by-moment invisible, was coating the fresh pink linings of his child's lungs, latently, blatantly carcinogenic. Their rugs no longer hid the splits in the threadbare linoleum, and the duct-tape-latticed seat of the sagging leatherette couch – always too large for the front room, a cast-off from a relocating friend – was no longer concealed by African-print throws. Yet despite all these evidences of poverty, Vone wished they weren't moving out.

Truthfully, though, it was time to go. Pandemic or no pandemic, for the past four years the gentrification of Fort Greene had been accelerating relentlessly, at times it felt exponentially. Their rent was being pushed up aggressively and consuming an ever-greater proportion of their meager, static incomes, and for the last eighteen months, though Vone and Jack were both employed, financially they had barely been clinging on. They had taken part in anti-gentrification protests, sometimes with Jay-Jay in his stroller; held up placards, yelled slogans and applauded as local activists railed through bullhorns against the developers, needing catharsis, all the while knowing it was as futile as bellowing at an incoming tsunami. Paying rich-people prices to carry on living in an apartment that was, objectively considered, a dump, had become an increasing source of resentment for both of them, and anyway Jay-Jay would soon need something bigger than his cubbyhole of a bedroom, in which the only storage space for his ever-accumulating mountain of toys and clothes was a pull-out drawer under his narrow bed.

Earlier that year Vone and Jack had both turned thirty, and it had seemed like a sign, or a warning, to get serious. The years of COVID had cast their shadow too, stripping the city of something that Vone, a lifelong New Yorker, would have hesitated to call innocence, but for which he could find no better word. And that was even though neither he nor Jack had lost anyone especially close: Jack a co-worker not much older than himself, African-American like so many of the dead in the beginning; Vone a diabetic aunt in Bed-Stuy he hadn't seen for a decade.

Several of Vone's friends and co-workers had been seriously ill, however, and some had even been hospitalized. The dearest of these was his homo homeboy Tarrell, who like Vone was a struggling artist – Rell was a painter; Vone a poet. Having no insurance, he had ended up in the short-lived, notoriously homophobic evangelical tent hospital set up by Franklin Graham in Central Park. He had survived both the bigotry and the virus, but even now, three years later, struggled – admittedly at times ostentatiously –with Long Covid, which manifested itself in spells of breathlessness and fatigue.

"Those fascist fuckers injected me with *something*," he wheezed, shortly after his discharge. "And girl, I don't mean antibiotics."

"It was either an Illuminati chip and drugs that work," Vone said as he helped Rell on with his coat, "or thoughts and prayers."

"Or Ivermectin and bleach. And child, you *know* we don't bleach."

"Amen."

Shortly after that conversation, two miracles occurred: a vaccine being approved (Vone and Jack took it the first chance they could), and Donald Trump being cast bellowing and bitching out of office. His replacement, though uninspiring, at least didn't run an alternate shock-jock persona on social media criticizing his own administration and calling for its downfall – which was, ridiculously, a relief.

Variant Omicron arrived, but seemed less severe than its predecessor, landing hardest on those keen to take any drug but the one their doctors recommended. The nation shrugged, businesses reopened and the virus, and people's most immediate and painful memories of the pandemic, began to recede. But as the song said, the thrill was gone. So when Jack was offered a placement in upstate Maine, for nine months initially, "but with a strong chance of funding being extended for at least a further two years," to set up and run a task force delivering training to local social workers and healthcare providers on issues around opioids, drug abuse generally, HIV/AIDS and other STDs, Vone had no real grounds for resisting a move that would offer their little family a fresh start in a new place.

No grounds, but plenty of reasons, though they sounded unconvincing when he said them out loud. For one, he liked his job. Well, not the actual *job*: he liked his co-workers. Slinging salad for an endless line of stressed-out office workers in Sweetgreen, a popular vegan takeout in Greenwich Village, was just work, and not particularly well paid. But it was also where he'd got to know Ellie, who had ended up being his and Jack's surrogate – which, since Jay-Jay was five, meant that Vone had been working there at least six years, which was if anything an argument *for* change, not against it. But he and the rest of the Sweetgreen staff had weathered the COVID storm together – the months of shutdown; the etiolated "open but most office staff are still working from home" months; the slow return to comparative normality – and were still there, and that felt like something to be at least partway proud of.

If that didn't count for much, more important, at least in theory, were the many poetry clubs, slam nights, workshops and cultural opportunities the city had to offer him, from the Bowery to the Nuyorican to Harlem Nights to Just Lorraine's. But when had Vone last actually performed anywhere?

"Granted, COVID totally fucked the scene for eighteen months," Jack said, not quite looking at his husband. "But since places started to open up again?"

"But I *could*, is the point," was Vone's weak comeback. Equally weak were his claims that he would be losing out on "great chances to network and build up contacts" when, after all, there was the internet. But there had been a trillion pandemic Zoom events he could have attended and didn't, and another trillion that were ongoing, or semi-ongoing, after the lockdown ended, and he hadn't attended those either.

Unspoken, because it was too painful and difficult a subject for them both, was Vone's breakdown, which, when they referred to it at all, he and Jack called "the episode" – mercifully brief, though it hadn't seemed so at the time, and now just over four years in the past. For either of them to use "the episode" in an argument felt like cheating, and it having happened shortly before the rupture of the pandemic made it feel curiously remote. Too, there was the feeling – on both their parts – that it *had* to be trivial compared to over a million dead in eighteen months.

Jack understood as well as he could how vulnerable Vone's psychotic break had left him; how unready his husband was to set foot in any amped-up environment. But how long could you keep your life on hold on the promise of the return of resilience when (unspoken, but thought) it might never come? And then there was Jay-Jay: shouldn't their son's needs come first, not those of (possibly perpetually) mentally fragile Daddy?

Easier to express, and more obviously legitimate, was Vone's unease at moving from one of the most racially diverse cities on the planet to somewhere that was at a conservative estimate 99.9% white. "We're a gay interracial couple with a kid, and I'm a Black man wherever we go," he said, when the possibility of relocating first came up.

"We're barely making rent here," Jack said. "You know that's only gonna get worse. It would be better for Jay-Jay."

"Jay-Jay's a Black boy," Vone said, reflexively adding, "a boy seen as Black," to head off a potential digression into his also-white heritage. "You know that matters, maybe more than anything, and it's gonna matter more as he gets older."

"And he'll have his Black daddy with him all the way," Jack said, attempting reassurance. "And we can affirm all that heritage and history as a family wherever we are. We'd have to do it if we stayed here. I mean, we're gonna have to negotiate him being a boy with two dads wherever we are. You tell me the shit they say in your barbershop."

"Not all of them," Vone said defensively. "Some of them. And only sometimes."

"I just mean nowhere solves all our problems."

"Yeah, but –"

And so the discussion had gone round and round. Unlike the rest of the several white men Vone had dated seriously, Jack didn't try to speak or wish the inconvenient fact of race out of existence: he knew he was part of a Black family, and that that had its joys, but also costs. And of course, Jack was right: they could create a home elsewhere as they had in Fort Greene, where Black art covered the walls, and Black and queer books crowded the shelves: a world of affirmation.

But without community, wouldn't such an endeavor feel embattled, even ludicrous and futile, in butthole, Maine? Wouldn't it somehow start to collapse in on itself, the way being out could do when you found yourself amongst churchy relatives on a (holy) roll? Vone had no desire to take on the missionary work of schooling the conservatively white and rurally straight citizens of upstate Maine, even if (and this was by no means guaranteed) they proved receptive to being schooled.

Then too there was the very real issue of being deprived of capital-C culture. Currently they lived just a subway ride (okay, yeah: with changes) from Harlem, and Vone made regular pilgrimages there, visiting the Schomburg Center, soaking up the remaining traces of the Renaissance with which he had been obsessed all his adult life, tracking what he called the spirit spoor of its many gay, bi and lesbian writers and artists. The prospect of losing that geographical connection, that groundedness, felt at times unbearable.

Yet the reality was that Harlem was being swallowed up by gentrification even faster than Fort Greene, and what good would it do him to cling on, mournfully and resentfully, until the bitter end; to see everything he treasured either entirely overwritten or else rendered down to a handful of commemorative plaques obscured by the awnings of generic chain stores? Wouldn't that be merely masochistic sentimentality – the desire to be wounded in order to feel and flaunt the pain of the wound; and didn't he in his poetry eschew the slightest taint of sentiment? And anyway, linger on to do or achieve what? He wasn't, and had no interest in being, an archivist, except perhaps of his own flickering states of mind. On top of all that, the reality was that many of the writers he most admired – Claude McKay, Zora Neale Hurston, Bruce Nugent – fled to the 'burbs when the area went downhill in the Depression; and others like Langston Hughes, who had held on then, bailed in the forties.

T/races
Kicked over
Places E-
Razed Ra
Space ain't it, baby

Vone himself grew up not in Harlem but in Bedford-Stuyvesant – a native New Yorker, as the song said – and he knew that part of his resistance to moving out was timid parochialism, and should therefore be resisted. Jack, who grew up being dragged around the featureless Midwest by his peripatetic single mother, and had come to New York to be bohemian, didn't understand Vone's fear – or rather he *did* understand it, he just didn't feel it. He was a roamer, a voyager: "Pirate Jack," Vone sometimes called him, and not just because of the Johnny Depp eyeliner he wore in his punk rocker days.

Sidebar: Of course, Vone knew the Midwest wasn't featureless. It was his projection, his condemnatory shorthand, his way of cranking up the contrast between his and Jack's upbringings for maximum dramatic effect.

He found himself staring at the water heater, which had never worked properly the entire seven years of their tenancy. He wouldn't miss that, nor the too-loud air conditioner they had wedged into the guillotine frame of the rotting, double-hung bedroom window. Though he and Jack had made the apartment a home, and filled it with love and joy, Vone now saw that to do so had been an act of defiance, rather than fulfilling something it naturally tended towards. Surely they could do the same in – what was it called again? Some mouthful of a name – Kwawidokawa County, upstate Maine. And if they were leaving friends behind, they could make new friends there, like people have always done everywhere. And wasn't it true that a lot of their once-bohemian circle were moving out of the city too, or had already gone, leaving behind them ghosts of friendships once alive, passionate, shallow declarations about staying in touch?

Don't be the last one at the party.

He knew the advice was good.

The house they were renting came fully furnished, which meant they could leave behind their major appliances (secondhand in the first place) and pretty much all the furniture, none of which was worth transporting, for the next tenants – or, more likely, to be tossed by whatever developer moved in to gut the place and quadruple the rent.

Presumably they'd replace the shitty water heater at the same time they wired in the recessed lighting.

Vone locked the front door for the final time, touched the cool glass bump of the spyhole with the tip of a forefinger in farewell, and headed for the stairs. He would miss the dim hallways with their underpowered striplights and suggestion of David Lynch psychodrama; the black-and-white tiled lobby with its dusty, wall-sized mirror, and the huge and equally dusty Monstera he had started to water because no one else seemed to be bothering. As he passed it by, he hooked a card over the rim of the pot, which read in what he hoped was a cheery hand, *Someone Please Water Me* ☺. He wondered if anyone would. He and Jack hadn't been close to any of their neighbors since "the episode."

It would be good to leave all that behind.

The landlord's representative, a tiny, elderly Jewish lady with mauve cotton candy hair, who wore smoked glasses indoors, blue latex gloves and a floral-pattern mask, had come round the afternoon before, to check on the condition of the apartment before they left and try to screw them out of the deposit. There had been some wrangling over wear and tear, but eventually she had signed off on the paperwork for the termination of their lease. Though Jack had been given an advance against his salary to help cover their relocation costs, he and Vone were counting on the prompt return of the deposit to pay for the hire of a second car, otherwise househusband Vone would find himself marooned in the middle of nowhere while Jack went to work. *No more needing some bay leaves and strolling down the block to the local store*, he thought gloomily. He liked to be able to walk places and not have to over-plan the small stuff: Jay-Jay took up all his capacity for scheduling and micro-managing.

After they finished loading up the station wagon Jack went round the apartment, filming with his phone to forestall any deposit-withholding claim by the landlord that they had trashed it after the representative's visit, holding up a copy of that morning's *New York Times* and zooming in on the date like a kidnapper proving his victim was still alive in order to extort a ransom.

And now Vone was saying his last goodbye, under the guise of an idiot check.

7:18 a.m.

The block's entry door clanged shut behind him. The sky was blue and cloudless, and his breath misted in the cold, still air. The street – wide, straight, residential – was at that hour on a Sunday deserted. Here and there leaves came fluttering down from the trees that lined the sidewalks.

Vone pushed down a sense of foreboding as he opened the passenger door of the heavily laden station wagon and swung himself in.

"All clear?" Jack asked, pressing the starter as Vone pulled his seatbelt across.

"Yeah. Ready to go, Junior?" Vone asked over his shoulder.

Their son was strapped in in the middle of the back seat, boxes and bags packed close around him. They had been piled so high he had no side views at all, though a narrow tunnel had been left above his head for the rear-view mirror. Jay-Jay held his favorite toy, a blue plastic diplodocus, and looked both forlorn and confused.

Seeing his son's expression, Vone felt a pang of guilt. He knew that all children value regularity and find change upsetting, but he also knew he was turning the move into a negative experience for his son by failing to mask his own ambivalence and persistent low mood. Yet even if he *had* managed to hide them, he was aware that depression, anxiety and other mental health problems were heritable, which was another reason for guilt, because though Vone was mocha dark and his son café-au-lait, it was obvious from Jay-Jay's features that it was Vone's sperm that had won the race when he and Jack mixed their samples for the insemination. *Should've just let it be*

Jack's. Should've set manly pride aside. Ellie brought the melanin, didn't need mine, not with –

He reached back and ruffled his son's large, unruly 'fro. "It's gonna be an adventure, Jackie-Jacks," he said, his smile only half-forced. "We're gonna have a whole house just for us with a big backyard. There'll be woods and nature and critters and everything."

Seeing Vone making an effort, Jack smiled. "We just need to drop off the keys and we're outta here. Say goodbye to Brooklyn, Jay-Jay."

Vone didn't look back as they turned the corner; didn't even glance in the wing-mirror.

Pillars of salt.

Two

O nce out of the city they took I 95, heading up into Connecticut, passing briefly through a corner of Rhode Island State, then Massachusetts, New Hampshire and on up into Maine. Their early start gave the rest of the day a hard-eyed, crack-of-dawn feeling that persisted even after noon had come and gone; and the monotony of the long drive, mostly on nondescript freeways, made time both stand still and spool on endlessly, its passing marked only by the hardening of their butts, the locking of their lower backs.

"The state bird is the chickadee," Jack announced as they crossed the Maine state line, but was unable to describe it. Vone looked on his phone. It turned out to be small, with a gray body, and a black head with white blazes under its eyes. "I'd imagined a chicken type thing," Jack said, as Vone showed the image first to him then to their uninterested son. "Or a sort of turkey."

Vone put his phone away and went back to staring out the window. Dull walls of brown-leaved trees slid by, cutting off any view of what lay beyond them. Once in a while the skyline ahead was interrupted by the brutalist hypotenuse of a concrete flyover, or by a semaphore burst of signage; the tree line by an off-ramp circling round to some suburban community or waystation. The monotony and the persisting low horizon magnified Vone's sense that they were getting nowhere, the signs displaying the miles to various destinations no more than abstractions, tauntingly disconnected from any sense you might ever actually arrive.

Initially Jack was to be trained in Bangor, a city Vone associated with Stephen King novels and nothing else, but they left the interstate well before then, taking Route 7 up into Kwawidokawa County and following signs to Collington-Osprey, the county seat, where Jack would be setting up, then running, his office hub. Having heard it was both largely geriatric and legendarily dull – and after online searches had confirmed the rumors – Jack had decided not to look for a house for them there. Instead he had opted for Gaugeville, which was a small lakeside town a further forty minutes' drive northwest. Gaugeville had summer and fall tourism, so would, Jack reckoned, be more bohemian and diverse than staid, 99.99% white Collington-Osprey. Vone, who had mostly nodded along with his husband's plans, was now wishing he had made more effort to learn about the area in advance.

Domed like loaves in a proving pan, and decked out in copper, gold and scarlet, the tree-covered hills began to rise around them; and ahead, though very far off, was a blue-smoke mountain range that Vone guessed was the Appalachians. The woods surged down to meet the road, and there was no question that even this final, past-its-best week of leaf season in New England was strikingly beautiful. Despite the presence of the highway, with its cars and vans and logging trucks, evidences of residency, tourism and commerce, it seemed to Vone they were entering a world indifferent to human endeavor and even to simple human presence.

The idea wasn't unwelcome to him. Though a lifelong city-dweller, he had always responded powerfully to nature, in particular to the shapes and forms of plants. In low moods, especially in the spring, he would go alone to one or other of the city's many parks and sit and quietly study the emerging greenery, intrigued by even the smallest and least special of the border-plants: the thrusting, near luminous spikes of bulbs; the way stems stretched up in search of light, leaves unfurled and budded, and the buds broke open and then the flowers arrived.

> *Nature patriot*
> *Flags of spring and*
> *Sun soaked chloroplasts*
> *Tendrils turn*
> *Clockwise, always*
> *Violent vigor of living*
> *Green*

He could feel the incipient pressure inside the buds at the gluey tips of the trees' twigs, and the sense of renewal gladdened his heart when people – even Jack, even Jay-Jay – didn't. And now there was this: the heady blaze of fall in

Maine. Sleepy though he had become in the closeness of the station wagon, Vone found himself sitting up and looking around as if there might be an answer in the endless woods: a response to his unspoken, unsung call.

Always alert to shifts in his husband's moods, Jack reached over and took Vone's hand, lifted it and kissed Vone's knuckles. The affectionate contact was a comfort, and images of the two of them hiking picturesque trails in butt-hugging shorts flicked up in Vone's mind. The images were appealing, albeit entirely confected from movies and TV; even from commercials for HIV medication – Big Pharma keen to show that the virus (if treated regularly with its products) needn't preclude a healthier lifestyle for the positive than the negative usually managed.

Pulling gently at his seatbelt, Vone lent across and kissed Jack on the cheek. "Thanks for doing so much of the gruntwork. I know I haven't been exactly..."

"It's alright," Jack said, keeping his eyes responsibly on the road. "I know it's more my thing than yours."

"It's *our* thing," Vone said. And as the forest's crimsons and oranges streamed past, enchanting and seemingly without end, he meant it. What was that Ursula Le Guin title? *The Word For World Is Forest*.

The spell was broken when they reached Collington-Osprey. Up until then they had only stopped for restroom breaks, to refuel, or to swap driving duties, and freeway gas stations by their nature feel removed from the rest of the world. Impersonal islands in empty seas, those who use them are perpetually in transit, mentally already elsewhere; and those who work there have the particular detachment that comes with knowing they will never see you again.

By contrast, Collington-Osprey was anchored in its history and geography. Yet its performative picture-postcardness – the self-consciously quaint "welcomes careful drivers" entry sign; the old-school population counter – gave it an unreal quality too, just of a different sort. Lawns were as neatly clipped as if Astroturfed, borders jaunty with late bloomers and white-picket-fenced. Homes were either genuinely pre-nineteenth century or looked it, and were clad in bright white clapboard. Any brickwork was oxide red, and freshly pointed with marzipan mortar.

Main Street, down which they were now driving, featured an Art Deco movie theater whose carefully restored façade advertised not something from Hollywood's golden age but a Sweetheart Fruit Pie Festival and monthly line dances. A carefully-silvered wooden fingerpost pointed the way to the Timber Mill Theater & Arts Center. Vehicles were unostentatious but on the costlier end, and most had recent plates. Public benches were plentiful and much used that sunny fall afternoon, and the numerous cafés were non-chain and well patronized.

As they crawled past an antiques market in front of which elderly white people rooted through small baskets and picked up things that glinted from trestles on which white tablecloths fluttered, Vone adjusted his hot pink du-rag. His expression was impassive, but he knew Jack would know what he was thinking without his having to raise more than an internal eyebrow.

Adjoining the market was a determinedly old-fashioned general store with a candy-stripe awning and, out front, next to a vintage gumball machine, tubs of carefully selected fruits and vegetables.

Older Kinder Blinder (A Place Dreams Of Itself And Sleeping Smiles Denial) – In Oils

"Do we need anything for dinner?" Jack asked. Food for the first night in their new home had been one of Vone's few responsibilities.

Vone shook his head. "We good." He twisted round to look at Jay-Jay and made a face. "Welcome to Stepford, Junior. Gibble-gabble, gibble-gabble!"

Jay-Jay laughed. "Gibble-gabble!" he repeated. "Gibble-gabble!"

"Neither of those references is even apt," Jack said, checking a street-name. "I think this is where I'll be –"

"GIBBLE GABBLE! GIBBLE GABBLE!" Jay-Jay shouted.

"Quiet, Junior!" Jack said sharply. "Stop winding him up, please, Vone."

Jay-Jay subsided; Vone resumed looking forward. "Goodbye to getting a decent haircut," he sighed as they passed a barbershop catering to the silver-haired and Caucasian, regretting in advance the loss of Clipz, the barbershop in Bed-Stuy to which he had been going for more than a decade, and the particular camaraderie it offered him; the loss of brothas, even when they ragged on him for his sexuality. "Yeah, but he a Omar," Vernon, the owner of Clipz, had said of Vone one time, in the middle of some silly but loud debate, referencing the legendary, defiantly gay antihero of *The Wire*, meaning masculine-presenting, and so the others began to call him Omar, mostly in a good-humored way, and new customers thought that was his name. *Given name a gift*. He had gotten a tight-ass Caesar-cut fade the afternoon before the move, only as he swung into the chair confessing that this was good-bye. "For the length of a pregnancy, anyway," he had added as Vernon flicked the cloth out over him.

"And could you have found anywhere more white?" he said to Jack, partly joking, partly not.

"Which is why this isn't where we're going to be living," Jack said patiently. "It's where my hub will be based. I just wanted to check out where the office is."

"I thought your first week is in Bangor."

"It is, but this is where I'm gonna be afterwards."

Though there was no oncoming traffic, Jack indicated before turning into a side-street markedly less quaint and more municipal than the main one. *A façade, then*. Jack looked up at a featureless office block, nodded, took a left, then another left and soon they were back on Main Street and heading out of town. At the limits they passed a sign that read, "Thank you for driving carefully whilst in Collington-Osprey – come again!"

"'Whilst'," Vone said, knowing Jack would have noticed the overly correct word-choice too.

North of Collington-Osprey was dairy country. Rolling acres of pastureland kept the woods pushed well back and the farms were tidy, with dully gleaming silver silos, red-roofed outbuildings and small, busily whirring windmills. Low stone walls, pale and crusted with yellow-flowering lichen, bounded their fields, and these seemed more an outgrowth than the work of hands. Black-and-white cattle chewed the cud and watched indifferently as Jack and Vone drove by.

A half hour later they had left the farms behind and were

once more in deeply wooded country. That far out, as it felt to Vone, there was little traffic, and on a long curve of road overlooking a small, tree-filled valley, Jack found a place to pull over for a pee-break that offered clear views in both directions. Standing in a row, with their backs to the road and facing the valley and thickly forested hillside opposite, fathers and son emptied their bladders.

From there on the road rose more steeply, though the surrounding trees mostly deprived them of a view. By the time they saw the first signs to Antler Lake and Gaugeville, the sun was low and striating epileptically through the treetops. Vone pointed out to Jay-Jay increasingly numerous signposts marking woodland trails. Some of these displayed encouraging silhouettes of moose, others unnerving silhouettes of bears and wildcats; and here and there were warnings for deer crossing, apparently always at a gallop.

Maybe this could *be something good*, he thought. Instead of admitting his own rising enthusiasm, however, he found himself saying dourly, "I hope the WiFi is decent."

Gaugeville, when they reached it, turned out to be a small tourist town on the southern shore of a large lake – Antler Lake. Its principal stores and businesses were on a main street three blocks long, at the center of which was a well-maintained church with a tall, shingled spire. A row of single-story restaurants, cafés and bars overlooked the lake. On the landward side of these, four-by-fours were pulled up in orderly diagonals, many with tow bars and trailers – evidence of a thriving market for sailing as well as hiking even this late in the season. Small powerboats sat on several of the trailers, and above the tarpaper roofs of the lakeside bars and diners the tops of masts were visible, guy-ropes thrumming in the breeze running in off the water. The northern, farther shore, which Vone glimpsed through gaps between buildings as Jack drove slowly by, was a long way off and seemed entirely wooded, suggesting that Gaugeville was a place on the edge of things, or at the end of things.

Those out and about were younger than the citizens of Collington-Osprey and mostly looked like tourists, but were no less white, and Vone sighed inwardly. Still, their blazoned ephemerality meant that, by comparison, he and Jack had a shot at being seen as residents, if not exactly locals, fairly quickly. Hopefully they would be at least partway accepted by whatever community there was there before winter came, with its storms and snows and the possibility of being pretty much shut in for long stretches, and having to lean on neighbors if necessities ran short.

The thought of all the ingratiation he would have to attempt made Vone feel exhausted in advance. *You can do this*, he told himself. The first in his family to go to college, he had been one of only two Black students in his class, and the other, a heavyset girl who seemed at pains to avoid him outside the classroom setting, had dropped out midway through the second semester, never to be seen or heard from again. He had got through that, hadn't he? Made white friends, connected with white tutors, charmed white administrators. By comparison this was –

But then you had a nervous breakdown, didn't you? Only got through it with a lot of allowances made.

Still: GPA 3.7, bitch.

And that was over a decade ago. *I'm better at dealing with shit now.*

Are you? What about "the episode"?

That was something else, and that's over too. Anyway, I'm on medication for it, so.

West of the town the road ran low and straight, to its left the woods, to its right a marshy expanse of sedge grass. Beyond this a line of pontoons floated, tethered together, dreaming of the coming summer's swimmers; and on the gentle curve of the western shore there stood what Vone guessed to be the most desirable houses in Gaugeville. Three-storied, clapboarded, from the 1930s or earlier by the look of them, each was sheltered by great oaks and chestnuts, and had a trim lawn that sloped down to the dark and dimpling water of the lake. Most had their own small docks; some had boathouses. The town's old money, Vone presumed. He imagined their inhabitants complaining about tourist numbers, vetoing helpful signs on the grounds that they lowered the tone, and opposing local businesses seeking to expand. But no question the houses were Gatsby elegant.

"Is our place on the lake?" he asked, feeling a surge of excitement. "I don't remember seeing –"

"We're not actually in Gaugeville," Jack said, glancing at the GPS. "Those are called Point Houses. They're crazy expensive, and none are ever for rent anyway. Ours is in Gaugeville Bounds."

"So, farther out?"

"Yeah. But with an option to buy if we like it, and at a price where you won't have to work."

"I can join the ladies who brunch."

"You can write."

Vone grunted.

"Especially once we find somewhere for Junior," Jack went on, adding, slightly defensively, "It's in the same district, Vone. Just a mile or two out."

"The 'hood part of Gaugeville."

"Well, they've got a drug problem here like anywhere," Jack said. This disconcerted Vone, who realized he had been indulging a romanticized view of the New England countryside as containing nothing but *Mayflower*-descended white farmers, tourists and service-industry workers. "You know the stats," Jack continued. "Rural and white drug-use exceeds urban and Black by a significant margin."

"Hence your new gig."

"And our fresh start," Jack said, not rising to what he knew Vone was thinking: that social work tended to be parasitical on misery more often than productive of solutions to it. Not that Vone, a poet for fuck's sake, would have had the bare-assed hypocrisy to say such a thing to his husband in anything other than the most joking tone. But his memories of social workers coming to the house when he was a child were ones of hostility and fear, at best resentment. And he did, deep down, just ever so slightly judge Jack for having given up on the struggle, impossible though he himself so often found it, to make art from the chaos of human experience; to wrestle something meaningful from the inhuman face of late-phase western consumer capitalism as manifested in a racist, homophobic (et cetera) nation-state the size of a continent.

When they first met, Jack was the bassist in Klamydia, an

underground art-punk rock band that was raucous, experimental and lyrically incoherent. Klamydia were having a moment – their peak, as it turned out, though that wasn't apparent then – sharing billings with the likes of the legendary Negrogothic M. Lamar and bands such as Cum Gutter. Vone couldn't say he had liked their music, but of course liking wasn't the point. He *had* liked Jack: punk pale and lean in skintight black PVC pants, dick and balls pushed provocatively to one plainly-outlined side, going commando in army boots and a cut-off tank top, peroxided hair spiked up and glistening with gel, eyes that turned out to be green hidden by narrow disco shades, a black rubber, faux barbed wire chain around his neck. He hadn't seemed gay at all to Vone, but he was. And Vone had bought him a beer after the set and they had talked, then more than talked. Klamydia's lead singer Biru, a Somali self-styled wild chick with a voice like nails on glass, was a friend of Tarrell's, which was how come Vone had been at the gig that night.

The band broke up six months later, after Biru overdosed. She survived but split the scene, going back to Minneapolis and the money it turned out she had come from. Jack had jammed with a few other bands after that, but none of them had gone anywhere, so he started volunteering at a couple of HIV/AIDS-related organizations, doing work around PEP and PrEP that after a year or so turned into a paying job. Soon he was on his way to becoming a healthcare professional, taking supplementary courses and gaining qualifications to boost his scanty CV and gloss over his patchy school record. He still dyed his hair but gelled it less spikily now, the eyebrow piercing was long gone, the junk jewelry less overt, the messy eyeliner set aside, his style of dress more button-down. Vone knew there was a side of Jack that regretted, even resented, his transition from would-be chaos agent to health-care professional; and however conservatively he attempted to present himself, something about him remained willfully off-key.

It was that off-keyness Vone still found attractive more than seven years later, even though Jack now wore a suit to work and dockers on weekends. And most of the time Vone was quietly proud of his husband for taking on the conventional shit he himself was so unsuited to; for sacrificing his wild self for his husband, for their son, for their family.

And after all, wasn't it time? Hand on heart, did Vone really want to get wasted and fuck in nightclub restrooms anymore? Weren't you supposed to do that in your teens or twenties, get it out of your system, grow up, move on? For sure he had learned this: that drink and drugs and constant kinetic activity solve nothing, and soon enough become the problem, not the solution. And if there was a glamor to seeing the dawn because you stayed up all night, there was a sweetness to the daylight too: an affirmation in prosaic commitment, in keeping on the rails. A liberation in functionality. Didn't every generation discover this? It was a theme replayed across the decades, probably even the centuries, with only the most minor variations. And then there was Jack Junior.

I'm a tethered balloon, Vone thought. And that was okay, mostly.

A random sign at the town limits proclaimed, "Elevation 1600 ft", and Vone recalled an online map that showed Antler Lake was at the slightly subsided center of a densely forested, roughly oval granite plateau around a hundred miles across, beyond which to the north were the Appalachians.

Past the sedge marshes were a succession of lanes and sideroads, leading on the left to residential homes without lake views that were, however, spacious and largely screened from passing traffic by groves of trees, and on the right to the Point Houses. Then there was nothing but the road, taking them somewhere or nowhere, like life, its black smoothness spattered with bright, fallen leaves. Like an Ezra Pound haiku, Vone thought, struggling to remember it. Faces... faces on the Metro? The subway? Wet leaves... Pound hadn't thought of brown leaves, though, and every shade of bronze, copper, redbone, butterscotch and ocher was here. *Tan faces/On the Elevated/Shades of Harlem in the rain/Chloroplastic Negritude/We the/Sun People/then/before rebirth/White Winter.*

He wondered how far the woods ran on; how many miles you would have to hike before you got to somewhere else. If you could easily wander lost and die of thirst or starvation.

Flicking on the indicator, Jack slowed to make a left turn into a sideroad next to a large sign. Opposite it was a logging site where diggers had carved a great black wall out of a rise of earth, creating a churned amphitheater that at its center was stacked with huge felled pines. Their chainsawed ends showed radial yellow wounds, they had been stripped of their branches, and the forest rose up behind them, dark and resentful in the glinting daylight.

An eight-wheeler was pulled up alongside one of the stacks, its tires taller than a man standing, presumably awaiting a load, though the crane that stood nearby was idle, and no one was visible in the cabs of either the crane or the truck. A light shone weakly in the mesh window of a nearby Porta-kabin, and Vone remembered from his few other trips to rural areas the odd sense that nothing was ever being done *now*. What was the word? Oh yeah: stasis.

Stasis Is this All there is.

The sign where Jack was turning in declared (meretriciously: the lake was over a mile and a half away), "Antler Lake Vicinity, an exciting new Community and Rental Investment opportunity." Beneath it a smaller sign urged, "Take care – children!" and another, more weather-worn, displayed the traditional glyph of a deer crossing at a run.

"Is this it?" Vone asked dubiously.

"No, and this *is* too *Stepford Wives*," Jack said. "We're out the other side, in the old section, the Bounds. Look for Cotton-wood Way. The GPS has given up on me."

The "exciting new community" turned out to be a grid of identikit two-story ranch-style dwellings. Each had a side-port with space for two cars, a porch that was oversized in relation to the house it fronted, a yard with a neatly raked lawn, small trees that hadn't got going yet, and sparse-looking, under-planted borders. In several of the ports SUVs were parked; otherwise there was no sense of anyone living there. Vone wondered how many of them were summer rentals; how many lights would show on dreary winter evenings. He wasn't sure whether he liked or disliked the idea that it would be few.

As they crawled along looking for street names, two women came jogging towards them, side by side and pushing three-wheeler sport strollers. Both were white, skinny, Vone guessed in their late twenties, and wore baggy sweatshirts, Lycra leggings and spotless white running shoes. Each had her straight blonde hair pulled back in a ponytail and wore a baseball cap, and both wore dark glasses – against the dazzle of the sun, maybe, though it was now behind them. Neither wore make up; both had sharp features.

As one, the women came to a halt and, jogging on the spot, watched Jack and Vone pass, their mouths unsmiling, their eyes concealed by the sunglasses. Hunching his shoulders, Vone sank down in his seat. Presumably their only experience of Black men would be from watching gangsta rap videos, episodes of *Law & Order* and *Fox News*. Maybe their husbands watched cuck porn. Maybe *they* did. He studied them receding in the side mirror. They kept on watching. *Pod people*, he thought. The idea was less painful, less frightening than seeing them as potential Karens in the Ramble, calling the cops on a brotha while faking being in danger. *That bird guy was gay too, wasn't he?*

Jack seemed not to have noticed the women. Craning over the steering wheel, he was peering up at street signs that were manufactured to look quaintly hand carved, but used needlessly small lettering that was hard to read – the more so when backlit by a sinking sun. Then he grunted an affirmation and turned into an unpromisingly narrow and rutted lane. Twigs squeaked against the sides of the station wagon as it slowly bumped along, and at one point it slithered sideways on a slippery mass of fallen leaves. The wheels spun for a moment, then gripped the road and jerked the vehicle forward, throwing those inside about. Jay-Jay laughed, then cried out: a box of books was threatening to disgorge itself onto his head. "Daddy!"

Vone twisted round to help his son wrangle the box back into place. As he did so, the station wagon passed into the blackness of an old-fashioned covered bridge. Beneath its wheels the planks thudded like the felt-clad hammers inside a piano. A moment later they were out the other side.

"We're here," Jack said.

Three

A slice of sun still showed above the treetops directly ahead, and as they emerged into the dazzle Jack and Vone raised their hands in tandem to shield their eyes. "Ours is number thirteen," Jack said as the station wagon nosed its way along the narrow curve of lane beyond the bridge.

The rutted lane, the close-pressing foliage and the antique covered bridge all led Vone to anticipate a tumbledown shack in the middle of a thicket. He had forgotten the photographs on the realtor's website – which, to be fair to Vone, had been just one among dozens of potential homes scouted out and thrust in front of him by Jack, and that more than six months ago. In fact, though it too was bumpy beneath the station wagon's wheels, likely due to the furtive incursions of tree roots, the short street that began where the lane ended was recently blacktopped and cambered, with drains and gutters for run-off, though these were currently clogged with fallen leaves. There were streetlamps too: three on each side, staggered on the diagonal. Their slender iron posts, four-sided glass bulb-boxes and spiky gothic canopies made Vone think of Narnia. The clapboarded houses of Cottonwood Way, all nineteenth century or older, were quirky, with porches that tottered on spindly, ornately carved or cast columns, high concave mansard roofs, diamond-paned upper windows and haphazardly thrusting gable ends. To one used to the historic architecture of Brooklyn they were much preferable to the soulless newbuilds of the Vicinity. Plots were bigger too, border plants well-established to the point of extravagance, the hedges between properties high and dense, and the trees in the front yards large and spreading.

There were seven houses on each side of the street. Number 13 was the last on the right, flagged by a bright white sign that read, they saw when they pulled up in front of it, "Another Home Let by Harris Realtors". Past it the road dead-ended and a trail ran off into wooded obscurity. A rusty, waist-high chain-link fence, sagging under years of dead growth, bounded the lot on that side. Beyond it was what looked to have once been a paddock, now grown up tanglesomely, and back of that was the wall of the woods.

Number 13's front lawn was large and subsided. In the middle of it stood a lone dwarf willow in need of pruning; the house itself was set back amidst a grove of pines. To the left as you faced it these dwindled to spindly stumpishness, but those around and in front of the house rose up tall as towers, broad-trunked, low-branched and massive. One that had perhaps been struck by lightning was entirely dead and slumped like a drunk against its neighbor, and Vone thought uneasily of storms and catastrophic collapses; and then that the some-what inward-leaning trunks created the effect of a monstrous bonfire awaiting a spark, with their home-to-be hidden inside.

Amidst the spiky treetops a chimney was visible. Tall and crooked, it made Vone think of the jaggedy illustrations of the witch's house in a book of fairytales his mom had bought him in a yard sale as a child. For some reason another picture in the book, illustrating a bubbling cauldron, had given him nightmares. Perhaps it was the scrawny hands, or more likely the disturbingly suggestive contents they stirred with what he remembered as a human thighbone. Eventually, because he returned to the book obsessively, his mother had had to glue a square of paper over that particular image.

The grass under the railing of pines that stood in front of the house was buried beneath a humped rug of demerara-brown needles; and through the columns of their silver-black, reticulated trunks Vone saw, above an erupting herbaceous border dotted with spidery orange blossoms, and below a smokey-blue swag of pine-branches, a whitewashed clap-board façade, pale green shutters hooked back from dark-eyed windows, and a wide wooden porch whose carved columns supported a slanted roof of silvered shingles.

To the left of the house and contiguous with it was a single story, flat-roofed breezeblock garage – obviously a later addi-tion, though its canopy door, pulled down and speckled with rust, had at some point been painted green to match the house's shutters and trim. The garage was reached by a con-crete drive. Jack turned in and pulled up in front of it, applied the handbrake and cut the engine. The sudden absence of vibration and the silence was both a relief and disconcerting.

Though cramped and achy from the long drive, Vone didn't at once get out, refusing for a pointless moment to step into his (their) future. Instead he asked, "Where's the realtor with the keys?"

Jack glanced at his phone. "We're ten minutes early."

"White People Time," Vone grumbled. But he gave in and opened the door.

The autumn air was chill and clear, traced with the sweetness of leaf-mold and an evocative hint of woodsmoke, and he found himself inhaling deeply as he never did in the city. Birds twittered noisily, concealed both by the golden foliage of the deciduous trees in the yards around them and the shadowy, blue-green pine-boughs. Everything seemed to Vone oddly hard-edged and detailed, as if very slightly magnified.

"Okay, then." Unfastening his seatbelt, he twisted round and unbuckled a suddenly fretful Jay-Jay, with a grunt lifting his whimpering son forward from among the piled cartons and bags. "Let's get you aired out, oh Feral One." Jay-Jay was now too heavy to lift easily, and the hours spent slumped in the passenger seat had told on Vone's lower back. "Come on, now. Help a brother out here."

He set Jay-Jay down, then got out himself. It was a relief to straighten up and be at journey's end. He rotated his hips and rolled his neck, then checked the overburdened roof rack. Nothing seemed to have worked itself loose from under Jack's competently tethered tarpaulin. Vone looked along the front path, of rough concrete like the drive. On one side was the house, its porch and its exploded herbaceous border, on the other the tall and somber pines; ahead was a laurel hedge that screened off the house next door.

He took another deep breath. It was strange to smell and taste pine, and for it to be the real thing, not a cleaning product or car freshener. He noticed fir-cones amongst the heaps of fallen needles, intriguingly half-buried. *Something cute to point out later.*

He noticed his son's sweater was snarled and squatted down to straighten it out. "Hold still, now."

"Dippy, daddy," Jay-Jay said worriedly. This was his lucky blue diplodocus, which he had evidently managed to drop down the storage well while Vone was hauling him out of the car.

Vone lent in and rescued the toy. "Your job is to keep track of him, okay?" he said as he handed Dippy over. Jay-Jay nodded, looking serious.

While Vone was attending to their son, Jack wandered along the front path, kicking aside fallen twigs and smaller, rotten cones. Turning to face the house, he leaned back and, with his hands on his hips, looked up at it, then looked round at Vone. "It's like my grandparents' place," he said, and smiled so simply that Vone was, quite unexpectedly, moved almost to tears.

Leading Jay-Jay by the hand, Vone went and joined him and took his hand, and together the three of them looked up at their new and perhaps future home. In the last of the sunlight it blushed pink and gold. The slanting shadows made by the porch-pillars were hard-edged, blue and long, and the windows sparkled like jet.

"We might get moose in our garden," Jack said to Jay-Jay.

"It's a step up from rats," Vone conceded as Jay-Jay looked up at his fathers in wonder: finding them screaming stuck to glue-traps in the kitchen had been a low point among a good many low points in their Brooklyn life. Unable to face killing them, Vone had thrown them alive into the nearest dumpster, knowing he was condemning them to slowly starve to death, and had been filled with self-loathing at his gutless cruelty.

On closer examination the paintwork was blistered, the gutters grass-tufted, the downspouts coming loose, but Vone reminded himself that taking on a fixer-upper was what married couples were supposed to do. Yes, Number Thirteen was a rental with a possible option to buy, not something they actually owned yet, but still. Both he and Jack were capable handymen; and given marriage equality had only been the law of the land for eight years or so, wasn't there something almost magical about two men setting up house just like straight people got to do?

At first he hadn't cared about marriage, arguing that workplace protections were more important than that single-issue and largely symbolic campaign – something he still believed, because you might have a partner or you might not, but Lord knows you had to have a job and a roof over your head. Only when the ruling came did he realize how much it meant to him; and yeah, that it had happened under a Black president – the first Black president, whatever Maya had said about Clinton in a swept-away moment – had sweetened it the more.

They had married for Jay-Jay, but not only for him. Jack had proposed and Vone had said yes without hesitation. They had chosen the rings together: white gold, plain. The service had been secular, which was both their preference. It was attended by few family members but many friends.

And now they were here.

Enjoy the moment, Vone told himself. There would be time enough to discover that the toilet backed up, the drinking-water pipes were made of lead and the neighbors were running a meth lab. *Maybe I* could *write here*, he thought. Lately he'd been considering attempting a novel, or at least a roman à clef, though that would require finding a way to handle the theme of mental illness that wasn't hackneyed and/or depressing, a theme he'd avoided that he could perhaps face now he was away from his old life, his old haunts.

Maybe.

Though the air was still, as they watched, one of the upper-story shutters swung slowly open, creating the illusion that the house was gently tilting towards them – though whether in welcome or disgorgement, who could say. Past it, and the guttering that underlined the roof, the upper part of the crooked chimney was visible, and on top of it Vone now noticed what he at first took to be an oddly bulbous chimney pot. Then he thought no, it was an owl, a hunched, immobile, dark gray owl. Or was it? It didn't move, and seemed too large. His mind went to the flues that fed the chimney. Probably some had been bricked up and forgotten about, like oubliettes: another childhood nightmare.

He blinked.

There was no owl.

No chimney pot either.

Okay.

He turned his attention to the porch, which ran the entire

width of the front of the house. Hanging from its trim were several empty wire planters. Bone-brown tendrils twined around their frames. *Gibbet caged exemplar end fall falls...*

Steps had been cut into the silvered wooden decking. These led up to the front door, which was centrally-placed, six-paneled, flanked by narrow, frosted sidelights, and was, like the shutters, painted a pale green. Above it was a classic New England fanlight and it had a plain brass knocker.

Overall, the house was square-set and large, and for its size the rent was, as Vone knew from Jack's exhaustive, indeed exhausting, research, unusually low. A bargain, in fact – though it meant a commute for Jack that he wouldn't have had if they'd opted for somewhere in Collington-Osprey, as well as a tediously long drive to and from Bangor during his initial training week. Vone wondered if its being number 13 knocked off a few dollars; if people cared about that kind of superstitious bullshit anymore.

"Sorry I've been a jerk about this," he said, and he kissed Jack on the cheek without first looking round to make sure they hadn't already become objects of neighborly scrutiny. Jack turned to him and they kissed on the lips, and Vone felt a flaring up of desire, though this was hardly the time, with the keys to get and the car to unpack, and their son standing right beside them. *Maybe later.* He couldn't resist pushing his tongue into Jack's mouth briefly before breaking the kiss.

Flushing, Jack looked to Jay-Jay and said, "We literally back onto the woods, Jackie-Jacks. How cool is that?"

Vone recalled the signs of cougars and bears they'd passed, and wondered how often they attacked people. He'd seen online videos of bears invading people's kitchens, which were sort of funny but also alarming, as even a small bear weighed more than a man. They could climb trees too. So could cougars. "Yeah," he echoed. "Cool."

"Let's do some exploring," Jack said.

"I'd better shovel this one into a coat first. Go ahead: we'll catch you up."

Jack vanished round the right side of the house as Vone returned to the car to dig out Jay-Jay's puffer jacket. Making airplane noises, Jay-Jay began to run in circles round the dwarf willow on the front lawn, and watching him Vone felt the seductive tug of this rural-suburban life. For sure he wouldn't wish his own shitty childhood on his son; wouldn't wish even the semi-gentrified Bedford-Stuyvesant of today on him (now all but unaffordable anyway). And if it turned out he couldn't write here, at least he was sacrificing his creative self-expression to be a good parent. Hadn't a billion women done the same thing down the centuries? Extracting the jacket, he turned to see fighter-pilot Jay-Jay, arms extended, running towards the road. Coming his way, on oblivious collision course, was a noiseless electric car.

"Junior!"

Dropping the jacket and ducking under the pine-branches, Vone loped quickly across the yard, catching up to his son just before he could run out in front of the car, whirling him round so his sudden pounce was more a game than a scare or a scold. "Don't run under cars, Jackie-Jacks," he said as lightly as he could. "Or you'll end up flat as a pancake."

Jay-Jay laughed as the car, a turquoise Prius, pulled up in front of them, and the driver, a smartly skirt-suited white woman in her forties, struggled out. To a degree that was, Vone guessed, accidental, her outfit exactly matched the car, as did her boldly-applied turquoise eye-shadow, her salmon-pink tie-neck blouse and lipstick a strident contrast. She was short, her hips were wide, and her very dyed, curly blonde hair was piled up and scrunchied on top of her head. She held a large bunch of keys, a clipboard and a wallet of, he presumed, documents, and advanced on him with a fixed smile, her blue eyes bird-bright.

Vone forced his body into passivity as she approached. It was almost, but not quite, a reflex, and the usual inventory ran through his head. He was with a child – respectable. A station wagon full of stuff stood in the drive – respectable. No bass-heavy, expletive-laden hip-hop boomed from the car stereo – respectable. But he was a man, a Black man, apparently alone with her, and not who she was expecting to meet. A mixed-race child wasn't respectable – evidence of sexual boundaries transgressed, Blackness pushed into whiteness somewhere along the way. He was gay – that was safe: she probably "loved" *RuPaul's Drag Race* and *Queer Eye* – but being gay wasn't respectable. Anyway, people never thought he *was* gay unless he said so, even if the do-rag he was wearing (not respectable) was hot pink and shiny. He was six foot one and broad-shouldered, and his build was evident through his joggers and light jacket. With no adult witness to the woman's responses the situation felt instantly unbearable, even dangerous. *Karen in the Ramble.* Central Park: that white woman had called 911 and claimed to be in fear for her life even while she was being filmed blatantly lying. And yet – and this was the most frustrating part – weren't any fears *this* woman might have at meeting an unknown man alone, legitimate?

Deeper down the well of history, he wondered if she felt conned, having assumed she'd rented the property to a white family, and now here goes the neighborhood.

"Hi," she said brightly, her eyes drilling into him, her smile tightening. "I'm, um – you're not Jack, are you?"

Putting Jay-Jay down and attempting a smile as natural as a model's in a Benetton ad, Vone said, "He's round the back, exploring. I'm DuVone Mapley-Stevenson," – adding with only the quiver of a stress, "Jack Stevenson-Mapley's Black husband."

He instantly regretted having given her so much: the emphasis on "Black," even if it was nearly subliminal; indeed saying "Black" at all, even as a joke. The woman instantly brightened up. "Wow, okay," she said. "Great! Well, I'm Sarah from Harris Realtor, your new home coordinator." Her accent was local, and strong. She reached out a hand and Vone shook it briefly. Her fingers were cool and dry. "And who's this little fellow?" she asked, hunkering down to befriend Jay-Jay.

"Jack Junior, aka Stealth Bomber." Suddenly shy, Jay-Jay turned away from her and buried his face in his father's thigh. "We just want to get in and get him settled," Vone added, trying out another smile.

Sarah straightened up. "Oh, am I late?"

"No, amazingly we're early."

"Well, okay. I just need Jack to sign –" She gave a little laugh. "Jack *senior*, I mean..." She gestured with the clipboard, to which various forms were attached.

Vone reached for it. "I can sign."

Sarah smiled helplessly, not offering him the clipboard. His own smile freezing over, Vone kept his hand held out. It was a duel without movement. For so many reasons he wanted to slap her.

The moment was broken only by Jack's bouncy return.

"Sarah?" he called from the corner of the house, ducking under the low-hanging pine-branches and jogging over to where they were standing frozen in place. "Hi, hi. I'm Jack. I was just doing some exploring."

Sarah's smile unclenched and she handed Jack the clipboard. Vone watched his white husband blithely scrawl his signature on various forms and initial the boxes by which a blue ink check-mark had thoughtfully been placed in advance. Sarah peeled off the pink carbons under each form, handed them to Jack, flicked through to check everything was in order, then handed him the keys.

"Welcome to your new home!" she said to them both. "I've written my cell on the top copy for if there are any problems, or you can always call the office number in office hours."

"The yard could do with some attention," Vone said, more flatly than he'd intended, though in fact the grass had been cut fairly recently, and some effort made to rake up the leaves under the dwarf willow, along with those that had blown in from neighbors' gardens.

Sarah pulled a face. "I know," she said. "We've had a few quiet years with this one, I don't know why really, I mean, it's a real classic. The owners are in Michigan, so..." She shrugged, as if that explained everything. "Vicinity – that's the new development – makes it more desirable, though. It's old but everything is up to code, and they had WiFi put in last year. It's pretty reliable, mostly, and is included in the rental. If you come by the office I can give you a bunch of information about the trails and beauty spots, or you can check out our website. Well," she ended brightly, "I'll let you get in!"

She shook Jack's hand, then Vone's, gave Jay-Jay a little wave, went back to her car and got in. They watched her do an oddly awkward three-point turn. "It's because she's literally already on the phone spreading gossip," Jack said.

Vone grunted an almost laugh. "Spilling the tea," he said. The sky above was deepening, and one of the streetlamps pinged into life. "You know we should've made her go in with us and check everything."

"It's not crazy here like in New York," Jack said. "They're not all rip-off artists."

"You hope."

"Let's just get in."

Unspoken was the truth that, as men, they both found that kind of prudent but nit-picking assertiveness impossible. And of course Vone had just wanted her gone.

While they were dealing with Sarah the sun had sunk below the tree line. Now the house looked drab and uninviting. Swinging Jay-Jay between them, they climbed the front steps. The planking was solid, slightly greened, slightly slippery. A few leaves had blown up onto the porch, but only a few.

Examining the bunch of keys, Jack tried a couple of plausible candidates. No luck. The third was the right one. The clack of the lock as it sprang back was oddly loud in the still air, in the dying day.

From somewhere in the woods, Vone sensed, more than heard, an echo.

Four

The door was swollen by damp, and Jack had to shove it sharply to get it open. He frowned.

"What?" Vone asked.

"It was like" – Jack smiled, shaking his head at the notion – "Like someone was on the other side, pushing back."

Vone half-laughed, but noted the impression had been strong enough for Jack to check behind the door as he went in. Vone followed, shepherding Jay-Jay. A few leaves, brown and curlicued, trailed over the threshold after him, catching playfully at his heels. He stamped on the mat to shake them loose as Jack found the light switch.

Low-wattage electric candles on a wagon-wheel chandelier threw a weak light over a square, wood-paneled hall crowded with tatty furniture. It was two stories high and overlooked by a three-sided balcony – the landing, reached by a steep, uncarpeted wooden staircase with a turn in it. The chandelier hung halfway down on a long brass chain. The furniture included an oversized coatrack with 'hooks' made of sharply protruding antlers and horns, a spindly occasional chair with a sagging seat and, across the way from it, obstructing the hall's one radiator (stone cold when Vone put his hand on it), was a chaise longue with water-stained, picky-threaded yellow silk upholstery. By the front door, on the opposite side to the coatrack, was an elephant's foot umbrella stand, in which were several knobbly, varnished walking sticks and a moth-eaten umbrella. Next to that was a grandmother clock, its fruitwood case decorated with touches of gilt and hand-painted sprays of pink and yellow flowers. On a low, glass-topped and badly frayed rattan occasional table was an '80s-era corded push-button telephone. A glass-fronted corner cupboard displayed plates and vases that to Vone looked like the sort of junk that gets old without ever becoming antique. Amateurish, cheaply-framed watercolor flower paintings dotted the paneled walls, and the darkly stained and polished floorboards were scattered with multicolored knotted rugs. Surfaces had been recently dusted, and furniture polish and bleach mingled in the moted air with trace odors of damp and must.

"Well, they said fully furnished," Jack said cheerily, closing the front door with a shove. The stairs to the second floor were directly opposite it; left, right and straight ahead were other doors, all paneled, all closed.

Vone watched his husband move about, opening the doors and looking in, and envied his boyish sense that this was all an adventure. Perhaps it was that Jack could – did – own all this in a way that he, Vone, didn't and couldn't. Or was that exceptionalism in reverse? Tragic Negro-ism? Maybe if he tried hard enough he *could* own this; imagine himself some Mayflower descendant, some possible, impossible, generationally free and never enslaved Black man.

Because there must have been some, right?

More realistically, if also more depressingly, wasn't it possible that some Puritan settler's blood might have (to phrase it with a grace it didn't deserve) commingled with that of some unlucky female survivor of the Middle Passage, some Tituba – Vone's many times removed great-great-grandmother, perhaps? If so, that would make all this his as much as Jack's – more his, if anything, for being bought at so great a price. But even if he held and claimed that right – itself asserted in despite of those whose land it was before – still he wouldn't own this place, any more than the Black cast of the much-lauded musical *Hamilton*, and its hip-hop styling, changed the brute facts of slavery: who owned, and who was owned. He and Jack had had the good luck to see a performance of *The Haunting of Lin Manuel*, the peppery Afro-futurist writer Ishmael Reed's rebuttal of the Broadway smash's deracinated fantasy, at the Nuyorican, a favorite venue of theirs, just before the coming of COVID, what felt like a lifetime ago.

Of course there were things here that Vone – that anyone – *could* own and enjoy. What was well-crafted and well-built was, after all, a universal pleasure. And weren't all cultural connections ultimately a matter of faith, not blood? He thought of Hotep bookstalls in Harlem, of Black men wearing ankh necklaces while dreaming of sparsely-documented Kemet and Meroë, ancient Egypt and Black Israel; and of how a white friend of his had always believed he had Cherokee blood

– had been proud of the fact, even at times militant about it – and then, when a DNA test revealed no such genetic heritage, had become clinically depressed. But what if he had never known; what if no one had ever known? Who would he have been then? Vone had written a poem about it: "Schrödinger's Fact and the All-Seeing (But Sometimes Closed) Eye of God."

Through the doors Jack opened then closed, Vone caught glimpses of, to the left, a cluttered, non-child-friendly front parlor, and to the right an unpromisingly dark, formal dining room. Out of habit he scanned the baseboards in the hall, to check the number of sockets that would need covers on them. The value of socket-covering was up for debate – he'd read several articles online about it being a waste of time – but as a gay parent, particularly a gay male parent, he felt an especial need to be beyond reproach.

No surprise, there weren't many sockets. None had covers on them.

Following a cable up from the baseboard, he pulled back a drape to reveal a WiFi hub sitting on a cushioned sill not quite deep enough to be a window seat. Its green lights flickered, reassuringly full of connections to life elsewhere. Okay, so Miz Anne ain't lied about *that*.

Jack opened the door next to the staircase, revealing a short, windowless passage that led to another door, also closed. There were earth-toned rugs on the plank floor, Native American in design. A small bathroom had been squeezed in under the stairs; opposite it were a pair of large, empty, built-in storage cupboards, their shelves lined with red-and-white checked paper.

Jack opened the end door and went through. Vone didn't immediately follow him. Instead, he turned to his son. "You wanna choose your bedroom, Jackie-Jacks?"

Jay-Jay nodded enthusiastically.

"You better go with him," Jack called from what Vone took to be the kitchen. "Those stairs are really steep."

"Yeah, I noticed. We should get a gate for the top."

"You choose bedrooms; I'll start bringing stuff in."

"Okay, cool."

Vone followed his son as, with difficulty, the five-year-old clambered up the stairs, the risers of which seemed unnecessarily high and the treads perversely shallow. They and the serpentine banister – a single piece of polished wood that seemed to float on the pierced iron spindles that supported it – once again made Vone think of a witch's house, or if not that, then a set from an Expressionist film. By the time Jay-Jay reached the landing he was climbing with his hands as well as his feet. "You're gonna have to be super careful coming down," Vone cautioned. "Maybe come down backwards or scoot on your booty."

Jay-Jay went round to peer over the balcony rail. He had to stand on tiptoe, so that at least wasn't a safety hazard, and the balusters were too close together for him to squeeze his head through, never mind the rest of him. Off to one side overhead was a ceiling-hatch; hanging on the wall nearby a pole with a hook on its end: presumably there was a pull-down ladder up there.

"This way, daddy." Jay-Jay caught Vone's hand and led him determinedly down a narrow passageway in the direction of the back of the house. At its far end was a small, diamond-paned window with, on its sill, a vase of dusty and cobwebbed dried flowers. Bits of dead flies were scattered round the base of the vase like metal shavings, the dinner debris of a hungry, long-dead spider. *Housekeeping only got so far, huh.* The walls were paneled to waist height and above the paneling were papered a pale yellow geometrically studded with pink roses the size of dimes. As well as more flower paintings there was an arresting portrayal of a staring owl, with behind it a full moon. It had a clumsy force, and Vone wondered if it was by the same artist. There were also eight doors, four on either side.

Passing the others without interest, Jay-Jay led his father to the last door on the right. Putting his hand on the knob, he looked up at Vone for permission. Vone nodded and Jay-Jay opened the door to reveal a modest-sized corner bedroom containing a pine-frame single bed with a blue-and-white patchwork coverlet, a large cedarwood pirate's chest, a bedside lamp with jaunty sailing ships and cheery, spouting whales on its shade, and a blue-and-red chest of drawers. Gold-painted fir cones were piled in the grate of a small, boarded up fireplace, and a couple of basic shelves had been put up on one wall, under one of which an area had been curtained off as a makeshift closet. The fabric, which was geometric white and navy blue, was the same as the drapes at the windows, which were catty-corner to each other. It was without question a boy's room, and more recently decorated than the rest of the house – in the mid-eighties, Vone guessed.

"Okay, well, this looks good. Do you want to check out the other rooms?"

"Nuh-uh. This one."

Jay-Jay went over to the back window. Vone joined him and lifted him up, and Jay-Jay put his arms around his father's neck. Being carried was something he was growing out of, but seemed to find reassuring in this unfamiliar setting. Together they contemplated the woods that ran away beyond the backyard fence, and watched them vanish beneath the encroaching tide of night. Jay-Jay had never experienced country dark before and his eyes were wide.

A rising wind stirred the massed foliage, rendering it sentient, and creating the impression that some huge, invisible something was rolling slowly toward them. *From the deep woods*. Viewed from safely indoors, the impression was fairy-tale-like, though the rattle of the window in its frame turned Vone's thoughts to the heating, or absence of same.

A thud came from below, followed by a muffled curse. Vone set Jay-Jay down. "Let's go help Dad out, okay?"

Heaving their possessions over the threshold and into the hall seemed enough of an achievement for that evening. They left for the morning unpacking the overfull cartons with their perilously sagging bottoms, the trash bags bulging with mismatched items packed late on in the process when discipline had broken down, the suitcases and straining travel-bags, the framed prints in bubble-wrap, the crates of books and Vone's folding workout bench, barbell and dumbbells, the combined weight of which had threatened to buckle the axle.

Food for that first evening had been boxed up and clearly labeled early on in the packing process – Vone's modest contribution to domestic efficiency – and so was easy to find. But it was disconcerting to be faced by how much they had hauled with them from Brooklyn. As Jack had observed wryly that morning, while struggling Tetris style to wedge their resentful, allegedly pre-decluttered possessions into the back of the station wagon, "At this point, none of it sparks joy." They hadn't rented a trailer – a conscious decision, to force them to be ruthless with junking stuff, but one that led to them seriously overloading the roof rack, *Beverly Hillbillies* style.

"They do have eggs in the countryside," Jack said as Vone stacked two, then three twelve-pack cartons on the kitchen counter. "Amazingly enough."

"I know, I just didn't want to –" Vone cut himself off. "You're right, of course," he said with an effort. "I brought this too," he added, producing a bottle of sparkling wine. Looking pleased, Jack took it from him and put it in the refrigerator, which was large and old-fashioned. Across its curving green-and-cream front "Kelvinator" was spelt out in go-faster chrome, and it hummed encouragingly.

Deciding that first evening to be cozy in the kitchen, they lit the stove's burners and turned the oven on, leaving the door open: they could tackle the central heating after eating.

The kitchen ran the width of the back of the house and had exposed oak beams. From these pots and pans hung amongst dusty bunches of dried herbs, giving it a rustic, low-ceilinged feel. A large picture window overlooked the yard.

To the immediate left as you came in were a pair of doors – cupboards, Vone guessed; then a nook with a built-in bench, a large pine breakfast table and four spoke-backed chairs arranged around it. Against the windowless left end wall, on the other side of which was the garage, were a large china hutch and a pair of low corner cupboards. Above the breakfast table was a pull-down light fixture of brass and china that reminded Vone of the time-warp house of an eccentric, rarely-visited aunt of his out in Long Island.

To the right an old-fashioned stove with eight burners sat in a large, brick-lined hearth, its tin flue disappearing wonkily up the wide throat of the chimney, and Vone had a sense that this part of the house was older than the rest. Facing the stove, under the picture window, was a Belfast basin set into a pale blue Formica-topped counter. This extended partway across the room, dividing the preparation of food from its consumption. The back door was to the right, on the side of the house.

When opened, the doors by the breakfast nook revealed, respectively, a utility cupboard with meter and fuse box, and a flight of steps that led down to the basement and, presumably, the heating and hot water system.

Through the window, lit by the light that spilled out from the kitchen, an expanse of tussocky grass was visible, along with the nubbly trunks of a group of tall and elderly fruit trees. At the far end of the yard was a head-height picket fence. In the middle of the fence was a gap large enough to step through, and Vone had an immediate desire, more intense than was reasonable, to see it blocked off. To the left was the chain-link fence and beyond it the overgrown paddock; to the right the laurel hedge, nine feet high, glossy, dark and dense.

Jack squatted down to search for something in one of the cupboards under the sink. "Wow, there's both rat poison *and* Drano in here," he said, taking out a bowl to whisk eggs in. "We're gonna need safety locks."

"There should be a couple in one of the cartons," Vone said. "I labeled it – um, I forget. Jay-Jay? Don't go in any of these cupboards, okay? Jay-Jay?"

Their son came in, carrying the purple plastic Buzz Lightyear lunchbox he kept his toy cars in – he must've been searching through the mound of stuff in the hall for it. Seeing nothing much was happening, he went over to the breakfast table, put the lunchbox on the bench and clambered up next to it. Once he was up, he turned and opened its chunky catches, unselfconsciously absorbed in his task.

"Well, *he's* loving it," Vone conceded. "I was worried he'd feel really alienated by the whole thing. You know kids love stability."

"Kids are resilient," Jack said, briskly cracking eggs into the bowl. For him stability had been a fantasy, not a reality; not, therefore, a necessity. He set a frying pan on one of the burners and rooted out a stick of butter from the provisions box.

"They can be smiling and still effed up on the inside, though," Vone said.

"I'd say that was inevitable. You wanna find some plates?"

Vone nodded and said to Jay-Jay, "Next task, Junior: go wash your hands. Sticky's good for geckos, not for boys."

Jay-Jay slid awkwardly off the bench and went through to the downstairs bathroom. A moment later there came the squawk of a faucet, then the gurgle of old pipework. This was followed by an alarming juddering like a decrepit washing machine on its spin cycle, the rush of water, and the sound of plenty of it splattering onto the floor.

Jack was by now pushing the rapidly solidifying eggs round the pan, so Vone set down the stack of mismatched plates he had found in the hutch and went quickly through to the bathroom. He found Jay-Jay standing on an upended tin wastebasket, face screwed up as with both small hands he tried to turn off a too-vigorously gushing faucet that was sending water spilling from the shallow sink onto the worn linoleum. Briskly Vone lifted his son over the rapidly widening puddle and set him down in the hall. Then, with an effort, he turned off the faucet, wondering as he did so how Jay-Jay had managed to turn it on in the first place.

Straddling the puddle and leaning on the basin, waiting for it to drain, Vone caught sight of his reflection in the bathroom mirror, his expression tense, his eyes haunted, his handsomeness – and he was, he knew, handsome – no protection from the chaos within. Why was everything so hard? So many didn't have his luck– up to and including a partner who stuck by him through his episode and didn't trade him in afterwards – so why did he have to repeatedly remind himself of the fact? First world privilege, maybe, though after all, each man's pain is his own, and not erased or even much offset by knowing that others suffer elsewhere.

He had hoped – he *still* hoped, while knowing it was against the odds – that this change of location might help his mental state; might somehow be a reset. But there was no way round the cliché that wherever you went, you took yourself with you, whack neurochemistry included.

He couldn't share any of that with Jack, of course. Because what is your partner supposed to say, or do, when you tell him that all his love and all his commitment fail to fill some fundamental hole in you?

One logical, and certainly self-protecting, response would be to admit defeat and file for divorce.

Just keep taking the meds.

The sink was empty now. Vone went in search of rags to mop up with, finding them eventually in the cupboard of poisonous things.

It felt late by the time they sat down to eat, though was in fact only 8 p.m. Despite Jack having to start his training first thing the following morning, they popped the sparkling wine. Why hadn't they moved on Saturday or even Friday instead of, of all days, Sunday? There had been some good reason, though Vone couldn't remember it now. Jay-Jay's head nodded as Vone and Jack clinked flutes – wedding gifts from Jack's colleagues at the Brooklyn HIV Prevent office – then Jay-Jay's juice-glass.

"To our overlord, and the reason for it all," Vone said. Pleased to be included, Jay-Jay took a sip of O.J., holding the glass in both hands, watching and imitating what his parents did.

"This could be good, if you let it," Jack said. "You always say you need boredom to create, and you haven't written anything for –"

"A year and three months. And two days."

"Roughly."

Vone looked at his son. "Minding this one's a full-time job, though." He ruffled Jay-Jay's 'fro.

"It's safer here," Jack said. "And you'll have way more headspace than you were ever gonna have chasing all those extra shifts at Sweetgreen. Out here we won't need to be on him 24/7. Will we, Junior?" He joined Vone in pushing their sleepy son's hair out of his eyes. Jay-Jay ducked his head, pretending annoyance, enjoying the attention. "Did you choose your bedroom yet?"

Vone answered on his son's behalf: "At the back of the house on the right."

"It's blue for boys!" Jay-Jay enthused.

"That's great, Jackie-Jacks," Jack said, adding to Vone, "Kids today are over-supervised, we both know that. We're giving him a chance to have what was good about our childhood."

"*Your* childhood," Vone said, then quickly revised his statement to, "Well, some of it."

Like many, perhaps most white rebels and outsiders, Jack had a background split between deprivation and privilege. Early on in their relationship, he had told Vone about growing up with a substance-abusing, alcoholic single mother, and how they had spent years living in nondescript motels in various dispiriting cities across the Midwest. "We stayed places just long enough for people to see through her," he would say summarily, and this oft-repeated narrative was so foundational to his identity that Vone would forget that Jack also had wealthy grandparents, and that at crucial times during his unstable boyhood he had been gifted idyllically recalled, mom-free holidays at their house in Bar Harbor, a wealthy and picturesque town on the Maine coast.

Vone now saw that Jack's memories of those holidays had primed him to arrive in Gaugeville already half in love with it, or rather his dream of it – something Vone empathized with in relation to his own sense of connection to the Harlem Renaissance, despite its being a cultural moment that had ended fifty years before he was born, and took place in a district where he had never lived. Vone dubbed this feeling paranostalgia. Yet his sense of longing and belonging was as real, it seemed to him, as an actual biographical or biological connection would be. And so he understood his husband's response to Cottonwood Way, at least by analogy.

Jack never squared the circle of how his apparently stable and loving grandparents had produced his damaged, peripatetic mother, and was forever blaming her and exonerating them, to the point where Vone sometimes wondered –

"A *good* childhood," Jack said, and he took Vone's hand in his and looked down at their intertwined fingers, contemplating the contrasting skin tones, hopefully seeing the combination as home. "And we both want that for him, right?"

"Right."

"And the apartment was too small and we couldn't afford anywhere bigger, or not where either of us wanted to live." That too was true: neither of them had been willing to relocate to some banal suburb. City or country, nothing in between. "And this is a promotion for me that comes with health insurance for both of us and enough of a salary bump that you don't have to get a job. You can write."

That was the deal, of course: *I'll support you, but you better crank out the verse or, being a man, why don't you go to work?* But then, what else could it have been? Jack had sacrificed the creativity within himself for this, for them, and Vone felt like a jerk for being other than grateful – including very concretely grateful that he and his various costly medications were included on Jack's spousal insurance – or would be once his probationary period was over. And Vone *was* grateful, though at the same time he thought of the way addicts react to those who care enough to make them go cold turkey: "We always hate the ones who save us" – a line for a poem, maybe, or did it sound too much like a Morrissey lyric? Hadn't he turned out to be racist or something?

Vone lifted his glass. "To new beginnings," he said, and Jack smiled and raised his glass too.

Jay-Jay folded his arms on the table and put his head down, clattering his plate and getting bits of scrambled egg in his hair. Vone slipped the plate out from under him, flicked away the egg.

"He can roam about and you won't have to fret," Jack said. "Fret" was code between them for anxiety spiraling into paranoia.

Vone said nothing, thinking of the steepness of the stairs, the gaping electrical sockets, the rat poison and drain unclogger in the unlocked kitchen cupboard: the known perils. And then there were the unknown ones, roaming the thousands of miles of forest behind the house, in which, as in a fairytale, a child could so easily get lost. Coyotes, bears, cougars, even wolves, probably. He squeezed Jack's hand. The wedding bands glinted.

Back in New York, Vone had been the native, Jack the visitor who stayed. In their bohemian, racially-mixed social circles Blackness, whiteness and brownness had existed mostly in a sort of parity, as had gay and bi and straight, hipness the trump card when who was in the majority could reverse itself from venue to venue, dominance at any given moment the product more of personal charisma than status in the outside world. But here all was monolithically white and hetero; here parity would have to be fought for, over and over.

Yet Vone knew there had been reasons to abandon

bohemia, which accelerating gentrification had both emblem-atized and laid bare. It was, for instance, a fact that those who had money in their background, whether acknowledged or disguised, began slowly – imperceptibly at first – to rise up the social ladder, and after a while you realized, as if startled from a dream, that they had, without apparent endeavor or even will on their part, drifted into middle-class property ownership, and you had not. And those who rose like jellyfish on an ocean current were, of course, mostly white. It wasn't, somehow, an accident that Vone was still slinging salad at thirty, while Jack was establishing himself in a career, albeit in the comparatively low-status field of social work; that Jack was salaried while Vone was merely waged.

And now not even that.

Jack's successes were Vone's too, of course: they were husband and husband; partners. But with two men you could never have the complementary, separate spheres that a man and woman might console themselves with: there would al-ways be an element of direct competition, of unavoidable comparisons and ranking. Like dick size, and how much you could bench-press.

With the stove turned off, the kitchen began to get chilly. "We'll have to figure out the furnace before we turn in or there'll be no hot water in the morning," Jack said without much enthusiasm.

"Maybe whatsername left instructions."

Jack flicked through the welcome pack the realtor had given him: no luck. "Maybe it'll be obvious," he said, not sounding convinced. He swallowed the last of his wine and got to his feet.

Vone followed suit. "I'll take Junior up," he said, lifting their sleepily protesting son down from the bench. "Time to get your fangs de-scaled, Wild Thing."

Jack went down to the basement; Vone carried Jay-Jay upstairs. Usefully, there was a shower-room next to his bed-room, with handbasin and toilet. Jay-Jay was now just tall and grown-up enough to do without a special step or inset seat, both unappealing and space-consuming items Vone had been glad not to have to try to force into the car that morning (lit-erally) on top of everything else.

Brushing his teeth, splashing his face with cold water and getting into his pajamas of course woke Jay-Jay up. "Monster hunt!" he shouted, jumping up and down on his bed. "Monster hunt!"

This was a game Vone had played with his son for as long as he could remember, in the beginning to get him over a fear of the dark that was threatening to become neurotic. Using his phone for a flashlight, Vone went through the usual routine, first pulling aside the drapes – "No monster moth hiding behind the curtains!" – then opening a drawer in the red-and-blue chest of drawers – "No folded underpants monster in the chest of drawers!"

"Under the bed! Under the bed!" Jay-Jay ordered.

Going down on one knee, Vone lifted the edge of the coverlet and peeked. "No dustball monster under the bed! Phew! All done for the night, Jackie-Jacks. Time for sleep."

"The chest! The chest!"

Vone reached for the chest, half-expecting it to be locked. It wasn't, and for no good reason he felt a spasm of unease. He lifted the lid with a quick, sharp movement. The chest was empty.

"No pirate-gold-guarding beach umbrella monster! Scoot under the covers." Jay-Jay did as he was told. "You are getting sleepy," Vone said in his best Transylvanian Bela Lugosi voice. "Very sleepy..." Jay-Jay obediently closed his eyes. Vone pulled the coverlet up to his son's shoulders, bent over and kissed his forehead. When he straightened up one of his knees clicked, and for the first time in years he thought of his father.

"Can I have the nightlight, please?" Jay-Jay asked with his eyes closed.

"We'll find it tomorrow. Do you want the lamp on?"

"Yes, please. And leave the door open and the passage light on."

"Okay, but only for tonight. Electricity costs money, honey."

"And makes climate change, Daddy."

"Greta'll get us if we leave the lights on too much."

"Like a witch!"

"Yeah. Well, a well-meaning witch. Night-night now."

Back in the kitchen, Vone went over to the cellar doorway

and called down, "Need a hand, babe?"

"I'll be up in a minute," Jack called back, sounding tense.

From the top of the stairs Vone could see nothing but a rectangle of concrete floor and one corner of an ominously old-fashioned washing machine. As he leant out over the drop, hanging onto the doorframe like a ship's figurehead, the knuckles of his right hand brushed something scaly.

Startled, Vone pulled himself upright. Nailed to the wall above the light switch was a snakeskin. It was around three feet long and had been hung vertically; another skin was nailed to the wall opposite.

Five

Vone's mind went at once to totems and warding spirits. Fighting the typical urbanite's squeamishness around hides and pelts, he examined the skins more closely. In their way they were beautiful: bead mosaic strips, one a column of flat bands of red, black and white; the other lozenges of amber and vermilion, both as vividly colored as if the animal was still alive. He leant in and sniffed the one he had touched. There was no odor. He had held a snake once, a small one, when he was nine or ten, at some show and tell at school. He remembered the girls squealing with overdone hysteria as the snake flicked its tail and wound itself around his wrist to make a living bracelet. Warmed by the sunlight, it had been muscular, smooth and dry to the touch, though some of the girls had insisted it was "slimy." He had almost liked it.

Still, snakes this large, and apparently home-killed, made him uneasy. He would have to Google poisonous snakes of New England and try to match the patterns up. He wondered if snakes liked to come in houses in winter to hibernate. On no evidence, he decided they probably did.

"I think the pilot'll stay on now," Jack said, coming up from the basement. "I overrode the timer, so we should get a build-up of heat overnight and hot water in the morning." There was a soot-smut on the tip of his nose. He didn't seem to notice the snakeskins, and for some reason, tiredness maybe, Vone didn't point them out to him. Instead he licked the ball of his thumb and rubbed the smut from Jack's nose. Jack smiled. "Thank you, Mom."

Next they lugged a first round of bags and cases up to their bedroom, which was at the front of the house, diagonally opposite Jay-Jay's, and chosen by Vone because it had an *en suite* with a separate shower and tub. Otherwise unmodernized, it was dominated by a big double-bed that had heavily carved, Jacobean style artichoke-shaped posts at its feet and a tastelessly mismatched, pink velveteen button-back headboard.

In the same style as the footposts were a large and solid

wardrobe and a chest of drawers. There was a faded cerulean velvet sewing chair in a corner, and under the side window a walnut dressing-table, before which sat a spindly stool with a plush, sage-green seat. More rag rugs, made, judging from the materials used, by the same hand as those downstairs, were scattered about on the polished but creakily uneven floor-boards. The wallpaper was flock, William Morris-y: large leaves and twining tendrils, dark green on pale yellow. It made Vone think of that Charlotte Perkins Gilman tale of creeping madness, and wasn't there a story by M. R. James he had read in college too? Something about faces peeping out as if from the edge of a cornfield. By contrast, the drapes were plain, of a pale green material that didn't quite match the green of the wallpaper. *A discordant eye*, Vone thought. Or else just poor, and making use of whatever was to hand or came for free.

The fireplace had a narrow mantelpiece, painted gloss white. The chimney was boarded up with a ventilation slot at floor level. A mesh guard stood in front of the grate. In the middle of the guard was a pewter medal featuring a, Vone thought, female face framed by wildly coiling hair. The mouth gaped, and Vone thought of pictures of Medusa's head on Perseus's shield.

Snakes on the brain, he thought. *Like Samuel L, or Caravaggio or Ray Harryhausen.*

The unaired smell was more pronounced here than downstairs: a latency of damp and plaster dust and something else half-familiar that he couldn't place. The *en suite* was an unappealing eighties salmon pink, and limescale crusted the fittings. Black mold crept up the grouting and fringed the shower-curtain, but when Vone spun the taps the water flowed obligingly and was instantly clear, and though the pipes juddered, the pressure seemed okay.

Jack opened the wardrobe to hang his zip-bagged work suits and plastic-wrapped work shirts – he'd checked in advance that Collington-Osprey had a decent dry-cleaning service. A mothball fell out with a clack and rolled away under the bed, the smell Vone had been unable to place. He looked round from decanting his meds into the bathroom cabinet as Jack knelt and felt about under the bed, with a grunt pulling out a large, old leather suitcase. It had rusted hasps and dragged heavily. Vone leaned in the bathroom doorway and watched Jack pop the locks.

If either of them was hoping for some intriguing mystery, or at least a talking-point heirloom, he was disappointed, as inside were only carefully folded velvet curtains. All were – or had been – dark green. Jack flicked through the layers of material, hoping for something more interesting underneath, but there was only more fabric. Damp dustiness touched Vone's nostrils, leaving him feeling slightly suffocated as Jack closed the suitcase and slid it back under the bed.

Later, after taking turns in a shower that was only slightly better than lukewarm, they got into bed. It was by then 11 p.m. The sheets were clammy, the mattress lumpy, and the pillows heavy and solid, suggesting that across the decades their feathers had been overwhelmed by the shit of a billion dust mites. The sage-green satin quilt smelled slightly of mold. Oddly, there was only one bedside table – on the window side, which Jack had commandeered, where there was also an electrical outlet – though above the headboard each of a pair of bordello-ish reading lights had its own cord-switch. Someone had once hoped for, maybe even had, a companion, Vone thought, then had given up.

Vone and Jack lay on their sides facing each other. Jack looked like he was going to say something, but instead he leant forward and kissed Vone on the lips. The soft, firm warmth was comforting and Vone kissed him back. Mirroring each other in the spirit of a sixties sitcom, they reached up and pulled their respective light-cords. Then Vone turned over and Jack spooned in behind him, sliding his arms around Vone's chest, crossing his hands over Vone's breastbone, his crotch warm against Vone's butt, and it felt good and safe.

Vone woke with a start, confused, for a moment thinking he was back in Brooklyn. Somewhere in the house he could hear Jay-Jay crying. Beside him Jack was asleep, a humped form in the dark. Funny how the gender dynamic played out when you had a child, he thought: the one who goes to work and doesn't hear; the one who doesn't, and does. Reaching over his husband he brushed a fingertip across his phone screen: 2:17 a.m.

Only, if he was honest, half-trying not to wake Jack, Vone turned back his side of the covers, rolled out of bed and, in undershirt and Calvin's, padded through to Jay-Jay's room. The air in the house was cool, and his exposed arms prickled, but a passing touch told him the radiators were warming up, and there was a slight smell of heating oil and burnt dust. The soles of his bare feet met bumpy rag rugs and cold floorboards.

He found Jay-Jay sitting up in bed and looking around tearfully. "Hey, Jay," he said, sitting on the bed and stroking his son's arm. "What's wrong? Did you have a bad dream?" Jay-Jay nodded. "Okay, well let's get you cleaned up." Vone reached for the Kleenex box that sat on top of the chest of drawers.

"There's a thing that lives in a hole," Jay-Jay said.

"Like a rabbit?" Vone asked lightly. "Blow."

Jay-Jay blew. Then, his face puckering, he shook his head.

"Maybe a fox?" Jay-Jay shook his head again. "Well," Vone said, recalling a documentary he'd seen about the burrows of tarantulas, and not wanting to seed such an image in his son's head, "I'm all out of ideas."

"Can I sleep with you and Dad?"

Vone gave his son a look. He and Jack had been trying to get Jay-Jay to sleep in his own bed for months now – "For the sake of what little remains of our sex life," as he had said to Rell in an unguarded moment. They had persevered, and nowadays Jay-Jay mostly stayed put. "*Please*, Daddy."

Vone caved. "Well, okay. But just for tonight. You have to get used to your own room, okay? That's why we let you choose it."

Jay-Jay nodded as Vone hauled him out of bed and slipped his hot arms around Vone's neck. "Don't forget Dippy, Daddy."

As Vone turned to pick Dippy up, balancing Jay-Jay on one hip, from inside the chimney-breast he heard a rustling: something falling or slithering down.

"Daddy?" Jay-Jay sounded scared.

"It's just soot, Jackie-Jacks."

"What's soot?"

"Well, in the olden days people would burn wood and coal in fireplaces to keep warm, and the smoke would go up the chimney and out through the roof. But now we have central heating we mostly board the chimneys up to keep out drafts. You've drawn with charcoal, right?" Jay-Jay nodded. "It's charred wood, that's why it's dirty. Charred like coal. The insides of chimneys get covered with the same sort of dirt. It's called soot, and sometimes it builds up heavily enough to fall down. And that's what we just heard."

Jay-Jay still looked worried, and Vone found himself thinking of the network of flues within the walls; how things might move around inside the house and go from room to room unseen. "I think I saw an owl on the roof earlier," he went on, "on top of the chimney. She's probably made a nest up there, and when she moves around, she knocks soot down. Let's go to bed, okay?"

He turned off Jay-Jay's lamp and carried him through. Jack was still asleep, and didn't respond when Jay-Jay burrowed in next to him. Vone went to the bathroom, emptied his bladder, and joined them under the covers.

To his surprise, sleep came easily.

The following morning was sunny and encouraging. The house was warm, and despite traces of hangovers, the mood determinedly cheerful as they all sat down to their first breakfast in the kitchen nook of Number 13, a little after seven a.m.

Today Jack was driving to Bangor to meet his department head for the first time in person, and begin his training. He was smartly suited and wearing a tie Vone had given him, a Paul Smith that was probably too high-tone for the job but boosted his morale. His choppy blond hair was spiked with gel, but not outlandishly, and in the golden morning light he looked handsome and primed for success, and only slightly in a "Category Is: Admin Realness" way.

Vone had on a fresh white tee, gray sweats, a silver du-rag, white socks and black rubber slides. The scent of laundry detergent always made him feel human. Funny how your funk didn't: the exact opposite of a dog loving its stinky basket. Or perhaps he felt more sharply than most that any sort of body odor or staleness or dirtiness might be the beginning of a descent into dereliction and mental disorder. And as a Black man, didn't he always have something extra to prove?

In his role as cheerleading house-husband, Vone served organic muesli and a jug of almond milk, wholewheat toast with organic maple syrup from the Whole Foods across from Sweetgreen, fresh orange juice, and fresh-ground Sightglass coffee for himself and Jack. Already the life of easy access to such upmarket goods seemed distant, though they had barely been able to afford them back in Brooklyn anyway. He thought vaguely of Amazon drones, wondered about their range.

Jay-Jay sat on the bench next to Jack, banging his heels good-naturedly against the paneled wall behind them as he spooned in his Cheerios – his parents' one concession to unhealthy but fuss-free eating. Dippy stood between the toast-rack and the coffee-pot, prehistoric and modern, a guardian: a Lares, or was it a Penates, or were those plurals? Mingus' *Ah, Um* played on Vone's MacBook on the counter, through the iPhone speaker that had been one of the first things he dug out when he got up that morning, needing something human to push back against the vastness of the woods.

Already he could feel the weight beyond the walls.

After a week's training in Bangor, Jack would be setting up an office in Collington-Osprey, out of which he would hire and train a small team to deliver the county's Prevention & Harm Reduction Strategy around HIV-AIDS and other STIs, opioids, and drug and alcohol abuse generally. This was clunkily acronymed PHRSt, pronounced "first". The team would spend most of their days visiting communities across the county, including schools and (some) churches, meeting back at the hub a couple of times a week to debrief and support each other. Once a month Jack would report to his supervisors in Bangor in person; once a week they would catch up by Zoom, to troubleshoot and course correct.

It was a lot of responsibility. Jack would be putting in long hours while setting everything up, and likely bringing paperwork and worries home, though hopefully his workload would ease once service delivery began. Vone knew he would be keen to make a good impression, not least so the funding would be more likely to continue. His own role, meanwhile, was to not bitch about having nothing to do, and not get bored and anxious while his husband toiled away at a demanding, stressful job with a long commute. It was all very fifties white suburban housewife.

They had been pill-poppers too.

"We pick up the other car next Monday," Jack said. "My bad. I mean Tuesday."

They had agreed to put up with having only one car until then because Monday of that week was the end of peak foliage season, and leasing rates halved once the majority of the leaves hit the deck. Inconveniently, the rental place was in Collington-Osprey, not Gaugeville.

When the move had been months away and therefore unreal, Vone had thought that being without a car for ten days would be no problem because he would be unpacking, settling in, getting to know neighbors and glad-heartedly using the stores in Gaugeville, which were good enough for the locals, and presumably stocked boujee items for tourists as well.

"It'll force me to mix and mingle," he'd said virtuously when he and Jack discussed it back in Fort Greene. The idea was less appealing now he was stuck with it.

"I'll get anything we need for dinner on the way home after work," Jack said. "Just text me if you think of stuff we're missing."

They finished breakfast. As Vone stacked the plates in the basin, Jack pulled on his jacket and picked up his phone and shoulder bag. Vone accompanied him out onto the porch. Jack gave him a look that was suddenly both very young and very nervous. Vone smiled. "You'll dazzle 'em, boo," he said, and he pecked his husband on the lips, performing unselfconsciousness at doing so while on display in front of their house, albeit only in the gaps between the pine trees.

Vone watched Jack back out of the drive, turn and go. Once the car was swallowed by the trees that hid the covered bridge, he looked round to see if anyone else was performing similarly housewifely duties.

In the middle of the road, staring at him unsmilingly and jogging on the spot, was a middle-aged white woman. She wore pink lycra leggings, pink running shoes, a baggy gray hoodie and a tinted sun visor. Her straight blonde hair was scrunchied back and she had AirPods in. She was skinny and knock-kneed and her iPhone was attached to her upper arm like a medical device. He didn't think she was one of the two from yesterday.

Trying to be easy, he gave her a smile and a neighborly wave. She looked down at her watch as if checking her step count, turned away from him and jogged off in the direction of the Vicinity.

Vone stared after her. *Standing on my own fucking porch while Black*, he thought, adding it to the ever-growing list of things that might get the cops called on you if, as Rell put it, you were of the melaninated persuasion. *Nine months.* He felt his face tighten. *No way we staying longer than that.*

Jay-Jay touched his leg. Vone turned to him, buckling on a smile. "Now Dad's gone to slave for The Man, let's you and me do some unpacking." Jay-Jay nodded but looked uncertain, and Vone hoped his son hadn't picked up on his sour mood. "That's our mission for the a.m. Okay, soldier?" he asked, faux gruffly.

"Okay, Daddy."

They exchanged salutes, a small ritual between them, then went inside and hauled some bags up to Jay-Jay's room. Vone briskly unloaded his son's socks, tees, sweaters and underwear into the chest of drawers, and hung coats and jackets in the curtained-off wardrobe space. *How does this child have these many clothes?* Some he noticed had never been worn, and Jay-Jay had almost grown out of them.

Leaving Jay-Jay to uncrate his equally excessively numerous toys and games and transfer them to the pirate chest, Vone went and sorted out his and Jack's bedroom, allotting and filling drawers, piling suitcases on top of the wardrobe, and as a final touch putting their silver-framed wedding photograph in pride of place on the dressing table. It had been a happy day, full of loving friendship, even if Jack's mom – by then three years sober – had been the only immediate blood relative there.

A wound
Wound into
Joy
Those who quote sermons
Smilingly

With unsmiling eyes
Declined to show
Blood thinner
Than love

Their respective unpacking done, father and son rendez-voused on the landing and went down together. After setting Jay-Jay up at the kitchen table with crayons and a coloring book, Vone worked his way through a list of tasks that included digging out the safety covers for the electrical sockets and the child lock for the cupboard of poisons. While putting away his and Jack's not particularly good quality pots and pans, (which it turned out they could have junked, as Number 13 had plenty), he found a small box of author copies of his chapbook, *What Does Not Break You: Poems for The Now by DuVone Mapley-Stevenson*. The cover was half his face, looking brooding and handsome, the publisher Xenith, an indie press in Brooklyn specializing in marginal voices. He remembered how pleased he'd been with the job they'd done: the little book looked great.

And here he was, six years later, forcibly disconnected from everything he needed to make a life as a writer.

No, this change was what I needed. Because he hadn't been writing in New York, had he? Or performing, or networking. *Live the life you've got,* as Brother Baldwin counseled: *You won't get some other life.* How did the rest of it go? Oh, yeah: "You won't have any life at all."

He looked around for somewhere to stow the books that would also put them on display, to low-key impress whatever guests he and Jack might eventually welcome into their home. His eye landed on a shelf occupied by some ugly cups that looked like props from a fortune-teller's caravan or a provincial production of *Beauty and the Beast.* He hid the cups away in the hutch and lined the books up on the shelf, proof that yes, I achieved something once.

The book had won a few favorable mentions here and there, even scored a capsule review in the *Village Voice*, along with a couple of enthusiastic online reviews by poetry bloggers, one too pretentiously garbled to be shareable however heavily he abridged it. It was just thick enough to have a spine rather than be saddle-stitched, thus escaping pamphlet status. He avoided counting how many copies he had left over. Rell had said, "Poetry is for poets, darling, not readers," and he was pretty much right.

At the bottom of the box were two copies of an anthology focused on Black gay men from eight or nine years ago that Vone had had a prose piece in, "Fire Flies in a Storm Cellar". He set them on the shelf next to the chapbooks. If he had kept on hustling, or at least producing, he might have had a reputation by now. But then "the episode" happened, his burden and his alibi.

Alongside his published work, Vone set the affirming volumes he treasured: the *Complete Poetry* of Langston Hughes; his autobiography, *The Big Sea*; collections of Hughes' correspondence with straight, Black, serious Arnold Rampersad and campy, white, moneyed Carl Van Vechten – polar opposites in every way save their abiding friendships with the poet; Essex Hemphill's *Ceremonies*; a thousand-page tome of Ralph Ellison's letters Vone was partway through and finding, if he was honest, boring; works by and biographies of gay and lesbian artists of the Harlem Renaissance – Zora, Claude, Countee, Wallace, Bruce: artists he claimed as his ancestors, and with whom – on good days – he believed himself in creative rapport.

Such a claim, easily made while wandering the streets of Harlem, felt specious here, like being some white kid in the 'burbs revering Tupac and Biggy, believing that through them he understood something of Blackness. And perhaps that white kid did, the communicability of experience being, after all, the foundational premise of art-making. But Vone had walked the streets Langston and Wallace and Zora had walked; had looked up at their houses – or the rooms they had rented in those houses, in that brief spring before the icy blast of economic collapse, and the stinging withdrawal of white patronage. He had haunted them, as they haunted him.

His dumbbells, barbell, weights and exercise bench waited in the hall, looking out of place. As he contemplated where to put them – he'd have to use them and be seen using them after making such a big deal about bringing them ("I'm sure Gaugeville will have a gym, Vone. Probably several," Jack had said, offering no proof. Vone could have Googled but didn't) – Jay-Jay wandered in from the kitchen. Running a small hand over the curves of various bits of furniture, he came to and opened the door of the grandmother clock, and stared at the brass disc of the pendulum and the lead weights that hung immobile inside. Vone wondered how you got it going. Carefully he closed the clock's casing. Norman-arched, it was like the door of a house where someone small lived.

"Okay, soldier. Time to reconnoiter."

Jay-Jay nodded, his expression serious as Vone opened the door into the front parlor. The hinges, needing oiling, cried like kittens, an unnerving sound, and Vone had the sense he was violating a taboo. The front parlor, after all, was the room you never used; were never even allowed to enter. He thought of his maternal grandmother: of the drapes drawn in perpetuity against the bleaching sun; the plastic couch-cover that had yellowed like old wax. The futility – the near-religious perversity – of protecting what lay beneath in such a way that it never was and never would be used or even seen. *God sees.* Vone had never been a believer.

The drapes of the parlor of Number 13 were closed too. Without crossing the threshold, Vone reached round and switched on the overhead light, a bowl of cut crystal on short brass chains.

The parlor, like the hall, was crowded with furniture, though it smelled pleasingly of beeswax rather than bleach. There was also an overpowering impression of green. The wallpaper was mint, pinstriped in lime; and the pale sage curtains featured large leaves the color of bladderwrack. The bulging sofa and armchairs were a matching greenish-brown, and over their backs were draped white lace antimacassars. They were Art Deco in style, and if originals, unlike the furniture elsewhere in the house, of museum quality. Yet more flower paintings dotted the walls, making Vone think of long empty days; of creativity dwindling to a nervous reflex.

The fireplace was white marble, the grate black-leaded. On either side of it were green and yellow tiles with a corncob motif, again in an Art Deco style. The throat had been neatly sealed off. Above the mantle a large square mirror hung in a frame of ebony and bamboo; in front of it was a brass carriage clock with a turquoise cloisonné face. Next to that was a cheaply framed postcard of the Golden Gate Bridge, its colors faded to yellow and pink. "Welcome to San Francisco!" it enthused.

Cut-glass and cloisonné vases stood around the room on lace doilies on occasional tables, and here and there were chrome and brass lamps with 1930s-style uplighter shades of yellow or green glass. Under a display dome on a windowsill a stuffed owl perched, amber eyed and frozen on a twig. Again Vone thought of guardians, though owls were predators too: their feathers, he remembered reading somewhere, structured to be noiseless when they swooped on something trembling in the dark.

A standard lamp with a huge yellow silk tasseled shade stood in a far corner like a gaunt church-lady in disgrace. Next to it was a wooden spinning wheel with a tuft of wool around its bobbin; and on a spindly walnut side-table next to one of the armchairs a large, blown ostrich egg sat on an elaborately carved ebony stand.

It was, Vone thought, an extraordinary room, and insane to leave it like that, not even locked, in a rental property that was supposed to be a family home. The realtor woman, what was her name – oh yeah, Sarah – must have known about it, but she hadn't said not to use the room; had just remarked that it was a fully-furnished let. Jack had signed a bunch of forms about the condition they found the property in, but nothing had stood out to him as weird or onerous, or he hadn't said so. Now Vone suspected the woman had avoided coming in the house for some reason other than the need to spread gossip about the miscegenated fag family as quickly as possible. But what?

Maybe he would box up some of the more fragile things and put them away. The stuffed owl's piercing eyes hardly made for a cozy atmosphere. What got people into taxidermy? His mind drifted to roadkill and then to Jeffrey Dahmer. Hadn't he started out doing taxidermy, or was Vone muddling him up with Norman Bates in *Psycho*? He and Jack had skipped the recent Netflix miniseries.

"This room is too full of breakables," he said. "I'm gonna rule it out of bounds, okay?"

Jay-Jay nodded. Vone wondered if there was a key for the parlor door. At least the stuffed owl hadn't freaked him out. Kids were funny about shit like that, either oddly unbothered or wearingly hysterical. Remembering the ceiling hatch on the second-floor landing, he said, "Let's go check out the attic."

As he shepherded Jay-Jay up the stairs, Vone wondered about the person the house had belonged to. Maybe he would amble over to the realtor's office after lunch and ask her – the address of the office on the paperwork was a Gaugeville one. She might even welcome the distraction on a slow afternoon. At least she hadn't been hostile to him like the Stepford Joggers – or no, Jack was right: they were more like the replicants in *Invasion of the Body Snatchers*: malignant pod people. Or the histrionic non-zombified humans in *Night of the Living Dead* – the original, that was, where the Black guy survives until the very end, then gets shot at the last second by a cracker vigilante, and you had to be grateful he *almost* made it out – progressive representation circa 1969. Vone had hated the recent remake, where the Black guy is murdered by the white woman, and she survives instead – a choice that seemed to him emblematic of the particular violence and incoherence of contemporary identity politics. But then, hadn't some white suffragettes opposed Black men being given the vote on the grounds that white women didn't have it yet, and should come first, being white though female? *Plus ça change.*

Taking the pole, he unhooked the hatch to the attic. A well-balanced ladder tilted down and slid smoothly towards him, catching correctly on its safety lock when half-extended. He set the pole aside, pulled the ladder the rest of the way down and, after making sure it was steady, let Jay-Jay lead the climb, following close behind him so he couldn't fall.

"Careful," Vone called as his son reached the top of the ladder, catching hold of the back of his dungarees to prevent him scrambling forward. "It may not be boarded out."

"It's okay, Daddy," Jay-Jay said. "It's safe."

"Okay, well, hold on anyway." Keeping a hand on his son's waist, Vone climbed a few more rungs and stuck his head up through the hatch. The attic was neatly boarded out and, to his surprise, empty: he'd assumed it would be rammed with junk. A large cold-water tank sat on bricks in one corner –

directly above his and Jack's bed, Vone realized uneasily; and in the center a square brick chimney column ran up through the roof. The air was cold and quite fresh, and the attic was underlit by daylight filtering up through the gaps in the eaves.

"Okay," Vone said, letting Jay-Jay clamber forward ahead of him. "Watch your head on the beams," he added as he followed.

There was nothing much to see. The boarding yielded slightly underfoot.

"What are these, Daddy?" Jay-Jay pointed at a scattering of small, whiteish things that lay among twists of dust beneath an eave-slant in one corner.

Vone squatted down to examine his son's find – seven or eight chalky cylinders. From childhood vacations spent with rural relatives down south he recognized them as the crushed, cobwebbed skeletons of regurgitated mice. Mustering matter-of-factness, he said, "Well, when owls eat mice they swallow them whole. Then they bring up the bones later."

"Why?"

"Because bones aren't digestible."

"Why do they eat them, then?"

"Because they don't have fingers."

"Like when we eat ribs?"

"Kinda the exact opposite, but yeah. Okay, well, there's nothing much here. Let's go check out the cellar."

Vone backed down the ladder ahead of Jay-Jay, so his son could have the adventure of descending under his own steam, but Vone could catch him if he slipped. *Must text Jack about the safety-gate for the top of the stairs*, he thought as he slid the ladder back up. It tilted away smoothly and the catch caught with a click. He and Jay-Jay went downstairs.

Uncertain about the state of the cellar steps – in fact, they turned out to be perfectly solid – Vone led the way, glancing at the snakeskins as he clicked on the light. He didn't draw Jay-Jay's attention to them – enough macabre joys of nature for one day – and, perhaps because they were quite high up, Jay-Jay seemed not to notice them, as Jack had not.

The cellar was small, about half the size he would have expected, and ran under the front of the house. There was a large, old-fashioned furnace, in the porthole of which a pilot light flickered, and by it a clunky but serviceable-looking Bendix washer-dryer. A plastic laundry basket sat on top of it, alongside an open box of powder detergent that Vone found, when he shook it, had set hard as cement. The entire back wall, the one that ran under the middle of the house, was shelved floor to ceiling with canned produce, all of it, judging by what was dimly visible through the dusty glass, extremely old. Together, father and son contemplated what Vone could only think of as laboratory specimens, most of them now unrecognizable. There was a faint odor of something – pickling vinegar turned foul, maybe. Like the owl pellets, it reminded him of visits south, a macabre version of his aunt and uncle's mostly cheerful canning bees.

That had been when he was nine or ten, his balls yet to drop – "Sweet," they had said, kindly enough; not yet a hell-bound homo who knew what he wanted to do with his genitals. Not yet 'buked and scorned.

"Let's have lunch," he said.

After bacon sandwiches and hot chocolate, Vone proposed a walk in the woods. The sun was bright, but a quick lean out of the kitchen door told him the air was extremely cold, so before they set out he bundled Jay-Jay up in a woolly hat, scarf and mittens, and wrapped up well himself.

Wooden steps led down from the side-door to a concrete area across which laundry lines were strung to a woodshed, behind which was the laurel hedge, densely evergreen and taller than a man. He wondered what the neighbors on the other side were like, but not much.

Though surely it was unnecessary, he couldn't let go of the habit of locking up carefully. The lock was stiff with disuse. He pocketed the key.

The backyard was large, tussocky and featureless, except for a clump of decrepit-looking pear trees off to one side. Late-season windfalls, half buried by fallen leaves, rotted at their feet; high up, a few last pears clung to the ends of twigs that bent beneath their weight. From a large, horizontally-extending branch two ropes hung side by side: evidently there had once been a swing there. Vone went over and gave them a tug. Both seemed okay. If he found a plank he could reinstate the seat easily enough. He noticed the ends of the ropes had been cut rather than fraying or breaking, and imagined a spiteful parent, a mean moment. Long ago.

At the far end of the yard was the fence, tall and white-washed, the gap in its middle an accidental doorway through which you could see, as in a folktale, a trail running off into the gold and scarlet woods.

Ducking under a twisted length of rusty wire, Vone and Jay-Jay stepped through the gap, a transition that did not then feel significant. The air had a mineral sweetness, and there was no wind.

In a short while they had left the house behind them and the woods might be all there was in the world, a sensation that was mildly unnerving but also exhilarating. The leaf-strewn loam was black and firm beneath their feet; and where the dead bracken and parched brown briars encroached, they crunched crisply as father and son trod them down. The trail ran straight, as if well-trodden; then, curiously, came to a stop before a wall of undergrowth. Vone was about to propose going back when Jay-Jay said, "There's more path on the other side, Daddy. Look."

Vone looked and saw that Jay-Jay was right. Rather reluctantly he led the way in pushing through the thicket, keeping Jay-Jay close behind him, making sure he was shielding his eyes from springing branches and spitefully jabbing twigs. The tangle grew denser, and Vone wondered if they would have to give up and turn back, but soon enough he was shoving his way out of it on the other side, and from there the trail ran clear again. They went on, the only noise their breathing and the swish of fabric on fabric.

Vone was struck then by the absence of birdsong – not a peep or cheep or trill or caw from the birds that had been so noisy on their arrival. It was as if they had migrated *en masse* overnight, which surely couldn't be true. Perhaps they were only vocal at dusk, though that didn't sound right either. His ignorance of their habits made him feel fraudulent in his padded, red check jacket, matching ear-flapped hat and too-clean Timberlands.

Category is: Rural Realness.

Though past its peak, the fall foliage was dense and still spectacular, running from amber, copper, caramel and rust to vermilion, crimson, orange and scarlet, interspersed here and there with glossy, viridian hollies and woodsmoke-blue pines. To attempt to make a poem of it felt both necessary and doomed to be a pointless echo of the dazzling reality – not to mention of the trillion other, already-written verses hymning the beauties of nature. *Blaze... blazing beech and burnished copper... bronze beech-leaves... gold-fed sunspot chloroplasts... heaped leaves like Inca pyramids...* Huh. Okay. Cut "like". And a zillion poets had used "blaze." And "bronze." And actually, are those beech trees? Be accurate. *Quiet – no – Silent Inca pyramids, (ziggurats) monuments raised (fallen/fall/fell) to (amidst) lost (sunken) green sun cities, ribs – veins – retreating, reverse (transverse) aquifers, sleepy brown now, a metallic – no, mineral absence, withdrawn/leached out, crumbling, slender barkskin pillars (pilasters?) in two-dimensional, labyrinthine diagrammatic halls...*

Jay-Jay scampered ahead, every so often jumping out from behind tree trunks; Vone, increasingly inattentively, pretended surprise. Twigs crackled like fire as his son rampaged about just out of view, enjoying making noise. *Maybe I actually will be able to –* "Jay-Jay?"

No answer.

"Junior?" Vone called, more sharply this time. "Boy, don't go running off on me now."

Again, no answer. No sounds of movement either. It was as if his son had been swallowed up by – "Jay-Jay?"

With rising unease and a crawling sense of defeat – *Jesus Christ, can't I even keep track of my own kid for all of –* Vone began to search about on either side of the trail, calling louder, "Jay-Jay? Jay-Jay!"

From nearby there came the crack of a rifle.

Six

S *hit.*

Vone blundered forwards, in the direction of the gunshot. Later he would think: how stupid: making a noise like some charging beast that would draw the rifle-sights towards him, that would tighten the finger on the trigger – *A black shape between two trees/A great white hunter/It's always the weaponized/Who feel terrorized/AK Also Known As/Stand your ground/less/Fear* – but at that moment he thought only of his son. "Junior!" he yelled, breaking into a run.

Thrusting through a hawthorn thicket, stumbling out the other side with briars tangled round his calves and ankles, he almost barreled into Jay-Jay, who was standing faced away from him in a grassy clearing walled in by trees. His arms hung at his sides and his head was bowed as if he were in church, neck bared as for an admonition, or the executioner's axe.

"Jay-Jay, what the fuck?"

Vone now saw his son was standing at the edge of a large hole and staring down into it. It was circular, eight feet across, brick-lined within, had no safety rail, and its crumbling lip curved down treacherously into the dark. A well, most likely. How deep was it? A small slip was all it would take; physics would do the rest. *A boy/a fly/a pitcher plant/stomach acid dissolution/below/meat broth: vegetable nutrition.*

"Jesus." Vone folded his arms round Jay-Jay and lifted him back. Small stones skittered down into the well mouth. No splash came, but for a moment Vone had the impression that something had stirred down there, though that too was a thought for later: right now all his focus was on his son. Vone turned Jay-Jay to face him. "Why didn't you answer when I called, Jackie-Jacks?"

Jay-Jay looked at him blankly, his mouth slightly open, and Vone wondered if he was having some sort of seizure.

Another gunshot cracked out, closer than the one before, though it was hard to tell the direction. *Should I call out?* But if he did, might the blackness of his voice bring hatred and harm rather than concern and alarm? *Like we all know/Too-Black names on job resumés/Cancel out/CVs/ Curriculum Vitae = Damnatium Mors*. Pushing back his son's hair, he said, "Let's go home, okay?"

The blankness left Jay-Jay's face, and he closed his mouth and nodded. He seemed unaware of the well mouth gaping behind him. Vone took his mittened hand and led him away from both it and the unseen hunter (or hunters), skirting the clearing until he found the spot where the trail entered it, rather than forcing his way back through the thicket with his small son in tow.

They hadn't gone far when Jay-Jay pointed at something white lying in the tangle of brown stickers and ground ivy next to the trail. "Daddy, look!"

Vone looked, and saw the cylindrically-crushed and regurgitated skeletons of three large rats or maybe possums. "Owls!" Jay-Jay said, proud to display his new knowledge.

"Yeah," Vone said. But the corpses were far too big for an owl to have swallowed them. *It would have to be the size of a hog to –* The image was displeasing, so instead he said, "Keep away from the well, okay? It's deep and the edges are weak. You get too close, they might collapse and you could fall in."

Jay-Jay nodded. "Who's the well for?"

"I don't know."

"Witches?"

Vone smiled. "Why witches?"

"For if their broomstick ran out of charge so they had to land."

"Ran out of charge?" Vone echoed, amused, then said, "Travelers, maybe. In the olden days before cars and roads. For them and their horses."

"Shouldn't there be a bucket?"

"There probably was, back then. Before people stopped going that way. What made you think of witches?"

Jay-Jay shrugged.

New England, Vone thought, *getting in his bones.*

Three more gunshots cracked out close together, or maybe four overlapping, and there was a male shout. It was distant but prompted Vone to hurry Jay-Jay away from the regurgitated corpses. He thought how gunshots heard in the woods had a different quality to gunshots heard in Bed-Stuy, and also how collateral damage was no less damaging than harm caused intentionally. A girl in his class had been shot in the leg in a drive-by; when she matriculated four years later she still had a limp. He thought of townies in rural horror movies, and of runaway slaves evading cracker patrols. *Hunting humans.*

He heard no other gunshots however; and gradually the fear passed from him, and a sense of proportion returned. How did meat get on the table, after all? Better a duck or rabbit roamed free and was cleanly killed than the horrors of the factory farm and the abattoir. To think otherwise was sentimental.

What today had made clear, however, was that Vone couldn't let his son wander at will, either inside or outside the house – so much for "minimal supervision" – and that was before considering bears or cougars or rutting stags or poisonous snakes. Just strangers who might shoot into the rustling undergrowth; who might mistake a boy for a rabbit. Who might not care about the wellbeing of a little Black boy. His mind fled to the rumored ugliness of brown babies with ropes around their waists being used to lure alligators from swamps in slavery times: piccaninny jokes on old tins that were at least maybe true; and for sure any hideous thing you could imagine had happened at least once, to someone, somewhere.

He wondered how Jack's day was going – the first time he had done so, he realized guiltily. Thinking of home, and yes, Number 13 was beginning to feel like home, he walked faster, catching at Jay-Jay's hand to encourage him to keep up.

Somehow they had gone farther out than Vone had reckoned, because dusk was falling by the time they got back to the gap in the fence. As he helped Jay-Jay clamber through, from the woods behind there came a panicky clatter of wings.

But there are no birds out there –

The clatter was cut off by an odd sucking sound that, as Vone looked round, ended with a glug or gulp like the release of the vacuum from a sealed bottle.

To the right of the trail, he glimpsed among the treetops not a bird, but something else bobbing or flitting about. It was too far off, and moved too quickly, for him to make it out clearly, but it was undoubtedly large, and his first alarmed impression was of a grayish ape, though one either lacking upper arms or straitjacketed, and curiously it seemed to float rather than clamber among the branches. A twisted tube of dirty gray fabric hung down from it and dragged about on the ground, and what he took to be its head resembled at that distance, and in the failing light, a puckered, lead-colored, partly deflated party balloon being jerked about on a string. A balloon caught in the trees. Except despite the trailing skein the thing was making its rapid way towards where he was standing, and for all its bobbing and weaving, moved with a sense of purpose that made his skin crawl.

Searching, he thought. *It's searching.*

He moved back from the fence a couple of steps. *On my own property. It can't* – Nearer it came. Shortly it would find the trail. The dead straight trail. Then it would rush towards him like some hideous predatory –

Jay-Jay tugged on Vone's belt-loop. As if in response the figure at once sank down out of sight, it seemed to Vone only just on the other side of the fence.

"Can we go inside now, Daddy?"

His son seemed not to have seen the thing. Vone nodded, but for a long moment he stood there, waiting. It didn't rise up again, nor did it peep round the edge of the gap, but he could taste its grayness as if he had put his tongue on the terminals of a battery with just a flicker of charge left in it. The sensation was akin to the synesthesia he had experienced during the height – or depth – of his breakdown, and which at times still touched him: the color of sound; the music of light, the three-dimensionality of words. That spring the buds in the parks had sighed and sung a shimmering chorale as they opened, and the overheard words of passers-by had tasted sweet or peppery on his tongue, the cries of children playing bright and zingy as limes.

Though alarming, for a time it had been ecstatic. But now he wanted to see things as they were; to not be, to choose a cute word, giddy; to get – though he knew this was both philosophically and neurologically nonsensical – his mind out of the way of his perceptions. And now here was this floating

gray hunter, this malignant – and he was sure it *was* malignant – kite, bobbing in a windless sky: anxiety made manifest,
the perilous old well the vector for it, maybe: the access point
to all that was alarming and buried at the bottom of his mind.

He leant through the gap and looked along the fence towards where the thing had sunk down. A tangle of branches,
suckers, twigs and briars met his eyes, and nothing else.

"Daddy?"

Vone nodded again. He turned his back on the woods.
Ahead the house waited, the pines around it gloomy and en-
closing, and atop its crooked chimney something formless sat
– the thing he had taken to be an owl the day before, he felt
sure, though it seemed larger today; bulkier; like a black sack
stuffed with rags, but sentient.

Can't not go in.

He gave his son an attempt at a grin. "Race ya!"

Side by side they ran, Vone pretending to sprint, letting
Jay-Jay get ahead of him, then catching him up so they arrived
at the side-door exactly together. He wriggled the key from his
pants pocket and gave it to Jay-Jay, but his small fingers
weren't strong enough to turn it in the lock. Vone did it for
him and ushered him inside.

Disappointingly, the kitchen was cold. Vone went and
checked the hall radiator: barely luke-warm. Resentfully he
clomped down to the basement and found the pilot light had
blown out. Turning the dial and keeping the sparker-button
pushed in, he managed to get it to come back on. *Good.* He
released the button. The flame vanished. He tried again, this
time counting to ten. Again, it went out when he released the
button, and he swore.

On the third attempt it remained stable. He watched it
distrustfully for a while. *Not a disaster. I coped.* But as he
turned away, Vone heard – distinctly heard – directly behind
him an exhalation of breath. The pilot light went out, and simultaneously, with a plink, the overhead bulb blew, leaving him
in the dark, sure he wasn't alone; that something was down
there with him. *If it slips round and gets between me and the
stairs I'll –*

He pulled out his phone, thumbed on the flashlight and
ran it round the low-ceilinged room, dreading in a child's way

some dwarfish figure darting forward with a snarl, but all he saw was the furnace, the Bendix and the wall of old jars, their dusty curves glinting in the sweep of the flashlight, their shadows swiveling. Giving in to childish fears, and because it was just about possible that someone or something might conceal itself there, he went and checked behind the Bendix. Nothing jumped up; no gray thing was crouching there.

Clamping the phone under his chin so he could see what he was doing, Vone awkwardly twisted the dial and pushed in the sparker. It took several goes, and left him with sore fingers, but this time the furnace stayed lit. That done, he went up to the kitchen, found a replacement bulb in a drawer, came back down and changed the one that had blown, all the while determinedly thinking mundane thoughts. He wondered if he should up his risperidone: the rapid onset of visual hallucinations and distorted psychology troubled him.

Jay-Jay's brief – what should he call it, mental time out? – worried him too.

There was no birdsong on Cottonwood Way that evening.

Thirty minutes later Vone was perched halfway up the front hall stairs, MacBook open on his knees, Skyping with Tarrell. Elsewhere in the house, like the nice warm convenient kitchen, WiFi coverage had turned out to be spotty, all stuttering, frozen images and audio drop out. Jay-Jay sprawled on a rug in the kitchen passageway, drawing dinosaurs and other, less identifiable creatures on a large pad of scratch paper Jack had carried off from his Brooklyn office.

Vone had meant to keep the call light and emphasize the positives because he knew that Rell, like himself a lifelong New Yorker, was skeptical of the move to Whiteurbia, as he called it – or sometimes "the Whiteyside", or, more grimly, "Whitecide."

Over time Rell had grudgingly come to accept Jack as Vone's life-partner, though still tended to talk of Vone's relationship choice as "depriving another Black gay man of a good Black partner." To which Vone would reply with some variant on, "Thank you, Jill Scott, and who are *you* dating at the moment?" – referring to Rell's preference for down low brothas who mostly struggled, or angrily refused, to admit they were gay, never mind commit to an actual relationship with another man, and often asked for financial assistance Rell couldn't afford, but gave anyway. And so the sparring would go on, mostly good-humoredly, sometimes spikily, as is the way with family, blood or chosen.

Unspoken by either was the blunt fact that being someone who'd had a psychotic episode and been institutionalized because of it (however briefly) did not make the marginally-employed Vone a straight-up catch.

Despite his best intentions, however, Vone soon found himself blurting out things to Rell that he had meant to redact from the record, or at least dress up a bit, and within thirty seconds had switched from tourist-brochure Maine booster to full-tilt bitch-and-moan mode.

"He could've fallen straight down that well – there was nothing roping it off, no warning sign, nothing – and broken his neck. Actually, we both could've. And that's before or after getting shot by local rednecks. So much for 'a safe environment for kids.' Even these stairs I'm sitting my bony ass on right now" – Vone swung the laptop around to give Rell a whirling view of them – "are a fucking – are a death trap. And then, and then out back I saw –"

"Don't take this the wrong way, baby," Rell interrupted. "But are you taking your meds?"

"Of course I am. *And* as prescribed." But Vone decided he wouldn't, after all, mention the thing he had seen in the trees, which wasn't, in any case, like the things he'd seen during his episode, a part of which Rell had witnessed; nor the misshapen black form crouching on top of the chimney.

"Because you know how you get."

"I'm gonna have to keep a constant eye on Jay-Jay, that's for sure," Vone said, changing the subject. "I don't know how I'm going to get any writing done," he added, defying Rell to read him on his lack of poetic output in the last eighteen months.

"J.K. Rowling was a single mom on welfare, and *she* got *her* work done."

"Yeah, but she was –"

"She was what?" Rell looked over his half-rim glasses schoolteacherishly and raised a finely-arched eyebrow. His paintings, large, brightly-colored and richly textured semi-abstracts with Yoruba motifs, filled the wall behind him.

"Basking in cis-het, able-bodied white Karen privilege."

"You're cis, Vone. *And* able-bodied. And male and even, dare I say it, buff. *And* with a degree, which puts you in the upper whatever percentage of –"

"Bitch, don't erase my illness slash disability just because it's mental," Vone said. "And you know how it is with white women and publishing: it's a total old girls' club, they all stick together and exclude –"

"Yeah, yeah, go tweet about it, get some likes. Have you been doing the Montessori stuff with Jay-Jay?"

"Blah blah, become his own person, self-contained blah blah. Obviously, yeah."

"Bitch, you so haven't. If you want him to be independent you have to actually encourage it. I bet you helicopter him."

"I do not," Vone said, though actually he had urged Jay-Jay to draw in the passage, where he might overhear things he shouldn't, rather than leaving him at the kitchen table, all of fifteen feet away.

"So how come I'm hearing the clatter of rotor blades as we speak?" Rell asked. "Never mind. When do you get the rental car and yo housewifely independence?"

"Ugh, can you believe not till next Wednesday. So I'm marooned in Guantanamo till then. And even then the rental place is miles and miles away, so I still have to wait for Jack to drive me there like some tradwife ditz."

"Wednesday's not long to wait, and you can walk to the local stores in the meantime, right?"

"Yeah. Gaugeville, the actual town, is only a mile and a half away."

"And aren't there nature trails all over the place, dripping with beauty and inspiration and shit?"

"Bitch, you hate nature."

"Yeah, but you don't. You're a poet. Poets love nature. Wordsworth, clouds, Gerard Manley um, Hopkins –"

"Yeah, yeah."

"Keats. Sappho."

Rell was looking down at his lap. "Bitch, are you reading off your phone?" Vone demanded.

"Of course not!"

"You so were... Anyway, so what you been doing in the forever since I left?"

"Baby, it hasn't even been thirty-six hours. Well, *since* you ask –" Rell launched into an excitable monologue about his upcoming one-man show, his first in a semi-name gallery, detailing the many obstacles and fuckovers, actual and anticipated, as he got the work ready. "The frames are all bespoke, but now the framer's bitching because they're non-standard sizes. Well, if they *were* standard sizes, why the fuck would I be paying him to...?"

Vone looked over the banister at Jay-Jay. Seen from that angle, the patterns on the rug on which his son was lying echoed those of the snakeskins nailed up on either side of the cellar door. *Must look up poisonous snakes*, he thought, as Rell shifted topic to prattle on about dramas at Sweetgreen, where he and Vone had worked side-by-side for close on six years; in fact it was Rell, already slinging salad there, who had recommended Vone to his manager when he was job-hunting. "...bitch won't wear a net over his beard. Says it makes him look like a sissy. So then *she...*"

Jay-Jay began to draw a spiral, grinding the pencil round until it tore through the top sheet of paper and cut into several sheets below. Just like all boys do; just like Vone had done himself, no doubt, but somehow that afternoon it troubled him: it was too much like self-harm by proxy. "Jay-Jay," he called, cutting across Rell, "stop that, okay?"

Reluctantly, Jay-Jay stopped.

"Jack! Junior! Dinner's ready!" Vone called. It was a few minutes of seven. No reply came. Hearing an odd whirring sound, he went through to the front hall to see what his husband and son were up to.

He found Jack, who had changed from his work clothes into a tee and track pants, turning a crank handle in a small brass-edged hole in the face of the grandmother clock, winching up the weights on either side of the pendulum while Jay-Jay watched, fascinated. Jack pulled out the handle and swept the hands round with his fingertip to the right time, then encouraged Jay-Jay to gently set the shiny brass disc swinging.

The mechanism clonked into life and a moment later the clock chimed the hour: seven melodic strikes. Jack put the handle up where he had apparently found it, behind one of the finials on top of the clock's housing. The ticking was reassuring in an Addams Family kind of way, and Vone supposed they would get used to the chiming and be able to sleep through it soon enough. Above the face there was a semi-circular painted tin disc that showed phases of the moon. Vone made a mental note to go out into the backyard later, see where the moon was at, and set it accordingly.

For their first proper meal at Number 13 they decided to eat in the dining room, which turned out to be a mistake. The ponderous furniture was sharp-edged and insufficiently cushioned, and the room markedly colder than the rest of the house. The atmosphere wasn't improved by the food: Vone's unfamiliarity with the stove meant the chicken was overcooked on the outside and only just cooked through enough on the inside to be edible; and the roast potatoes, despite appearing golden, being seasoned with garlic, rosemary and parsley and pleasingly crusted with sea salt, were not as soft within as they should have been. He and Jack split a bottle of red wine that was also somehow a disappointment, possibly through guilt by association.

As they did their best to ignore the reality of the meal, Vone found he had to force himself to show an interest in Jack's day, which was frustrating because he *was* interested. He certainly didn't want to talk about his own day, mostly because he didn't want to mention that he had been seeing things; also he doubted he would be able to switch off the moaning that was threatening to become his default mode when he had already bitched disloyally for an hour to Rell.

"You'll see how white he is now he among the white folks," Rell had said towards the end of their call, albeit mostly to be irritating.

"They do have *one* African-American staffer in the Bangor office," Jack was saying. "Tanya. You'd like her."

"Why, because she's Black?"

Jack gave him a look. "Because she's likeable. We should have her over."

"Sure," Vone said, forcing himself to be open to the idea.

After all, if Rell had mentioned befriending the only other Black member of his new staff, Vone would have been ready enough to meet her – pleased, even. "Yeah, let's do that. My next culinary effort won't be such an abortion, hopefully."

"Abortion!" Jay-Jay repeated, as Jack loyally jabbed a fork at one of the potatoes sitting round the carcass in the roasting tin. It was too hard for the tines to penetrate easily. *Oh well*, Vone thought. He could boil the bones for stock or something. Do a Spanish omelet with the potatoes.

He turned to his son, who was pushing a chicken-bone around his plate with a fork. "Are you done with that, Jackie-Jacks?" At Jay-Jay's nod he gathered up the plates, took them through and got yogurts from the fridge. They ate the banal dessert in silence, Jay-Jay grinding his spoon round the pot till Jack told him to quit it.

"Have you met any of the neighbors yet?" he asked as Vone took the pot and spoon from their son.

"They stare from a distance, then run away."

Jack reached for Vone's hand. This wasn't how he wanted the world to be either, of course. At least he didn't offer a bromide, or, worse, attempt a partial exoneration. To his credit, Jack never did. "Eff 'em," he said.

"Eff 'em," Vone echoed.

Seven

"**D**o you think it's the meds?" Jack asked, his voice carefully neutral, as it was regrettably often these days. Vone stared up at the bedroom ceiling, limp dicked and hard-eyed with frustration.

After lullabying Jay-Jay to sleep – they both had pleasant voices and enough skill to harmonize – he and Jack had tiptoed through to their bedroom, where one sort of harmony had suggested another, and they began to kiss and caress each other. It was Vone who made the first move, and for a while he was into it, enjoying the intimacy of the contact, but nothing built up in him, and eventually he broke the embrace and rolled onto his back with a sigh.

"I don't know," he said.

Jack traced Vone's profile with a fingertip: forehead, nose, lips, chin, Adam's apple, studying him as he did so. "Okay," he said. Then again, "Okay."

"Sorry."

"It's alright."

And after all, maybe it *was* the meds, though over the last twelve months Vone had, to his great relief, been tapered off those with the worst side effects. Now he was down to modest daily doses of risperidone and clonazepam, for the management of paranoia and anxiety respectively, along with omeprazole to manage the acid reflux they caused. Once less heavily medicated, he had found the willpower to get back to the gym, shed psychotropic and pandemic blubber, and restore his physique to its firm, near-six-packed pre-episode shape. The interregnum of flabby torpor had made him feel unattractive, though Jack had worked hard at seeming not to notice the deterioration. Any sexual desire Vone had felt during that time had been oddly abstract, like rewatching an OnlyFans session you filmed a year before at the same time as you were performing it. Disconnected from his own body, he had, unsurprisingly, felt disconnected from Jack's body too.

How much sex were they supposed to be having anyway, after seven years of marriage? Such a blogpost-level question was no help, of course: the fact was that to repeatedly fail to give your lover what he needs makes you – and him – more alone. And the more you both performed not noticing your aloneness, the more you became exactly that: performers. Not – what would the word be? Participants.

From somewhere inside the house there came a sharp cracking sound, breaking in on his thoughts, or, more exactly, his evasions from thinking. He and Jack exchanged a look. Not quite holding their breaths, they listened for any follow-up. From somewhere downstairs there came a creak that was maybe nothing or could have been a stealthy foot on a warped floorboard: someone moving from the back of the house to the front. *Looking for a way up.* He thought of the floating gray thing in the woods, and now it seemed to him in its pulpiness like the arm of a huge beached squid, a pallid, groping tentacle with a wider, diamond-shaped tip.

Our Brooklyn apartment made noises all the time and they were nothing, he reminded himself. *This is an old house made of wood expanding because of the heating being run for the first time maybe in years, even decades. Not –*

There was another creak. Someone or something was definitely creeping about below. "Maybe it's Jay-Jay," Jack said, and Vone thought uneasily of how he hadn't reminded him to buy a safety gate for the stairs when he, Vone, was in the house all day to notice, repeatedly, its absence.

As one they turned back the covers, got out of bed on their respective sides and went along to the landing. Jack mimed he would go check on Jay-Jay; Vone nodded and looked down into the hall. Despite the darkness, he found the shadowy shapes of the furniture were already familiar to him, and he could see the parlor and dining room doors were closed.

A hand on his shoulder made him jump. "He's asleep," Jack said quietly. From below there came another a skittering sound. "Maybe some animal's got in."

Vone nodded, though his mind had already flown beyond the plausible incursion of some stray cat or innocuous woodland critter to imagined klaverns of local racists or – more believable – drug-trashed, latently psychotic teens, bored and full of homophobic hatred for his queer swirl family; for what he and Jack did in bed (however infrequently). Psychos who could hurt a child and laugh.

A clatter came from the kitchen like a dog-dish being kicked about. A raccoon, maybe, or a skunk. How vicious were those kinds of animals? When he was a kid, his mom had sometimes fought rats in their Bed-Stuy apartment, yelling curses and jabbing at them with the mop. They had arched their backs, bared their incisors, and tried to jump at her. She used a hammer to smash the heads of the ones that got stuck squealing to the glue-traps, and made Vone carry the flattened carcasses to the dumpsters round the back of the block. Sometimes he had actually thrown up. It was why he had been unable to kill the ones they caught the same way in Fort Greene. But he reckoned he could kill a critter here. He wondered if rabies was a thing in New England.

Wordlessly, they descended to the hall. Vone took two walking sticks from the elephant's foot stand, keeping hold of one and passing the other to Jack. At least they were both men, he thought, and robust, therefore less vulnerable than they might be as a same-sex couple: two women would have so much more reason to be afraid. The grandmother clock clonked and whirred, readying itself to strike the hour as they entered the kitchen passageway.

The door to the kitchen, which Vone was sure he had closed when they went to bed, stood open, and moonlight spilled brightly across the room's interior: disliking coming down to dimness in the morning, he had, as was his habit, drawn back the curtains before going to bed. Entering ahead of Jack, he switched on the overhead light. Nothing moved, and nothing appeared to have been disturbed. But had the sudden glare caused whatever it was to freeze? Might it be watching them from a hidden corner?

He went and checked the back door. It was locked and the key was in the lock. He removed it and set it on the counter. While he did so, Jack rummaged under the furniture with his stick, then under the drapes, aiming to flush out their unwelcome visitor. How could it, whatever it was, have got in? Gnawing? Burrowing? Squeezing? Mice could compress the bones of their skulls, Vone knew. There were no obvious holes in the baseboards, but perhaps behind one of the –

From inside a low corner cupboard by the breakfast table

there came a scratching sound, quick and furtive: rat-like, or
– claws on wood, anyway. Exchanging a look with Jack, Vone
positioned himself next to the cupboard on the hinge side, so
he would be behind the door when it opened. Facing the cupboard, Jack struck a baseball batter's pose and nodded he was
ready. Vone yanked the door open and jumped into critter-
bashing position alongside his husband.

Nothing emerged.

Slowly they lowered their sticks. Vone squatted down.
"Careful," Jack said as he reached in and felt about. Touching
something soft and somehow animate, he withdrew his hand
sharply. "What is it? Did you get bitten?"

"No, I..." Vone reached in again and pulled out a dusty
wooden hoop maybe six inches across, from which feathers
and slender wooden rods hung on twine. The feathers were
gray, white and brown. "A wind-chime?" he guessed. But the
rods weren't metal or hollow, so would clack, not chime.

"I think it's a dreamcatcher," Jack said.

Vone nodded, put it back in the cupboard, and closed the
door on it.

A small sound behind them made them look round. Jay-
Jay stood there in his peejays, holding Dippy and rubbing his
eyes sleepily. Before either of them could scold him for coming
downstairs on his own, he said, "Where's the crying lady?"

"What crying lady, Jay-Jay?" Jack asked.

"She lives in the cellar. She eats mice and she cries."

"No one lives in the cellar," Vone said. "It was just a
dream. Let's get you back to bed, okay?"

He picked Jay-Jay up and the three of them went through
to the front hall, the presence of their son making him and
Jack act fearless, and deny the atavistic unease to which even
adults are prey in unfamiliar places, in the small hours of the
night.

As they passed it, Vone noticed that the moon-dial on the
clock had rotated to a new phase, one fifth off full.

The following morning found Vone and Jack baggy-eyed on
the front porch, sipping mugs of coffee in the bright sunlight
and looking through the pine boughs at the as-usual-deserted
road.

"It's like living in a graveyard," Vone said dourly.

"It won't be so bad once you've made some friends," Jack said – rather mechanically, to his husband's ears.

"Who with? The KKK Stepford joggers?"

"Well, why don't you set up your weights and at least burn off some nervous energy?" Jack glanced at his phone. "Okay. I gotta go." He handed Vone his mug and pecked him on the lips.

"Knock 'em dead, mister man," Vone said as Jack hurried down the steps, beeping the car lock open as he went. It was a golden fall morning and the sky above was cloudless, but Vone struggled to feel anything but beat: "low cotton," as his great-aunt used to say.

Once Jack had gone, setting the mugs on the rail to take in later, Vone went round to the garage and, with difficulty, wrenched up the door. One of the springs dangled uselessly from the cantilever. With patience and pliers he reckoned he could reattach it. Another thing for the list.

The garage was built of breezeblock, had a concrete floor and tarpaper roof, and though it shared a wall with the house, there was no way through. Old paint tins, rusty kerosene cans, a metal workbox containing grimy-looking tools, and a couple of crates of what looked to be trash were lined up against the back wall. Above them an axe lay across two lugs, alongside loops of rope and hose and wire. Along the party wall were a mildewed wooden hutch with a chicken-wire front, a standing faucet with a tin bucket under it, and a lawnmower rusted solid as a fossil. Next to the lawnmower were two adult pushbikes and a child's one with training wheels, all tangled together, rust-scabbed and with pancake-flat tires.

"Junior!" Vone called. "Junior? Come to the garage and see!"

When Jay-Jay didn't appear, Vone went back round to the house, collecting the mugs along the way. He found his son once more lying on the rug in the kitchen passage. He was drawing a spiral in the scratch pad, with a blunt black crayon too soft to tear the paper.

"Leave that and come see what I found."

Jay-Jay left the drawing easily enough – Vone was always on the lookout for signs of obsessive behavior in his son, as that was how his own breakdown had begun – and let his daddy lead him to the garage. He was gratifyingly excited by the discovery of the bikes, and he and Vone spent an enjoyable morning fixing up the child's one. After wiping it down with soapy rags to clean off dirt and spiders' eggs, Vone tackled the rust-spots, using steel wool he'd found in one of the boxes of junk, along with a dented, half-full can of light oil. After a further hour's work he was able to get the initially seized-up pedals of the bike, now upside-down on the driveway, turning smoothly and set the back wheel spinning. The sunlight sparkled on the links of the chain as he applied the oil, rusty orange transformed to juicy black as it whisked round. Though the frame was a metallic purple, arguably an effeminate color, the bike had a top tube. For a boy, then. A boy's bike, and a boy's bedroom.

Why should that strike Vone as disquieting rather than welcoming? Perhaps because what seemed like a welcome could in fact be – what was that word to do with birds of prey? – a lure.

In one of the crates he found a pump. "The rubber of the inner tubes is probably too rotted to hold the air," he warned Jay-Jay as he knelt and screwed the pump-head onto the back wheel valve, enfolding his son from behind so he could use the plunger to make some awkward initial thrusts before daddy took over. But the tires inflated, and stayed inflated when Vone squeezed them. Jay-Jay imitated him, and smiled because Vone had smiled. The wheels were wonky but not hopelessly so: a few turns with a cresent wrench helped steady and straighten them; and there was still some rubber on the brakeblocks. The training wheels didn't turn very well, but weren't completely seized up.

"What did you mean about the crying lady?" Vone asked, a shared task being as ever the man's way into a serious discussion. In the morning sunlight the question seemed harmless enough.

"She lives in the cellar, and she cries."

"I think that was just a dream you had."

"Nuh-uh. She *does*. And she eats mice and she says she's my friend."

"Oh. Okay. Well, that's cool, I guess. Well, not so much the eating mice part."

As he spun the back wheel, Vone wondered how common it was for kids to have imaginary friends; whether it was considered "normal" or a worrying predictor of future mental illness. He couldn't remember when he himself had begun to feel detached from other people and the everyday world; to live what others would consider excessively in his imagination. Early on, for sure. But wasn't that the story of every artist? Too, he knew that Black men were massively over-diagnosed with schizophrenia, and also that a sense of alienation was common among incipiently gay kids: the anticipation and fear of rejection, a fear based not in neurosis but in fact – though Jay-Jay surely wouldn't feel *that*, however he turned out. And despite Rell's scoldings about Vone's helicopter parenting, Jay-Jay was generally self-possessed. A little shy, perhaps, but perfectly sociable – if anything more confident with grownups than was usual at his age, due to being around them more than most kids were. The benefits of a too-small apartment, Vone thought. Then: *not anymore.*

He only slightly judged himself for wanting normalcy for his son. Or not normalcy, exactly: just the fewest internal obstacles in a world so full of external ones. He imagined the sentiment fairly much universal. Setting the bike right side up, he said, "Wanna try your wheels out, soldier?"

Jay-Jay nodded enthusiastically. Vone steadied the bike as he clambered on, then straightened up and watched Jay-Jay pedal round the concrete drive, growing in speed and confidence with each orbit, his quick acquisition of the skill one of those commonplace but gratifying miracles of childhood.

"Wanna go once round the block?"

Coming to a wobbly stop, Jay-Jay looked up at Vone and nodded.

There wasn't a block, of course, but they made their way down the street in the direction the covered bridge, a stooped-over Vone laboriously shepherding his son around potholes, towards which he was drawn as if magnetically, and away from the leaf-clogged gutters. Somehow the other houses on Cottonwood Way looked more cheerful today: characterful, well-maintained, *established*; and that was a good thing, right? But generations of owner-occupiers implied a community of white people whose roots reached back to seg-regation times, and, beyond that, way on down into the deeper, darker soil of America's racialized history – a history that was perhaps less likely to be repudiated if it had in no way been interrupted.

Vone tried to imagine the reverse of his current situation: him and Jack having chosen, at his urging, to move into an all-Black community instead of an all-white one. And there he would have been, with his white husband, his mixed race son born to a paid surrogate, and his secular self, wondering if he – if they – would be welcomed or shunned; wondering what negotiations and accommodations he would have to make with those other equally, if not equivalently, unforgiving and persisting histories.

Jay-Jay seemed to be enjoying himself, so where Cotton-wood Way ended they continued down the short curve of track that led round to the covered bridge. It was leaf-strewn and muddy, but the mud had dried out enough for Jay-Jay to pe-dal along okay, though Vone had to steer him away from the deeper ruts. Several times the fallen leaves clumped in his mudguards and he ground to a halt, and Vone had to pull them out.

On the other side of the bridge, suddenly, there was bird-song, and Vone recalled how silent the woods had been the day before; how there had been no birdsong in Cottonwood Way that morning. He looked for some flapping thing to point out to his son, though his knowledge of birds ran no farther than crow, eagle, buzzard, seagull, owl – and now of course the chickadee. Perhaps he could bluff it with his phone – there was bound to be an app that identified birdsong, an avian Shazam. How did people make money out of that kind of shit? His lack of understanding of business always left Vone feeling an outsider to systems of power and prosperity.

A little way along, they emerged onto one of the smoothly blacktopped streets that gridded the Vicinity. Several of the houses had "sold" signs in their yards, some by Harris Real-tors, but not all. He wondered if there was feuding between the old and new realtors of Gaugeville: surely there wasn't enough to go round.

Leaves had been raked, and filled garden waste sacks

stood in orderly rows by carports awaiting collection: probably there was an ordinance against burning them. To Vone the
houses were depressingly devoid of personality, though he
supposed they would have more reliable heating than Number
13, better water-pressure and less drafty windows.

It was as he stood with his hands on his hips surveying the
street that the police cruiser turned the corner.

Eight

Vone couldn't help himself: as the cruiser drew nearer he turned away from it and attempted to shepherd Jay-Jay back towards the covered bridge. As he did so, a siren whooped. Wearily, and with his chest tightening, Vone took his hand from his son's shoulder and straightened up. Jay-Jay looked round at him, confused, as, with his back to the approaching cruiser, Vone stood blankly waiting.

A car door opened, then closed. Vone could hear the staticky sound of a police-band radio, though couldn't make out the words. Keeping his hands open and his arms hanging limply at his sides, very slowly he turned to face the uniformed cop now ambling towards him.

Male, white, middle-aged, heavyset and cleanshaven, the cop wore a Kevlar vest and mirrored sunglasses. He had a slit for a mouth, freckles, and his short hair was gingery blond. Slung around his thick waist was the bulky paraphernalia of violent law enforcement: a revolver; next to it a taser, with which it could so easily, it seemed, become confused; pepper spray, cuffs and an extensible baton.

A second officer, also male and white, cleanshaven, younger, fleshy-faced and dark-haired, stayed sitting in the cruiser, a radio relay held up to his mouth. He murmured something into it as the older cop came to a stop just over an arm's length from Vone, his right hand resting would-be casually on the taser. He wore no body camera and Vone wondered if there was one in the cruiser and, if there was, how wide a field of vision it captured.

"Do you live round here?" A strong local accent.

"Do I have to?" Doubled in the lenses of the cop's reflective shades, Vone's features bulged back at him. With an effort he conceded, "We moved in yesterday."

"What address?"

"Don't you believe me?" Vone asked, and in his tone the *What the fuck you harassing me for?* was all too obvious.

"Sir, what address?" the officer repeated flatly, a slight flush in his cheeks the only giveaway the conflict was turning him on. Why else, after all, would you become a cop?

"Through there. In Cottonwood Way."

"Number?"

"Thirteen."

"Name?"

"Why?"

"Name."

"Mister Mapley-Stevenson."

The officer produced a notebook with a pencil slid through its spiral binder. Laboriously he noted the name down, whether out of borderline illiteracy or to wear on Vone's nerves, Vone couldn't tell. He was in a different zone now, the blank zone where you aren't there anymore, your responses as preordained as a catechism.

"First name?"

"DuVone."

"Jew-vone?"

"D-U-V-O-N-E."

The cop slowly printed the individual letters. "He yours?" He indicated Jay-Jay with the blunt end of the pencil.

"I'm not the maid," Vone said tartly. Then, immediately regretting making a remark that could be taken as camp, as gay, as engaging with the situation, he added, "Yeah. He's mine. My son." He looked down at Jay-Jay, who was looking worriedly between his father and the cop, trying to make sense of the slithering power dynamics, the repressed but naked hostility on both sides.

"He should be wearing a helmet," the officer said.

Vone looked past him along the street. No one was jogging, there were no faces at windows.

"You seem uneasy," the officer said, patting the taser as if absentmindedly.

Vone felt the surge of anger it was impossible to keep down as a Black man, an anger too tangled up with too awful a history to be disavowed and still be a man. "I'm angry, not uneasy," he said tightly. "I'm angry because apparently someone round here, someone in this street called you because I'm walking while Black. With my little boy." Phone footage leapt into his mind – of George Floyd, Sandra Bland, Eric Garner, Tamir Rice above all, but so many, many others – along with memories of encounters with cops in his adolescence: vivid and wretched for sure, but he and his friends had always been stopped in groups – "gangs." It had never, he only now realized, been just him on his own. Him and two cops.

Him with his son.

"People just want to be safe, sir."

"Safe from what?"

"Calm down, sir, or I'll have to take action."

"Why should I be calm at being interrogated by you for no reason? If I was a white woman –"

"Sir, I instructed you to calm down."

"Or what, you'll taser me in front of my son for asking you why you're questioning us like criminals for no goddamn reason whatsoever?"

Keeping his mirrored eyes on Vone, the cop signaled to his colleague in the cruiser, who at once got out and started towards them, leaving the door open. His hand was on his gun grip: no middle-ground tasering for him.

"You're scaring my son," Vone said levelly.

It was true: tears were starting in Jay-Jay's wide-open eyes. "Daddy?"

From inside the cruiser came the crackle of the police radio. "Bill? Joe?"

The second cop trailed back to answer the call. Vone, Jay-Jay and the first cop stood as still as a taxidermy display while a quick exchange took place. "Joe," the second officer called. "We got a 10-54."

The first cop left it a beat before saying, with a blunt finger pointed warningly at Jay-Jay, "I want to see a helmet next time, okay?"

Vone refused him the satisfaction of a nod, just looked at him blankly, the offense once known as dumb insolence. He knew the cop wanted to make something of it; knew he should just knuckle under because to not do so would only make things worse, but he couldn't. Some lines –

"Joe!" the other cop called, impatient now there was a real crime to deal with.

With what was clearly an effort, the first officer turned away from Vone and Jay-Jay and made his ponderous way back to the cruiser. It did a three-point turn and drove off fast, lights spinning.

Once it was out of sight, Vone squatted down in front of Jay-Jay, took his son's hands in his, and searched his eyes for that primordial wound: the first time you realize you're Black in a white world. He saw puzzlement, a little fear, but not that. Not yet. "Let's go home, Jackie-Jacks," he said, trying not to tremble; trying not to cry.

Jay-Jay nodded, and they went back up the track, leaving the Vicinity and its treacherously joyous birdsong behind them. They passed through the old bridge in silence. A stream tinkled unseen below. *To cross over running water*: that was something witches weren't supposed to be able to do, he thought.

Cottonwood Way now felt like a sanctuary, even if that meant the housing development had become a gauntlet he would have to run to reach the rest of the world. How the hell could he ever be happy here, when there would always be bullshit like that to deal with? He was relieved to see no pale faces at neighbors' windows; no white female joggers on their way to or from the moose trail, because surely it was one of them who'd called the cops on him.

The house waited. Whatever had been hunched atop the chimney was absent now. Away. Doing – what? His mind went to the regurgitated bones by the well, the ones that were too large for owls.

He and Jay-Jay went and stowed the now-tainted bike in the garage. The rental car would insulate him from some of the bullshit, he thought, though he wondered how many times he would be pulled over while driving it. Just as well he and Jack didn't have the funds for anything flashy, though that was a fucked-up way of having to think. He supposed the cops would get used to him after a while and leave him alone. Or would they never stop goading him, keeping it up until they got the explosion they had tried and failed to provoke today?

He sighed. Those were the kinds of calculations Jack never needed to make. Sure, as a gay man he could find, in fact *had* found himself in situations where the straight world turned nasty, and he too knew the cops couldn't be trusted: there weren't *no* comparisons. But you couldn't read Jack as gay. At least not while sticking your nose out from behind a curtain.

He wanted to call him and tell him.

He couldn't tell him.

He had a duty to tell him.

If I don't let him know, how can I expect him to –

Maybe later.

After fixing a scrambled egg and wheat toast lunch where he cooked the eggs too hard, Vone lay on the passage rug with Jay-Jay, getting indigestion as he and his son drew dinosaurs together.

"Daddy?" Jay-Jay asked tentatively.

"Uh-huh?"

"The policeman said I should wear a helmet."

"The policeman was right," Vone said, not looking at his son, concentrating on the sweeping skull of a pterodactyl, or was it a pteranodon: the one with the elongated hollow crest, anyway. With a sigh, he put the crayon down and met Jay-Jay's eyes. "The police aren't our friends, Jay-Jay. Don't believe anyone who tells you they are."

"They were mean," Jay-Jay said, going back to his drawing.

"Yeah. They were mean. Okay, let's get this guy colored in. What is he, a stegosaurus? What color's a stegosaurus?"

"Purple."

"Purple? Well, okay."

Later, staring bleakly at his reflection in the bathroom mirror, Vone took an extra clonazepam.

An hour after that, feeling less about to fly apart mentally, he found himself once more perched on the front hall stairs, Skyping with Rell.

Of course Vone instantly told Rell about the fuckover encounter with the cops. It wasn't so much that he knew Rell would get it and Jack wouldn't; it was more the reassuring certainty that whatever he said, Rell would be entirely on his – their – side; that he wouldn't for one second make excuses for, or enter the minds – or souls, if they had them – of Blue Lives, or even of wypipo in general, when maybe Jack would; would be unable not to.

"That's why you've got to have your phone with you at all

times," Rell admonished. "Film the fuckers and hit upload before they snatch it off you. You got that app, right?" – he was referring to the Mobile Justice app, the one that sent your footage directly to the ACLU. "Right?"

"Man, if I'da tried to get my cell out I'd've been tasered. Or shot. In front of my son."

"Did you at least get their names and badge numbers?"

"No. I just wanted to get the hell away from them."

"Vone –"

"I know. Don't shower before the rape kit."

"Exactly. Because now what do you have? Their word against yours."

"I didn't want to escalate shit. There were two of them and no witnesses except Jay-Jay. 'Gimme your badge numbers.' How was *that* gonna play out?"

Rell sighed. "You should write a poem about it."

"You know it doesn't work like that."

"Well, maybe it should."

"Yeah."

"Maybe it will."

"Maybe," Vone said grudgingly. "Anyway, I should go. Thanks for listening, man. It really helped. It really helps."

"De nada, girl. Any time, okay?"

Vone reached out and pressed his fingertips against the screen. White fields pooled around them as the pixels spread beneath the gentle pressure. Rell matched his fingertips to Vone's, and they said their goodbyes.

That evening Vone was at the kitchen counter, aggressively chopping vegetables while Jack, still in his work clothes, and with files and folders piled in front of him, watched from the nook. Having decided he wouldn't tell Jack what happened, Vone had found himself ranting on about it anyway.

"And Jay-Jay's only fucking *five*," he said in a choked, wobbly voice. "And he had to see *that*!"

His voice strangled in his throat, and Jack got up and came to him and gathered him into a hug, and it felt good and just then safe; and Jack smelt of citrus and cinnamon and Vone buried his face in Jack's shoulder and let himself cry, and when eventually he lifted his head he saw tears were bright in Jack's eyes too. And of course they were: Jay-Jay was his son too, and Vone was his husband. He had married into Blackness: this was his family, and harm to them was harm to him, even if that was something others couldn't see when he was apart from them.

"I'm sorry I'm sorry I'm sorry," Jack said. "Love you love you love you."

That evening they ate dinner in the kitchen, which managed to be cozy despite the central heating having to cope with a considerable drop in temperature – the result of several days of clear skies. The meal, a Spanish omelet using last night's potatoes and fried-up cubed roast chicken, was a success, and made further inroads into the cartons of eggs Vone had brought in his burst of survivalist-in-reverse urban neurosis. Tomorrow he would walk with Jay-Jay into Gaugeville, check out the stores. Being seen around the place would be some sort of protection from the police, perhaps – oh, a local – and cowering inside could only worsen his mental health.

They were drinking hot chocolate – Jay-Jay sipping from his special double-handled mug, each handle an ear of Simba the Disney lion cub – when Jack surprised Vone with a gift, a gold cardboard box about a foot square and the depth of a shoebox, tied with purple ribbon. "Just in case house-husbanding was making you feel kind of, you know," Jack said as he handed it across the table.

Glancing at Jay-Jay, though surely Jack wouldn't give him something overtly sexual in front of their son, Vone untied the ribbon and opened the box. Inside, wrapped in mauve tissue paper, were sparring gloves and, beneath them, a pair of silky Mohammed Ali boxing shorts. Vone smiled. Jack smiled back. "I thought we could... try them out in the bedroom first," he said.

"The gloves?" Vone asked suggestively, teasingly.

"The shorts."

"I thought you had a mountain of paperwork to do."

"The mountain can wait on Mohammed Ali."

Vone turned to Jay-Jay. "Time for bed, oh feral one."

That night the sex was good. The shorts allowed some fun

into it, a moment of play that removed both of them from their everyday roles as dads, and allowed their intimacy to be an act of liberation rather than the discharge of a spousal duty. Even their repeated attempts to stifle the pinging bedsprings and mute the rhythmic creak of the antique bedframe as Jack thrust vigorously into Vone brought a welcome sense of adolescent intensity to their lovemaking. Vone had been careful to jam the back of the sewing chair under the bedroom doorhandle, thus preventing their son wandering in while he rode his husband's dick like a horny bitch and enjoyed doing so.

Afterwards he lay back on the bed, tremors running through his aching thighs, glistening with sweat, his hole joyously used. Jack slid on top of him and kissed him on the mouth, pushing his tongue in boldly to elicit a final gasp from his husband, kissed Vone between his pectorals, then moved down the groove of his twitching stomach to taste his come; then rolled out of bed to go and wash up.

Vone studied Jack's back and ass and legs as, naked, he crossed the room. A good V; a solid butt, perky for a white boy's; skin smooth, no flab. Jack was as much of a gym-bunny as Vone: keen to offset the mostly sedentary work he did, he had already found a gym in Bangor. *Still a hot couple*, Vone thought, and though perhaps that shouldn't have mattered it did, because beauty was a power in the world, a form of resistance to the forces that would call him and Jack ugly and dirty for how they loved; for how they fucked.

He thought vaguely of reactivating his social media accounts and posting cute images of, and anecdotes about, their new life online. Then he thought of the hostile pile-ons that came in response to the most anodyne post by anyone Black and/or gay, especially if they had the temerity to have a white partner and thereby betray the race – and also of the chasm that could open so easily between façade and reality, down which one's self-esteem could so readily tumble – and parked the idea.

The bathroom faucet squeaked, the pipes gurgled, water rushed forcefully into the basin, and Jack cursed as some of it splattered onto the floor.

Now he was a sexual being again, and had been properly fucked into the bargain, Vone could smile at the wonkiness of their new home. Pulling on the Mohammed Ali shorts, he got out of bed and went through to check on Jay-Jay, his pumped-up, radiant blood temporarily insulating his bare torso and legs from the chill of the hallway.

Before opening it, for a moment Vone stood listening at his son's door, for what he didn't know. Gently he turned the knob. As the door swung open, and before he saw the room beyond, which was lit only by Jay-Jay's Jack Skellington night-light, he found himself looking through the hinge-gap widening between the door and the frame. As a child that gap had at times seemed to him a window onto another world, an enchanted space that was both theatrical and revealing of what went on backstage, though later he would swear that at that particular moment he had had no such thoughts or re-membrances.

Through the expanding gap he saw – would swear he saw – hunched over Jay-Jay's bed a mannish, heavy-set old woman in a grimy black overcoat. Her lank, gray hair was tied back in a messy plait that straggled down almost to her waist, and in it feathers and chicken bones were tangled. Her eyes were in shadow, though tears glistened on her pouched brown cheeks, and a dirty, bony hand with split claw nails rested on the coverlet directly over Jay-Jay's breast. As she leaned in, the old woman's cracked lips moved fast. They were dotted with spittle and showed a glimpse of threaded, yellow-gray teeth, and Vone thought he caught the unfamiliar words, "Kwidôbawô nia…"

Then she belched. A rat tail spilled pinkly out of her mouth and began to flick about. The old woman gagged and hacked and swallowed it back down.

Nine

Heart surging, Vone wrenched the door open and stepped in fast, right arm drawn back, fist bunched, ready to yell and –

There was no one there.

Just Jay-Jay, peacefully asleep.

Vone looked around wildly, but there was nowhere the old woman could have hidden herself, and in any case no time for her to have done so. Puzzled and troubled, he went back out into the corridor and swung the door back and forth, to see if its framing generated some sort of obvious-when-you-saw-it optical illusion. It didn't, though the clothes-rail curtain was pulled back, and just conceivably, in the dark and uplit by Jay-Jay's nightlight, the clothes that hung there could have produced the momentary effect of a hunched-over figure; and maybe he, Vone, had in an unguarded moment somehow mixed his son's mention of a crying, mouse-eating old lady with – what? The dream catcher in the kitchen cupboard? – to create a disconcerting chance illusion.

Maybe. But Vone found himself unable to shake off the feeling that what he had seen had been real. If so, then might she somehow, impossible though it seemed, have quickly concealed herself in the chest? Warily he went back into the room and opened it, but saw only Jay-Jay's toys, pleasingly tidily put away.

He lowered the lid, then knelt and checked under the bed, lifting the coverlet so he could see all the way to the wall behind, Monster Hunt for real this time.

Of course there was nothing there.

Vone checked the windows. All were closed and their catches were fastened: nothing could have left that way, and the fireplace, too small for a human being to squeeze down anyway, was boarded up. Where the old woman's scrawny hand had lain on the coverlet there was no indentation, no trace of anything having been there.

Bending over his son, Vone lightly kissed Jay-Jay's forehead. His skin was clammy, as if its heat had been drained away, and Vone thought he could smell a trace of something like licorice in the air.

There being nothing else to do, he left the room, checking the hinge-gap again as he closed the door, resisting the urge to carry his son through to sleep with his daddies. *Don't let Jack and Jay-Jay know you're seeing things. Don't burden them.*

As he stood there, he began to shudder. He told himself it was the coldness of the air on his bare, goose-bumping skin.

After emptying his bladder and popping an extra risperidone Vone got back into bed and cozied up to Jack. Closing his eyes, he tried not to listen out for strange sounds in other, supposedly empty rooms; tried not to turn a fleeting trick of the mind into something significant – either an actual sinister presence (and what the fuck would *that* mean?) or, infinitely more likely and hardly less frightening, the resurgence of his mental illness. He'd hoped he wouldn't need to hurry to find a psychiatrist; now, abruptly, it was a priority. He guessed he would have to go to Bangor. When did Jack's spousal insurance kick in? Not till his probation period was over, that was for sure. Vone hated the sense of vulnerability being medicalized induced in him: the way his diagnosis marked him out as officially broken, as the legitimate subject – or object – of institutional concern. But the truth was, if it wasn't for Big Pharma he'd probably be dead.

Outside, as if to torment him, the wind began to stir, building fast as he lay there vexingly wide awake until it was rattling the window frames and droning in the chimney like some atonal bagpipe. Where they were hooked back, the outside storm shutters clonked repeatedly against the clapboard façade of the house. Getting out of bed and opening the windows in order to reach out and pull them closed seemed like too much effort, and wouldn't doing so during a gale let the wild wind in, to make tempestuous mischief? Pine branches swished against the glass like the brushes of coniferous jazz drummers, and the surrounding deciduous forest hissed in alarm as the intensifying gale stripped the trees of their dying, desperately clung-onto leaves. Then the wind seemed to rise up cyclonically and blew directly down the chimney, as if it was eager to spread soot and disorder within the house. Vone turned over in the dark restlessly, listening for Jay-Jay to wake and cry out. How could he sleep through this? How could Jack? The drapes ballooned in phantom pregnancy, subsided, bellied out again.

The well, he thought suddenly, and for no particular reason, though it seemed to him then that it had been the start of something: the small stones Jay-Jay sent skittering down its maw causing an awakening in the darkness below, a rising up. *That gray thing in the trees, floating, following.*

A well in the woods. Wasn't that the title of a fairytale, or a poem? He thought so, or maybe. A lonely old well. Could a well be lonely? Or there was the quainter word, "lonesome". Why would there even *be* a well in the middle of the woods? Who would have dug it, lined it with bricks carted from somewhere along some track or trail, and once upon a time used it to draw up water? A waystation for witches, Jay-Jay had said. Had Vone seen a witch tonight? *She lives in the cellar.*

Eventually the wind quieted and he drifted off to sleep.

The next morning, though baggy-eyed, Vone was determined to perform cheerfulness. To some extent it worked, and Jack went off to Bangor not having to worry about his husband's ability – or inability – to hold things together as a solo parent for all of nine continuous hours. The storm, which hadn't troubled Jack at all, had blown many leaves from the trees: both front and back yards were carpeted with them, copper, gold and crimson, as were the drive and road, a spectacular effect. Handfuls lay along the front porch too, so bright as to be almost luminous, as if scattered for the arrival of some stately, autumnal bride of twigs and roots. Above, the sky was blue and cloudless.

A minor upset occurred while Vone was clearing away the breakfast things: Dippy had gone missing.

"Well, where did you last see him?" he asked his wailing son as he stacked the plates in the sink, wondering if they could get a dishwasher plumbed into a system with such uneven water pressure. There was space for one, but no pre-installed pipework. He couldn't imagine the letting company being very interested in the idea.

Jay-Jay broke off from wailing, thought about it and said, "On the window."

"You mean on the windowsill in your bedroom?"

"Uh-huh."

"Have you checked he didn't fall down the back of the radiator or behind something else, like the toy chest?"

"Yes!" A wail began to build up again.

"Well, you know what? I think you should go check again. Give me a minute to finish clearing up, then I'll come look with you, okay?"

Sniffing back tears, Jay-Jay nodded and headed off in the direction of the front of the house.

"Careful on the stairs!" Vone called after him. Then he noticed the blue plastic diplodocus standing on the floor in front of the basement door, turned towards it, its diminutive forehead pushed up against the bottom rail as if to keep the door from opening.

Vone bent over and picked the toy up. Just as he was about to call Jay-Jay, he thought he heard a furtive movement on the other side of the door. Pressing his ear against a panel, he held his breath and listened. There came what sounded like a brief flurry of wings. Maybe a pigeon had got in, or a crow or a jay or –

An owl.

But weren't owls' wings silent? Something about the feathers... Straightening up, Vone opened the door. A pale oblong of concrete floor waited grave-like below, and the kitchen light behind his head threw his shadow down into it. As he reached for the basement light switch he touched one of the snakeskins. This time he didn't flinch.

There were no more flapping sounds, and the light revealed no mess, no droppings. Reluctantly Vone descended. He found no panicky trapped bird with its head turned sideways on, one eye watching unblinking.

The pilot light burned steadily in the furnace port. Remembering the cold breath that blew it out the day before, Vone went back up to the kitchen more quickly than a grown man should and called, "Jay-Jay! I've found him!"

The rest of the morning was spent putting his son's

abundant but messy 'fro in cornrows. Vone scolded him intermittently for squirming, and did his best to distract him by
telling him prettified tales of his rural childhood visits, de-
scribing relatives Jay-Jay would likely never meet. That done,
Vone fixed them lunch: cold ham and pickles on rye. Pulling a
face, Jay-Jay left the rye. More connected than usual to memories of what being a kid was like, Vone didn't scold him.

Afterwards, without much help from Jay-Jay, who was
markedly less enthusiastic now it wasn't his own bike they
were working on, Vone cleaned up the two adult pushbikes,
picturing as he did so a wholesome (if slow-moving) family
excursion on the coming weekend. Then he tackled setting up
a home gym in the garage, lining up the dumbbells by size and
weight, lugging round the barbell weights, and reassembling
the bench and stand. Last came filling the hollow base of the
punch-bag at the garage faucet. Jay-Jay pedaled around on
the drive while he did all this, keeping close.

Vone decided to christen the gym with a short workout:
there was enough warmth in the afternoon sun for the garage
to be pleasant to exercise in with the door up. Activity always
helped clear his mind, and soon he began to feel hopeful
again, as, dressed in basketball boots, the Mohammed Ali
shorts and a mustard singlet with African Nation trim, a gift
from Rell, he began to work up a sweat.

As he exercised, he noticed how often Jay-Jay gave him a
worried look, seeking confirmation that what he was doing
was safe. Vone did his best to smile back reassuringly as he
jerked the dumbbells harder, fighting the battle within himself that he guessed pretty much every Black parent has to
fight, over whether to choke his feelings down or reveal them
and risk causing his child pain to no useful end. His own father had been emotionally closed off, and perhaps that was
because he had wanted to protect his children, but in the end
what good had it done them – or for that matter himself?

Other than those of anger, Vone had always found it hard
to guess his father's feelings, but that was at least partly because, beyond the emotional masking that most men do as a
matter of reflex or upbringing, his father had lived an actual
double life; had sneaked off and had kids with another
woman. Well, hardly "sneaked," since everyone in the

neighborhood knew about it – even, as it turned out, Vone's mom, though she kept the truth from him and his sisters – Duree, who was four years older than him, and Toree, two years younger – as long as she could.

So his mother had worn a mask too.

Over time he had become friends with his half-brothers Mason and Danton, who were five and six years younger than him respectively. Neither had turned hostile when they realized he was gay, and Vone came to view their mother as an honorary aunt. At times his father treated her badly, much as he had Vone's mom, so Vone couldn't hold onto much anger at her, this other woman who was the victim of the same selfish man. And by his early twenties he had learnt enough to know that a man can't be "stolen" unless he wants to be. He couldn't say whether he forgave his father's double-dealing or not, since his father never sought, nor gave any sign that he wanted, or would be capable of accepting, forgiveness.

Vone doubled the rate of his jerks. *Sweat that shit out.*

Just then a woman came walking by in the direction of the moose trail, white of course, in her late forties maybe, trim and attractive in a one-procedure-too-many kind of way. Her blonde hair was pulled back in a ponytail, she wore purple joggers, hiking boots and a white quilted jacket, and beside her trotted a small brown wire-haired terrier on a leash. Vone continued his jerks as if she wasn't there, getting ahead of the snub curve for once, but Jay-Jay, still on his bike, dawdled to a halt and gazed at her and the dog, which was prick-eared and alert.

To Vone's intense surprise, the woman stopped at the bottom of the drive, smiled and waved. With a clonk he set his dumbbells down and stood there, his chest heaving.

"May I?" she asked, gesturing for permission to step onto his property. He shrugged in what he hoped was an amiable way and she started up the drive. The dog kept alongside her rather than straining tiresomely at the leash, its tail wagging. Jay-Jay, who had been bugging his daddies for a dog for at least the last year, and been fobbed off with the to-be-fair entirely legitimate, "We can't because we're in an apartment," awkwardly got off his bike and shyly approached the visitors.

"Do you mind?" the woman asked Vone. "She's really

friendly." After another shrug from him, she squatted facing Jay-Jay and said, "Her name's Pepper. Sometimes we call her Pep. She likes it if you scratch behind her ears."

Carefully Jay-Jay touched the top of Pepper's head. She closed her eyes as if in pleasure. Vone watched his son reach behind one of her ears. The little dog yawned.

"I'm Aurora," the woman added. She had only a trace of a local accent. "Awful, isn't it? Friends call me Rory." Off Vone's lack of a clear response she added, "So call me Rory. We're pretty much neighbors – three along, at number five." She gestured in the direction of the Vicinity.

"I'm DuVone."

She came to him and they shook hands politely. Her hand was cold but dry, the contact unexpectedly welcome.

"Well, it's nice to meet you, DuVone."

She took in his physique a beat too long, flushed slightly, and withdrew her hand. Vone felt the usual tiresome pull between wanting to make her feel safe in the way white women so often needed to feel safe, by somehow getting in that he was gay and so not a sexual threat to her, and keeping her out of his business.

Past that was his human longing for a moment of simple, undistorted social interaction of the sort she probably assumed they were having, and he knew they weren't.

He had no reason to trust her, and perhaps she was only being friendly because she'd heard the gossip about the fag family. But faced with a nothingy afternoon, he found himself saying, "D'you wanna maybe come in for a coffee or something?"

"Oh, are you sure?" She glanced back along the street.

He felt a spasm of irritation. Was she afraid for her white-lady reputation? Surely the presence of a child was insulation against – "If you want to," he said, with a slight shrug that was almost a flinch.

She wavered. "Can Pepper visit too?"

"Sure."

She smiled, it seemed genuinely. "Then that would be lovely. Thank you."

Vone smiled too. "Come on round."

He made himself leave the garage door up, the way people

do who know they live in low-crime areas.

They sat at the kitchen table with mugs of coffee and a plate of cinnamon toast – another last taste of Manhattan Vone had brought with him, sealed in silver foil – while Jay-Jay and Pepper rushed round the house and up and down the stairs, Jay-Jay's feet thudding, Pepper's claws skittering on the polished boards. Vone dropped "my husband Jack" into the conversation early on and Rory took it in her stride. Perhaps to test her further, or perhaps because it preoccupied him, he found himself telling her about his encounter with the police.

"I can't believe they did that," she said. "I guess they didn't know you lived here."

"Why would I be cycling at zero miles per hour with my kid if I *didn't* live here?" he asked irritatedly. "Anyway, there's literally a trail at the bottom of the road with a moose sign. People must come through here all the time, right?"

"Some of those women are total paranoid bitches."

"Yeah."

"I know," Rory said. "'Not all white people'..."

Vone gave her a look. "And you would have voted for Obama a third time if you could," he said, quoting *Get Out*.

"I would have," Rory agreed, maybe getting the reference, maybe not. "But they *are* bitches. Trust me, I know. They're not even locals. I mean, not *real* locals. And I mean, they didn't even know you're gay." Vone winced. Rory noticed. "I mean, that you're nice."

"Yeah, well," Vone said with an effort, thinking it ought to be self-evident that you shouldn't have to be "nice" to not be interrogated by the police for no reason. He changed the subject. "So how long have you lived here? How long to become a real local?"

She laughed, he presumed with relief at getting away from the subject of race, and with a real live Black person too. "God, it feels like forever. Let's see. Ted, he's my husband, he – it'll be twelve years this Thanksgiving."

"Do you have any kids?" She looked away and shook her head. "Sorry, is that, um –?"

"No, no, it's fine. We just – it never happened."

Pepper ran into the room with Jay-Jay in hot pursuit,

dashed round the baseboards and darted out again. "Be gentle with her, Jackie-Jacks!" Vone called. "Don't scare her!"

"He's named for your – husband?" Rory leant back and touched her back hair and ever so slightly arched her spine.

"Yeah." Odd how the simple use of the word implicitly relegated him to being the wife. Or of course not odd at all, just heteropatriarchal: the linguistic corollary of a husband is a wife. "It's also Jack's granddad's name, so. But his middle name's Dupree, after one of my uncles."

"He's a sweetheart. Real bright."

Vone nodded, trying not to bridle at her choice of words: she might have said that of a white child, after all. "Do you know anything about this house?" he asked. "I mean like, its history?"

"It's been a rental forever," Rory said. "There's been the odd couple or even single guy in here, mostly short termers. One time a young woman writing up her doctoral thesis, something to do with the witch trials, kind of stand-offish, you know? But you're the first family to take it since we've lived here, which is ten years, pretty much. Ted'd know more. He's old stock, he's got family all round Gaugeville, a real native Kwawidikowan. Did the rental people tell you anything?"

Vone shook his head, though of course they might have told Jack stuff he hadn't bothered to pass on to his overtly uninterested spouse. "What does Ted do?" he asked. "Don't tell me – chief of police."

She laughed. "Actually, his dad was on the force, till he retired. He died a couple of years back, of congestive heart failure. No, Ted's on the town council. His thing's fiduciary oversight, mostly keeping an eye on the developers, balancing stresses on service provision with bringing in tourist dollars, new housing and infrastructure with wildlife and environmental preservation, encouraging newcomers while maintaining what it is people actually want to come here for." She smiled. "He knows where all the skeletons are buried."

A clonking sound from beyond the cellar door made them both look round. It was followed by gurgling, then the audible rush of water through pipes. Rory laughed again, and Vone had the sudden sense that she was uneasy. Not uneasy at being with him: something about the house; being in the house.

"Do you work?" he asked. "I mean, if that's not rude."

"I run a mail-order beauty business. I don't really need to – Ted's salary is enough for the both of us – but I'd go nuts otherwise. All-organic face-packs and rejuvenating creams, skincare generally. High season they sell pretty well at the general store – the one on the waterfront, Fancy's, do you know it?" Vone shook his head. "It sells, you guessed it, fancy stuff for incomers, on top of things you actually need. Out of season it's mostly mail order, off of the website. I'll give you a sample. Not that you need rejuvenating." She smiled. Again, a near flirtation.

He smiled back and said, "Well, you know what they say." Then, since he didn't know if she knew what they say, he filled in the punchline: "Black don't crack." Possibly he was leading her on, ever so slightly. Not that he'd been with a woman since he was fifteen, and he had no urge to revisit the experience.

"They're actually really good quality," Rory said. "The parent company's in Canada. And what about you? What do you do?"

"Um, I'm a poet. And a parent."

From the front of the house came the clatter of something wooden falling onto bare boards, accompanied by a sharp bark.

"Shit." Followed by Rory, Vone went through to the hall and found the parlor door open and Jay-Jay and Pepper inside. The little dog's tail and ears were down, and she looked more guilty than his son, who was attempting guilelessness. The spindle-legged bamboo table had been tipped over, and next to it, alongside its carved ebony stand, lay the ostrich egg, shattered.

As Rory got Pepper back on her leash, Vone squatted down in front of his son, lifted his chin and looked directly into his eyes. "What did we agree about the front parlor?"

Jay-Jay looked down and swung his hands, his little fists clenched. "Don't go in."

"Because?"

"Stuff can get broken. But it was Pepper!"

"Did she open the door?" Jay-Jay shook his head. "Well, then, it can't be her fault, can it?"

His face darkening, Jay-Jay shook his head again. "Maybe

we can stick it back together?" he said, tears thickening his voice.

Vone softened. "We can try."

"I'd better go," Rory said. "And gosh, I'm really sorry about the egg."

Vone straightened up and managed a wry, "I guess that's why they don't rent to families."

"You can probably get another one off eBay," she said as he saw her out. "I mean, if it was that valuable they wouldn't have left it in there, right?"

"I guess not."

In the doorway she turned. "Why don't you and Jack come to dinner tomorrow? You could bring Jay-Jay too. I'd love for Ted to meet you. He's a good guy, and it's nice to have some interesting neighbors for once. What do you think?"

"Sure. I'll tell Jack we've been invited."

Jay-Jay pulled at Vone's hand. "Can Pepper visit again?"

"If Mrs – if Rory says it's okay. But you have to not let her get in the parlor if she does."

"Of course it's okay," Rory said. "And I *am* sorry about the neighbors." Impulsively, she kissed Vone on the cheek. He didn't respond. Blushing, she turned away from him and hurried off down the drive, pulling a now resistant, backwards-looking Pepper after her.

"The lady kissed you, Daddy!" Jay-Jay said in wonder.

"She's just lonely," Vone said. "Okay, let's see about the egg. You go to the kitchen, fetch the breakfast tray and we can put the pieces on it to fix."

Jay-Jay did as he was asked, and watched as Vone began to gather up the broken bits of shell, starting with the bigger ones. Underneath one of them he found a small cork – plugged into the base of the blown egg, he supposed; under another, a small key.

"Huh. Look, Jackie-Jacks. What d'you reckon this is for?"

"A door?"

Yes, but a door to what?

Ten

I t was later that afternoon. Jay-Jay lay on his back on the rug in the kitchen passage, holding Dippy up at arm's length and making a deep-throated noise that Vone, compiling an ever-expanding To Do list on his Macbook in the kitchen, found both irritating and unnerving. Then, abruptly, he fell silent, and that too was unnerving.

"Jay-Jay?" Vone called.

No reply came. With a sigh he got up to go check on his son. He found Jay-Jay staring blankly at the ceiling and breathing heavily, as if he'd been running. Then, for no apparent reason, he started screaming, piercingly.

"Junior? Boy, what's wrong?" Vone knelt down next to him, his hands moving over his son's rigidly outstretched body. "You hurt? Where you hurt?" Jay-Jay's pupils were unnaturally dilated. Vone thought of brain hemorrhages; of oxygen starvation; of cri du chat syndrome, where the sufferer wails mindlessly like a mewing cat. Apart from the screaming mouth, Jay-Jay's face was expressionless, and his skin had a gray undertone.

"Skog Madoo!" Jay-Jay yelled. "Skog Madoo!"

"What do you mean? What you talking 'bout?"

"She's coming!"

Not knowing what to say or what else to do, Vone hugged his son to him, Jay-Jay's fresh cornrows ridged and silky-tight against his cheek, between them the heat lines of his bare scalp, radiant. "Ssh, ssh... Hush now... Hush..."

Jay-Jay fell silent, and when Vone tilted him back to study his expression the blankness was gone, but now he looked scared.

"Do you hurt anywhere?" Vone asked. Jay-Jay shook his head. Vone's mind now turned to more commonplace but equally grim parental fears: of meningitis, epilepsy and other congenital childhood blights – fears that were in his case amplified by an underlying, rarely admitted sense that he and Jack had gone against God in order to contrive this child, and so deserved punishment, or at least to fail and be miserable.

Thankfully, in defiance of Jack's mother (and to be fair, many of Vone's farther-flung relatives) they'd had Jay-Jay vaccinated against everything there was a jab for, so it couldn't be measles, mumps, rubella, scarlet fever, diphtheria, pertussis, polio, whooping cough, tetanus or Hep B.

"Well, okay, that's good. So what was all that noise about, then?"

Jay-Jay didn't answer. His pupils seemed normal now, his skin tone close to its usual butterscotch. Vone touched the back of his hand to his son's forehead. No fever. His breathing was regular and he wasn't trembling or shaking. Nor was his manner confused, though he didn't seem to realize he had been screaming his head off. What was it he had yelled? Already Vone couldn't remember. He thought of phoning Jack, but Jay-Jay seemed okay now, meaning there was nothing that couldn't wait until after work hours, and attempting to describe what had happened over the phone would either worry his husband to no useful end or sound hysterical.

He could, he thought, go over to Rory's for advice, but she didn't have kids, and being a woman didn't in and of itself grant her better insights into childcare than his own. Too, he recalled the stonewalling moms at the nursery he used to take Jay-Jay to in Fort Greene. It had been advertised as "queer friendly" but wasn't, at least not to a masculine-presenting Black gay dad whose presence disrupted what was otherwise a utopia of lesbian parthenogenesis. Any casual observation he had shared was greeted with a cold look, a skeptical raising of the eyebrow, a determined turning away. His mom had been hostile to him and Jack having a child, so knocking on that door wasn't going to happen – on top of which she'd recently gone overboard with religion, and he didn't need to be advised to "pray on it"; and his sisters (each of whom had two kids apiece) were too keen on point-scoring for him to consider calling them. What would they say anyway? Either: call an ambulance right now, or shrug, dissolve a half aspirin in a teaspoonful of water and give his son that.

Jay-Jay wriggled free of Vone's embrace, got to his feet and went and picked up Dippy. His upset seemed to have passed from him as inconsequentially as a bowel movement. Even so, Vone had him sit at the kitchen table and draw while he took care of emails and admin. After a while of side-eyeing Jay-Jay's aimless scribbling, Vone set him to writing the alphabet. If Jack's funding got renewed past the initial nine months they'd have to think about schools, but Vone was happy enough, and felt competent enough, to homeschool their son through the coming winter.

Behind the walls the water pipes began to clonk and gurgle as if performing some strange acoustic dance. There was definitely something odd about it – the washing machine wasn't running and no faucets were on inside the house – so Vone concluded his day's business by mailing the realtor to ask for a plumber to come check things over, and while he was at it take a look at the erratic pilot light. Sorting out everyday shit grounded Vone, and he knew Jack would appreciate it more than some corny romantic gesture. *Married life.* He looked up ostrich eggs on eBay. There were plenty of them, and Rory was right, they weren't expensive – you could get one for around $40 – though none of the dozens he clicked on quite matched the one Jay-Jay had broken either in color or texture. All seemed smaller, and his memory of its shape was that "his" egg was more pointed than any of those on offer.

He went through to the parlor, brought the tray of shell fragments he had left there earlier in the day back to the kitchen, and dug a small tube of half-used superglue out of his utility kit. It had a pin in its nozzle, and the glue inside was still mobile when he squeezed the soft metal casing. Looking round for Jay-Jay, he saw him leaning his forehead against the basement door, his arms hanging at his sides, echoing how he had stood at the edge of the well.

"What's going on, Jay?" Vone asked, bracing himself for another fit or screaming episode.

Without looking round, Jay-Jay said, "The Owl Lady wants us all to sleep in the basement."

"Hm," Vone said lightly. "It's pretty cold down there, so I don't think that's a good idea.'

"She says –"

"And damp and smelly too."

"Uh-huh. But –"

"And there's no bathroom and it's too small for a bed, so we couldn't all fit, could we?" Jay-Jay shook his head. "Okay, come and help me with this."

Jay-Jay came to the table without any fuss.

"Pick out the biggest bits first and lay them out to make a shape."

The rest of the afternoon was consumed by the task. Though the glue was fast-drying, Jay-Jay wasn't yet dexterous enough to hold two pieces together long enough for it to set, his fingers more often getting stuck to one or other fragment of shell, or to each other, than the fragment to its neighbor. As there was no hope of restoring the egg well enough to fool anyone it didn't really matter, and was more about Jay-Jay learning that it was virtuous to try and make good when you fucked up, and appropriate to put up with being bored for a while as a consequence, rather than just pleasing yourself and expecting others to do the work of reparation for you.

By the time they'd done what they could the shadows outside were lengthening and the sun was lowering. Needing some fresh air, Vone togged Jay-Jay up and took him out for a walk. This time they left by the front door and went down to the start of the moose trail. Richly carpeted with gold and scarlet fallen leaves, and littered with twigs brought down by last night's gale, it ran away like something from a fairytale. Though the day had been dry there was a damp, loamy smell, and Vone's and Jay-Jay's breaths misted thickly.

That afternoon there was a little birdsong, though it ceased as soon as they left Cottonwood Way behind them. It was as if there were some invisible boundary beyond which no flying thing dared trespass, or if it did, it went in silence, and fast.

Boundary, he thought. *Bound. Bind. The Bounds. Beating the bounds. Gaugeville Bounds. Bounding along.*

The air was still, the trail ran straight, and there was no sound of anything moving about in the dried-out brush beneath the trees. At first neither father nor son registered that silence, that stillness as odd. Then they did. Jay-Jay took his daddy's hand when the day before he would have rushed ahead, and Vone felt sure it wasn't out of a suddenly-remembered fear that there might be holes he could fall down, or unseen hunters with loaded rifles.

Vone's eye was caught by white things the size of golf balls dotted about strikingly among the fallen leaves: the fruiting bodies of mushrooms, pushing up through the moist black mulch. "Look," he said, pointing them out to Jay-Jay. "Fungi. Don't touch," he added as his son knelt in front of a particularly large specimen that had grown up in a cleft among tree-roots, its creamy-brown sombrero cap more than six inches across. "Some are poisonous, even just to touch. You have to know which ones are safe."

"Don't you know, Daddy?"

"I know some of them. Like if you see a red one with white spots, that's super-poisonous. Or there's one that's stinky with flies all over it and kind of with a veil."

Jay-Jay made a face. "Who'd eat a stinky one, though?"

"Well, no one. And it's called a Destroying Angel, so. But some of the most poisonous ones look really similar to the edible ones."

"Like they want to fool us?"

It was an intelligent question to which he had no answer. "Kind of. Let's leave them all alone, okay? Just to be on the safe side."

Jay-Jay nodded. They went on. The talk of poison mushrooms had flattened both their moods, and Vone intermittently urging his son to keep an eye out for moose failed to lift them. After twenty minutes' monotonous trudging, and with the dusk coming on, they came to a halt and turned back: the woods had defeated them, for today at least. Tomorrow, Vone decided, they would do what he had half-intended to do that afternoon: walk the mile and a half to Gaugeville, which promised, if not exactly civilization, at least other human beings gathered together in defiance of the wilderness. He had, he reminded himself, thought the lakeside town pretty when he first saw it. "They have sailboats and everything," he added. Jay-Jay looked pleased.

From the bottom of the drive, Vone looked up at the house. The tall pines pressed close around and overshadowed it, and the thing atop the chimney looked larger than ever, a bulky black sack backlit by a colorless sky. As he watched, it tipped backwards and tumbled down behind the house. But when he went round and checked, he found nothing in the backyard.

He didn't ask Jay-Jay if he had seen anything. Its presence and then its absence seemed neither good nor bad.

Over dinner that evening Jay-Jay told Jack about Pepper and Rory (without, Vone noted, mentioning the egg-breaking incident), rushing on to conclude, melodramatically, "And then she kissed Daddy!"

"She's just lonely," Vone said, in response to Jack's raised eyebrow.

"And curious about BBC, it seems."

Jay-Jay looked between his fathers for an explanation of the acronym. "Never mind Dad, Jackie-Jacks," Vone said. "He's just being silly. Anyway, I said yes to dinner."

"When?"

"Tomorrow night. Is that okay? I know you'll have work to do."

"It's fine."

With a lengthy creak that drew all their eyes, the door of the small cupboard containing the dreamcatcher swung open. Nothing more happened, and after a while Vone got up and closed it. As he did so a sharp odor made him wrinkle his nose. "D'you smell that?"

Jack sniffed and made a face. "It's like vinegar."

"Pooh!" Jay-Jay said, sniffing in imitation of Jack.

Vone went and opened the door to the cellar. The smell was stronger there. He switched on the light. The snakeskins glistened on the jambs. Were they wards against snakes coming up, he wondered, or totems of serpent power, energized by the sacrifice of the living snakes? Why was he the only one who noticed them? *Maybe I should say something.* But then Jack joined him in the doorway. The two of them went down together, followed at a distance by a wary Jay-Jay.

The bottles of decades-old, home-canned produce waited for them, and as Vone and Jack looked on, with a delicate plink a hairline crack forked its way across a jar of gray, shriveled things that had once been zucchinis, perhaps. A drop of pickling juice beaded at the head of the crack.

"All this stuff seems like it's ready to blow," Jack said. "And if one goes, it's bound to set off the others." He turned to Jay-Jay, who was hanging back on the stairs. "Stay there,

Jackie. This could be dangerous." Then, to Vone: "We can clear it all out this weekend. Hopefully nothing'll actually explode in the meantime."

Vone nodded. "I saw a couple pairs of workmen's gloves in the garage," he said. "I'm going into town tomorrow, I'll get us some safety goggles."

They went back up to the kitchen. Once again, Jack didn't notice the snakeskins. It was a small thing, but added to Vone's sense of existing in a parallel universe of portents and meanings that his husband wasn't a part of.

While putting Jay-Jay to bed that evening, Vone found himself swinging the bedroom door back and forth, peering through the hinge-gap and trying to reproduce the collision of triggers that had summoned the grotesque figure the night before. After a while he realized his son was watching him and stopped. "D'you want to play Monster Hunt?" he asked. Jay-Jay shook his head. "Do you want Olly?"

"Yes, please."

Vone reached for a plush turquoise octopus, another favorite toy, and tucked it in with him, careful to put four arms over the coverlet, four under, kissed Jay-Jay's forehead and, leaving the night-light on and the door ajar, left the room.

Though it wasn't late, Jack had already come up, and after a quick trip downstairs to check the front and back doors were locked, Vone joined him.

The bedroom had always been a space where they could talk more freely, particularly as, for different reasons, both felt a duty to police their feelings around their son. Jack's mother had shielded him from nothing as a child – drunkenness, drug-taking, and transient partners who were, if not actually physically violent toward her, certainly psychologically so; and Vone's mom had torn his dad down verbally in front of him and his sisters so relentlessly that both Duree and Toree had acquired ingrainedly negative attitudes towards Black men, while still seeking them out as partners. Vone believed that masochistic mentality had poisoned their romantic relationships, and both were now embittered single mothers. It was as if they had drawn to themselves the men they dreaded but believed to be their destiny. Only Vone seemed to have escaped the trap – though perhaps his habit of choosing white partners, which to him felt more contextual than intentional, (majority-white university; majority-white bohemia), reflected his mother's dismissal of Black men as worthless too. Certainly, embarrassing though it was to admit even in private, to him white men tended to emblematize larger possibilities, or at least an escape from overbearing constraint. But he also had Black male friends he loved deeply, like Rell; and he didn't, he thought, hate himself. Or at least, not in that way. *After all, straight men don't get involved with women because they hate themselves for being men.*

Jack had just showered and was sitting on the edge of the bed with a towel around his waist. Vone clambered onto the bed, knelt behind him and pressed the balls of his thumbs into the knots in Jack's shoulders, expelling grunts from his husband as he did so. The peach tones in Jack's butter-pale skin were heightened by the heat of the shower and his wet, tangled hair was shiny and smelt of rosemary. Vone tilted Jack's head back, stretching out his throat, arched over him and kissed the tip of his nose. Jack smiled, and his dick, which was large, twitched visibly under the towel.

Vone went back to massaging Jack's shoulders, using an elbow to disperse a particularly solid clump of tension. "You're very hunched up," he said. "It's like there's a metal bar between your shoulder blades."

"I'd forgotten what it's like to be the only one in the office," Jack said. "You'd think with it having an HIV focus it'd be different, but – uh! Yeah, that's it, there. Ow!"

"Should I –?"

"No, it's good, don't stop. I mean, obviously I'm 'accepted' and they know I'm married to you, but it's still tedious. Demeaning. Well, not that exactly, but you know. Having to watch out for being condescended to all the time."

"Microaggressions."

"Yeah. It'll be better when I'm managing my own team. Then I'll be the boss, so –"

"Tolerance being by definition a power relationship, it won't be an issue."

"Exactly."

"We can skip dinner at Rory and Ted's if you want."

"No, it's alright," Jack said. He twisted round, pushed Vone onto his back and slid on top of him. "Even if she does have designs on your body."

"You got no worries in that department, mister man," Vone said, slipping his arms round Jack's back, enjoying the feel of muscles moving under hot skin. "Just keep slinging me the D the way you do..."

Encouraged, Jack hooked his arms under Vone's knees and hoisted his legs, pressing his hips against Vone's instantly receptive hole.

"Fuck me," Vone said breathlessly, feeling Jack elongate rapidly against his perineum.

"I'm gonna fuck you hard," Jack responded throatily.

"Yeah!" Vone gasped. "Make me beg!"

"I'll make you beg!"

But just then frightened cries came from Jay-Jay's room.

With a sigh Jack rolled off Vone. Managing their erections awkwardly, they pulled on underwear, sweatpants and tees and went through to their son's bedroom. They found him sitting up in bed, screaming as he had screamed earlier while lying on the rug in the hall – Vone felt a stab of guilt, realizing he hadn't mentioned the fit, or the screaming, to Jack: sex had got (had tried to get) in the way – staring at something unseen that, if it were there, would be floating in the middle of the room.

"The Owl Lady! The Owl Lady!"

Eleven

"**Y**ou just had a nightmare, Jackie-Jacks," Vone said, once he and Jack had comforted their son a little. "But she says we've got to go in the basement!" Jay-Jay insisted.

Vone groaned. "Not this again."

"What again?" asked Jack.

"She, she says – she says *she's* coming back!" Jay-Jay went on.

"What? Who is, Jay-Jay?"

"Skog Madoo!" Jay-Jay said, looking around panickily. "Skog Madoo is coming back!"

Jack sighed. "You'd better sleep with us tonight," he said. Vone nodded agreement and Jack picked Jay-Jay up and carried him through to their bedroom.

Before following them, Vone swung the door a couple of times. No Owl Lady. No – what was it? – Skog Madoo.

Snuggled between his dads, Jay-Jay quickly fell asleep. Vone then told Jack about their son's not-exactly-a-seizure earlier, and his demand that they all go and live in the cellar with the Owl Lady.

"Do you have any idea where all this stuff has come from?" Jack asked. Vone shook his head. "Not from playing Monster Hunt?"

"No, that's just silly stuff. You've seen me do it. Jay-Jay loves it."

"Maybe stop it anyway."

Vone nodded, though grudgingly. Why was Jack's judgment to be deferred to more than his own? And why was he, who was with Jay-Jay all day, deferring to it? Sometimes when they fucked Jack would say, "You're my bitch," and that kind of shit could be hot in the bedroom, but he didn't want it to escape into the rest of their lives, and even there he only enjoyed it because neither he nor Jack took it seriously. A man being fucked was still a man: that was what being gay meant. And Vone liked it both ways, even if Jack was more of a top.

But he was probably right about Monster Hunt.

At least he hadn't mentioned doctors, though that was an-other thing on Vone's to-do list: as well as a psychiatrist for himself, a pediatrician for Jay-Jay – there must be one in Gaugeville. Perhaps he could discuss the Owl Lady business with him or her.

But who, or what, was Skog Madoo?

She's coming.

"Shit!" Jack yelled from the bathroom.

"What?" Vone asked sleepily. It was six-thirty a.m. and barely light outside.

"There's no hot water."

"Shit," Vone echoed, though without much feeling: his husband had showered before they went to bed the night be-fore, and Jay-Jay's freak-out had prevented them having sex and getting their sweat on.

Jack came through in his Calvins. "The pilot must've conked out again. Can you call Sarah and get her to send someone to fix it or clean it out or whatever?"

"Yeah, sure, I'm on it." Vone turned to Jay-Jay, taking his little hand and shaking it gently. "Time to rise and shine, Jackie-Jacks. Breakfast gon' need eating, and that's your job." Jay-Jay stretched and yawned theatrically. "Go get dressed, okay? Call Dad when you need help with your laces."

Before starting on breakfast, Vone went down to the base-ment to restart the pilot light. The smell of vinegar was stronger, he thought. After several goes he got it to stay on. Before going back up, he took a moment to check on the state of the jars. Seven or eight of them now showed hairline cracks, and where the pickling juice had dripped down it made small dark pools on the dusty concrete floor.

As Vone watched, a finger of the rancid liquid slid towards him from one of the pools, moving quite fast, as if the floor was being tilted in his direction.

He blinked.

The finger was gone.

His gut clenched as if he had been punched. The move-ment of the liquid had been serpentine.

*

Vone sat at the table after Jack left for work, his coffee cold in front of him, breakfast things not tidied away, and stared into space. The day outside was almost dark, the sky lowering and turbulent with fast-moving rainclouds. Inside, the house was chilly and the air stirred strangely, as if unseen presences were dallying in the rooms and hallways, passing always from the front of it to the back, as though heading for the woods. Presumably it was just the wind hitting the building at a very particular angle, one that happened to penetrate every gap and chink all at once. He knew that happened sometimes, like when it blew straight down the chimney, spreading soot and unease.

After how long he didn't know, Jay-Jay tugged at his arm. "Daddy, let's go outside."

Vone turned his head in the direction of the kitchen window just as a spray of rain dashed itself against the glass. Leaves whirled and flew about outside, some attaching themselves froglike to the wet pane, and at the far end of the yard branches waved wildly above the uneven, vibrating pickets of the back fence. Upstairs the window frames rattled, then rattled again. "Maybe later," he said. "Daddy just needs to..." He tailed off mid-sentence, went back to staring into space.

Jay-Jay, who in the months following his father's release from the hospital had grown used to him blanking over, gave up and wandered off in the direction of the front hall. Vone tried to care but he hadn't the strength just then, not even to feel guilt. Odd that the impossibly moving fluid, the most trivial hallucination he'd had since coming here, was the one that had derailed him most. Perhaps it was because, being so minor, it was something he could admit to Jack without risking everything, and so he had a decision to make about disclosing it, whereas he couldn't tell Jack about the other things: Jack would leave him; would take Junior and go.

No, he wouldn't.

Maybe.

Closing his eyes, Vone pressed his fingertips against the lids until he saw stars. *Don't be a slave to this.* In his mind the pill bottle waited, but he didn't want to take another tablet, didn't want the drugs to be what saved his sanity. *Don't be so goddamn weak.*

And so he sat there until the low mood passed, using logic and reflection to inch his thinking along. The hallucinations he'd been experiencing in the Bounds were disconcerting, but they were also very different from those he had experienced during his breakdown. The latter had mostly been fizzing, crackling, whirling amplifications of real phenomena that to his pinwheeling mind had promised plummeting insights into the nature of the universe. He remembered the stars shouting boisterously, and the synesthesic, shimmering music of the plate glass windows of department stores. Daffodils in parks had barked like dogs, at first joyous; later, threatening. He had known there was a mental tsunami coming from the way the birdsong began to appear before his eyes as a rolling screed that became increasingly jagged and scrawly, and had felt his brain boil over like a saucepan of milk.

By contrast, the hallucinations he'd experienced here had been brief and geographically contained, hadn't escalated, and, when considered later, were, though disquieting, fireside stuff of the sort you'd expect an old house in New England to generate: folk images of spirits prowling the woods and witches in bedchambers; Puritan fears seeded by centuried timbers, psychic echoes caught in glass, vitreous vitrines of unease: the isotopic decay of what were once sincere beliefs into distorted, flickering, half-familiar mental debris.

Such analysis helped, and though he still felt anxious, his mind stopped racing. The stress of the move had, as he had feared it would, caused an imbalance in the delicate neuro-chemistry of his brain – a *temporary* imbalance: hold onto that – and as a result his imagination (and wasn't he a poet, a being whose entire existence was about making unexpected connections?) had synthesized that imbalance into a handful of striking images. Encouragingly for his sanity, they seemed not to be building in extremity. The bag-like thing on the chimney grew but didn't *do* anything. The puddle of vinegar was far more mundane than the witch he had conjured up two nights ago, and she, though inside the house, was less alarm-ing, less fully weird, than the floating gray thing he had seen on his first full day at Number 13. The fact he hadn't seen ei-ther the thing or the old woman again suggested that the witch might have been the peak, or the trough, of the mental wave.

Or so he hoped, anyway.

With an effort he got up and cleared the table. As he did so the rain spattered the windows hard as hail, crazing the glass outside with tears, and the wind tore the last few leaves from the backyard pear trees. Blankly he did the dishes. By the sink the key that had been hidden inside the ostrich egg waited. He dried his hands and picked it up. From its size it was for a door or a larger cupboard, rather than, say, a jewelry box or a teenage girl's diary.

Regretting his failure to engage with his son earlier, Vone went and found Jay-Jay idly rattling the walking sticks in the elephant's-foot stand in the front hall. Together they went through the house, trying the key in every door, drawer, chest and cupboard they could find. Vone even ran a hand over the walls of the front parlor for unnoticed panels that might conceal secret storage spaces. The activity lifted both their moods, but the key unlocked nothing, and so the quest lacked a resolution. Outside, the rain fell unrelentingly.

After the search had petered out, not giving himself time to get overwhelmed by his usual dread, Vone called the realtor – something he could cross off his list despite the shitty weather, and that Jack would notice had been done when he got home. Sarah answered and said she'd seen his email and would send a plumber round the following morning. She asked after Jay-Jay, then asked how Vone and Jack were finding the house with what Vone felt was a slightly forced brightness but might just have been her usual manner. He responded bromidically.

Afterwards he Skyped Rell but got no answer. Probably doing gallery shit, or else on shift at Sweetgreen. Much as he'd bitched about the long hours, low pay, no benefits and asshole management, Vone found he missed the camaraderie; even – despite their multiple allergies to, and intolerances of, pretty much every foodstuff known to man – the customers, whose accents hailed from every corner of the globe, with an intensity he knew was ridiculous. And now he would be missing Rell's private view.

Though we could drive down for it. I could persuade Jack. Rory could babysit, maybe. We could stay over somewhere. Gaugeville isn't Mars. But somehow the idea of returning to New York only for a visit appalled him.

Hunching against the rain, he scurried round to the garage and worked out for ten minutes with the punch bag. It helped, and while he was doing so the downpour, quite abruptly, stopped. Disconcerted, he looked up. Above the gables and gambrels of the house across the way, the clouds were heading north. They moved fast, as if sped up time-lapse style, and drew other clouds after them – an unending gray wagon trail that all but guaranteed more rain soon.

Vone had left Jay-Jay at the kitchen table, playing a game on the iPad. It was something he felt only a little guilty about: keeping their son away from the technology everyone else used constantly wouldn't be great parenting either; and hopefully his and Jack's ongoing parental input would offset the quasi-English accent he was picking up from *Peppa Pig*. Deciding to risk a quick jog round the block in the gap between downpours, he went along to and up the front steps, opened the front door and called, "Daddy's just going for a quick run. I'll be back in ten, okay."

"Okay, Daddy," Jay-Jay called back.

Vone jogged up the street in the direction of the Vicinity. He didn't ask himself why he was risking the development instead of opting for the moose trail. Defiance, maybe, or the aversion felt by a city boy brought up poor to getting dirt on his Nikes. Then too, there was the dread of encountering one of the white women joggers in the woods, alone and away from witnesses. As he kicked at the scads of wet yellow bark-flecked leaves he realized he needed this: just a little time where he wasn't having to perform for anyone.

Skirting the muddy track, he bounced through the tangle of ground ivy that bordered it, sped up as he passed through the covered bridge, and on the other side kept going, as he did so brushing against a dense, twiggy wall of hawthorn that scattered water droplets over him like diamonds and darkened the left shoulder of his dove-gray hoodie.

He was moving fast by the time he reached the blacktop beyond. He turned left and ran straight, keeping to the middle of the road, turned right then right again. One last right completed the circuit. More cars were parked in their ports than the day before, though no one was out raking up the last of the autumn leaves, and of course the grass was too wet for a final end of season mow. He thought he noticed a curtain twitch in one of the windows as he passed. Vone set his jaw, and accelerated. The ludicrousness of his fear – that they would call the cops on him every time he left the house – only left him angrier and more stressed.

But *was* it ludicrous? Every day he saw videos of Black people being victimized – for being estate agents, hiring bicycles, asking someone white to leash their dog to protect nesting birds, on and on. Fleetingly he imagined being arrested for Jogging While Black; imagined Jay-Jay, left home alone, coming to harm of some sort; Jay-Jay getting taken away by agents of the state "for his protection." Trying flailingly to explain to a stony-faced Jack that it wasn't *him* who was in the wrong because, as a general principle, when a thing happens to you over and over isn't it you, not the world, that's at fault?

He did a second, faster circuit. It helped, and fifteen minutes later he was back at Number 13 far less tense than when he set out. He ended with a mini sprint up the drive that set his calves burning, and afterwards took a minute to stretch on the front steps. Before going inside again he took a few steps back and looked up at the front of the house. Nothing crouched on the chimney today, but to his surprise, the absence wasn't particularly reassuring. The clouds rolled on behind the stack, charcoal dark and pregnant with rain.

The house had been waiting for him, but did it welcome? Then again, how welcoming had their old apartment been? They had made it so with books, art, personal photos, Jay-Jay's scrawls stuck to the fridge with campy magnets in the shape of pineapples, melons and paw-paws, colorful rugs draped over tired furniture, but most of all by building memories together. Number 13 could be home too: it would only take time and willpower. Because everywhere had its shadow side, didn't it? Jack had been robbed at knifepoint in Fort Greene the year before; someone in a neighboring block who they knew slightly had been murdered in a home invasion.

"Jay-Jay?" he called as he stepped into the front hall. "I'm just gonna take a quick shower, then if the rain holds off we can go out." No reply. "Junior? Boy, what you up to? You better not be in the –"

He opened the parlor door. No Jay-Jay. Went through to the kitchen, unease rising. *I said I'd be ten minutes, I was gone twenty. More than enough time for...* For what? No knives were reachable, the kitchen scissors were safely put away, the safety lock was on the cupboard where the rat poison and Drano lived. The laundry pods were out of reach on top of the refrigerator. Jay-Jay wouldn't go down to the basement in the dark, and he couldn't reach the light switch.

The iPad sat on the kitchen table, its screen asleep. *At least two minutes, then.*

Glancing out of the window, he saw a small figure making its determined way towards the gap in the fence. *An entrance; a doorway.* Above the pickets the storm-stripped branches of the trees, now still as stone, rose like the charcoal frame of some torched cathedral: a place once spiritual, now a pagan echo of its former self. Going quickly to the side-door, Vone found it unlocked. How had Jay-Jay got it open when the key was too stiff for his fingers to turn? *I guess I didn't –*

Another thing to not tell Jack.

Then again, maybe it was Jack who'd unlocked the door while Vone was out of the room, determined to embrace carefree country living.

"Jay-Jay!" Vone called as he jogged across the tussocky yard in pursuit of his son. Jay-Jay didn't seem to hear him. Vone caught up to him just as he was stepping awkwardly through the fence-gap, determined, it seemed, to follow the trail. He had on his sweater and dungarees, but no coat or mittens or hat, and his indoor shoes were already sopping from the wet grass. Vone caught him by the shoulder. "Boy, what you doing out here?" he asked, more roughly than he had intended. "Didn't you hear me calling?"

Jay-Jay looked up at him. "Do we have to go in the woods, Daddy?" he asked.

"Don't you want to?" Jay-Jay shook his head. "So why did you come out here?"

"*She* wanted me to."

"The crying lady?"

"Nuh-uh."

"Who, then?"

"The other one. She was calling me. She said I had to."

Vone looked through the gap in the fence along the trail, half-expecting to see a face peering out witchily from among the trees, or worse, some distorted figure taking a determined stance in the middle of the path and facing their way, lank hair obscuring its features. "What other one?" he asked.

"I don't know."

"Skog Madoo?"

Jay-Jay didn't answer; maybe didn't know. Briefly Vone wondered if there could somehow be an actual real person – apparently a peculiar woman – around the place. Unfairly he thought of Rory, the bitter, barren woman of fable. But Jay-Jay knew Rory: she wasn't some mysterious crone creeping about in the wet woods. "How did you get out of the house?" he asked. "Did you come out the front way?"

Jay-Jay shook his head.

And now Vone had to ask: "Did Rory...?"

But his son's expression told him it hadn't been Rory.

From some way off along the trail there came a curious sound, a vibrating rattle that might have been the persistent knocking of a woodpecker.

But there are no birds in these woods.

Maybe it was something mechanical, then: an irrigation system kicking in, perhaps, or the vanes of a small windmill whirring in the breeze. He'd noticed several of those in the farms they'd passed on the drive from Collington-Osprey: mechanisms with fans of blades at the back like a turkey's tail-feathers, mounted on little derricks. But he didn't think so.

The rattling faded away. In the damp cold, Vone shuddered. Whenever he was outside, if he stood still for more than the shortest length of time, his core temperature crashed. He had always been that way. *Black man's genes. We Sun People.* He took his son's hand. It was cold and Jay-Jay was shivering too. *My son.* Did Jack ever resent the fact?

"Let's get inside, okay? Hot chocolate and toasties?"

Twelve

That evening Vone and Jack trailed over to Rory's with Jay-Jay leading the way, excited by the prospect of seeing Pepper again. Jack carried a bottle of red wine, Vone a six-pack of beer that Jack had picked up on the way home, both of them wanting for inadequate reasons to make a tolerably manly first impression on their new acquaintances, and irritable as a result. The rain spat in their faces in the dark and the wind blew wet leaves against their legs. Under their coats both men wore chinos, plaid shirts and yellow Timberlands – the nearest to a conservative semi-formal ensemble Vone could muster, though annoyingly it meant he and Jack would be presenting as one of those clone couples who dress exactly the same. There was no need to express to each other their unease at going to the home of heterosexual strangers as a gay couple, perhaps the only gay couple Rory and her husband would have ever met. Long experience had taught them that a progressive woman didn't guarantee an equally progressive male partner.

In Brooklyn they had felt – had *been* – normal; here they were not. To be Black in Cottonwood Way was abnormal too, as was, parallely, being a white person partnered with someone Black. Which meant that Vone knew Jack would have his back. But since the thought necessarily included its corollary: that his white partner might *fail* to have his back, it made him tense.

That was so even though Jack had from the beginning understood the simple premise that if your partner – your family, therefore – is Black, there is no middle ground: you're either on his side or you're against him; and, without self-delusion, you have to give up at least most of what is called whiteness. And Jack had done that. But removed from the environment where those insights had formed in him – the environment that had in part formed those insights – might he drift back into shabby accommodationism? Vone knew that people who had therapy for arachnophobia and ended up exultantly holding tarantulas at the zoo could snap back to their previous mental state if they didn't happen to see a spider for ages, then suddenly saw one. The new thinking, the new imprinting could be entirely lost. And who hadn't denied his version of Christ at some family gathering or workplace get-together or job interview, if by nothing worse than omission?

Vone trusted Jack: it was only his sense of being mentally off-balance that was making him think that way. Had Rory's husband voted for Trump, he wondered, but didn't say aloud.

Rory and Ted's house, which was three along from theirs, was built in a similar style but better maintained, with a neatly-pruned cherry tree in the front yard, a trim lawn, and herbaceous borders that even that late in the year were full of color. The clapboards were pale blue and the trim white, giving the house a lakeside feel that Vone was surprised the designers of the Vicinity hadn't ripped off, given its "practically on the water" marketing patter.

The porch light was on to welcome them. A white cruiser with a recent license-plate sat in the drive. Prominent in its rear window was an NRA sticker.

"Oh, joy," Vone said as they climbed the front steps.

"It was you who said we'd come," Jack said, dragging up a smile as he pressed the bell. "Surely she wouldn't have invited us if the husband was a total –"

Rory answered in a knee-length, sleeveless red velvet evening dress that flattered her still-good figure. She was carefully made up, effusive and already slightly drunk. She kissed Vone on the cheek, shook hands with Jack, and squatted – somewhat hobbled by the fit of the dress – to fuss over Jay-Jay. Then, with Vone's reached-out-for assistance, she straightened up and stepped back for them to enter. As they hung their coats Jack managed to whisper, "Plot twist: they're swingers," and Vone suppressed a snark.

Taking Jack's proffered bottle, Rory led them through to a large lounge-diner decorated in oranges and browns, where her husband stood waiting to greet them. He was a ruddy-faced, clean-shaven white man in his late fifties with cropped silver hair. Heavy set, maybe six two, like his guests he had on chinos and a plaid shirt, and made a humorous gesture acknowledging the fact. "If I was my wife, I'd have to go up and change. I'm Ted." His Maine accent was strong.

He shook their hands vigorously, then sat with a grunt on a leather footstool to introduce himself to Jay-Jay on his eye-level. His considerateness towards their son made Vone warm to him. Pepper pattered in from another room, wagging her tail, and pushed her head under Jay-Jay's hand.

"Junior can watch TV in the den if he likes," Ted said. "Grown folks' talk is boring for a yowun. Take a seat, why don't you. Now, something warming on a cold night. What'll you take?" He crossed to a small bar that was like something from a bygone era, its curving, orange glass front jailed behind bent copper spirals.

Vone offered his six-pack, which Rory carried with the wine through to the adjoining kitchen, and, after a shared glance, he and Jack opted for the large, brown leather sofa so they could sit as a couple, allowing, with extreme self-con-sciousness, the outer edges of their knees to touch as they spread their legs masculinely. Vone's thoughts went to the madhouse paradox of trying to prove yourself sane by self-consciously performing normality in a situation so abnormal that weirdness was the genuinely sane response, but not the one that would convince them to let you out. The mental hos-pital was of course, *per* Foucault, quintessentially the place where the power of the minds of others was made both con-crete and inescapable. But then, wasn't it inescapable wher-ever you were? Church. The ballgame. The locker room. And so he and Jack manspread almost without thinking about it.

The dining table was large and fancily set, with an elabo-rate centerpiece that featured heaped squash, dried flowers, seed pods and gilt-rubbed pinecones. A pair of solid-looking candles, visibly embedded with twists of dried fruit, cloves and other spices, had already been lit, and the wine and water glasses and silverware sparkled pleasingly.

Following Ted's lead, Vone opted for a Jim Beam, Jack a beer, Rory a glass of the wine they'd brought. She fetched Jay-Jay a tumbler of orange juice from the kitchen, and together they toasted good health and good neighbors. Logs crackled in the open fireplace, which had a flaring hood of beaten cop-per, and the room felt cozy, the more so when, behind the drapes, the wind rattled the window frames. The walls were wood-paneled and hung with well-intentioned oil paintings attempting, but Vone thought failing, to capture the spirit of the woods in different seasons; and around the fireplace were mounted several sets of antlers.

"All mine," Ted said, looking satisfied. "Hunting season runs from the last day of October through November, limit of one deer per bag. Using a rifle, that is. Archery it's all through October as well. Rabbiting's good any time."

"We heard some shots in the woods when I was out with Junior our first day," Vone said, trying not to sound like a timid townie. "I was worried we'd end up as collateral damage." He forced a laugh that didn't come out right because, of course, it wasn't funny.

Ted waved a dismissive hand. "Folks are pretty careful round here." He looked over at Jay-Jay, who was kneeling on the rug in front of the fire and playing with Pepper's silky ears. "He'll soon be shooting up a storm."

"Maybe they won't want him to," Rory said, taking a big swallow of wine. "Not everyone likes killing things." Vone noticed her glass was already nearly empty. She got up and went over to the table for a refill.

"City gal," Ted said amiably. "So how'd you both end up being Junior's dads? Last I heard it was one sperm, one egg."

"Ted!" Rory clonked the bottle down on the dining table. Then she turned to Jay-Jay. "Come watch some cartoons in the den, Jay-Jay. We've got all sorts. Tex Avery, Disney, even some of that Japanese stuff."

"Anime," Ted said as, slightly unsteady on her high heels, Rory led Jay-Jay through an arch to a small side-room, picked up the remote and switched on a large but old and boxy television set.

The men watched in silence as Rory set everything up, put a dvd in the player, turned the volume down low, and left Jay-Jay sitting on a large leather beanbag between a pair of saggy, big-armed armchairs, holding the remote, with Pepper's head in his lap. The wall behind the TV was shelved out floor to ceiling. On the shelves, as well as dvds and even some video cassettes, were books – mostly of a practical nature, though there was also a row of Judith Krantzes and similar romances – framed family photographs and several rows of life-size duck decoys, each a different type. On the right-hand wall fishing flies had been hung behind glass, decoratively, like butterflies; and there were taped-up storage boxes stacked in a corner.

"I apologize if I caused any offence," Ted said as Rory sat back down with the bottle in her hand.

"You can be a bonehead," she said.

"I was just asking a question."

Vone and Jack exchanged the flicker of a glance. "It's alright," Jack said. "Of course you're curious. We had to find out ourselves. At first we wanted it to genuinely be both of us, but it turned out that to try and mix our actual genes would be – we did look into it to start with, but it's really expensive. And in a world where there are already stepfamilies and adoption, how important is the genetic thing really? So we decided to mix our sperm and let the best swimmer win. Our surrogate was mixed race, so however it turned out, both sides of us would be represented. No one would be able to go, 'That can't be your kid.'"

"I don't know how a woman could do that," Rory said, going for another refill.

"Aw, honey," Ted said.

"Well, I *don't*. Sorry," she added, catching herself, waving the glass about. "I mean, I *get* it. For the money. I've been broke. But doesn't that make you kind of like a –?"

"Rory. Go check on dinner, please."

"I'm just saying, I guess there's those that can, and those that can't. Do something like that, I mean."

She hauled herself to her feet and disappeared into the kitchen. "We tried for years," Ted said as the oven door clanged open and there was a sizzling sound. "IVF, AI, everything. Tests up the wazoo, both of us. She's got a loose womb or something. The placenta comes away early on. Nothing you can do, just lay still and hope. And we did, over and over. But no joy. Now we're too old."

"I'm sorry," Jack said.

Ted shrugged, perhaps uncomfortable at having had to reveal so much. "It leaves a hole, as you can imagine. We've got nephews and nieces, and we love 'em, but it's not the same."

They fell silent as Rory banged about in the kitchen and Vone wondered whether the meal would be a culinary disaster as well as a psychological minefield. He remembered how he'd felt as their baby grew inside Ellie, the nervy fear that surely she'd change her mind and refuse to give it to them; that precisely because she was a kind, decent person, she would at the last second be unable to hand over the baby she'd carried and birthed. And who could have blamed her? Who denied her?

They had chosen Ellie because of her good qualities as a human being; because she was healthy and didn't smoke or do drugs; and most of all because she was chafing at her various jobs, of which Sweetgreen was only one, none of which paid her enough, or left her with enough time, to pursue her acting career. She wanted to move to LA and take a shot at the Hollywood dream. And to do that, she needed money.

Vone couldn't remember who had started the conversation – it might even have been Ellie herself – but he did remember talking it out with Jack, checking online to find out what was typical for such an atypical process, and agreeing that between them they could pay her $25,000. Having a reliable (and at least slowly increasing) salary, Jack paid the lion's share. Vone contributed what he could – probably a higher proportion of his crappy income than Jack, but still, not more than $5000.

A lesbian lawyer friend had helped them with the legalities, trying to keep that side of things as unobtrusive as possible: they were afraid that formalizing the process might make Ellie skittish. Even so, they had had to accept that, if at any point she changed her mind, they had no moral right to try and take a child from its mother; and also accept that whoever it turned out was the biological father would then have to pay child support for the duration, with access or without. And so their stress levels rose throughout the pregnancy, which, barring a scare early in the third trimester that turned out, thankfully, not to be pre-eclampsia, had proceeded in an orderly way.

Vone had learned more about the minutiae of women's bodies than he had ever expected to, and, he didn't doubt, knew more than most straight men, certainly most husbands, by the time the baby came.

It wasn't until they had watched Ellie wheel her suitcase through the departure gate at Newark that they had looked at each other and known they really had a son. Even then they had hung around the airport for an hour after the plane took off, just to make sure she hadn't bailed at the last second, and wasn't rushing back through the terminal to say she had changed her mind – a romantic movie denouement in reverse – before heading back to Brooklyn and their new life as parents.

They had had little support from biological family – Vone's mother and sisters were disapproving; Jack's newly sober mom was ready with plenty of unsolicited advice (mostly culled from whatever she'd just read online) but offered no practical assistance. Women friends, straight and gay, were often ambivalent, even skeptical, until they met Jay-Jay, and found a happy, well-cared-for baby boy. Then they softened and rallied. Gay male friends – they had no close straight male friends – were initially delighted for them but lacked sustained interest. Of Vone's friends, Rell was the most attentive and supportive, and their friendship had deepened since Jay-Jay's birth and his appointment as fairy godfather. *I must get Junior in on our next Skype session*, he thought, though that meant it would have to be one that didn't include talk of hallucinations, sex, racist cops or hating the house and the area. *Maybe that would be a good thing*.

Rory brought in a sizzling rack of lamb, carrying it with lobster-claw oven mitts. She set it down on a trivet, went out again and returned with a tray of roast potatoes. "French beans'll be ready in a minute," she said. Then, evidently following a line of thought that had been in her head since she went through to the kitchen: "Junior's a lovely boy."

"Thank you," Vone and Jack said at the same time.

"Have you had him baptized?" She caught herself. "Oh, I suppose you can't..."

"They're gays," Ted interrupted her, "not Satanists."

"They could be both," she said, attempting a joke.

Jack glanced at his watch. Ted noticed. "Let's go to the table," he said. Vone called Jay-Jay through from the den.

The business of sitting and serving and passing plates allowed for a change of mood, and the food provided a new subject matter. Rory's drinking slowed, and eating settled her down. She became affectionate with Ted, and Vone remembered why he had liked her. Ted talked easily about

159

Gaugeville, the home of his family all the way back to his great-great-grandparents, and Antler Lake: "Great for fishing. There's rainbow trout, salmon. Lamprey's a thing too, if you can get past the look of it."

"Ugh, those circular teeth," Rory said. "The way it latches on and burrows into a living –" She shuddered.

"Tasty stewed, though. Like eel."

Ted talked about the growth in tourism, and the conflict between generating income and despoiling the natural beauty that drew visitors there in the first place – the semi-despised but much-needed "leaf peepers". Dessert was a cobbler crammed with autumn fruits that had everyone coming back for second helpings, and the coffee that followed was freshly-ground, strong and hot, and Rory thought unprompted to make a cup of cocoa for Jay-Jay too.

"My wife said you were interested in the history of your house," Ted said. They had moved back to the lounge area by then, and this time, feeling less of a need to assert the validity of their relationship, Vone and Jack took the armchairs, allowing Rory to curl up with Ted on the couch. Jay-Jay was back in the den, once more engrossed in cartoons, sitting too close to the screen and watching the politically incorrect and anarchic antics of cigar-chomping, womanizing Felix the Cat, for whom, despite his blackface origins, Vone had a soft spot – Felix the street version of the square and sexless, therefore more palatable Mickey Mouse.

"Yeah, definitely," he said. "Is there a story to it?"

"Any ghosts?" Jack asked.

"I never head of ghosts," Ted said, relishing his role as tale teller, taking a moment to reach another log out of the basket and lob it onto the fire. "But it's a sad story, that's for sure."

"It used to belong to a kooky old spinster named Mamie Place, isn't that right?" Rory encouraged.

"Ayup. Local character. Claimed to have Native blood in her, though I never found out if that was true. Abenaki, maybe it would be, I don't recall. You could see it in her features, which were, you know, kinda heavy. Mannish, if you're allowed to say that these days. I remember seeing her a couple of times – I was very young back then. She'd come in the general store smelling of drink, with this long, dirty gray hair.

Sometimes it was tied back in a long plait with feathers in, pretty much to her waist. Kinda like the uh, the dorsal fin of some big lizard."

"What kind of feathers?" Vone asked. Jack gave him a look.

"I don't recall. Brown and white, I think. I didn't know my birds then, so I wouldn't trust my memory on that point. I want to say owl feathers. She died sometime in the early seventies. The house went to a distant relative, living I forget where."

"Idaho," Rory said, unobtrusively refilling everyone's cups from a green and brown coffee-pot.

"Anyhow, they never cleared the house. I heard some story about how she – I think the relative was a she – didn't want to set foot inside it on account of some family feud. And then there was something in the will, some clause saying whoever inherited couldn't do this or that with the property. Whatever it was, the relative never showed up, just had it rented out as was. Gus Harris took care of it. Old Gus. Young then, of course. He's been retired a long time now – Sarah, who would've let you in, she's his, what would it be? Great-niece. She runs the business now. Got in bed with the developers early on. Shrewd lady." He rumbled disapprovingly.

"Ted, you know that's how it goes in business," Rory said.

"You're a newcomer," he replied mildly. "For us it's different."

"See?" Rory turned to Vone and Jack. "Newcomer – and that's after fifteen years!"

"So that's how come the front parlor's like a museum," Vone said.

"Ayup. Or so I hear."

"Jay-Jay's room looks more recently decorated though."

"Well, yeah. That's the sad part." Ted glanced in the direction of the den before continuing. "It was all over the news at the time – even went national, though I doubt anyone would remember it now. It was crazy, but not crazy enough, you know? I was about to turn fourteen, so it'd have been '86. My dad was a police officer, and he was one of the first on the scene. He said it was the worst thing he'd ever seen."

Rory shivered and rubbed her bare upper arms, though

whether because she was cold, genuinely disquieted, or from melodramatic anticipation Vone couldn't tell.

"Their names were Rick and Nancy. The kid was called Tommy. They seemed pretty much of a model young couple to start off with. He'd been a star quarterback, she'd been the homecoming queen. They married straight out of high school. The kid must've been four, five when it happened."

"It was drugs," Rory said. "They got into drugs."

"Not at first. They rented the house – your house," he added to Vone and Jack. "It was old and tired, so it was cheap. They did it up a little – the boy's bedroom; maybe had the bathrooms done. But Rick turned out to be a nasty bill of goods and Nancy, well, she was his doormat. That equation where people are drawn to each other, you know, but in a bad way."

"Enablers," Rory said.

"I guess Tommy must've seen a lot of what went on. The police were called to the house more'n a few times."

Vone looked round to check Jay-Jay was still absorbed in the cartoon. He wasn't paying the screen much attention; instead he was looking down and rubbing Pepper's tummy. He didn't seem to be listening.

"He was dealing; soon enough they were both using. The usual mess. Anyhow, story is, Tommy got into Rick's stash, had a real bad seizure and died. Rick took the body off into the backwoods, they reckoned to throw down the old well out there. That's another story, by the way, a lot farther back, but interesting. Lead piping poisoned the groundwater and caused an outbreak of mental retardation – I mean what would you say now, difference – and madness, and this entire village –"

"Now, Ted," Rory warned.

"And there was a preacher showed up there," Ted continued, "by the name of Nehemiah Light, one of those freaky Appalachian snake-handling –"

"Ted!"

"Okay, okay: another time for that one. So Nancy followed Rick into the woods with an axe and – well, you couldn't blame her for not being in her right mind with the kid being dead. She hacked him to death. The papers called her Gaugeville's answer to Lizzie Borden. No surprise, she was found unfit to stand trial."

"They put her in a mental hospital in Bangor," Rory said. "She was young, so she's probably still alive. Or did she get let out?"

"Not that I heard," Ted said. "But I didn't follow the case afterwards. It wasn't like now, when you can just type a name into the computer every so often and see what comes up. And it was only because my old man was a first responder that it stuck in my head the way it did. He didn't say much about it, then or later, but he allowed there were things about it that didn't add up."

"What things?" Vone asked, too quickly perhaps, because Jack gave him another look.

Ted shrugged. "It's nearly forty years ago. I don't recall. Them not finding drugs in the house, maybe. I mean, not even a joint. Or the coroner said they weren't on drugs, or the boy wasn't, so how come he died. I recall someone saying something about mercury poisoning."

"Mercury?" Vone echoed.

"Ayup. Like you get in thermometers. It gets in through the pores if you touch it. I suppose it was a mix up in the paperwork, most likely."

"And that's why the house has been empty since?" Jack asked.

"Well, there've been short-termers," Ted said. "Most of 'em okay, I guess. Some undesirable."

"You're the first family in forever," Rory said, and she smiled.

"And it's our pleasure to welcome you," Ted said. "You are now a part of the real Gaugeville Bounds – the Vicinity don't count." He flung his coffee dregs into the fire.

It was after ten p.m. by the time Vone was buttoning Jay-Jay's coat, and he and Jack were waving cheery goodbyes and insisting they would host the next get-together and yes, it would certainly be soon; and in the warmth of the moment, well-fed, jazzed on caffeine and a little drunk, they meant it.

The rain had stopped and the sky above was cloudless, black and starry, but the wind blew speckles of bark into their eyes they turned into it for the short trek back to Number 13.

"I can't believe Rory said us having a child 'only' a year after getting married was rushing things," Jack grumbled. "I mean, would she have said that to a straight couple?"

"She feels like she failed, I guess," Vone said. "That's why she suddenly went into that routine about 'breast beats bottle'. At least they weren't anti-vaxxers."

"And 'what if he saw us having see ee ex?' Like who *wouldn't* be scarred seeing their parents do it?" A beat. "You never did, did you?"

"Bitch, we weren't *that* ghetto." Vone was about to add, "What about you?" but then he recalled Jack's tales of his mom's sloppy drinking and sub-Tennessee Williamsesque gentleman callers, and didn't.

"Bitch!" Jay-Jay repeated.

"That's not a nice word," Jack said. "Daddy didn't mean to use it, and he won't use it again. Isn't that right, Daddy?"

Vone felt that sudden vexing contraction of his life to a tiny dot of "proper" behavior, suitable at all times for a child to witness. But what was the alternative? Having seen domestic violence as a child, and been beaten by both his mother and his father, as a parent he wavered between tough love – "I turned out alright, didn't I?" (bar clinical depression and a psychotic breakdown, that was) – and a liberal "let's be emotionally open and always center our child's feelings" approach that risked producing a neurasthenic brat.

"Right," he said, as amiably as he could. The wind came barreling down the moose trail, and he thought, despite the clearness of the sky, *another storm is coming*.

They were about to turn into their drive when, up ahead where the trail began, there came the sound of some large animal crashing about. They stopped and stood there in silence, watching to see what would emerge from the shadows. It should have been a magical moment, alive with the possibility of seeing a moose or buck or doe, but somehow wasn't.

The one thing out there that's moving, Vone thought. He wished he'd asked Ted about the apparent lack of bird and other animal life during what he said was hunting season, because it was as if they had all vanished overnight; as if the woods had –

As if the woods had swallowed them up.

He thought how there had been birdsong that first day. It was as if their arrival at Number 13 had triggered –

He squinted into the miasmic night as the sounds of movement receded. The thing's non-appearance, whatever it was, was a relief. A damp leaf blew onto his cheek and stuck there like a clammy kiss. Jack reached up and peeled it off. "Let's get inside," he said.

They found the house pleasantly warm, though occasional drafts of chilly air slipped in through unseen gaps, triggering a sudden shiver. Vone and Jack put a very sleepy Jay-Jay to bed, locked up, then took turns to shower, Vone first that night. The pressure was low but the water was hot. The pipes clanked ferociously all the time the shower was running, a new development, but stopped the instant it was turned off.

"I can hear something moving inside this one," Vone said as Jack toweled himself off. He was bent over and pressing his ear against a pipe that ran up external to the wall and was for some reason capped at waist-height. He thought he had heard something stirring inside it. Then came another sound, something so like an exhalation of breath that he moved his head back sharply. "The fuck?"

"The plumber's coming tomorrow, right?" Jack said inattentively, going through to the bedroom.

"Yeah, tomorrow morning." Vone suppressed a groan at the thought of having to deal with a (no doubt) white stranger as a Black man, and a (likely) macho tradesman as a gay man. *Where's a good lesbian handyperson when you need her?* He shook out a couple of clonazepam, swallowed them with a mouthful of water from the faucet, dried his hands and left the bathroom.

He and Jack lay in bed with their bare shoulders touching warmly, staring up at the web of fine cracks in the ceiling-plaster. They seemed more numerous tonight, as if something with a heavy tread had been pacing back and forth in the attic.

"I hate that a child died here," Jack said.

"Me too."

"I guess in an old house someone'll always have died."

"Not that way, though."

"No."

"It's weird, you know."

"What?"

"When she came in the house the other day Rory made out like she didn't know the story. But tonight she was kind of prompting Ted."

"I guess she was being tactful, not blurting, 'Hey, this is a murder house, oh, and by the way your kid's sleeping in the exact same room as the kid who got killed.'"

"I wish you didn't have to go to that fucking conference tomorrow." Vone was referring to a weekend-long series of seminars that had been sprung on Jack that afternoon – or that he had told Vone about then, anyway.

"I wish I could skip it too," Jack said. "It's always 90% shit you already know, and then most of the rest is irrelevant to your particular field. But I gotta look willing. Network, build up contacts blah blah. Once I'm off probation I can slack off."

Vone smiled. "Like you actually would."

They shared a kiss; then, like synchronized swimmers, reached up and switched off their reading lights. Vone closed his eyes. He tried not to listen out for furtive movements in the pipes.

Time passed in the dark. The wind began to circle the house, setting the downstairs shutters clattering against their catches, then falling silent, then clattering again, like the gills of some enormous prehistoric fish. Then the bedroom windows began to rattle excitedly. The chimney flue droned, and all around the house the pine boughs creaked like the masts of a storm-tossed sailing ship.

We could be pulled up in a vortex, he thought, knowing such a fear was both fantastical and absurd. He imagined the woods rushing by below, and then the image of a witch on a broomstick came into his mind – mention of Mamie Place, he supposed, or, more likely, Margaret Hamilton in *The Wizard of Oz*.

The windows rattled again, this time more violently. Vone wondered if Jay-Jay was awake and scared, and tried to listen out for him calling through the racket of what was evolving into a storm. How bad would it get? There had been no hurricane warnings: he would have seen them on his phone, or Jack would've. Ted and Rory hadn't mentioned anything, and they seemed the types to know that kind of shit. Since when did Maine have hurricanes anyway? This was just a windy night. Just another windy night and he should relax into it: any lost shingles were the landlord's problem. But the pines were taller than the house, maybe older than the house, and were creaking and straining ominously. Vone could feel the tension, the ache beyond the walls. One of the pines was dead, a great weight barely propped up by its fellows and just waiting for the chance to come crashing down and split the house in two. Vone's southern relatives, whose homes were in a hurricane corridor, had a proper storm cellar, and outbuildings they tethered with guy-ropes when the warning came. Here there was nothing like that. Because there was no need. Or was there? One day in the storm cellar his older cousin Vernal had exposed himself to Vone, and tried to get Vone to do the same.

The wind came rushing, rushing down the moose trail, swerving to twist around their house like a great invisible serpent. Was the breath of a serpent cold, he wondered abstractedly; would it mist a mirror?

Skog Madoo.

He should've asked Ted about the name, though it was only now that he remembered it, and anyway he wouldn't have wanted to bring it up in a situation where Jay-Jay might overhear whatever Ted had to say.

Something slithered down the chimney, soot he guessed. More followed. Though the fireplace had been boarded up, set into it at floor level was a vent, for access if a bird fell down it, maybe. How did birds weather hurricanes, he wondered. Did they get torn from the sky, from branches; get battered and buffeted? Did they cling on, or did they release themselves to it; ride the windways thrilling to the wildness, the chaotic buoyancy?

The branches of the firtrees pawed excitedly at the windows, their cones clattering against the glass.

Wanting to get in.

He remembered then that the cold-water tank was directly above their bed, ready at any moment to come crashing through the ceiling and crush their vulnerable, outstretched bodies. He thought of Puritan settlers huddled by their hearths, afraid of wolves and bears and pissed-off Native tribes, but also and perhaps more intensely afraid of what Cotton Mather called the *Wonders of the Invisible World*, which never were wonders, but only horrors. Vone knew about Mather because of Jack's mercifully brief Wiccan phase. He still had a regrettable pentagram tattoo, discreetly placed between his shoulder blades – provocative on the rare occasions Vone fucked him: sexily othering.

Somewhere a gate swung on unoiled hinges and clanged. *Not our house*, Vone thought. *We don't have a gate.* It went on: clang... clang... clang... *Why don't they get up and –*

He didn't realize he had fallen asleep until he started awake. He'd been standing at the top of the cellar steps, looking down into the dark, and had reached out to touch one of the snakeskins nailed to the wall. The scales had risen towards his fingertips as if it were flexing sensually, enjoying the attention. Or else it was bristling, like hackles along a spine: afraid, if snakes manifested fear that way. If they had emotions at all. He was –

He was in bed. *Just a dream.* But he had the uneasy impression that something was moving across the floor, keeping just out of sight beyond the foot of the bed. Sitting up, he glimpsed what might have been a thin line of silver fluid slithering away under the fireguard. Was the vent open or closed? Closed, surely. He stared at the fireguard. Which was the greater concession to madness, to go and check behind it, or to refuse to check and lie there defiantly, unreassured and anxious? He listened for any sound of the slot being drawn back; for something that had crept in in secret to let itself out again.

Down in the hall the grandmother clock chimed five. Vone sighed and decided to take another clonazepam. As he crossed the room to the bathroom he allowed himself a brief glance at the fireplace, just enough to reassure him that nothing lurked there and that the slot was closed. The floorboards were cold beneath the soles of his feet, almost burningly so, and that was odd, though perhaps a flickeringly present side-effect of the medication: his doctor said he had been lucky to avoid permanent peripheral neuropathy. Avoiding looking at his reflection, he shook out a pill and swallowed it. He couldn't take many nights like this. Turning off the light, he fumbled back to bed in the dark. The wind continued to coil around the house, intending, it seemed to Vone, to take hold of it and draw the building and those inside away into the maw of the woods.

He had no memory of when he finally fell asleep.

Thirteen

The plumber arrived mid-morning, and Vone felt from jump that he was pissed at being called out on a Saturday. His name was Everett Sterling, he was 6'3" tall, white, solidly built and in his late fifties, with nicotine-yellow, gray-streaked hair tied back in a ponytail, a full beard, and Germanic tattoos on his forearms that Vone guessed meant he'd been a Hell's Angel, or at least wanted people to think so. The two of them were down in the basement, standing side-by-side, contemplating the furnace. Everett leant back with folded arms, a bag of tools at his steel-toecapped, booted feet, and Vone found himself imitating the workman's pose as he assessed the job. The rules of machismo forbade him from mentioning the potential danger posed by the exploding pickling jars, though the smell of rancid vinegar was stronger than ever.

"You got a joint supply, see," Everett was saying. Vone nodded as if he understood. "What that means is, other people run a bath or a shower in their place, even if it's a couple houses along, your pressure goes haywire."

"Oh, okay. Yeah, that would pretty much explain it. Can you –?"

"Nothing to be done about it."

"Oh, okay."

"Soot in the valve is why you keep losing your pilot light," Everett went on. "I'll clean that out for you. Not a big job. The rest of your problem is likely tree roots, and that *is* a big job. Major excavation all the way to the street. Trenching, relaying, lining, sealant."

"Tree roots?"

"Trees grow as big under the soil as the branches get above it," Everett said. "As a rule of thumb. And sometimes there's stumps that get buried and forgot about. They're dead, basically, but they keep on after a fashion. Last year I opened up a washing machine for Abby Warren – she's the lady lives opposite you." Vone nodded, though he had yet, as far as he knew, to set eyes on the woman. "Good Christian, minds her own business – and what do you think?"

Vone made an "amaze me" hand gesture.

"Roots. Right the way up to the drum."

"I thought I heard movement inside one of the pipes in the upstairs bathroom last night."

"Not likely. No animal could survive inside a pipe. Water pressure'd do it in like that." He didn't bother to snap his fingers. "I can put an optical cable up there, though. Have a look about. It runs fifty feet, so pretty much to the main drain out front."

"The bill goes to the realtor, right?"

Everett nodded. "Landlord's responsibility."

"I guess we should, then. Or do you wanna check with her first?"

Just then Vone heard Jay-Jay piping "Daddy! Daddy!" in a scared voice. Leaving Everett, he hurried up to the kitchen, taking the steps three at a time. Jay-Jay ran to him as he emerged, grabbed him around his legs and buried his face in Vone's thigh. Staggering after him was an alarming scarecrow of a figure: a gaunt, unshaven, very elderly white man in a greasy gray-green suit. He wore carpet slippers and his bony feet were sockless. Pinned to his lapel was a laminated label that caught the light and flared unreadably. His eyes were dulled by cataracts, his pale skin traced with purple threads, and what was left of his tufted hair was white and wild. His lower teeth were yellow and jagged, and he reached out for Jay-Jay with dirty, arthritically distorted hands.

"Hey hey hey!" Vone said, shuffling Jay-Jay round behind him. "Sir, I'm gonna need you to –"

"You – you better get outta here," the old man threatened, jabbing a buckled forefinger at Vone's chest. His accent was local and strong, and he smelt of cigarettes, sweet liquor and mothballs.

"Sorry, who the fuck are you?"

"That bitch. That goddamn bitch. I *told* her."

"What? Who? Told who what?"

"She shouldn'ta let this place. Not to you!"

"Why? Because I'm Black? Because we're" – Vone paused for the usual closety millisecond – "gay?"

"Because of the boy," the old man said, spittle flecking his chapped and scaly lips. His skin was waxy, blotched red, fundamentally unhealthy, and wiry white hairs protruded from the corners of his mouth. Vone had never been this close to an elderly white man before, and he wasn't enjoying it. "Goddamn it, because of the *child*."

The old man sank into an unsteady crouch, getting level with Jay-Jay, who was now watching him from around Vone's leg. "Go down to the cellar, yowun," the old man said breathlessly. "You'll be safe down there. Trust *her*. And, and, and beware the other."

"Sir –" Vone said.

"'Cause everyone's got two mothers, see," the old man continued. "The black and the white. You just gotta figure which is which is all. Well?" he asked snappishly. "What you waiting for? Go down!" And he reached for Jay-Jay again.

Instinctively Vone pushed the old man back, in his alarm harder than he had meant to, and he fell weakly to the floor. He turned as he fell and the side of his head hit the lino as heavily as a dropped bowling ball. "Shit. Sir –?"

A throat was cleared. Vone looked round to see Everett watching from halfway up the cellar stairs, like the head of John the Baptist on a platter. At once Vone knelt, to help what was now all too obviously a confused and frail old man. "I'm really sorry," he said. "You came in my house and frightened my kid. I didn't know what you were doing." The old man avoided meeting his eyes, covering his face with his hands as if to ward off a blow or, like a child, hide himself. Vone now saw he was trembling, which might be a permanent condition, or caused by fright. "I didn't mean to..." He turned to Everett. "Help me?"

"I reckon maybe he needs an ambulance," Everett said stolidly, staying put.

And there Vone was: a muscular Black man who had assaulted a frail white senior, and he couldn't undo that, couldn't expunge it from the record in which all Black villainy and all white fears are set down. "He's fine," he said, on no evidence. "He's gonna be fine. He's just a bit shook up. C'mon, man, give me a hand with him. Please?"

Grudgingly Everett came up, and between the two of them, each taking him under an arm, carefully they lifted the old man from the floor, supporting his weight – guilt-inducingly little for his height, which was a shade over six feet – until he found his balance, then slowly letting him go. He said nothing, avoiding their eyes and looking down at his feet, but was, to Vone's relief, able to stand unaided.

Also to Vone's relief, he didn't reflexively try to bond with the tradesman against his dark assailant.

Vone hoped the fall – the shove – hadn't sent the old man into shock. A very minor stumble had sent his proudly independent, eighty-seven-year-old grandmother to hospital for a couple of days, to be "checked over" by the doctors, and by the time she came out again she had somehow lost all her confidence, became permanently confused, and died just a few months later.

Somehow the old man belonged in the parlor– *a guest; an elder* – so, rather than sitting him at the kitchen table, with Everett's help Vone guided him through to the front of the house and sat him down in one of the bulky armchairs that flanked the fireplace. He was now quite placid, as if he had already (as Vone fervently hoped) forgotten the details of what had happened to him. Nothing in his movements suggested a sprain or fracture, nor did he seem in any pain, but where he had hit his face on the floor a horribly eye-catching spatter of purple was already spreading beneath the translucent parchment skin.

Vone now had a chance to read the label on the old man's lapel: *Mr Harris suffers from Alzheimer's*, it read. *If found wandering* – it gave an address, 158 Timber Road, and a cellphone number, which Vone called as Everett, satisfied it seemed that Vone wasn't intent on further elder abuse, returned to the basement. To his surprise the female voice that answered said, "Hello, Mr. Mapley-Stevenson, how are you today?"

"Um, hi, um, I found an old man in my house, scaring my kid. This number is on a plastic thing on his jacket. He fell over and – he's okay, maybe a bit bruised, but anyway he's sitting quietly now."

The woman sighed. "That's my great uncle. I'm so sorry. I'll come right away. I thought you were calling about Everett. Is he there yet?" Vone now recognized the voice as belonging to Sarah the realtor.

"Yeah. He's down in the basement."

"Is he okay?" From the shift in tone, Vone assumed Sarah meant her great uncle.

"Yeah. He's just a bit – quiet." (No need to mention the bruise before she saw it.)

"Okay. Well, could you just keep him calm and let him know I'll be there as soon as I can?"

"Yeah, of course. Should I give him something to eat or drink, in case he's dehydrated or in shock? He's quite confused."

"Water, maybe. I think he forgets to drink enough. He usually makes it to the bathroom when he needs to." She hung up abruptly.

Vone filled a glass at the kitchen faucet and brought it through to Mr. Harris. "I thought you might like something to drink, sir." He offered the glass. The old man showed no interest in it, so Vone set it down on a stained glass coaster, on the table next to him. "I called Sarah and she said she'd come as soon as she can." Again, no response. "You know, Sarah, your great-niece? And once again, I'm so sorry about earlier."

The old man didn't respond to the apology either, but suddenly seemed alert to his surroundings, looking about him with evident interest. "Do you know where you are?" Vone asked.

Mr. Harris's watery eyes landed on the carved stand where the ostrich egg had been displayed. "You found the key, then?" he asked.

From the basement came the squawk of a pipe being wrenched that set Vone's teeth on edge. "Yeah," he said. "How did you know –"

"I put it there."

"What's it for?"

"A door, of course. *Her* door."

"Who?"

"Mamie. Mamie Place. You know Mamie?"

Vone nodded slightly.

"She made me promise. A long time ago. Made me the guardian. Well, not *the* guardian: that was her, you know. Likely still is, some way. Because energy carries on, don't it?

Maybe not focused, mostly. Maybe just about enough to raise the hairs on a cat's back and we say looky there, they seen a ghost. What you need, you need a, a lens or just an angle, moonlight on a mirror, or shining through an old window, and then I don't know... Anyhow, if you *do* know a thing, especially if it's a bad thing, you got a duty, don't you? So: caretaker. Okay. Yes. Caretaker. I can go with that. That's how come I, I..." The elderly man trailed off but kept looking about him. "She put it in her will, you know," he said confidentially. "This room and, and the other, of course. In perpetuity. Legal term, that is. Until all laws are done. By then it won't matter. Nothing will matter."

"What other room? Do you mean the bedroom? My son's room?" Mr. Harris said nothing. Impulsively Vone asked, "Have you heard of Skog Madoo?"

Mr. Harris didn't answer, nor did he speak again. But he began to tremble all over, and inclined his head as if in contemplation, and mumbled as if in prayer.

A half hour later Vone opened the door to Sarah in a baggy pink jumper, blue jeans and pink sneakers. "I'm so sorry about this," she said. "He doesn't normally get this far." Her hair was tied back and she wore no make-up. Vone pictured her having coffee with her husband when his call came; imagined her reluctance to spruce up for a client on a weekend.

He showed her into the parlor, where the old man was now hunched forward in his chair. Sitting opposite him, mirroring his pose and looking solemn but unafraid, was Jay-Jay. Vone was pleased. Aware that his son lacked grandparents who were present in his life, never mind great-grandparents, he had thought it important to give him a chance to move from a prudent fear of strangers to accepting oddness as something that was usually harmless, so had led him through to the parlor and introduced him to Mr. Harris by name. The old man had been responsive and friendly, and had extended a hand to gently shake Jay-Jay's, apologizing for his arthritic fingers – "I know, they look like you're seeing 'em through a water glass" – and Jay-Jay hadn't freaked out, as Vone had feared he might, perhaps in part because Mr. Harris's presence meant he got to sit on one of the special chairs in the forbidden room.

Apparently they had been talking, because Jay-Jay said in a serious tone, "Mister Harris knows the Owl Lady."

"Does he? Well, you remember Sarah, right? She helped us find this house, and Mister Harris is her great uncle. Go see if Everett needs a glass of water or juice, please."

"Okay, Daddy."

Jay-Jay slid off the chair and headed for the door. From there he looked back, but the old man's eyes had retreated, their irises now more china than glass. Hanging next to the door was a print of a Medieval painting Vone hadn't noticed before. It was narrow and featured a doll-like Adam and Eve, their genitals shielded by awkwardly-placed hands, and coiled round the trunk of a small tree that stood between them was a serpent with an angelic face.

Gently Sarah straightened her great uncle's lapel where the laminated note was pinned, as if he were an eccentric academic about to go up to the lectern at a conference. "You mustn't wander, Gus," she said. "We were really worried."

The old man looked up at her blankly. "Who are you?"

The question seemed simply sincere. Sarah's face tightened. "I'm your great niece Sarah. You live with me."

Partly to check how steady Mr. Harris was on his feet, Vone suggested they all go to the kitchen for coffee. Though he needed help to get out of the chair, the old man shuffled along without particular difficulty. Sarah could hardly have failed to notice the purple stain on his cheek, which seemed to be darkening as well as spreading, but hopefully she was relieved it was no worse than that: a subcutaneous bleed. She wouldn't want the hassle and possible expense of a doctor, much less an ambulance, he guessed; wouldn't want hard questions asked about how the old man had wandered so far while supposedly under her care.

The sound of hammering came from the basement. Reckoning a confession rooted in protecting his child was better than being exposed as a violent hoodlum by the tattletale tradesman, Vone told Sarah what had happened, leaning into his reading of Gus Harris's words as racist, and emphasizing his own (irritating but expedient term in the circumstances) over-sensitivity to such things.

"It's not about you," Sarah said. "I mean, not like that. Really it's not. One of his best fishing buddies was, um, African-American. Well, a mix. Part that, part native, part...' She ran out of circumlocutions, blushed and changed tack. "Gus co-founded the company way back when, in the late seventies. After buying out his original business partner, that would have been in the late eighties, he ran it on his own for almost thirty years. Then he began to lose it mentally, slowly at first, but after a while me and my husband had to step in to stop him from going broke. He always had a thing about not renting this particular house to families with kids, so when he saw your son, he..."

"Except the once," Vone interrupted. He glanced round at Jay-Jay, who was playing a game on his iPad with the sound down low and seemed fully absorbed in its candy-colored on-screen world.

"You heard about that?"

"Yeah, some neighbors told me."

"It was horrible," Sarah said. "And maybe I should have said something, but you know, it was practically forty years ago. I mean, that's more than fifteen years before 9/11, and it didn't actually happen in the house. Gus fixated on it, I don't know why. When he got – frail – we had his trailer towed into our yard. It means he's still semi-independent. He can prepare his own meals if it's not too complicated. He comes and showers in the house. I put up post-its every morning for things he needs to do. Mostly it works." She smiled a tight, bright smile. "But they don't get better, you know?"

Vone felt uncomfortable sitting next to Mr. Harris while his grand-niece talked so freely, but supposed the old man was used to it, and after all it was the reality of their situation. Certainly he didn't frown or object, just quietly sipped his coffee. "It's good for us to know," Vone said. "That way if he wanders again we'll know not to freak out. Do you think it's because of what happened that he came here?"

"I think he goes out for a walk then forgets where he lives or where he was going," Sarah said. "I don't think there's anything more to it than that."

Everett came up then, hefting his tool bag. "All done, Mrs. Anderson."

"Drop your invoice off at the office," Sarah said. "I'll get it paid first thing Monday."

Everett nodded. That brought things to a natural conclusion, and Vone saw him, Sarah and Mr. Harris out. Sarah helped the elderly man to laboriously navigate the six steps down to the path. To be that old was unimaginable to Vone.

Jay-Jay stayed on the porch and watched as Everett slid the side-door of his van open and slung his toolbag in. Sarah had parked up right behind him, penning him in. She opened the passenger door for her great uncle, and Vone took the old man's hand to steady him as he sank into his seat. His grip was surprisingly strong. "You doing okay, sir?" Vone asked as Mr. Harris lifted first one skinny leg into the car, then, with an effort, the other.

"She tied it to this place," he said, looking down at his bony knees.

"Tied it?"

Mr. Harris looked up at him. "Tied, tethered, bound." He gestured vaguely. "Put it in a – a – a whatsit. Wrestling. Sleeper hold. But it wakes up, and once it's woke and et it has to come here, see. Here to this house. Because. And maybe that was a bad or a foolish thing Mamie did, but she only knew what she knew, being quarter-breed or not even that. If that matters, if blood's a thing. Like say you're quilting. You got a quilt all pieced out, you've got your thread and a notion how it should look, but there's pieces missing. That's what she had when she got to stitching the words. So she put the house inside, you see. That was her mistake. Inside with the mice and rabbits, not on, on, on the right side, the safe side. Like a whatchamacallit, a tank, a vivarium. Mind you, even if she'd got it right, there's always gaps. Because nothing's ever really sealed, is it? Not in the end. Balloons deflate. Sealant splits. Then the dark things looking in, looking for the dark on our side, they can get in because it's there. What's the word? Bridgehead. Long as they live that will be the case. That's why I left the key, see. Just in case. So anyone who needed could break the egg and... so..."

"So?"

But the old man had lost his thread, and after a querying look from Sarah there was nothing for Vone to do but make sure Mr. Harris had drawn his elbow in before closing the door on him with careful firmness. Sarah leaned over and awkwardly tugged the seatbelt across her great-uncle's lap. He didn't help her. Eventually she got it done.

As she backed out, Everett turned to Vone. "You're lucky I didn't say nothing."

"It was an accident," Vone said flatly, fighting an urge to punch the plumber out, Hell's Angel or no Hell's Angel.

Everett grunted, heaved his van door shut, got in, started the engine, reversed out into the street and drove away.

Followed by Jay-Jay, Vone went back inside and through to the kitchen. He spun the faucet. The water gushed, then spurted unevenly, and the pipes began to judder inside the walls. With a sigh he turned it off, hoping Everett had at least sorted out the pilot light problem.

After lunch, though it would likely be muddy underfoot from the rain the day before, Vone decided he and Jay-Jay should go for a walk in the woods back of the house. He wanted to discourage irrational fears from taking root in his son's mind, the more so after the odd incident of lucid dreaming or sleepwalking that had led to him leaving the house on his own the other day: *She said I had to go in the woods.* Jay-Jay's worried, confused face had surely mirrored something in Vone's own, back when unreal things had clustered around him, transparent entities like giant stained cell-slides that had quivered and pulsed and sometimes urged him to harm himself in happy, squeaky voices.

Today, however, Jay-Jay seemed happy to go out through the kitchen door. Vone dressed him up in rubbers and a bright yellow slicker that would announce to any lurking hunter that this was a child, not a fawn or – what was a baby moose called? He looked it up on his phone. A calf, disappointingly.

The sky was blue and scumbled with puffy white clouds, the air mild and damp, and there was no wind as they crossed the yard together. The grass was wet and tousled beneath their feet, like a white boy's hair after a shower, and beyond the fence the branches of the trees showed bare. Vone helped Jay-Jay through the gap, and hand in hand they started up the trail, which that morning was buried beneath a carpet of fallen leaves, scarlet and orange and so vivid they glowed.

As Vone remembered it, the trail ran pretty much straight, without forks or crossroads; however, after only a short while he found that he didn't at all recognize the narrow, ivy-bordered defile along which he and Jay-Jay were ambling. His error surprised him. Looking back there was no sign of the trail, just a floor of red and orange leaves. He wasn't unduly worried, however: he and Jay-Jay hadn't gone very far, and could retrace their steps easily enough. He had the curious sense of being inside a snow-globe: a small, Narnia-like world compassed by the distance a child could walk.

The defile began to arc round to the east, and he was glad: he hadn't wanted to end up back at the well, and it was surely prudent to avoid an area where he knew people hunted, even though there now seemed nothing for them to actually hunt. Once more he felt a sense of connection to the landscape. Reaching out with a gloved hand he touched the trunk of a random tree, then, removing the glove, he touched it again, and the bark, rough against his palm, was somehow vital.

Sleeping sap suspended/Dreaming/Tension of trunks... trunks of... what? Next time he would bring his phone (knowing there would be no reception, he had left it charging in the kitchen), take photos and study up on tree types, at least enough to teach his son the basics. There was something pleasing about all tree names, he thought: elm, ash, oak, larch, birch, poplar, pine, plane, cypress, beech, hickory, maple, hawthorn, holly. Even monkey puzzle. As the names rolled off his mental tongue, he felt like a poet again. *Phoenix like spring sap capillarized, reborn from brush fire ash, catastrophic fertilization, benign dry winters, black forms dance powdered white, predictive shamans port de bras stiff, winds fan sparks spiraling/up/rise/lift up your eyes arise, arise...*

"Come *on*, Daddy!"

A little way ahead of his preoccupied father, Jay-Jay was kicking his way through heaps of orange leaves and sagging, sodden underbrush, scattering droplets of water from briars and suckers, soaking his corduroys dark where they bunched like pirate pantaloons at the tops of his rubber boots. Vone was pleased to see him rediscovering his independence and fearlessness.

Putting his glove back on, he caught up to his son. He found himself cheered by Jay-Jay's childishness – no: *childness*. He had written very few poems about him, and just then that struck him as odd. Perhaps Jay-Jay was too present, too much himself to be reduced to marks on paper, keystrokes on a computer screen. *Son sun orbit...* The swish of their coats was loud in the pristine air.

And then, abruptly, Vone's mood tilted. The silence around them began to feel intentional, like a breath being held so he and Jay-Jay could be tracked by anything with ears. They trudged on, both of them somber now, almost tense. *Don't let it beat you.*

Through the trees to the right Vone saw the steep, grass-covered side of what appeared to be a small hill or ridge. It stood alone, unconnected to the Asiwi range to the northwest, or the farther-off, bluesmoke Appalachians.

Following the curve of the trail, Vone and Jay-Jay found themselves circling a dome-shaped mound perhaps one hundred feet across and sixty high. Its summit was crowned by a grove of pine trees, their wind-distorted trunks spreading outwards from a central point like the fingers of an arthritic, up-turned hand, as if awaiting some benison from above.

Vone felt a sudden impulse to climb the mound. "C'mon, Junior. Let's go up."

"Nuh-uh."

Vone was surprised: Jay-Jay was rarely reluctant to take part in a physical activity, especially something new and different. "We'll get a great view," he encouraged. After a further moment's hesitation, Jay-Jay let his father lead him over to it.

As they began to clamber up the slick turf incline, Vone felt unseen eyes were on them. But even if they were, so what? They weren't doing anything illegal, were they? Anything –

Wrong.

He glanced round. Jay-Jay was a little way behind him, concentrating on not slipping back down: the side of the mound was steeper than it had looked from below. Father and son were soon on their hands and knees, grabbing hold of tufts of short, wet grass that threatened to tear away from the shallow topsoil, and sometimes did. What was beneath felt hard and granular, like dirt frozen solid. Though the gradient grew gentler as they breasted it, Vone found himself heaving for breath by the time he got to the top of the mound.

It was flatter than he had expected, and among the pines the squirming tree roots formed a gray-brown lattice. The center was subsided like a fontanelle, suggesting the possibility of some collapsed interior space. Oddly there was a disc of frost there, as if no sunlight had reached it.

Vone reached back to haul Jay-Jay up the last few feet.

He was struck by the mound's symmetry, then by the word "mound" itself, with its funereal associations. He wondered where the well was in relation to it. A half mile or so west, maybe.

A well and a mound.

How come there was a well out in the woods anyway? Perhaps there had once been an inn there for travelers – Jay-Jay's witches' waystation guess – or maybe a hamlet or village. Ted had said something about it, though Vone didn't remember what. Something to do with lead in the water, wasn't it, like in Flint. And madness, and snakes.

Now he thought about it, perhaps the well wasn't as isolated as it seemed. It was possible that had he and Jay-Jay gone just a hundred yards farther, they would have hit a road and houses – though from his memory of the (admittedly only briefly studied) local map there was no such road, no such suburban community, and looking in that direction he couldn't see one now, just trees and more trees and, beyond the plateau's edge, heaped blue hills.

"Do you reckon you can find our house?" he asked, squatting down next to Jay-Jay and facing him in what he reckoned was roughly the right direction.

Jay-Jay pointed vaguely. "There," he said, too quickly to have given it any actual thought.

"You think so? Well, maybe. But why don't we..." Vone squinted. "See over there, that church spire? That's Gaugeville." Using it as a reference point, he reckoned he could figure out roughly where the Bounds was, and therefore their home. His knees began to ache from the squatting, and putting a hand on his son's shoulder for balance, he straightened up. His therapist had said he should try yoga and of course she was right, though if he hadn't got around to it in Brooklyn, was he likely to do so here? "Boring," he had said.

"Remember that boredom can be a tool," she had replied, "if you resist distraction."

Though heterosexual, Kimberlé was Black, and that had mattered to Vone. All the things you didn't have to explain, however differently you might process them as individuals – some Black people had voted for Trump, after all, and would again if given the chance; and look at Kanye, or Clarence Thomas, or Candace Owens. But still.

Even before Vone had officially outed himself to Kimberlé as both gay and a one-time psychotic, she had gifted him a biography of the painter Beauford Delaney, the gay mentor to James Baldwin who had also struggled with psychosis. Kimberlé: someone else left in Brooklyn: Skyping with her wouldn't be the same.

Anyway, right now she was on vacation, somewhere in the Caribbean.

He wondered who had built the mound, and when, and what for. His mind jumped to the phrase "Native American burial mound," but there were other reasons for raising such a structure, he supposed: as a fortification, say; and other people who might have done so. Having no sense of what the interior might look like, assuming there *was* an interior, he thought vaguely of Egyptian pyramids, with their golden masks and sarcophagi, his impressions mostly *Indiana Jones*-level semi-nonsense mixed in with a dash of teenage hoteppery.

Though the sun was still an hour or so from setting, the moon had already risen, its disc slightly flattened on the right side, meaning it was a day or two off full. How large it was, Vone thought; and how strange that even without a telescope you could make out continents, craters, waterless seas; that it was that close.

Jay-Jay stamped his feet. "I'm really cold," he complained. "Daddy, can we go back now?"

Vone's feet were icy in his boots too, so he nodded and carefully led them down the shadow side of the mound, resolving to Google Indian/Native American burial mounds in Kwawidokawa County when he got home, alongside trees of New England and venomous snakes. Oh, and poisonous mushrooms and bird migration and the hibernation patterns of the larger New England mammals.

They slid down the last and steepest part of the mound, getting damp patches on their backsides that didn't matter at the time but slowly soaked through as they trudged along, making Vone feel like he'd soiled himself, and Jay-Jay pull repeatedly at the seat of his pants.

Helpfully the trail looped back on itself in the shape of a teardrop or a breast, steering them homewards without Vone having to search about for a way back amongst the fallen leaves. His thoughts turned to the cryptic warnings of Gus Harris. What, if anything, did they amount to? The old man had known the key was in the egg because he had put it there, and had known the woman who owned the house back in the sixties. Vone supposed that what happened to the little boy back in the eighties had gained prominence in the old man's mind because of Alzheimer's deleting the rest of his memories, and got mixed up with the previous owner being a grim old maid who hated kids to produce a cautionary tale of sorts. While Vone was out of the room Jay-Jay had mentioned his invisible friend the Owl Lady to Mr. Harris, and Vone had happened to come in on the old man mirroring his son – the cold reading medium's parlor trick, performed by accident.

"There was an old woman called Skog Madoo," Jay-Jay chanted, kicking through the fallen leaves.

"What?"

"There was an old woman called Skog Madoo," Jay-Jay repeated, as if expecting Vone to chime in. When Vone didn't, he went on rhythmically, "She had one tooth and she wore no shoes. She was so hungry, she was so cold, she looked at the moon and swallowed it whole!"

"Who taught you that rhyme?" Vone asked. "Was it Mister Harris?" But Jay-Jay had said the name Skog Madoo before meeting the old man – had screamed it, in fact, though he seemed cheerful repeating it now.

Jay-Jay shook his head. "Nuh-uh. *I* told *him*."

"Do you know any more of it? *Is* there any more?"

"Uh-huh."

"Well, so do you wanna tell me?"

"Okay." Jay-Jay took a breath and began, "Skog Madoo

had a silver hen –"

"A silver hen, huh?"

Jay-Jay nodded. "She kept it in a cattle pen," he chanted.

"That was a weird thing to do."

"Sh! Daddy! I'll get it wrong!"

Vone made an apologetic face.

"The poor little hen, it had no legs. So Skog Madoo had to lay the eggs!" Jay-Jay finished, and laughed.

"That's some rhyme," Vone said. "Poor old Skog Madoo." Jay-Jay's laughter meant he felt no particular unease at saying the name himself. "Who taught you?" he asked again. Jay-Jay shrugged. "Well, did you make it up?"

"Kinda."

"What do you mean, 'kinda'?"

"I just thought it and there it was."

"The Owl Lady didn't tell it to you?"

"No, I was just thinking about the well, and..." Jay-Jay's brow furrowed. Vone cursed himself for mentioning the Owl Lady. Once again he felt eyes on them: two small wanderers in the wide and endless woods, heading home, naïvely hoping nothing would catch up to them along the way.

Nothing did, and no lumpy black thing crouched atop the chimney cowl of Number 13, awaiting their return – though as before, Vone had the sense something had tumbled down and swooped away into the trees, a movement so fast as to be almost subliminal. If the thing were a guardian, was it benign or malign? Was it protecting him and Jack and Jay-Jay, or were they intruders to be driven off? And if protected, from what?

Skog Madoo?

A minute later he and Jay-Jay were sitting damp-assed on the side steps, tugging off their boots with cold-numbed fingers. They went in and Vone fixed hot chocolate for them both. Afterwards he re-examined Mr. Harris's secret key. It was, he felt sure, a door key, but he had tried every door in the house. Jack called just then to say the conference was running over, and that he'd be late getting home.

At first, though he did his best to hide it, Vone was irritated. But then he realized that if he put Jay-Jay to bed when he was supposed to (since the move they had let him stay up well past his usual bedtime, a habit Vone didn't want to become established) he would have a couple of hours to himself.

The thought was almost intoxicating.

After fixing Jay-Jay an early supper Vone ran a tub in his and Jack's bathroom and bathed him – or rather, helped him bathe. As so often, he was gratified by Jay-Jay's rapidly growing physical competence and desire for independence, though Vone still had to shampoo and, more particularly, rinse out his hair. Afterwards he dried him off, briskly moisturized him – *can't have my boy be ashy; gotta represent now I'm out in the boonies* – got him into his peejays, oiled his cornrows, wrapped them in a du-rag and put him to bed, at Jay-Jay's request leaving the nightlight on, the door ajar and the passage light on.

Though he spent most of his precious post-Junior/pre-Jack time scrolling idly through Black Twitter, to do so connected Vone to a larger, Black-centered reality that was affirming. He knew that racial isolation would destabilize him unless he was both mindful and resistant, and downing tranks couldn't be the answer. A brief image of an enslaved man running flashed into his mind, alongside half-remembered tales of Native Americans helping those who fled the Peculiar Institution.

Sometimes, anyway.

He didn't think he'd heard of afro scalps being taken.

With an effort he put down his phone. Having nothing else particular to do – Jack had said he would bring takeout – he found himself wandering the downstairs rooms. Something was somehow slightly off, though he couldn't put his finger on it. As always he had first to think, is the feeling, the unease, only inside my head? "The brain is structured to find patterns and derive meanings from those patterns," Kimberlé had said to him in one of their earliest sessions. "All theorizing, all world-building derives from that fact. In some people, the impulse to seek for meaning is more active than others. And then sometimes the gas pedal gets stuck, and even wrenching up the handbrake doesn't stop you from accelerating out of control." Which was where the meds came in, of course. *Neurochemical brake/ synaptic break/ homolecular divide/ broke/ n-word/ connections –*

In the front parlor his eye was caught by the cheaply framed postcard on the mantelpiece, the one thing in the room that hadn't been carefully curated. *Something off.* He picked it up and studied it. A generic photograph of Golden Gate Bridge, its colors were faded in that particular way that happens when one element in the emulsion has deteriorated ahead of the others, the cyan maybe, as what remained was overly yellow and pink. He turned it over, unclipped the frame and slipped the card out. The back was, as he'd hoped, written on. It had been through the mails: the five cent George Washington stamp was blurrily canceled; and it was addressed to 13, Cottonwood Way, though there was no named addressee, and the only date given was "Friday," with no indication of month or year.

Vone squinted at the tiny but neat copperplate handwriting that crowded the space to the left of the central divide and made out:

> *Another foggy day! Business going well: many Friends of D here, & they will spend on antique & fancy furnishings & you know I have an eye for authenticity at good prices. So does David (smile, 2 Davids, we are known as "the Davids"). Since his discharge from the navy we share the apt. & get along well. I think I said he is Negro tho light enough most assume him Spanish (tho even that is too much for several neighbors, who cut us at stores &c which is as he says their loss). I hope life is smiling on you at least somewhat. Don't let 'em get you down!*

He slid the card back into the frame and returned it to the mantelpiece – something to show Jack when a light moment was called for, he thought, as he closed the door on the parlor.

Halfway up the front stairs he saw Dippy, standing sideways on as if to block the way. *Huh. You sure do get around for an inanimate object.* He thought he remembered Jay-Jay having the toy with him when he put him to bed. *Guess not.* Raising a child could be mind-numbingly repetitive, of course, and Vone supposed that was a memory from a previous day. He placed Dippy on the window shelf by the front door, so Jay-Jay would see it when he came down in the morning. As

he did so, something on the window seat caught his eye–
something small and dark and dirty: a clump of mucky leaves.
They had been trodden into mud, peeled off the sole of a boot
and for some reason placed there on the cushion, sort of but
not quite out of sight.

*Not me, not Rory, not Jack, not old man Harris or Sarah.
Neo-Nazi Everett, come back to –?*

Quickly – quicker than he'd meant to – he went through
to the kitchen and checked the back door was locked. It was,
but then he noticed the knife drawer was slightly open. *I know
I didn't* – He closed it, then watched to see if, as happens
sometimes, it tended to slowly open by itself.

It didn't.

A scuffling sound came from the direction of the basement. *Had* someone got in the house? Opening the drawer
and taking out the largest of the knives, Vone went down to
check it out before his anxiety ballooned unmanageably. He
saw no one there and was about to leave when he recalled that
someone dwarfish, or a child, could just about hide hunched
down behind the Bendix. Knife at the ready, he went and
checked.

Nothing.

Overhead a floorboard creaked. Since it might have been
Jay-Jay out of bed for some reason, Vone held the knife behind him as he came back up to the kitchen. *No need for Junior to see Daddy acting cray-cray (again).* No one was there.
Vone put the knife back in the drawer, closed it carefully, and,
after a moment's indecision, went through to the front hall.
Not for the first time he had a vague impression of things having been moved in his absence, or at least touched, though of
course "touched" was paranoid thinking.

From somewhere upstairs there came a flat clack, uniden-
tifiable but singular. Vone collected Dippy and went up to investigate. As he did so, the pipes began to judder in the walls.
Neighbors running their washing machine, he told himself:
nothing to do with this, whatever "this" was. He had the feeling that he was being led or lured somehow.

Going first to Jay-Jay's room, he found his son asleep, the
radiator warm, nothing out of place. Setting Dippy on the
chest for Jay-Jay to find when he woke up, he went back out

and through to his and Jack's room.

There he saw something concrete to disquiet him, though it was a small thing: their silver-framed wedding photograph had been turned face down on the dressing table. He stood it back up. The stand was stable, and even if the brace had come loose the picture would have fallen backwards, face up, not forwards, face down.

Maybe some scurrying creature had knocked it over, which would explain the sound he had heard, and some of the other sounds too.

That, or someone *was* in the house. Someone hostile, in particular, to his and Jack's marriage. One, or maybe more than one of them, making sounds in different places, trying to fuck with his head. Hoodlums who had heard about the fag household from Sarah or Rory or, yeah: that Nazi fuck Everett. *Runic tattoos*. Which was worse, Odin or Satan?

Sensing a slight movement from the passageway, Vone went and looked out.

Where before it had been closed, the hatch to the loft hung open.

There had been no noise.

Heart thudding, Vone held his breath and waited. There was no sound of movement overhead; nor did anything slowly lower itself or drop abruptly into view. He could circle round to where the pole hung, he reckoned, use it to close the hatch before anything had the chance to –

No. You have to check it out.

Keeping looking up, he edged round to the pole, took hold of it and, very quietly so as not to wake Jay-Jay, hooked the sliding ladder and pulled it down. Warily he went up. As he did so, he thought of going to get the knife, but climbing a ladder while holding it wasn't practical, and while he was away anything up there could creep down; could make its way to Jay-Jay's room and –

He clicked on the light, ready to jump if someone or something – but no: there was no hidden stalker; no rolled up sleeping bag; no tool for drilling holes in ceilings, plastic bags of undisposed-of shit or video village of camera feeds. Still, he checked behind the chimneystack, though there wasn't really room for anyone to conceal him- or herself there. Then he turned off the light and went back down to the landing.

After pushing the ladder up and shutting the hatch, he went downstairs and made sure the front door was locked, then did a fast round of the first-floor windows, making sure their catches were fastened so no one could get in without audibly forcing them or smashing glass.

Last came the kitchen. Passing the black block of night the picture window framed, and imagining unseen gunmen drawing a bead on him, briskly he closed the curtains. His mind swung wildly between "don't be an idiot" and surging paranoia. Because wasn't that what everyone told themselves who subsequently turned out to have been stalked for real? After a while of that, he went upstairs and took a clonazepam.

The medication and some CBT-informed self-calming mantras meant that a half hour later reasonableness won out. Drafts could blow stuff over, swing doors open, push drawers out a little way; the loft-hatch catch had slipped because he hadn't closed it properly before; Everett (probably not a neo-Nazi) had put the leaves on the window seat before leaving that morning, or Jack might have picked them up absent-mindedly from where they fell off someone's boot, and Vone hadn't noticed them till now.

He checked his phone. *Tweets aren't loading right now.*

Jack got home a little after nine, with a large, decent-quality pizza they reheated and ate to the accompaniment of a bottle of equally decent red wine. After hearing all about his husband's networking tribulations and triumphs, Vone told Jack about his encounter with old man Harris, and Everett's parting threat.

"He didn't call the cops on me," Vone concluded wryly. "I guess by local standards that makes him a social justice warrior."

"So long as we've got hot water, I'd give him a pass for being in the KKK," Jack said, tipping the last of the wine into Vone's glass. "Not really, obviously," he added, darting Vone a look. Would he have felt the need to say that back in Fort Greene? For that matter, would Vone have thought he needed to? But power flowed differently here in this all-white county, where klaverns were far more readily conceivable. "I don't think Maine *has* a KKK," Jack said.

"I bet it does," Vone said, looking on his phone.

Jack waited.

"Huh."

"Well?"

"It did."

"When?"

"In the 1920s," Vone said, disappointed in point-scoring terms. Determined to find something damning, he scanned the Wikipedia entry and read aloud, "'In 1987 a cross was burned in Rumford, Maine. Anti-Klan rallies were held in Portland, Bangor and Augusta, and there were 150–200 anti-Klan demonstrators in Rumford, including representatives of the governor and Maine's two senators. To show their displeasure, neighbors surrounded the farm with chicken manure.'"

"Displeasure with the Klan or the anti-Klan?"

"The Klan, let's hope." Vone yawned. "Let's go to bed."

They tidied the dinner things away and went upstairs. Vone managed to resist re-checking the windows, and he managed not to tell Jack that he thought there might have been people coming in the house.

Fourteen

V one found himself standing in front of Jay-Jay's door. He had no sense of what time it was, nor any memory of how he had got there. Moonlight streamed through the small end window, its diamond lattice making him think of bucket hats and witch trials; of rage born of repression; of frightened, senile old women burnt in bonfires, emotions and memories caught in the bubbling glass as in the lenses of dying men's – or women's – eyes. He wondered if the window really dated back to those times, as perhaps, who knew, the cellar did, as the rest of the house obviously did not – a foundation re-used, perhaps; an old end wall, by chance still standing, incorporated into the later structure with its window miraculously or profanely intact. Could moonlight shining through old glass somehow reactivate what was trapped inside? Could it reactivate old memories, liberate old spirits and energies? Or, more relevantly, since moonlight for all its uncanniness was really just sunlight reflected, might the pull of the moon operate on levels other than the gravitational, two days from the full?

Thou shalt not suffer a witch to live. – Exodus 2:18.

At heart Vone had always been a pagan, aligned with shamans and sangomas, not preachers or pastors; drummers and chanters, not choristers. He would, he believed, have found himself at the rope's end, or among the stacked firewood, never a part of the torch-bearing mob; never in the congregation of the ecstatically hating, the psychopathically afraid. But then, against what had he ever really been tested?

He realized his hackles were up. How *had* he come to be standing there? With a click, Jay-Jay's door swung silently inwards. Dread rose in him, and he was unable to move. *Sleep paralysis*, he thought, though the thought, the fact, did him no good. Like the passage, his son's room was bathed in moonlight, the curtains drawn back as if in anticipation of – what? The shadows cut oddly across each other, and Vone had the intuition that the room was lit by not one but two moons: the moon now and a moon of the past, in another part of the night sky. Everything was somehow stylized, like a stage set; and bent over a sleeping Jay-Jay, as perhaps she had bent over that other boy back in 1986, was the old woman in the raggedy coat, the old woman with the dirty plait of hair into which were knotted feathers, beads and the bones of small animals, the latter now more numerous, Vone thought. As before, she was whispering into his son's ear, but this time Jay-Jay was stirring restlessly, as if struggling but unable to wake up.

I am asleep and he is asleep, Vone thought. *She has trapped us in sleep.*

The old woman's jaw was slung forward and contained the gray-brown stumps of teeth. She leaned in closer and still Vone couldn't move, though when she reached out to cup Jay-Jay's face in her thin, dirty hands, he managed to say, "No." His voice was toneless and without authority.

The woman looked round at him and she had the huge black, disc-like eyes of an owl. As she turned she screeched, a wholly inhuman sound. Simultaneously, and with great force, the door slammed in his face.

Vone woke so abruptly that he sat up in bed. His heart was hammering and sweat was trickling down his armpits. His crotch was wet, and for a mortifying moment he thought he had urinated on himself. Jack was asleep next to him and it was still night. Vone reached over him to check the time: his phone sat next to Jack's on the nightstand. 4:01 a.m. Perhaps the chiming of the grandmother clock had woken him. *Just a bad dream*, he thought, though it had left his mouth dry, and there was no glass of water on the nightstand.

As a child he had sometimes had night terrors. This had been similar: paralysis, combined with a sense that something of critical importance was being revealed to him. It was more than two decades since he'd had such a nightmare. As a child, they had left him with a dread of going to sleep for weeks afterwards. Perhaps that had been the beginning of his nocturnal habits; had made him a

A night owl.

He decided to go check on Jay-Jay, then get a glass of water from the kitchen: the water from the bathroom faucet had an unpleasant metallic undertone.

He found Jay-Jay asleep, the room warm, the curtains closed. Dippy stood sentinel on the pirate chest and no moonlight shone through the window at the end of the passage.

As he descended the stairs, however, Vone thought he sensed stealthy movement coming from the kitchen. Still prickle-skinned from the nightmare, his first impulse was to dismiss it as sensory bleed-through. But what if someone had got in the house after all? *Just because you're paranoid...* He had pushed the idea of hostile locals out of his mind; now it came surging back. Local kids looking to rob or vandalize, or maybe just creepy-crawl the fag house for a dare. Teenagers who might terrorize for kicks.

He couldn't wake Jack again: in no partnership is neuroticism or paranoia an asset or appealing. And if there *was* someone, well, he could yell, and he was six foot tall, strongly built and 170lbs; and after all, weren't white people cravenly, ludicrously afraid of any and all Black men?

But lynch mobs aren't. Meth-head thieving psychos aren't.

Breathing through his mouth, he made his way through to the kitchen. The grandmother clock ticked and tocked behind him, a sound from another era, a misleading romance of reassurance. He found the kitchen curtains open, but remembered Jack had pulled them back before going to bed, as he, like Vone, preferred to get up to light rooms. The key that had been hidden inside the egg waited on the breakfast table in a shaft of moonlight, and Vone once again found himself inside a dream-world latent with symbols and riddles. Defiantly he snapped on the overhead light, forcing the room back into normality; forcing the moonlight to withdraw into the cold abyss of space, or at least into the night outside. Pointedly ignoring the key, though only he was there to see himself doing so, he filled a glass from the faucet, drank it down and refilled it. The pipes squawked, gurgled and fell silent.

Just as he was about to leave the room, a tiny movement at floor level caught his eye: in front of the basement door something small was quivering. It was a feather, about six inches long, dark brown, with white tufting near the pen-end. It stirred in the draft that flowed out from under the door, which Vone could feel chilly on his bare ankles. He bent down and picked it up. There was a dark speckle on the quill like a scab, suggesting it had been torn from a living bird.

He thought of opening the basement door, going down to investigate.

He didn't.

After breakfast the next morning, Sunday, Vone made the mistake of trying to express his jumbled night fears to Jack, who had to drive all the way back to Bangor for the second day of the conference, and lacked patience as a consequence. Vone knew he was triggered in advance by the subject, which was the corrosive impact of addiction on those around the addict. Yet instead of engaging with his husband's anxieties and offering support and reassurance, he found himself going on narcissistically about himself and his own – well, weren't they neuroses?

"So you didn't actually find anything?" Jack asked rather shortly. They were standing on the porch with their mugs of coffee, the pines tall and cool in front of them. In the front yard, beyond the trees, sunlight slanted across the lawn. A cone fell onto the porch roof with a thud and bounced and skittered into the herbaceous border.

"There was the feather," Vone said.

"I mean evidence of someone coming in the house, like a lock or window forced or broken or even just left open." Vone shook his head. "If you really thought you'd heard something," Jack said, "you should've woken me."

"I know. I just – I wasn't sure, so I didn't..." Vone wished he hadn't said anything. But then what was the point of a relationship built on evasion and hidden shame? How, ultimately, was that any different from being alone? It just looked like you weren't, to those on the outside.

"Are you taking your meds?" Jack asked. "I mean, do we need to –?"

Somehow Jack asking that was more annoying than Rell asking the exact same thing, and this morning his otherwise laudably in-this-together use of the word "we" grated on Vone. It also reminded him that he had yet to find a local physician – an evasion of responsibility that could reasonably be considered self-harm by default. *Why can't I just –?* At least he had never suffered from any R.D. Laing-esque delusions that the medication was a suppression of his true self – a subject on which he had had to school several would-be radical friends, as well as the pray-it-away brigade amongst his blood relations, a good proportion of whom had also tried, with an equal lack of success, to pray away his sexuality a few years earlier.

"I'm fine," he said, trying to conceal the effort it cost him. "I just need a bit of time to get used to a new place. You know I hate change."

"Okay," Jack said.

"Once we've got the rental car I'll be better. I promise."

He and Jack kissed gently on the lips.

After Jack had gone, Vone once again found Jay-Jay leaning his forehead against the basement door, this time with his eyes closed. He decided not to make an issue of it. Instead he would perform a mundane domestic task: he would test out the washing machine with a small load of laundry, involving his son in the most natural way by asking him to move aside from the door. Jay-Jay obeyed with nothing odd in his manner, and followed his daddy down the steps.

Once he'd loaded the drum, Vone lifted Jay-Jay up so he could tip lumps of the damp-solidified powder (broken up by Vone with a few sharp bangs of the box on the floor) into the detergent compartment, and consulted him about the possible meanings of the time-worn, half-erased symbols on the wash-dial. After a silly conversation sparked by the appearance of the laundry powder about Snow Cones and feeding the monster's maw, they left the machine churgling away, seemingly efficiently, and went back up to the kitchen. The pickling jars seemed no more cracked or odoriferous than the day before, clearing them thus no more urgent.

It was by then mid-morning. A glance through the window showed a blue sky scattered with wispy white clouds. These moved fast, though at tree level the branches were as still as wrought iron. How abruptly the golden season had ended, he thought. The fallen pear-tree leaves needed picking up out back, the willow leaves out front, and he hadn't seen a rake in the garage. Another something for the list, for when they went to town. Jay-Jay could help him bag up the leaves.

"Let's get some air, little monster," he said. "Go find your shoes." Jay-Jay scampered off to the front hall, where Vone had lined up the family's footwear beneath the antler-horn coatrack, and returned with a pair of sturdy lace-ups.

The doorbell rang just as Vone was wiggling Jay-Jay's shoes onto his feet. It was a jarring sound and he flinched. Leaving Jay-Jay he went to answer it and found Rory on the step. Today she wore a faun coat, belted at the waist, just a little make-up, and her hair was loose. She had Pepper with her on a leash, and held a large paper bag containing something bulky but light. Her expression was uncertain.

"Hey," he said, not letting her in.

She didn't seem to expect it. He supposed her memory of the dinner party was hazy, and that her hesitancy came from Ted scolding her the day after. "When I was in town I saw this," she said, offering the bag, "and I just thought..." Vone looked in and brought out a child's cycle helmet, gray with blue and yellow lightning bolts on the sides. "The man said it was adjustable, ages four through eight."

"Aw," Vone said, genuinely touched, "that's so sweet of you, Rory. How much did it cost? I ought to –"

Rory waved his offer aside. "Please. It's a gift. My shot at a better welcome to the Bounds." She smiled, and Vone felt bad for holding her at arm's length. "Jay-Jay!" he called. "Come see what Rory brought you!" Then, to Rory, "Do you want to come in? We were going out, but..."

"Oh no, I've got a bunch of errands to run. Do you think Jay-Jay might like to walk Pepper?"

"Sure. He'd love to." The idea of a pet that came to visit and wasn't full-time was appealing, and Pepper was, as Rory said, a sweetheart.

Jay-Jay came slip-slopping through from the kitchen, kicking out his laces so he wouldn't trip on them. He studied the helmet with great seriousness and stood as upright as a soldier on parade as Vone tried it out on him. Happily, with only a little adjusting of the chinstrap it fit. Vone lifted it off him, made him thank Rory properly, then had him sit on the stairs and play with Pepper's ears while he talked with Rory out on the porch.

"Um, can I ask," he began awkwardly, "I feel like we might have kids coming in the house. They're not taking anything, or I don't think so. I just feel like the odd thing's been moved. I mean I'm not even sure, but is that a thing that happens here?"

Rory looked doubtful. "Every kid round here is scheduled pretty much 24/7," she said. "They don't roam, not like we did."

"Maybe teenagers, breaking in for a dare?"

"I guess it's possible. It only takes one or two bad apples to make you feel like there's a crime wave. But I'm not aware of anything like that, and in a place like this, as you can imagine, you get to hear about pretty much everything that's going on. In summer you sometimes have teens getting drunk and tearing up, but even then I haven't heard of them going in other people's houses. There's the odd prank at Halloween, I guess – someone's house getting egged, stuff like that. And it is Halloween tomorrow."

With all the business of the move, Vone had forgotten all about Halloween. Maybe he could dress Jay-Jay up as something cute and take him trick-or-treating. It might cut through some of the bullshit with the neighbors, at least in Cottonwood Way, if not the Vicinity: Jay-Jay would be just another kid with a jack-o-lantern candy bucket, being shepherded along by an over-anxious parent. His mind flicked to razor blades hidden in candy apples, LSD in sweets, but those were just urban legends, weren't they? Back in Fort Greene, Jack had always loved Halloween; funny how he hadn't mentioned it here. Too preoccupied, Vone supposed.

"I guess break-ins do happen," Rory was saying, "but none that I can think of. Kids getting into holiday homes in the off season, that could happen, and the Vicinity's more than half rentals, so maybe. Have you reported it?" A look from Vone reminded her of his low opinion of the police. "Has anything been taken or broken?"

"Like I said, no."

"Well, I guess all you can do is make sure you lock up." Rory smiled apologetically and offered Pepper's leash. "Thanks for taking her. She gets lonely when I'm out."

"My pleasure. She comes when she's called, right?"

"Yeah, and she keeps close when she knows people."

"We'll bring her over after."

Rory left, and Vone and Jay-Jay put on their coats, hats and gloves and set out, again through the gap in the backyard fence. Overnight the temperature had fallen to not much above freezing, and where the sunlight hadn't reached the heaped leaves yet, they sparkled like mica. The tree branches were black against the bright blue sky, a calligraphic effect that made Vone think of the spilled ink paintings he'd made as a kid, where you wetted the paper, droppered the ink, and tilted the sheet this way and that. Maybe he could show Jay-Jay how when they got back.

Leaves leaving left fall's leavings, departing departure diasporic retreat quiet silent grave of the year branch hands folded over breast of year... Mud, muck.... What was that word? Mulch. *Mulch memory forgotten, individuals fade, absorbed in greater memories of race and place, recall...*

Today Vone wanted to break new ground and so he avoided the paths that he knew led either to the well or the mound. Somehow there seemed more choice today; more forks and crossroads. Perhaps the night-winds had scattered the fallen leaves and exposed them.

Pepper looked round at him as if for guidance, her tail wagging uncertainly. Vone sighed. He missed Jack. This should have been a delightful family-with-beloved-pet vignette, not a single-parent-making-the-best-of-it one; and it should have followed a good Sunday morning fuck, or a sticky, full-on sixty-nine, jizz washed down bruised throats with good coffee afterwards, and freshly-made French toast.

When a student, Vone had read Betty Friedan's *The Feminine Mystique*, as part of a Gender and Sexuality in Literature course in which the latter took a back seat to the former, but was interesting even so. Friedan explored how, after World War II, suburban isolation drove relatively affluent white housewives to dose themselves en masse with tranks: "mothers' little helpers". Their white flight, from chocolate city centers to vanilla suburbs, had left them alienated from themselves – a lack of Black, he had thought back then; almost, though he had resisted the conceptualization even as he believed in it too, a lack of soul. He had been unable to articulate this admittedly tenuous notion to his uninterested, all-white-women tutors, and now, ironically enough, he found himself relating to those anomic Caucasian housewives, who were themselves (in a further twist) precursors to the "diet" pill-popping, perpetually "on" amphetamine crazies of Warhol's Factory and a thousand other suburb-fleeing New York punk and post-punk scenes, on the fringes of several of which he had found himself in the already remote-seeming 2010s.

At least his own flight from the city had taken him somewhere beautiful, with the wild woods at his back door, rather than some dreary tract home or suburban grid.

Jay-Jay jumped out from behind trees, picked up and hit fallen branches against their trunks, and Pepper bounced her way through the tangled underbrush, now and again barking, apparently at nothing.

It was pleasant to amble along in no particular direction, moving just briskly enough to keep warm, yet after maybe a half hour Vone found that, against his intentions, he had led them back to the mound. Somehow it seemed a less easy presence today, and he didn't suggest they climb it: instead they trailed around it in silence. Oddly, Jay-Jay didn't give it a glance, instead keeping his eyes on the scampering Pepper, and it occurred to Vone that his son was deliberately avoiding looking at it. He wondered if anyone had ever opened it, and if so, what they had found inside. He supposed that to do such an excavation now would be illegal. Apart from the specific issue of the violation of Native sensibilities, weighted by history as it was, there was the more general question as to when a grave turned from a place where loved ones were interred, and therefore sacrosanct, into an archaeological site, and therefore a legitimate area of scholarly inquiry. Should the mummies of the pharaohs have been left reverently undisturbed forever, rather than being stripped of their wrappings by curious Egyptologists?

He supposed it was like jokes: once everyone directly involved in, say, the Holocaust, had died, how people referred to it would change. And in time everything, however awful, becomes just another chapter in the endlessly accumulating record of the past. Was that shitty, or okay? Forgetting our history makes us lower than animals, Malcolm X said. But wasn't holding onto everything paralyzing? Fifty million people died in the Spanish Flu pandemic of 1917 (as Vone knew from its being endlessly used as a comparator during the Covid pandemic): who wept for them now? Nobody. Nor were there monuments or novels, songs or services of remembrance. A mass cataclysm, nowadays it was referenced only as a rebuke to those thought to be over-sentimental about the number of deaths caused by the novel coronavirus.

By contrast, Vone had friends so haunted, so consumed by the horrors of chattel slavery that they were disabled by it. He understood, but it troubled him how such passionate engagement, such holding of the past in the present, seemed also to open them up to conspiracy theories and paranoid thinking, and he, of course, knew what paranoia was, and wasn't. One of his uncles was like that, and it was exhausting to spend time with him once his theorizing expanded to include CIA conspiracies to effeminize The Black Man via "homo vaccines" and, per Frances Cress Welsing's *Isis Papers*, program him to commit non-reproductive racial suicide through homosexuality. *Well, I've got a son, so so much for that*, he had thought, but not said, the last time he saw him.

Their circuit of the mound completed, they started for home. His head full of his own thoughts, Vone let Jay-Jay and Pepper choose the way, and the way they chose was winding and indirect.

After a while he noticed the sun was dazzling him, which meant they were heading west. As their home was pretty much due south of the mound, he began to look for left-hand forks or turnings, so they could loop round and get back on course. Uneasily he realized that unless he happened to recognize the moose trail when they crossed it, they could get seriously lost. It would be night in a couple of hours and then they'd really be screwed. There was no need to panic yet, but he moved up to lead the way, and started to walk a little faster.

"Is Pepper with you?" he asked, glancing back at Jay-Jay.

"Yes, Daddy."

"Good. Keep up, okay?" Vone didn't want his son to see that he was worried, or find out he was as capable of leading them in circles as the dimwits in *The Blair Witch Project*.

A little later the western skyline flared, and as it did so the shadows lengthened, or seemed to lengthen, with unnatural suddenness, like candles deprived of oxygen, and everything felt suddenly heightened – like, but not like, his dream of the Owl Lady, bent over his son in the light of two moons, whispering her dirty secrets. He wished there were landmarks in the woods other than the mound and the well.

Ted had started to talk about the well the other night, but Rory had cut him off. There must be books of local history, Vone thought, or websites, telling of settler villages reclaimed by the wilderness. Such sources would also give, no doubt, the white man's views on "Indian" cultural activities like the raising of the mound. The Puritans left Vone cold, but he had the intuitive sympathy for Native Americans that many Black people do, though their epic romance with the unowned and unownable land of their forebears could never be his. One day, he thought, he would go to Africa – sub-Saharan Africa, that was, not Hoteppy, Arabicised Egypt. He would visit the kingdoms from the interiors of which his ancestors had been sold by vicious, avaricious kings to infinitely more vicious and avaricious European traders. Step backwards through the Gate of No Return on Gorey Island and break down in tears, or not.

He thought vaguely of berdaches – or was that word offensive now? He'd read an online post recently complaining that "Inuit" was – which was the upgrade from Eskimo, which was now definitely unacceptable, though he forgot why. He forgot what the approved word was supposed to be if berdache wasn't. Two Spirit? Perhaps the scolding was in relation to white people culturally appropriating the term under the non-binary umbrella – the "2S" at the end of the LGBTQQIAAPP2S riff. Androgynous shamans, anyway, kin to South African sangomas, who he'd read about, and seen short documentaries about, at various LGBTQ+ film festivals, and might be considered – or consider themselves – gay or trans.

Pepper barked sharply. Vone was pleased: it would alert any unseen hunter to a human presence nearby. Bounding a little way ahead of him and Jay-Jay, she came to a sudden stop in the middle of the trail and began to growl at something off to the left – that particular low rumble in the throat that makes your skin crawl; that reminds you dogs are kin to wolves. Jay-Jay looked scared and moved close to his daddy's side. As they caught up to the little dog, Vone tried to keep his tone casual, reassuring. "What you found, girl? What is it?"

Pepper's hackles were up and her ears lay flat. Vone's eyes followed the direction she was pointing in and his heart lurched: unquestionably, something large was moving about out there. His mind went to a bear. Google said there were bears in Maine. Okay, fuck, so do what then? Stand still and hope it ambled by? But Pepper's barking would draw it to them. A bear might ignore a small dog as not worth the bother, but wouldn't it want to kill and eat a boy? A boy and a man? An odor coated his nostrils and the roof of his mouth that was hard to identify, something like the grease on old machinery.

"Daddy?" Jay-Jay asked tremulously.

"It's probably a moose," Vone said quietly, trying to re-member when rutting season was, and failing. "Let's keep real still, okay? We do that, it may just go about its business." But he had a sense that the thing, obscured though it was by the trees, moved too close to the ground, as perhaps a cougar might slink along, though it was far larger than a cougar, longer and bulkier: if anything the size and mass of several cow-carcasses being dragged along in a rough gray sack. He wondered if yelling would help or make things worse. Pepper continued her monotone growl.

"Okay," Vone said as calmly as he could. "We're gonna keep facing it. Then we're gonna walk backwards real slow. Then, when we've got a little way and given ourselves a head start, we can turn and run. I'll tell you when."

"What about Pepper?"

"We'll put her on the leash. Pepper?" Vone called softly. "Come here, girl. Pep –"

Barking excitedly, the little dog darted off in the direction of their unseen stalker, and in an instant had vanished from sight.

Fifteen

"Fuck's sake! Pepper!" Vone called, frightened and exasperated at the same time, half starting forward, half hanging back. Would he find himself trying to wrestle her mangled corpse from the jaws of an eight-hundred-pound bear or a snarling cougar?

Out of sight in the dense underbrush, the little dog barked repeatedly. Then came an odd sound more than anything else like a truck tire being stabbed at full pressure, a noise Vone knew from his street-running days as a teen in Bed-Stuy, followed by a yelp and a pitiful whimper. At the same time something large moved off fast, tearing through twigs, briars and bracken, and he caught a glimpse of a shapeless gray mass like a great heap of sacking heaving itself rapidly away.

Keeping Jay-Jay close to him so the thing, whatever the hell it was, couldn't circle round behind them and somehow snatch his boy away, Vone came forward. He didn't want Jay-Jay to see, but –

They came upon Pepper almost at once, lying on her side in a tangle of ground ivy, whimpering and shivering. Keeping Jay-Jay back, Vone knelt down by her. In her little breast was a singular puncture wound from which a shiny metallic liquid beaded. It was as if she had been injected with mercury, impossible though that had to be. With gloved fingers Vone spread apart the ginger-brown hair around the wound. The skin showed pale, and beneath it black threads radiated outwards from the site of the wound. They didn't seem to follow blood vessels but made a pattern of their own, nerves perhaps.

From the direction the thing had lumbered off in there now came an entirely unexpected sound: the crackling in the undergrowth receding so rapidly it was as if its source were being dragged away at high speed by a motorized winch or an accelerating tow-truck. This was accompanied by a noise like the clatter of ropes against a flagpole in a high wind, and in under a minute it seemed the thing was swallowed by the distance, because all was once again quiet. Vone thought it had gone in the direction of the well, and wondered if it had left a trail a hunter could follow. *Maybe. But not now.*

Keeping his eyes on the patch of scrub where he had last glimpsed the thing, Vone carefully scooped Pepper up. "Go ahead of me," he said to Jay-Jay, indicating the direction with his chin. Wordlessly his son obeyed.

There followed a sweaty nightmare jog of maybe two miles, Pepper whimpering in Vone's arms, a small trickle from her bowels spattering down his coat-sleeve, and she grew heavier, as if dying had mass. In his mind was nothing but the thought, "Oh Christ she's gonna die, she's gonna die in front of my son and I'm gonna have to bring her to Rory dead and how fucked is that." Out loud he only swore. There seemed no hope of saving her, but he had to try. He couldn't carry both her and his son so their progress was slow, as no way would he let Jay-Jay fall behind, even by a couple of steps. The blood pounded in his ears, blotting out any sound of pursuit. How impossibly fast the thing had moved!

Later his mind would turn to thoughts about mercury and needles. He would tell himself it had to have been some skulking crazy in a raggedy gray coat, a grotesque scarecrow with a hypodermic who lived in the woods, who lurked on the outskirts of things, a deranged survivalist and/or drug casualty. That was an ugly thought because it meant the person was still out there, but also ludicrously unlikely. An animal bite seemed more plausible, but there was no question it had been liquid metal dripping from Pepper's chest. Well, what *could* be an explanation, then? When he asked Jack that night if mercury was a thing with junkies, he said no.

Pepper was small, but Vone's arms felt strained by the time he and Jay-Jay were hurrying along the side of their house and cutting across the front yard. It seemed to have taken forever to get back: Jay-Jay was too small to run for more than a short time and fell often, crying not out of physical pain but from being emotionally overwhelmed. And then, finally, they were on Cottonwood Way, walking fast, heaving for breath, breaking into a run up Rory and Ted's drive.

Giving himself no time to feel the dread, with Pepper cradled in one arm, Vone hammered on her door and shouted, "Rory! Rory!"

As he waited for her to answer, he looked down at the little dog. She was shivering violently and looking up at him with unnaturally dilated eyes. A moment later an alarmed-looking Rory opened the door, disheveled in a baggy jumper and leggings. "Something in the woods bit Pepper," Vone blurted.

Rory glanced at Pepper, snatched car keys from a dish by the door and jammed her feet into a waiting pair of Crocs. "There's a vet in Gaugeville," she said, pushing past Vone and Jay-Jay and hurrying round to the driver's side of her cruiser, beeping it open as she did so. Only once they were all inside – Jay-Jay in back, Vone holding Pepper in front – did she take a moment to look at Pepper properly. The little dog was quivering but now not even whimpering. Rory, whose perfume, heavy and musky, filled the car's interior, stroked her head.

Vone twisted round and gestured to Jay-Jay to pull his seatbelt across, which he struggled to do as Rory reversed jerkily into the street. Supporting Pepper awkwardly like a swaddled baby, Vone reached round, tugged the belt across Jay-Jay's midsection and forced the tongue into the buckle.

Rory thrust her cellphone at him. "The vet's under Eric: call him and say –" But even as she crunched the stick into drive and the car lurched forward, Pepper let out an excruciating howl, kicked and stiffened and was still. "Tell him we're gonna –"

"Rory."

"Aw, no." She took her foot off the pedal and the car drifted to a stop, its front wheel bumping softly into the gutter. "Aw." Rory took Pepper from Vone with gentle, futile care, buried her face in the little dog's side and burst into tears. Behind her Jay-Jay was crying loudly, and Vone's own eyes were wet as he put a comforting arm around Rory and bent her to him, at the same time reaching back to squeeze his son's shoulder.

Holding Jay-Jay's hand, Vone watched as a red-eyed Rory jabbed the spade into the black earth beneath a peach tree in her backyard. Pepper was wrapped in a plaid blanket from her basket in the kitchen.

It was unbearable, Vone thought, in the precise way the death of a pet *is* unbearable: they are there to be the repository of all our sentimental feelings. They have none of the failings of people. They don't disappoint you by marrying the wrong person, desiring the wrong person; by getting failing grades; by not getting their career together, not providing grandkids. Any way they annoy you is because of their simple animal natures and therefore not blameworthy. And Pepper wasn't just a companion to Rory's kids, an object lesson in responsibility: she *was* her kid. And she had trusted Vone, and Vone had let her come to harm; had let her die.

"It's not your fault," Rory said blankly, after the little grave was filled in, the modest hump of earth the size of the animal below, and she had laid upon it a bunch of late-blooming flowers from the front yard. They were yellow, long petalled, with centers the color of old beeswax, and by chance Vone knew they were called black-eyed susans.

Now they were sitting at his kitchen table, sipping coffee. Rory had brought a bottle of whisky with her, and she added a large slug of it to her mug. She offered the bottle to Vone, who shook his head, but offered her by way of compensation a pill from his stash.

"What is it?"

"Clonazepam. Anti-anxiety. Heavy duty, pretty much non-addictive."

Rory took the proffered pill and swallowed it with a mouthful of whisky-braced coffee. Wrung out himself, Vone took one too. Outside the shadows were merging with the dusk and the sunless sky was pale as a pearl. Despite the hot coffee the kitchen began to feel chilly, and Vone realised the pilot light had blown out again. *That fucker Everett.*

Jay-Jay stood on tiptoes at the kitchen window, looking out. Giving Rory's arm a brief squeeze, Vone went and knelt behind him and hugged him. He smelt of chocolate and boy and somehow the woods. Vone kissed the top of his head, pulled a leaf from one of his cornrows, and stood up again. Together they gazed into the deepening dusk, Vone's hands on his son's shoulders. Once they had the rental car they could drive far enough away to be free of whatever waited out there, he thought: the great gray thing that dragged itself laboriously between the well and the mound; that could also, when it wished, somehow move impossibly fast.

*

Rory left at seven, saying she expected Ted home from his fishing trip around then. She and Vone hugged, and ever so slightly she pushed him away. Of course she blamed him. He wondered if their friendship, so fledgling, could survive this trauma, and doubted it.

From the porch he watched her make her unsteady way up the road, the whisky bottle glinting in her hand. The sky was by then a deep and darkening blue. No lights showed in the windows or porches of the houses across the way, but one of the streetlights fizzed into life as Rory passed it by, creating an illusion of significance or meaning. Vone waited a little, then went in to fix dinner.

Jack got back when he said he would: eight p.m. Vone was relieved: he had more than half-expected another call to say that a conference post-mortem was too good a networking opportunity to pass up. Perhaps the subject matter of addict parents had turned out to be too personal, as Jack was subdued and said little about his day.

As usual they ate in the kitchen, the dining room having been consigned without further discussion to Thanksgiving and Christmas Day use only. Which, along with the front parlor being kept for display, made Vone think that Number 13 was, against the odds and its own inclination, a very Black home as he fixed the gravy for a pot-roast at the stove. Jack had got the pilot light to stay on, which Vone, to his considerable vexation, had been unable to, and the house was warming up reassuringly: his husband had literally brought coziness with him, as well as pleasing manly competence. Jay-Jay was lying on the rug in the passage, drawing odd-looking birds or possibly pterosaurs in the big scratch pad.

"I think it was a snake bite," Vone said as he sprinkled corn flour over the meat juices, stirring vigorously as the surface began to steam and pucker. "I mean, it was definitely poisonous."

"It couldn't have been something she ate?" Jack asked, scrolling on his phone.

"It was a fucking snake bite, Jack."

Finding what he was looking for, Jack read out, "There are no water moccasins, cobras or other exotic venomous snakes native to Maine."

"Junior, it's ready!" Vone called. "Put your drawing stuff away and go wash your hands!" Then, to Jack: "Maybe it's an escaped pet."

Jack shrugged but couldn't deny the possibility. Like everyone else, they'd watched *The Tiger King* in lockdown, and been shocked by how many dangerous animals were privately owned by rural whackos.

Jay-Jay came through, carrying his drawing pad in both hands, letting the middle sag to gather together all the crayons and colored pencils he'd been using. He put it down on the floor in front of the cupboard containing the dreamcatcher. Once he had gone back out to wash his multicolored hands Vone said, "Do you think it might come in the house?"

"Why would it?"

"Warmth."

"Why this house?"

"Why not this house?"

There was the tinny clonk of the waste basket being turned upside down. The faucet squeaked and water splashed in the basin. Then it squeaked off again. When Jay-Jay came back, Jack picked him up, sat him on his knee at the table, and gave him a hug. Then he met his son's eyes seriously. "Daddy told me about Pepper. I'm sorry, Jay-Jay. It's really sad."

Jay-Jay looked away, at the now-black rectangle of the kitchen window. "The Owl Lady says not to go in the woods," he said.

"Well, okay. She's –"

"And she says we have to let her out. Or else."

Sixteen

Jack frowned. He touched the back of his hand to Jay-Jay's forehead, and just then Vone thought their son looked much more like his husband than himself. "You're a little feverish," Jack said. "Let's have dinner, then we'll get you tucked up in bed, okay?"

Jay-Jay nodded. He didn't eat much, and was silent as Jack talked in a keep-it-going way about how funding problems were already constraining his vision for the hub – along with ideological conflicts that limited the number of schools in the county prepared to allow frank discussion of STIs and drug abuse as part of their sexual health curriculum.

"It's the same arguments over and over," he said. "Even though a majority of parents want these classes, the educators are mostly on our side, and the facts repeatedly show that classes like the ones we offer lead to fewer infections and fewer underage pregnancies and therefore fewer abortions, there's still a 'we've got to please the Christofascist wingnuts' thing going on. And if I question it and say we have to push back, I'm told I don't know the lay of the land, so."

Still, he liked his team, he said – who were, apart from himself, all women, mostly late middle-aged, and one, he mentioned again, was Black.

It was in its way the real world, which Vone had never been a part of, and which Jack hadn't either when they first met, both of them back then doing shitty service jobs and shiftwork so they could make their art. And maybe they had been butterflies on a wheel, but weren't butterflies as real, as much a part of the ecosystem as, say, beef cattle? For sure they were more a part of the natural world than those steroid-distorted, genetically augmented beasts that were factory farmed and butchered for burgers. And their marginal, poorly paid lives had in a way been far realer than the funded, salaried life they lived now, because directly connected to the precarity of an unconstrained free market; to all the shit that left you longing for a revolution you knew would never come.

And maybe, Vone thought, it really *was* just a coincidence

that of the two of them it was Jack, not himself, who had become respectable. After all, it wasn't like you *couldn't* be Black, come from poverty, and become middle class: as the first in his family to attend university, he had never bought into *that* excuse – that copout, as he'd at times uncharitably thought it, looking without much compassion at the bullies he'd left behind, who in adult life still hung out on their corners, or were in jail, or absent because dead: Hiroshima shadows, if even that, smiling out of fading family snapshots. And here he was, in a spacious, historical house near a prosperous holiday resort on a picturesque lake, seven years married, with a son he adored, and a husband he adored too, when he remembered to, and who supported him in every way he could. Who accepted the fragile side of him, the side that came unwound in the workaday world.

Plenty, Vone knew, wouldn't.

He reached for Jack's hand and paid better attention: his work was important and deserved to be treated as such. Now Vone asked questions, making an effort to memorize the names of people he hadn't met but in due course supposed he would, probably at some awkward office party, and did his best to picture the space the hub would be in. He had at least seen the block when they drove through Collington-Osprey on the day of their arrival.

After putting Jay-Jay to bed with half an aspirin dissolved in a teaspoon of water they cleared up, showered, then turned in for the night. They avoided further discussion of the Owl Lady or the death of Pepper. What more was there to be said? No venomous snakes were native to Maine, no news of escaped wild animals was to be found on the internet (Vone had tried quite hard to find some), and the Owl Lady wasn't new, nor Jay-Jay's report of her demands.

In one way it was a relief not to talk about any of it; still, as he lay there, Vone felt frustrated. He knew Jack thought he was filling their son's head with creepy nonsense; that he had somehow induced both the Owl Lady and Skog Madoo in Jay-Jay's mind, and triggered his fixation with the cellar. He knew too that there was a side to Jack, amplified by the pragmatic nature of his current job, that was suspicious of, even rejected, having an imagination. He had, for instance, while enjoying playing in a band and enjoying being in front of a crowd, never contributed any lyrics to their songs. For him it had been more about camaraderie and the cathartic thrill of performance. The songs were just the excuse for that; the catalyst.

At first Vone had been surprised that Jack had never tried to write a song, but had then accepted it, though to him to be wordless was to be dead inside. He tried to imagine a world where he held down some dreary admin job and supported Jack in his music-making but couldn't.

That night he dreamt something was trapped inside the boarded-up fireplace; something that had tumbled down the flue as through the entrance to an oubliette, those hideous medieval dungeons which had no doorway, just a hole in the ceiling through which you were lowered and then forgotten about. Whatever it was was crying to be let out, flapping and clattering in desperation. *A bird*, he thought uneasily, *a bird in the chimney*. But when he woke there was no bird and all was silent.

Careful not to disturb Jack – it was an irony that his husband slept as heavily as if he had been drugged, while he, Vone, though actually sedated, woke repeatedly – he got out of bed and went to check on Jay-Jay. With a determined effort he avoided looking through the hinge-gap as he opened the door. Jay-Jay was sleeping peacefully. Vone went over to him and touched his brow with the back of his hand. The fever was gone. He went downstairs and wandered about, checking the rooms. That night he had no sense of any unseen presences. His circuit made, he went back to bed, and this time slept through.

The following morning, Monday, Vone and Jack woke early and had fast, hot, cathartic sex. Vone sat on his husband's face and deep-throated him, swiveled round and, in push-up position, fucked his face, then moved back, sat on his dick, and rode him to completion, clamping his hand over Jack's mouth as he did so to stop him yelling out and waking Jay-Jay.

The sun was bright that morning, and though frost fringed the kitchen windowpanes, the house was warm. These were small reasons for optimism, but after serving breakfast, seeing

Jack off and putting on another load of laundry – their messy bedsheets this time – Vone's mood slumped. Unease crowded his thoughts, and once his few tasks were done he found himself sitting halfway up the front hall stairs, Skyping Rell for company. The washing machine sloshed distantly. Jay-Jay was playing dinosaur parade at the kitchen table, making small and mercifully normal animal noises as he marched the colorful plastic creatures along.

Today Rell wore a Kente cloth headwrap, his locs up Nina-Simone-high-priestess fashion.

"It's making me wanna write poems about growing up in Bed-Stuy," Vone was saying. "About my dad in particular."

"Maybe because you're away from it," Rell said. "Like when Baldwin went to where was it, that village up in the Swiss Alps –"

"Löeche-les-bains."

"– so he could finish *Go Tell It On The Mountain*."

"Except here they *have* seen a Black man, and they don't like it."

"Any more b.s. from the feds for breathing while Black?"

"No," Vone said. Then: "No, nothing like that."

"Well, you sound bothered by *something*, honey. Break down, let it all out."

Vone sighed. "There's this woman, a neighbor a couple of houses along."

"Okay."

"She was actually friendly, which was a novelty. She kind of looks like she might be a cougar type, but she was nice to Jay-Jay, so. Anyway, we went round for dinner the other night. Her husband's already drafting him into the NRA."

"Well, I guess he doesn't object to an armed Black man."

"He was nice too. I mean, they had us over to dinner and didn't make too many gaffs, considering. And of course they're gonna ask stuff."

"Did they tell you they voted for Obama?"

"She did, but can we jump straight past the *Get Out* references –"

"Ooh – they tryna get you to throw yo keys in the dish? Serve you some freaky suburban swinger shit?"

"Jack beat you to that punchline. No, it was: they told us

that back in the eighties a kid died in our house. A little boy."

Rell's expression turned serious. "Was there – I guess there was a story?"

"He was five. He was killed by his drug-fucked parents, apparently. The dad fed him something. Then the mom killed the dad with an axe and ended up in the loony bin."

"Okay."

"But it's not even that. It's –" Vone took a breath. "She let me walk her dog yesterday, while Jack was at some conference. This cute little dog, a wire-haired terrier or some shit. Gets on well with Jay-Jay, and you know he's always wanted a dog. So I'm thinking this is actually ideal. So we go for a walk in the woods back of the house, and she starts barking and runs off in the bushes and gets bitten by something – a snake, I think – and we had to – I was literally carrying this dying dog, her dog, to her front door and she doesn't have kids, so it was more than a pet, you know? It was just fucking awful, and Jay-Jay was really upset."

"It's a rough life lesson for a kid."

"He's been a lot quieter than usual since we moved, and now this – and on top of that he's been talking about seeing this owl lady."

"Owl lady?"

"It's ever since I said to him there had been owls in the attic because there were pellets up there – thrown up mice bones, you know? So I feel like I put owls in his head."

"Well, you know he's imaginative. That doesn't sound like too big of a –"

"Yeah, but then – okay, what it is, is: I think I saw her once. I had a dream about her. But I think I saw her before that."

"What you mean, 'saw her'?"

"Through a gap in a door. This witchy old woman with feathers in her hair, and I guess chicken bones and shit, and big black eyes. I mean, freakishly big, like, like, like – an owl. She was in Jay-Jay's room, whispering to him while he was asleep, in some language I didn't know."

"Chile, you're starting to freak me out," Rell said, and he meant it, though his tone was dry.

"And then there's Skog Madoo."

"Skog what now?"

"This nursery rhyme character – an old woman with one tooth and a silver hen, and Jay-Jay said –"

"Honey, what's going on?" Rell interrupted. "We've gone from someone else's kid died what, forty-fifty years ago, to the dog died to Jay-Jay's upset about moving to he says there's a witch in the house and then you see her too. Do you mean a for-real old woman broke into your house and crept upstairs and you caught her in Jay-Jay's room? Because bitch, I would be outta there like *that*." Rell snapped dramatically. "Or at least I would call the cops, toxic as they are, because you gotta get shit on the *record*, girl. Women can be pedophiles too, you know."

"No, she – I opened the door and she wasn't there anymore. I saw her through the hinges. You know, the gap between the door and the frame. But then this old man *did* come in the house."

"This old man Skoggydoo?"

"No, that's completely different."

"But the old man is, forgive me, honey – real?"

"Yeah, absolutely. That was the day before yesterday, and he knew about her, I mean he knew about the Owl Lady, even though she's been dead for like a half century or something."

"So, wait, he's who, exactly?"

"The grandfather – no, the great uncle of the woman who rented us the place."

"So not a witch – warlock, whatever."

"I don't think so."

"Don't think so?"

"He used to be the realtor, then he lost it, I mean got Alzheimer's, and she took over. But –"

"Vone, honey –"

"Because of the Alzheimer's he wanders around, and she said it was a coincidence him showing up at our house, but then he came out with stuff, like – I dunno, warnings, you know? At first I thought it was racism. Then shit got fucked up because I shoved him – I thought he was going for Jay-Jay – and he fell and hit his head, and the asshole neo-Nazi plumber saw me and –"

"Neo-Nazi plumber?"

"He's got rune tattoos on his arms, Odin shit, so – The old guy was okay, thank fuck, but I was lucky not to get charged with assault. And then the dog died. We'd been out near this old – I think it's a burial mound. The top of it's kinda sunken in, like there was a space inside that caved in, and I was gonna Google it and –"

"Vone," Rell cut his friend off. "You know I love you, but sweetheart you are gabbling and you need to see a professional before you *really* unravel. Because chile, you and I both know it's a hundred times harder to climb up out of it *after* you fall down the rabbit hole."

Vone glowered at his friend. He knew Rell had seen him bug-eyed, hallucinating and babbling shit he had no memory of later; that Rell and Jack had one time pulled him back when he clambered out onto the fire escape of the apartment naked, in the middle of an electrical storm, yelling at the diamond-hard downpour as the thunder boomed and he saw the sky crack open and the universe turn itself inside-out in a celestial prolapse. Afterwards, after he'd got better, he had asked them both, separately, what he had said in his fugue state, and neither would tell him.

As a result of that episode he had been committed to the Kingsboro Psychiatric Center for two weeks, following which, assisted by the stabilizing fruits of Big Pharma, he had had therapy until his meager insurance ran out. After that he had been at the mercy of sliding-scale counselors with very variable levels of insight, and with a hard-to-manage monthly pharmaceutical bill. But somehow, with the support of Jack and Rell, and having lucked out with Kimberlé, he had regained his balance and, he had thought until the move, expelled his demons. Now he wondered: were they all still inside him, roving like Pacmen round and round his fritzing synaptic map and waiting to rise up again, roaring? Was the disjointed list of phenomena he had just described to Rell, which, before he had spoken it aloud, he had started to believe was somehow a singular, unified uncanny event, a resurgence of the same old craziness in brand-new drag? He wished he'd said nothing. "You won't tell Jack?" he asked suspiciously.

"Honey, you can lose the hangdog look," Rell said. "You know I wouldn't get between yo business and yo man."

Vone nodded. Still, he felt uneasy. If Uncle Rell thought Jay-Jay was in danger he might break his word. And wouldn't he be right to do so?

Rell then asked a series of practical questions about Vone's meds; whether he had found a doctor like he said he was going to a couple of days ago; if he'd found a psychiatrist, either in Collington-Osprey (ideally) or Bangor – all of which reminded Vone that as yet he hadn't even got to Gaugeville, which was within easy walking distance, so the lack of a car was no excuse. He would go there this afternoon, he decided. Take Jay-Jay with him. The thought cheered him up, and he relaxed enough to allow Rell to tease his various anxieties apart and help create more commonsense narratives.

"Okay, so..." Old Mr. Harris had known previous tenants. No surprise there. Of course his granddaughter – great niece – hadn't wanted to mention the violent death of a child in the house. The death explained why it was cheaper than average to rent. Sad as Pepper's death was, likely someone's unwanted venomous snake had escaped captivity, and they hadn't told anyone. Being non-native, it would likely die over the winter. Certainly there was no reason to think it would head over to Number 13. The larger thing was probably a moose that had coincidentally wandered over during the snake attack and then, spooked, likely by the snake, galloped off fast. And of course the move had given Jay-Jay, and for that matter Vone himself, strange dreams. Presumably it was the Puritan setting that had put witches in both their minds – hadn't the crooked chimney made Vone think of a fairytale witch's house on that first day? Maybe he said something to that effect to Jay-Jay and forgotten about it.

Despite a nagging feeling that at least some of those things had happened in the wrong order for such explanations to make sense, Vone allowed himself to feel relieved by them. As Rell pointed out, just because Jay-Jay had only recited the Skog Madoo skipping song (as Rell declared it to be) in Vone's hearing after they moved to Maine, it didn't mean he had learnt it there. Why couldn't he have heard it back in Brooklyn? Or on YouTube? Maybe they recited it on *Peppa Pig*.

"You're a poet," Rell reminded him. "Poets make strange connections." He glanced at his phone. "Okay, well, I gotta go to the gallery and chivvy those lazy-ass white bitches. As the iconic Essex said, take care of your blessings, child, and –" He ended the call with a jab of a flawlessly manicured, clear-varnished forefinger.

Vone closed the laptop. Almost at once the improved mood Rell had managed to inflate in him began to wobble and subside. *Stop thinking*, he told himself.

Down in the basement the washing machine thundered to the end of its spin cycle. He went to the kitchen and found Jay-Jay still playing dinosaur parade, with Dippy at the parade's head. Vone ran his hand over his son's mercifully still-tidy cornrows. "Daddy, don't!" Jay-Jay complained, moving his head out of his father's reach.

Vone blanked the snakeskins as he went down to the basement and, once the washing machine had juddered to a halt, hauled the wet sheets out of it into the basket and came back up. Unlocking the kitchen door, he went down to the side yard. The air was cold and dry, the sky bright, and there was a breeze. Clotheslines left by a previous tenant stretched from the house to a small, moss-stained woodshed, its backside embedded in the dense, statically surging laurel hedge that ran all along that side of the property. Vone hadn't thought to check it out before. Laundry basket under one arm, he went and peeked in. The shed was empty except for a stump that, judging from the cuts on its flat surface, had been used to split logs on. The cuts were old and greened. He remembered the axe hung up in the garage and felt uneasy, though he knew there had been other tenants since the killer mom, probably dozens of them, and the cops would hardly have returned the murder weapon to the property for future use.

Something soft brushed his shoulder: hanging on a hook on the back of the door was a bulging, dirty velvet drawstring bag. When he lifted it things clicked inside: plastic clothespins. Their springs when he thumbed the mouth of the bag open were rusty, but the pins still gripped. Taking it, he closed the door and went to hang out the sheets. Though clammy to handle, once pinned they flapped and snapped and billowed pleasingly. The air felt clean in a way it never did in the city, and was laced with the subliminal scents of unseen, late-blooming flowers. It was by then a little after eleven a.m.

The sheets cast sharp blue shadows slantways across the whitewashed clapboard, and swelled in unison like some great bellows, or the sails of a long-ago schooner tacking on the tide, hoping to catch – what were they called? – trade winds, and be borne away to far-off, unknown lands. Vone thought to call Jay-Jay; to see if he would be open to the magic of the sheets. They could act out some pirate adventure, some Hotep *Treasure-Island*-meets-*Wakanda* scenario that Vone would make up on the spot – a place where a mixed-race boy with two dads could play without inhibition; a Neverland untainted by knowing anything about Michael Jackson, or even, quite likely, J.M. Barrie himself; one without (as Vone had been disconcerted to find when, as an adult, he finally actually read *Peter Pan*) the "redskin" Piccaninny Tribe.

Maybe he'd write a children's book someday, he thought. To be part of the forming of the mind – the spirit – of a child, a person, when they first fall in love with the written word: that would be something wonderful in a way that was different from being an actual parent, where your sense of wonder was so often dragged down by the quotidian.

The sheets billowed, rose, sank down again. The air stilled. Now they hung flat as plate glass, dazzling in the sunshine. He had pegged them out at full stretch, and they were as smooth as if they had been stapled to a frame.

Then the face pushed through.

Seventeen

V one started back with a shout. The face that pushed through the sheet was skull-like but oddly elongated, and the damp material sucked into its eye-sockets, its nose-hole and its widely gaping mouth, in the upper jaw of which a single fang flexed against the material like a hard-on in underwear. Then, as abruptly as it had appeared, the face vanished, as if it had been violently yanked back.

Snatching up a piece of broken plastic guttering that lay discarded by the kitchen steps, a pitiful weapon but at least something, Vone bent over and lifted the bottom of the sheet, bracing himself for the hideous thing behind it to rush out at him, but there was nothing there. Squatting on his haunches, he quickly checked under the other sheets, lifting their hanging hems with the length of guttering, keeping whatever might be there at arm's length the way you do when you're searching for something vicious or venomous or just scuttling. Again, nothing. There was nowhere the thing could have gone to in the second it had taken him to get hold of his weapon – not behind the shed (he checked anyway: the foliage pressed against its backside impenetrably); not round the corner of the house – too far off. The wall wasn't climbable, nor were any of the upper story windows open to provide a point of entry. Anyway, he could hardly have failed to notice some man-sized creature scuttling up the side of the house like a gekko.

A rolling breeze set the sheets billowing again. Vone stepped quickly from one side of each sheet to the other, this time to check that nothing was, in some impossible way that required casting no shadow, concealing itself by clinging there with its feet drawn up. He realized he was sweating heavily.

"Daddy?" Jay-Jay stood in the kitchen doorway, looking worried.

"Go back inside, Jackie-Jacks," Vone said. When his son didn't obey at once, he added sharply, "Do as you're told!"

Flinching, Jay-Jay stepped back and closed the door.

Okay. Go check the backyard. Just in case.

Guttering in hand, Vone went to the corner of the house

and surveyed the still patchily frosted back lawn. He thought he could make out a trail running across it over to the gap in the fence, but even as he watched, as in a time-lapse film, it was absorbed into the general melting of the frost in the sunlight.

Replacing the guttering where he'd found it, Vone went back inside, locking the kitchen door behind him. He was aware his mind was racing and his thoughts were getting jumbled. Leaving Jay-Jay at the kitchen table, he went upstairs, took a clonazepam with a handful of tepid water from the faucet, then came back down again. He didn't think Jay-Jay had seen the face but didn't want to ask him. Instead he joined him on the bench in the nook, so they were sitting side by side.

"I'm sorry I was angry just now," he said. "I was worried a cougar might have come in the yard." Because a cougar, however unreal, was part of the sane world; a way of making his son wary of what might wait outside that didn't involve garish tales of floating skulls. Or would this new, factually-unsupported object of alarm suck Jay-Jay farther into his daddy's resurgent delusional thinking? The idea appalled him, but just then he couldn't think of anything to do except sit with his son at the kitchen table, watch the window and the door, and wait for the meds to kick in.

I should get a shotgun, he thought. Maybe he could borrow one from Ted, though the thought of Rory answering the door to him was excruciating. And Jack would freak when he saw it and heard Vone's loony-tunes attempts at justification. *I could hide it somewhere. I could –* No. No gun.

What *was* he going to tell Jack? Jay-Jay was bound to mention the supposed cougar to him. Then again, maybe not. Maybe he was humoring crazy Daddy who sees shit that isn't there, and so wouldn't say anything to sensible, non-crazy Dad.

Not a good thought, all told.

Jack would tell him – as Rell had already told him – to start seeing a shrink again, and would be right, of course. But this wasn't like the other time: that had been a sensory chaos, fractured and liquid, through which dissonant images had swooped with neon intensity, and on some level he had known it was all unreal. By contrast this was a sequence of singular, concrete intrusions into an otherwise solidly everyday world: the gray thing in the woods, rushing and floating; the black thing on the roof that swooped silently away; the witchy old woman in his son's bedroom; and now a living skull-face that, like the old woman with her outsize saucer eyes, wasn't quite human. He sensed that it too was female. Was it Skog Madoo? What was the line –

She had one tooth and she wore no shoes.
She had one tooth.

Both creatures seemed predatory. Predatory and female. What would Freud say about that? At college he had read out-dated crap about homosexuality and dominant mothers. Despite that, he had found the murky ruminations of Freud and in particular Jung intriguing – albeit more as a sort of poetry than factual information about how the brain worked. He was especially intrigued by the notion of the collective uncon-scious – the more so since recent discoveries in neuroscience demonstrated that the trauma of slavery was passed down as a collective stain on Black people's chromosomes, leading to, among other things that might seem of greater significance, a poor quality of sleep. And didn't he sleep badly?

Jay-Jay got down from the bench and, holding Dippy, went over to the window, looking out for lurking predators, perhaps. Guiltily Vone made them both hot chocolate, hoping the quotidian and the sweet might heal or at least distract; try-ing to figure out how he could unsay the cougar, root it out of his son's mind. He sniffed the milk: it was about to turn, but was still just about drinkable. He tipped it into a small copper-bottom pan he and Jack had treated themselves to one anni-versary, in a spasm of aspirant domesticity.

As he lit the stove, he recalled what Jay-Jay had shouted the other night: "She says she's coming back." The meaning was plain: there were two shes: the Owl Lady and Skog Ma-doo. Maybe that was why, on no other evidence, he had read the face in the sheets as female. He dumped a couple of spoon-fuls of cocoa powder into the milk and stirred. As it dimpled and started to seethe he found himself explaining the face away: the sheet had billowed against a knobbly tree trunk, making a weird shape. There wasn't a tree close enough, but it sounded believable if you hadn't been there. Almost.

"Here we go, Jackie-Jacks," he said, pouring the contents of the pan deftly into two mugs. The smaller of the pair, another Disney Store purchase, was in the form of a manic-looking blue rat. Lilo, or was it Stitch? He brought the mugs to the table and gestured to Jay-Jay to come over. "But let it cool a bit first, okay?"

Once again they sat side by side with their backs to the wall, facing the window. Jay-Jay had a little difficulty climbing up, but managed without Vone's help. *I swear he's taller than when we got here.* The speed of their son's development was one of the things that made rearing a child bearable: every day something new. That, and the emergence of a distinct personality, regardless of parental attempts to mold or impose one on him. Vone didn't seem – so far – to have infected Jay-Jay with his neuroses, and was proud that he was a robust little boy who liked to cycle, run around, fall, shout, treat his toys badly at times (though never Dippy), and he knew Jack felt the same.

Of course he'd love Jay-Jay however sissy he was, but while it would in no way feel like a failure if he turned out femme, the idea that it would be seen by others as the result of his being raised by two gay men – well, the stereotype grated, and set uneasy thoughts about inadequate role-modeling sliding around inside his head. He loved being a man and he loved being fucked, and now he was a stay-at-home parent, a role he was mostly happy in. Did the three things complement or contradict each other? His father had made him box as a boy, briefly, and he hadn't been any good at it; had in fact hated it. He had disliked team sports too, and had never bought into exercise until he discovered the estheticized, homoerotic world of the gym. Which, ironically, had led him to take boxercise classes and work out regularly with a punch-bag. But so what? Women could box. Men could sashay. And lord knew if you were a queen you had to be ready to throw a punch. *All I want is for him to be his ownself.*

As he sat quietly with his son, Vone began to put together what he could recall of what Jay-Jay had said about the Owl Lady and Skog Madoo, and figure out how they had become mixed in with his own dreams and – what? Mental projections, let's say, keeping it neutral. Then there was what the old

man had said: the disconcerting way it seemed to tie in with
the rest.

Treat it as a story.

Okay.

She's coming. Not the Owl Lady. The Owl Lady sleeps in
the cellar. She cries in the cellar. The old man said we'd be safe
in the cellar. Jay-Jay said we should sleep in the cellar. And he
said: let her out, she wants to get out. What had she been whispering to him while he slept? What subliminal messages had
she been implanting in his mind? She had said a word or
phrase, but he couldn't recall it. Ka-something.

Okay. So. The cellar. The cellar with nothing in it but a
washing machine and a wall of canned preserves that should
have been cleared out decades ago, but hadn't been. The cellar
that was small for a house that size; that was maybe half the
size you would expect.

Half the size.

After setting Jay-Jay up with his drawing pad and crayons
at the kitchen table, Vone went down there, returning the
laundry basket his alibi. The stink of pickle juice had intensified: more of the bottles were cracked, and the dark puddles
under the bottom shelf were wider. He went back up to the
kitchen and got a pair of tough rubber workman's gauntlets
from the cupboard of poisonous things. "Daddy's just doing
some clearing up in the basement," he said. "Some of the bottles may break, so I need you to stay up here, okay?"

Jay-Jay looked round at him, nodded and went back to his
drawing. *Not strong enough to turn the kitchen door key,*
Vone reassured himself. The front door was locked too: he'd
made sure. He could leave his son alone for a short while without him getting out, or anyone else getting in.

Pulling on the gauntlets, Vone contemplated the shelves of
preserves. Getting rid of them was a job that wouldn't need
explaining: he and Jack had talked about doing it over the
weekend. That hadn't happened, so why not now?

First he took down the jars that appeared uncracked and
so least risky to move. The larger ones on the upper shelves he
had to pull forward, tilt toward him and cradle. They were
heavy, and the curved glass was dank against his biceps and

chest. The things inside sloshed about, some sinking darkly down, others bobbing to the surface like dead goldfish, and each jar clinked as, carefully, he set it down on the rough concrete floor. He thought of carrying them upstairs one at a time and putting them out in the backyard but didn't: that wasn't why he was clearing the shelves.

That done, more warily, he began to lift down the bottles with visible thread lines in them, starting with those at waist height. He thought it would be sensible to put goggles on, though it would have to be his swim goggles, and he had no idea where they were. He carried on without them.

Once he had moved four or five jars from the center of the middle shelf he saw what he had guessed would be there: behind the shelves, a door.

It took him a further half hour to take down all the remaining jars. None broke, though several dripped on him unpleasantly. The shelves were plain plank boards that sat on brackets and were held in place by screws. Not wanting to wrench the brackets out of the plaster along with the shelves, Vone came back upstairs, poured Jay-Jay a juice – "Pooh! Daddy, you stink!" – went round to the garage, rummaged in the toolbox and came back with a screwdriver that had been used to stir paint. Unscrewing the screws manually put a blister on first his right, then his left palm, but eventually he had lifted the shelves – seven in total – off their brackets and stacked them against the wall. It was grimy, sweat-inducing work. Decades of dirty dust and grit tipped over him as he tugged the boards loose, setting him coughing and sneezing and thinking of the asbestos that had been discovered in an apartment where an aunt of his lived. She had developed a persistent cough, way before Covid.

The door he had exposed beyond the shelves was narrow, four-paneled, visibly warped by damp and had a dull brass knob, below which was a keyhole. As he had expected, it was locked. He went upstairs to get the key that had been in the egg and found Jay-Jay at the window. He had brought the wastebasket in from the downstairs bathroom to stand on. Vone went over and kissed the top of his son's head. "We're okay in here," he said.

Jay-Jay looked round worriedly. "She's getting closer."

"Who?"

"Skog Madoo."

Vone knew he should say something to head off that line of thought, or at least offer a "she can't get in" bromide. Instead he nodded and said, "Come get me if you see anything. Okay, soldier?"

Jay-Jay nodded. Vone went back down to the basement, to the hidden door. As he slid the key into the lock he had a sense of something moving on the other side. His scalp prickled, but for all he knew the room beyond might have long ago been burrowed into, and be filled with commonplace critters.

At first the key didn't seem to be the right one. The fit was too loose, it had an uncertain bite and wouldn't turn. He pushed it in more firmly and twisted harder, risking snapping it. After all, worst case he could get a crowbar and –

The lock turned.

With the tips of his fingers, Vone pushed at the door. It swung inwards, into darkness.

Eighteen

T he cloying smell of dust and rotten plaster met Vone's nostrils. Instinctively he opened his mouth to breathe, though that meant mold spores coating his upper palate and lining his lungs.

The room beyond the now-open door was dark and windowless, and before crossing the threshold he reached in and felt about for a light switch. His fingers brushed a cord. He pulled on it, and a bare bulb splashed the low-ceilinged room with weak yellow light. What met Vone's eyes made him think of the zillion serial killer movies he had seen, for suspended from the ceiling on twine like car air fresheners were dozens of snake skeletons, each three or four feet long, their spines wired, their fangs thrusting forward aggressively from gaping jaws. Amongst them hung dried or shed skins like those at the top of the basement stairs. Opening the door had caused a shift of air: the skeletons rotated slowly and the skins, paper light, stirred.

As Vone had expected, the room took up the other half of what had originally been a large basement. At its center was a lumpy single bed with a curlicued brass headrail. A caramel blanket embroidered with zig-zag motifs in white wool and black thread covered it, and across the blanket there lay a hefty iron chain around five feet in length. One end of it was padlocked to the bedhead; at the other was a businesslike pair of handcuffs. One cuff was closed around the last link of the chain; the other lay open receptively, suggesting perversity, or captivity. From under the bed the curved white lip of a chamber-pot protruded, with its sordid connotations.

Black paint had been used to daub motifs like those on the throw on the damp-discolored, whitewashed walls. The bed had been pulled forward from the back wall and a chalk circle drawn around it. The circle was divided into neatly-ruled segments within which were marks or letters, though these were now very faint. Something about them made Vone think of the tattoos on Everett's forearms. In the sections where nothing had been drawn, mismatched candlesticks stood: random

junk picked up cheap in yard sales, Vone supposed. In the nozzle of each was the stump of a cheap white candle. Here and
there feathers, brown, black and white, lay on the concrete
floor in among twists of dust, and these, like the snakeskins,
stirred in the subtly shifting air.

A small side table – the one missing from Vone and Jack's
bedroom – stood by the single bed, which Vone presumed
came from one of the spare rooms into which he had, as yet,
barely glanced. He supposed the double mattress and frame
would have been too heavy and awkward for one person to
drag down. The sides of the table bloomed white with nitrous
precipitates. On top of it was a pile of damp-stained and yel-
lowing newspapers, books and magazines. Behind the pile, on
what appeared to be a small safe, were stacked a chipped
enamel mug and plate, next to which were a matchbook and a
candle stump. The matchbook was for a bar called the Waterfront Dive. Attached to the safe, covering it where the keyhole
would ordinarily be, was some sort of clockwork mechanism
with a butterfly winding key.

"Daddy!"

Jay-Jay's voice was sharp. Switching off the light and closing the door on the secret room, Vone clomped up to the
kitchen and joined his son at the window. "What is it? What
did you see?"

"I heard something," Jay-Jay said. "It was scary."

"Where did you hear it?"

"Outside."

"Like, right outside the house?"

"Nuh-uh. Further away. In the woods. A wail."

Vone relaxed a little. "It's probably just some animal," he
said. "Vixens – girl foxes – can sound like babies screaming
when they're in heat." He scoped the tree line, glad his son
hadn't asked what "in heat" meant. Whatever Jay-Jay had
heard was silent now. Vone thought how bolts for the doors
would be a good idea: that way any intruder would have to
break the frame to get in, not just trick the lock. And then
there was the secret room: that too should be bolted, he
thought, high up, so Jay-Jay couldn't get in; and maybe so
some unseen something else couldn't let itself out.

A jarring buzzing sound made both father and son jump

and look round. It was Vone's cell, vibrating on the counter-top. The ID showed it was Jack calling. Vone answered, care-ful to keep his voice level. "Hey, honey, what's up? They fire you already?"

Jack laughed drily. "Not yet. I've got to stay late tonight – my presentation to the big boss is first thing tomorrow – but I'll bring takeout so you don't have to cook."

"Okay, cool. Jay-Jay can have leftovers so he can eat at his usual time. D'you know when you'll be back?"

"Not really. Sorry."

"It's okay," Vone said. "You gotta make a good impres-sion." And of course he meant it: this was their future; and of course he felt a flicker of irritation too, along with something akin to, if anything, betrayal, though that was a ludicrous overstatement. "Do you know, is there a hardware store in Collington-Osprey?"

"Sure, there must be. What do you want me to pick up?"

Vone wavered. "Actually, forget it."

"Are you sure? I can make time."

"Yeah, no, I'll take Jackie to Gaugeville and see what they've got. It's crazy I haven't even gone there yet."

"How is he today?"

"Fine."

"Okay. I better go," Jack said. "Kiss him for me. Love you."

"Will do. Love you too." Vone turned to Jay-Jay. "Dad said to give you a kiss."

As he kissed his son on the neck, which normally made Jay-Jay squeal and giggle, the little boy said seriously, "Don't tell Dad about the scary stuff."

"No? Why?"

"He doesn't understand."

"I won't tell him."

"Promise?"

"I promise. Okay, let's go see what the town is like. We can check out the lake and the boats. Find a diner and get some lunch, how does that sound?" There would be bound to be a hardware store in a boating community, and Vone hadn't wanted to ask Jack to buy heavy-duty bolts before he saw the hidden room; saw proof that something was going on that wasn't only happening inside Vone's head. He would see if they had a stairgate too. Somehow resolving that practical, tangible safety issue had been forgotten amidst the other, stranger occurrences.

"Is it through the woods?" Jay-Jay asked worriedly.

"No, it's in the opposite direction. We go through the Vicinity" (Vone sighed inwardly) "then keep on for a mile and change. There's sure to be a trail, or we can just follow the road. We'll have to keep our eyes peeled for traffic, though."

"Peeled – ew!" Jay-Jay said, and laughed.

They put on their coats – Jay-Jay could now just about do up the chunky buttons on his – and matching deerstalkers with faux-fur earflaps. Vone wore suede gloves, Jay-Jay woolen rainbow ones from some LGBTQ+ Pride Brooklyn street fair. "Are we taking our bikes?" Jay-Jay asked.

Vone shook his head. "The road's too dangerous," he said, not adding that he didn't relish shepherding a wobbly Jay-Jay along it for a mile and a half, then doing the same thing coming back, possibly while also carrying a stairgate.

Taking what he mentally compartmentalized as a responsible city dweller's care to lock up the house, rather than a paranoiac's, Vone took Jay-Jay's hand and together they set off for Gaugeville.

To his relief there was no car outside Rory and Ted's.

Leaving the Bounds behind them, they kicked their way along the leaf-strewn track that led to the covered bridge and passed through. A little way beyond, the Vicinity waited. It was deserted, which was a relief, and soon enough they were out the other side, standing uncertainly at the turn-off from the main highway.

In the timber yard opposite, great pines lay, stacked and somehow desolate, the wounds of their chainsawed ends amber-bright, the incised rise of mud black behind them. The space was deeply shadowed despite the sun at that hour being almost directly overhead. As on the day of their arrival the crane lacked an operator, and no light was on in the mesh window of the dirty white portacabin.

The main road had no verge, and of course no sidewalk, but there was what appeared to be a track a few feet into the trees to the right. Probably there was a more picturesque and

properly signposted trail running from the Vicinity to Gaugeville that he hadn't found yet, but today they could trudge
along beside the main road safely and easily enough.

Having finally got round to Googling trees of New England, Vone could now point out to Jay-Jay poplar, chestnut
and birch, and farther back spruce and white pine. Excited to
be on a mission with a definite goal, Jay-Jay didn't wander but
instead walked beside Vone as much as the somewhat overgrown track permitted, determined to keep up. *My little man.*

In due course they reached a sign saying "Gaugeville welcomes careful drivers," above an artist's impression of a
bearded fisherman on a pier, pulling an outsize salmon from
the water on a looping line. The bright pink fish floated above
him like a blimp. Here the track rejoined the road, and they
went on in single file, with Vone leading. The next sign, fifty
feet on, said "Welcome to Antler Lake," and just past that were
a succession of turnings into residential lanes, most of which
were also marked as moose trails or "scenic" trails or just plain
trails. One or two of the lanes, always to the left, were marked
"Private: access only," and the houses Vone glimpsed along
those were larger, on larger plots. Past the lanes came the
sedge flats and pontoons, and then the town.

When they drove through it that first day, Gaugeville had
seemed small to Vone, a village on a pond. Just a week later it
seemed like a city on a bay. Main Street, along which they soon
enough found themselves ambling, was broad. It followed the
curve of the shoreline, and on the waterfront side the mast-
tops of dozens of small boats were visible above an uneven line
of single-story bars, eateries and bait shops. On the inland
side were four short blocks of brick buildings that included a
car dealership, a bank and three churches of various denomi-
nations. One of these had a strikingly tall spire – the spire
Vone had spotted from the top of the mound. Farther along
on the waterfront side, glimpsed between boxy administrative
buildings, a surprisingly large passenger ferry waited at dock
to take travelers farther north; and at the far end of the street,
where the road bent round to skirt the lake, signs announced
This Way To Snow Country. Another, smaller road continued
on pretty much due east: a local airport was signposted in that
direction. So it turned out that Gaugeville was both a tourist

hub and a significant waystation.

The realization was encouraging to Vone. Once they picked up the rental car he would be able to escape here whenever he wanted; maybe find a café to write in and people-watch. The flow of tourists would mean a more cosmopolitan mix of people, even if the image of himself as a sweaty Cuba Gooding Jr. in *Snow Dogs*, entering some redneck bar in a too-hot ski suit, came swimming up into his mind.

Wandering back from the eastern end of Main Street, Vone and Jay-Jay cut through an alley with beached buoys at its entrance, in search of the waterfront and somewhere to eat. They found themselves on a long, undulant boardwalk lined with mostly contiguous cafés, restaurants, bait shops and bars, all of them flat-roofed and built of tarred wood. They faced moored fishing boats and sailboats, piled crawfish pots, rusted hawsers, poles with regulations and warnings nailed to them, lifebuoys, hauled-up orange floats, nets and tangles of blue nylon rope; and there was the particular smell of the lake, fresh and clean, muddy and rotten all at the same time. The dark blue water dimpled, reflecting the depth of the sky, and the ropes on the masts of the sailboats slapped and clanked in the stiff breeze coming off the lake. On the opposite bank the distant gray-brown woods ran down unchallenged to the water's edge, to drink or drown.

Jay-Jay needed a comfort break so they went into a long, low café-diner called the Crab Pot, which had small-framed windows that looked out over the lake. Mid-afternoon on a weekday at the tail end of the season it wasn't busy. The presence of a few ruddy-faced older men at the counter suggested it was well enough thought of by the locals, despite the plastic crabs caught up in nets staple-gunned to the ceiling and a plethora of poorly-executed harbor views, mostly priced at around $40, "frame included!". Vone only got a few looks as he closed the door behind him and Jay-Jay, and they seemed indifferent rather than hostile.

At the counter Vone ordered a crab melt and fries for himself, and a cappuccino; a hot chocolate and small fries for Jay-Jay. The waitress, a chubby girl with a permanently flushed face, was cheery as she pointed out the restrooms. "The boys' is a lobster," she said, her accent local and strong, "The girls' is a crab." He raised an eyebrow and she laughed. "It was the owners' idea. People get 'em mixed up all the time, though."

She rang up the sale. He felt only a little guilty at using the family Amex to pay for a meal at which Jack was not present. Jay-Jay chose their booth. Plastic pumpkins sat on the windowsill, and a very fake spider taped to a sagging Silly String web reminded Vone that tonight was Halloween. Jay-Jay didn't seem to notice, seeing crabs in nets and spiders in webs as the same sort of thing, perhaps. *Next year for dress-up*, Vone thought. *If we're still here.*

Maybe he should get some candies though, in case trick or treating was a thing in the Bounds. He and Jay-Jay could hand them out together, maybe both dress up a little. Blacula and Son of Blacula. Or no, what was the sequel? Rell would know – oh yeah, *Scream, Blacula, Scream*. They had face paints somewhere, and plastic fangs.

I should get a pumpkin too, he thought, low-key affronted by the plastic ones in the diner, which were presumably shipped all the way from China to a land full of real, actual pumpkins that weren't even expensive, and in due course would wind up in landfill and last forever. *We can carve it together. Wrap the pulp in old newspapers if we can find any.* Other than the rotten old papers in the secret room, that was. *Get a candle to go inside.* He thought of the stumps of wax in the basement candlesticks, but mixing the kitsch with the genuinely creepy seemed like a bad idea: the sort of thing that might somehow open a door. He wondered if the Karens of the Vicinity would come helicopter-parenting their kids down Collingwood Way, where the houses were authentically Halloween spooky; if he would be able to drag up the energy to open the door and smile and make them feel "safe."

Whatever happened or didn't happen tonight, it seemed prudent to give the community a year to get used to them being there before he and Jack did their Mardi Gras scare act, with zombified blue-gray skin, white contacts and sausage-link entrails. Who had Rell been last year? Oh yeah, zombie Dolemite – or Eddie Murphy as zombie Dolemite, in a sequined green pantsuit. As a dubious homage to Prince, Rell had cut out the ass-cheeks.

When the waitress brought their order Vone asked about

a hardware store, and she was chatty and asked where he lived, and they talked about that for a while, and the "stuck-up" folks in the Vicinity. Vone was reminded that he was capable of being charming, and the waitress seemed quite regretful when the cook dinged a bell and hollered that another order was ready to go. The food was mediocre, but it was cooked by someone else and served in a pleasant atmosphere, so he didn't care, and the secret room in the basement of Number 13 seemed as remote as something in a book he had been reading and set aside.

Buying the bolts brought it back to him, however. The old white man behind the counter in the hardware store was amiable, offering him various options. Naturally he asked Vone why he wanted six of the heaviest duty the store carried.

"Critters have been getting into some of our sheds lately," Vone said, feeling self-conscious at using the folksy word. Did people out here really say it? But the old man nodded, dropped the bolts in a brown paper bag, rolled its mouth closed and rang up the sale, which Vone once again put on the Amex, because didn't spending on a card build up your credit rating or something? From a neighboring store he bought a modest sized (real) pumpkin, regular plain candles and a couple of packets of cheap candies.

As he and Jay-Jay started for home, Vone recognized a name: Dock Street. That was where the letting agent's office was. He thought of going in and asking how Mr. Harris was doing, but left it: now he had the bolts, he wanted to get home and put them up.

Once he and Jay-Jay had left the town and the sedge flats behind, and passed the residential lanes, and were trudging through the woods again, Vone's spirits once more began to sink. He tried to hide it from Jay-Jay, but worried that his attempts at lively conversation sounded horribly false – though at the same time he knew that children were used to being spoken to in a way that to adult ears sounded grotesquely overdone. He thought of childless aunts who had tried too hard.

The air was lively with the twittering of small birds and the cawing of crows, which Vone supposed sounded melodic to other crows, or, if not that, at least lusty and assertive. On that stretch of the road the fallen leaves were dull copper; and here and there amidst a sea of gray-brown trunks hollies gleamed, glossy and dark, their ruby berries anticipating Thanksgiving. Vone had to concede that to cut their own holly and cedar boughs for Christmas would be charming. They could source their own tree too: saw it down, carry it home between them, put it up in the front parlor, and take a family photo in the manner of Norman Rockwell (or Charles Addams), to charm or nauseate loved ones back in the city, according to temperament.

The pumpkin was soon a chore to carry, and Vone wished he'd thought ahead and brought a backpack. A logging truck clanked past, unladen, heading for the town and what Vone now thought of as civilization. Between that civilization and the wilderness was his home, Gaugeville Bounds. *Bounds, boundary*. Had the peoples of the First Nations feared something in the woods other than wolves, bears and the weather? Looking up mounds online he had found a reference to the Red Paint People, who had lived in Maine thousands of years ago, and left behind them only their burial sites and a handful of stone and bone tools. A people gone and forgotten before the birth of Christ, which was, somehow, and for no clear reason, a disconcerting thought.

Fuck. He had forgotten the stairgate.

The sky was paling and the sun below the tree line by the time they got back to the Vicinity, and everything was leached of color. As yet no jack-o-lanterns had been lit and placed on porches or windowsills, though here and there cottony spray-webs covered the panes, and in front of one house a life-size puppet witch in a black conical hat and striped socks sat slumped on a rocker, cradling a whisk broom. Its turnip head lolled unpleasantly. No kids were around. Perhaps there were no children there out of season, and the Halloween gestures had been made by the developers, to create an illusion of community for marketing purposes.

Cottonwood Way, when they reached it, had given itself over more enthusiastically to tradition, with real, not plastic pumpkins glowing in the windows of maybe half the houses. Guiltily, Vone thought of Rory. He could imagine her overdoing the gushy door-answering: the outthrust dish of candied eyeballs, tongues, worms and green snot, Ted hovering behind her, dressed as Uncle Fester, maybe: a good sport. But there was no pumpkin in their window.

No kids were out here either.

Probably 4 p.m. was too early.

Once inside, he dumped the pumpkin and candy down on the kitchen table, hauled out the bag of bolts and set it on the counter, helped Jay-Jay off with his coat, and went to hang it alongside his own on the antler spikes in the front hall.

Before he had removed his shoes, he remembered the sheets needed bringing in.

Reluctantly he fetched the laundry basket up from the basement, unlocked the kitchen door and went out to the side yard. The sheets hung waiting. He touched the nearest one. It was cold but pretty much dry.

Casting a glance in the direction of the backyard, he began briskly to unpeg the sheets, as he did so bundling them into the basket, to fold properly once he was back in the warm.

As he took down the last sheet, he heard a sound so strange, so unpleasant that it made his hackles rise.

Nineteen

I t was some way off yet all too near: a whirring rattle into which was wound what sounded like the sobs of terrified children. Vone's skin goosebumped and his chest tightened. The sound became harder, a cicada vibration that was almost mechanical in nature, then sharpened into a hissing like sand on a windswept beach. The sobbing shrilled and thinned and passed beyond the range of human hearing, leaving behind it empty air and a sense of dread and desolation.

Vone went inside fast, set the laundry basket on the counter and closed and locked the kitchen door. His hackles were stiff, an unpleasant feeling, like having grossly swollen lymph glands on the back of his neck. Jay-Jay was somewhere else in the house. Vone was certain – absolutely certain – that the sound hadn't been a hallucination. Nor, he was sure, had it been some natural emission – a burp of shale gas; some muted seismic event – or mechanical: an innovation in windfarm technology, say. It had been something animal or at least animate, and he knew, though the knowing was impossible, that it was connected to the face that had pushed itself through the sheet.

We have to move into town, he thought, futilely, because they couldn't afford to. Well, no: there'd be, because there always was, wasn't there, some shitty shack, overpriced but at a rent they could just about cover if he, Vone, got a job too. *I'd just need to convince Jack that –*

The whirring and sobbing began again, neither nearer nor farther off, built up, then subsided. It was the sound of whatever had silenced the birds and beasts, the thing that wandered between the well and the mound, bound, maybe cursed to do so. Or perhaps that was only its corporeal aspect, and for a brief time its mind, its will, had broken free and thrust a psychic projection of its face against Vone's wet sheets – the same mind that had tried to summon Jay-Jay to it the morning after they first discovered the well, and had almost succeeded. Vone thought of the seemingly multiplying trails in the woods, and then of the web of invisible threads a tarantula spins at the entrance to its burrow, in which it lurks, still as stone, waiting for some unlucky cricket to wander by and set a silky line vibrating. Were those trails such a web; was the well a burrow?

He stood in the middle of the kitchen, listening, but there was no further repetition of the sound. Jay-Jay came in then, carrying his Buzz Lightyear lunchbox. He seemed untroubled. Vone rubbed his prickly upper arms. *Keep it together.*

The paper bag of bolts caught his eye. He went out to the garage and fetched an electric drill he'd seen in the toolbox the day before. It was battery-powered, and the charging cable ran into the battery not the drill, meaning it couldn't be run directly from the mains – which was why he hadn't used it to take down the basement shelves that morning. The battery was of course long dead. He slotted it into the charger and plugged the unit in. A red light flickered half-heartedly.

There was nothing to do but wait.

Dusk drew on and the kitchen sank into shadow. Vone kept the lights off, as a besieged man will. Jay-Jay played with his dinosaurs at the table uncomplainingly: he understood. After an hour had dragged by, Vone tested the drill. It whizzed briefly, but gave out after a few seconds. He could, of course, hammer a nail into the wood to start a hole and laboriously wind the screws in manually, but the palms of his hands were still blistered from taking down the shelves. Better to be patient.

He realized he couldn't face carving the pumpkin. Jay-Jay didn't react when he moved it from the table to the sideboard and put the candies away with a clatter in a drawer. Though several times Vone thought he heard the laughter of children in the street, no one came knocking. But then, as well as there being no lit pumpkin on the porch, the lights were off, and there was no car in the driveway.

Jack got home with dinner a little after eight, just as Vone was about to put Jay-Jay to bed. He was bullish – the presentation had gone well – and Vone was happy to let him take over in the tooth-brushing and pajama-suiting department while he, Vone, put the boxes of Chinese takeout in the oven to warm, set the table and broke out a bottle of wine – the last of Brooklyn.

His sense of relief at Jack being home was yanked from under him when his husband appeared in the kitchen doorway, holding up a bottle of pills that Vone recognized at once as his anti-psychotics. "I found this on Jay-Jay's windowsill," he said. "Next to Dippy."

Vone was puzzled and troubled. "He didn't manage to open it, did he?"

"No, but that's not the point. He could have."

Vone felt his face twitch. "Jack, I really have no idea how he got his hands on the bottle. You know I keep my pills in the cabinet. It's way too high for him to reach, even if he took the wastebasket upstairs and stood on it."

"You must've left it out on a table or something."

"I didn't. I'm always super-careful."

Jack placed the pill bottle on the kitchen table between them and looked down at it. "What are you saying? That someone else did it?"

"No, obviously not."

From the oven came the faint smell of cardboard beginning to singe. Jack sighed and said, "Let's just agree to be extra careful from here on, okay?"

Glowering and choked, Vone took the medicine bottle from the table, went upstairs and returned it to the bathroom cabinet. He knew he hadn't left it sitting about anywhere Jay-Jay could find it. What, then? Was something playing games? No, not games, because if Jay-Jay had swallowed even a single pill – Something trying to make him look nuts? Break them up? Drive them out?

When he came back down he found Jack setting the take-out boxes on the table, and went and dug out some chopsticks and a nearly empty bottle of soy sauce he had almost not bothered packing.

They ate in silence, facing each other but looking down at their food. Vone knew he had robbed his husband of sharing his workplace victory, but somehow couldn't turn the talk that way. When he tried to, he found himself saying instead, "I found something today."

"Oh, yeah? What?"

"It's easiest to show you."

They set their cartons aside – another unspecial meal –

and Vone led Jack down to the basement. The snakeskin brushed the back of his hand as he turned on the light. He was used to it now; expected it, just as he expected Jack not to notice. He led Jack to the hidden door, unlocked and opened it, reached in and switched on the light, then stepped back.

His husband stared at the dangling skeletons and skins; at the chain laid out across the bed, its handcuff open and waiting; took in the chamber pot. "The Owl Lady lives in the cellar," he said.

"Yeah."

"He doesn't know about this, does he?"

"No, I made him stay upstairs in case the bottles blew."

"Then how did he –?"

"I don't know."

"I think we should lock it up again," Jack said. "Put the shelves back up and forget we ever saw it."

"Aren't you curious?"

"I'm creeped out," Jack said. "And I don't want Jackie seeing it."

"He never comes down here on his own," Vone said. "He can't reach the light switch and he wouldn't come down in the dark. I bought some bolts today. I can put one on the basement door, high up enough so he can't get to it."

"Why did you buy bolts?"

"I just – I wanted to make sure the house was secure at night."

"But we already lock everything, don't we?"

"Yeah, but – yeah, I guess."

"I don't wanna – This is feeling like it could be a spiral."

Vone felt his face harden. "It's not," he said shortly. Then, knowing it was a terrible gamble, he added: "This is real."

Jack sighed. "I'm worried putting bolts up everywhere'll frighten Jackie," he said. "It'll make it look like we're living under siege." Once it became clear from Vone's expression that his husband wouldn't give ground, he changed tack: "Oh well, I guess it can't do any harm. I'm gonna go shower."

He left Vone to lock up. Vone took four quick steps into the hidden room and, setting aside the things on top of it, picked up the small safe with the clockwork device on its front – the heap of papers could wait – carried it upstairs and set it down on the kitchen table. Then he cleared the supper things away.

A little later, Jack came in wearing a monogrammed robe – Vone had a matching one: wedding gifts from the guys at Sweetgreen – and found his husband sitting at the table, contemplating the safe. It was dull pewter, with a brass crest on the front that read 'Generic Safe & Lock Co.', and a brass handle. Where you would expect the dial for the combination lock to be, a clockwork mechanism had been soldered clumsily. From it a butterfly key protruded.

The shower had improved Jack's mood, and he kissed Vone on the top of his head. "What's this?"

"I don't know," Vone said. "I mean, obviously it's a safe, but" – he indicated the mechanism – "I don't know what this thing is." There seemed nothing to do but wind it up, and he began to do so. The key was stiff but turnable.

"Why are you doing that?" Jack asked, a slight edge to his voice. But since the answer was self-evident and likely to reignite their earlier argument he went on, "Oh, never mind. Leave it and come to bed. No more morbid shit till the morning, okay?"

Vone let Jack lead him from the room, leaving the device ticking like an old-fashioned alarm clock or a time bomb. Did Jack really not wonder what it was for or what was inside? Perhaps he was only pretending incuriosity, trying to divert Vone from becoming the cat who got himself into shit. *Drowned among the goldfish.* From the doorway he looked back. In the darkness, the light on the drill's battery shone a steady green.

He would put the bolts up in the morning.

Vone woke with a start, thinking he had heard Jay-Jay cry out, and for a second he saw the skull face rushing towards him from the foot of the bed, its jaws open wide; and then, in the heaving darkness of the room, it was gone as if it had been violently yanked back. *Up the chimney?* Vone's heart hammered as he listened for a slithering withdrawal, but he heard nothing. *Just a bad dream.*

The Medusa head medallion on the fireguard glowed gray in the scotopic dimness, a ward, he hoped, for all the fury of its expression. He listened out for Jay-Jay but heard only Jack's breathing, deep and peaceful beside him.

It seemed part of Vone's particular punishment in Cottonwood Way that he woke while Jack slept through. Had it always been like that? He didn't think so, and they had shared a bed for close on a decade. Maybe Jack's almost unnaturally heavy sleep since they moved wasn't a coincidence. But even if some poltergeist was playing games with pills, there was no moment when anything could have been slipped into Jack's food or drink; no way Vone wouldn't have noticed. Once, maybe, just about: not night after night.

And then he wondered, with crawling unease, *But what if it's me? Blanked out like Jay-Jay? Externally controlled, taking the bottle and tipping out pills and* – It was an alarming thought. *What if I'm the danger?*

Almost angrily he turned back the covers on his side of the bed and swung his bare legs out. The air was cold on his skin. Maybe the pilot had blown out again, or maybe it was the timer or thermostat or some other shit he didn't know how to reset. Pulling on a pair of shorts and a tank undershirt, he went into the bathroom, opened the cabinet and contemplated his pill bottles. He would count their contents tomorrow, figure out if any were missing.

If they were, would that make things better, or worse?

Feeling restless, he went to check on Jay-Jay, passing on the way the chilly chasm of the stairwell, with its dark suggestion of thalassophobia. He found his son sleeping peacefully, the room lit cozily by the Jack Skellington night light.

Feeling the house was somehow not at peace, Vone left Jay-Jay and looked in on the two spare bedrooms. Both had closed-up fireplaces, pinecones piled decoratively in their grates, plain, dark furniture, faded floral wallpaper, polished floors and rag rugs. With a bit of sprucing, guests might feel welcome enough in them, if not for – well, everything. Could all this end somehow? He couldn't picture Rell dumping his knock-off Versace bags on the bed ("Ver-sayce, bitch!"), looking round and being at home. *He'll never visit.* One room contained a single bed; the other would have done if it hadn't been dragged down to the cellar.

Vone went downstairs and tried the front door. Locked.

He checked the catches on the windows in the parlor and dining room, then went through to the kitchen. The mechanism was still ticking. After checking the side door, for want of anything else to do, he switched the drill charger off at the wall.

"What are you doing?" Jack's voice made Vone jump.

"Just checking."

"Didn't you do all of that already, before we went to bed?"

"Yeah, but I just, I —"

With melodramatic aptness the clockwork device stopped ticking. Vone and Jack looked round as something clunked inside it, and the door of the safe popped partway open.

Twenty

E xchanging glances, Vone and Jack approached the safe, moving apart so both would be out of the line of fire of anything inside when the door was fully open. Vone took a battered aluminum ladle down from where it hung from one of the ceiling beams. Watched by Jack, he used it to hook the door open. Nothing happened: there was no deadly dart, no booby trap. Together they looked in. The safe was empty except for a tiny key. *Another fucking key*.

"It looks like it's for the handcuffs," Jack said.

"Why's it in there, though?"

"Because she was fucked in the head?"

Vone winced internally. Mostly he didn't mind – even encouraged – throwaway talk about madness: a big part of how he and Jack had got through his episode was by using gallows humor forbidden to outsiders, and by never being linguistically pious – they both threw "batshit cray-cray," "nuts," "nut house" and "whack job" around unselfconsciously. But just then it grated on him. "She?" he said.

"Mamie Place, presumably."

"Do you think she's the Owl Lady?"

Jack sighed. "Vone, I – Let's just put this stuff back in the cellar so Junior doesn't see it."

"Yeah. Okay." Taking out the key, Vone closed the safe and carried it down to the secret room. The soles of his bare feet cringed on the wooden steps, and suddenly he was a kid again, afraid that something would reach through from behind them, grab his ankles and –

Unlocking the secret room, he went in and put the safe back where he had found it, carefully matching its edges to the outline of dust on the side table, as if to do so might arrest a process that, now it had begun, could turn out to be dangerous. He would bring up the pile of papers tomorrow, after Jack had gone to work.

Before leaving the room, he tested the key in the handcuffs and found it sprung them with ease. Out of some wary fastidiousness he left it inserted in the post. Then he turned out the light, locked the door and returned to the kitchen. He placed the key to the secret room on the work surface by the stove, and he and Jack went back to bed.

While Jack checked in on Jay-Jay – a sign Vone had induced irrational unease in his husband as well as himself – Vone sneaked an extra clonazepam. *Remember to deduct it from the tally tomorrow.*

Though he fell back to sleep quickly enough, it wasn't the end of a troubled night for Vone. He woke again, he didn't know how much later, only that it was still dark, and lay there listening, at first to his own heartbeat, then with an effort out beyond that. *Why did I wake up?* His chest tensed: somewhere he heard, definitely heard, the creak of a floorboard under the weight of a stealthy step. Then another. He shook Jack's shoulder and said quietly, "There's someone in the house."

Jack was instantly alert, revealing both that he wasn't as doped up as Vone had begun to assume, and that he wasn't as skeptical of Vone's frets about intruders as he had acted earlier. This, after all, was a man who as a kid had had to hide under motel beds when people his mom owed money to sprang the flimsy lock of the door to their room with the point of a knife, or came creeping in through easily-jimmied windows.

As one they got out of bed. Both wore shorts, Vone a tank undershirt; Jack took a moment to pull on a tee. Without discussion they went to Jay-Jay's room. They found their son's bed empty. Vone quickly searched under the bed, behind the wardrobe curtain, in the toy chest, then moved the drapes aside to check the window hasps. They were closed, and in any case no tree with boughs large enough to support a person's weight grew close enough for an intruder to get in that way.

No *person.*

Vone looked out at the night. The moon had set, and beneath the frozen stars the woods were as darkly immobile as quarried jet. Devoid of light pollution, the yard was a sea of ink, the fence an uneven black band that divided blackness from more blackness. It was an oddly depthless optical effect. *Rothko at night*, Vone thought. One time in the Whitney he had become mesmerized by a Rothko, the somber bands of floating color making him tip forwards and eventually stagger in the dimly-lit gallery. He felt a similar sensation now.

Jack touched his arm. "C'mon." Wordlessly they made their way to the landing and looked down into the shadowy hall. "Jay-Jay?" Jack called, but softly, as if he didn't really want to be heard.

"He might be sleepwalking," Vone said as they went down. For some reason he resisted joining Jack in calling their son's name. Something to do with it being bad to shock a sleep-walker awake, perhaps. *His heart could stop.* Surely an urban legend, but still. He tested the front door: still locked. Jack glanced into the front parlor, Vone the dining room. No Jay-Jay. They went through to the kitchen, the most obvious place their son would go, of course, but he wasn't there either, and the side door was, when Jack tried it, locked.

The cellar door was closed, but light leaked out around the edges of its frame. Vone knew Jay-Jay couldn't reach the switch, and he was sure he hadn't left the light on, but then he had thought the same about his meds. He opened the door and he and Jack hurried down. There, at last, they found their son, in his peejays and barefoot, leaning his forehead against the locked door of the secret room with his eyes closed, his arms hanging at his sides.

"Junior?" Vone said quietly. When Jay-Jay didn't respond, he said to Jack, "I tried to get a gate for the stairs at the hardware store today but they didn't have one." *Why am I lying?* "He must've sleepwalked."

Jack nodded. "D'you think it's alright to –" he reached out for Jay-Jay's arm. It was so delicate; their son was so little and vulnerable.

Bolder than his husband and in mama mode, Vone lifted Jay-Jay away from the door, scooping him off his feet and into a fetal position. Jay-Jay didn't wake up, which was troubling, but on the plus side he didn't see the door either, and his head turned reflexively into Vone's chest as Vone carried him away. Jack followed, looking worried.

Once they were back in the kitchen Jay-Jay stirred and woke, stretching and yawning and looking around him in a confused way. Vone put the back of his hand to his son's forehead. It was damp, slightly chilly. "No fever," he said.

"Good," Jack said.

Jay-Jay put his arms round Vone's neck. "We think you sleepwalked," Vone said as he carried their son through to the front hall. "Remember that time at Auntie Delores' at Thanksgiving?" Jay-Jay shook his head. "Well, that's because you were asleep." Vone nipped Jay-Jay's nose between his thumb and forefinger and Jay-Jay giggled. He had several times caught Delores, who was old-school about hair texture and "fineness" of features, stroking the sides of Jay-Jay's not-especially-broad nose "just to make sure it grows straight."

They had Jay-Jay in bed with them, so he couldn't go wandering again in what little remained of the night. Once he was asleep, and he fell asleep so quickly it was as if he had been drugged, they quietly talked things through, deciding first that, as he seemed well and not distressed, they didn't have to call a doctor or go in search of an ER. Unsurprisingly this led to a repeat discussion of the fact that Vone hadn't yet found Jay-Jay – or himself – a doctor.

"I'll get the stairgate tomorrow in Collington-O," Jack said. "I Googled and they have a Mamas & Papas. But why do you think he went all the way down to the cellar?"

"It's all that 'she sleeps in the cellar' b.s.," Vone said. "I still don't know what old man Harris said to him while I was out of the room, and you know how kids can fixate on stuff."

"You really didn't show him the room?"

"No. Anyway, the Owl Lady stuff was happening before I even figured out it was there. I mean I found it *because* of stuff Jackie was saying, and then what the old man said about the key."

Jack looked thoughtful. "It can't hurt to put those bolts on," he said. "That way he can't get back down there or outside."

Vone nodded, relieved his husband was supporting him. "It's weird because he's not strong enough to turn the key," he said, "but at least once I..." He didn't finish his thought, which was that he had already found Jay-Jay out of doors, in a trance, going towards the woods; going towards, he was sure, the well, and apparently against his will. Was this dream summons the same as that? It felt different somehow.

He yawned jaw-clickingly and checked his phone. It was five a.m. Jack had to be up by seven.

Breakfast was a largely wordless affair, which saw both Jack and Vone punchy from lack of sleep. Coffee did little to lift their energy levels, and they chewed toast without relish. Jay-Jay seemed untroubled, if thoughtful, as he ate his Cheerios.

"Are you gonna be able to drive okay?" Vone asked as Jack finished his second mug, black and sugared. "The timber lorries on that road are huge."

"I'll be careful," Jack said. "Oh, and tomorrow's the day we pick up the rental car." He turned to Jay-Jay. "We'll all go to Collington-Osprey first thing and pick out a nice car for Daddy. Then you guys can go exploring all over the place." Jay-Jay didn't respond. "Okay, well, I've gotta go." Jack pecked Vone on the lips, stroked his son's cornrows a touch warily, picked up his shoulder bag and went out. Vone didn't follow him: already their little habit of coffee on the porch and Vone waving Jack off had fallen by the wayside.

After his husband had gone and Vone had washed up, he took the drill and put up the bolts: three on the front door, two on the back, one on the door to the cellar. The bits were blunted and tended to skid out of the screw-head crosses even when he leant in hard, but he managed to get the job done without too much ill temper. All the bolts were out of Jay-Jay's reach, and all moved back and forth easily when he tested them: a competent job.

Sunlight spilled in through the kitchen windows. What was the point of locks and bolts when glass shattered so easily? In the supernatural realm the lack of an invitation to pass a threshold (emblematized by the presence of the bolts) seemed more important than the physical strength of the barrier to which they were attached, but beyond that? At least they would stop Jay-Jay wandering. Well, probably.

Leaving his son playing on the rug in the kitchen passage, Vone went down to the basement and collected the pile of papers from the hidden room. Coming back up, he took care to bolt the basement door after him, though Jay-Jay seemed to have no interest in it that morning. Again Vone had the

suspicion that his son was actively pretending a lack of interest, as he had at the mound the day before last.

Dumping the papers on the table, Vone fixed himself a
mug of chamomile tea. The tea, the warmth, the slanting sunlight, all were a reassuring contrast to the dank, windowless
cell below: the everyday, frontal-lobed world literally and fig-
uratively on top of the murky, subconscious one; the Apollo-
nian covering over the Dionysian.

Topmost in the pile were newspapers and magazines, and
as he peeled them apart, he thought of the TV show *Extreme
Hoarders*. All were yellowed, wrinkled, stained with water-
marks and in places frosted with nitrous salts. Dirt slid off
them onto the tabletop, gritty and unpleasant. Blocks of pages
were damply welded together, so couldn't be opened or read,
and most of what could be read was of no interest: torn or cut
from local newspapers dated between 1966 and 1969, it
mostly comprised recipes for cakes and pies, "how to" advice
on making handicrafts, and flyers for craft fairs and other minor local events. There was a partly filled in, undemanding
puzzle book, below which were several Sunday supplements,
one of which commemorated the Apollo moon landing,
though that was mostly rotted to pulp. Vone held each of the
supplements by the spine and gave it a shake. Nothing fell out
but a small dead spider, pressed flat as a flower in some unlucky moment over a half century before.

Next in the pile was a hardback book of local history with
a dull cover and a manually typed spine label that read "Prop.
Coll.-Osp. Pub. Lib. 973 LOC." The due date, stamped wonkily
on the brown paper cardholder glued onto the inside cover,
was 08/07/66. It hadn't been borrowed much before then: the
preceding stamp was for a date in 1957.

Vone flipped through the book without much interest, but
his eye was caught by a black-and-white photograph of a
group of haughty-looking old men in traditional Native American clothing, one wearing a large feather headdress. The image was overly solarized, so there wasn't much detail to be
made out, and the text beneath it read, *Elders of the Pennacook tribe, 1883. The land on which our town was built was
ceded in perpetuity by the Pennacook in 1782, though they
continued to trade, especially in furs and pelts, until the*

commencement of World War I. Note the ceremonial head-dress of owl feathers, which is said to be symbolic to them.

The leaden, passive phrasing, carefully avoiding mention of white wrongdoing, and the lack of actual information – symbolic of *what*, for fuck's sake? – reminded him of history lessons at school; of the evasions around everything to do with slavery, so eager were the educational authorities to gloss over past white cruelty – and that had been in predominantly Black Bed-Stuy, not (say) cracker-controlled Alabama. Actual Black history was largely left to parents to pass on, either at home or at after-school clubs, and if they didn't it was down to you to fill in the gaps yourself, later. His own parents had had pride in Black New York in general, in old school rap and hip-hop in particular, and in the idioms and fashions of Black urban life; they name-checked Malcolm and Martin, Angela Davis and Mohammed Ali, Spike Lee, Tupac and Magic Johnson, but delving any further back they had left to him. And of course their focus had been entirely on the heterosexual.

Stifling a yawn, he closed the book, stretched, got up and wandered over to the kitchen window. He expected to see nothing unusual.

He was wrong.

Looking over the backyard fence was a cowled figure all in gray. Taller than the pickets by at least a head, it was, therefore, more than seven feet in height, and was freakishly narrow-shouldered – so much so that, like a trompe l'oeil seen from the wrong angle, it appeared optically stretched and distorted. The hood hung forward like a grotesquely excessive gray foreskin, entirely concealing the figure's features, and a robe of the same material hung down like a cloak.

Vone closed his eyes, took a breath, counted to ten and opened them again.

The figure was still there. Its color was the same as that of the shape he had glimpsed when Pepper had been bitten, and similar to, if darker than, the thing that had floated in the trees, though it was now as solid and unmoving as a statue.

At least it hadn't darted forward while his eyes were shut.

Vone looked round to check on Jay-Jay, who was obliviously playing dinosaurs in the kitchen passageway, and came to a decision. Stepping over his son, he went through to the front door, self-consciously slid back the bolts, unlocked it, and went round to the garage. The canopy door clanged noisily as he swung it up, making him look round, but the street was deserted. The axe waited on its lugs. Vone took hold of it. The head was heavy but the haft well-balanced. *Might've been made for me.* Axe in hand, he headed back along the front path.

Watching him from the street, as suddenly present as if she had arrived by teleportation, was an unsmiling white woman in lycra leggings and a pink hoodie. In her forties maybe, she wore dark glasses, her dark blonde hair was pulled back in a scrunchie, and she was jogging on the spot. Whether she was one of the women he'd seen before he didn't know.

Forcing a cheery tone, he announced loudly, "Just gonna chop some firewood! Don't call the cops on me!" She turned away as if he hadn't spoken and jogged on in the direction of the moose trail. "Fucking bitch," he said under his breath, half hoping she would hear and try to make something of it, but she was too far away and he had no time for white nonsense anyway, not right then. Surely she wouldn't call the cops on him for carrying his own axe on his own property. Or would she? He thought of the footage he'd seen of the Black teen held at gunpoint by seven white cops for picking up trash on his own lawn with a flimsy plastic claw.

Re-entering the house, he heard the bloop-bloop-burble of a Skype call coming through on his Macbook, which sat open on the chair by the coat stand, and showed a ludicrously over-Photoshopped and therefore bone-structureless image of Tarrell as the caller I.D.

Vone ignored it and went through to the kitchen. When he stepped over his son, seeing Daddy carrying an axe, Jay-Jay looked scared. "Don't worry," Vone said flatly, crossing to the window.

The figure was still there. A part of him had assumed it would be gone, because that would once again make him look crazy to his son; another part knew that this, whatever it was, was his destiny, and so was unsurprised. "Just stay inside," he said – Jay-Jay had followed him through, and was twisting Dippy in his hands. "It'll all be fine, but I just need to go check on something."

Jay-Jay nodded, watching with large eyes as Vone pulled back the bolts on the kitchen door, unlocked it and went out. He locked the door behind him and pocketed the key, thinking as he did so, *If I need to get back in in a hurry I'm fucked.*

That was better than putting Jay-Jay's life in danger. But in danger from what, exactly? The sun was high, the sky a cloudless blue. The backyard grass glowed green, scattered with yellow leaves. Here and there copper-colored windfall pears added a pleasing, Pointillist contrast. It was as far removed from a scary scene as could be imagined. Nothing was vague or shadowy; everything was hard-edged and clear, the waiting figure too.

Hunching over the axe and thanking god the yard wasn't overlooked by nosy neighbors, Vone scurried forward. He had no thoughts then about what it was that he was confronting. Mad and sane, possible and impossible, sleeping and waking jumbled together in his head.

He had never been one of those people who knew they were dreaming.

His heart thudding hard, he reached the gap in the fence. From that angle he couldn't see the thing and, unless it moved, it couldn't see him. Glancing back, Vone saw Jay-Jay was at the kitchen window, but couldn't make out his expression.

Ducking under the twist of rusty wire that held the tops of the pickets together, Vone stepped through the gap. On that side of the fence the bushes pushed close, cutting off any view to right or left. Giving himself no time to think, he forced his way along to where he reckoned the thing stood, one hand on the axe; with the other shielding his eyes from springing, thorny twigs and briars. Even now he expected there would be nothing; that it would turn out to be yet another projection from his misfiring mind, another secret to be hidden – badly – from his husband, if not his son.

But no: there it was, now with its back to him, freakishly tall, dressed in a textured gray robe that trailed in a twisted tangle along the ground. Vone's tongue clove to the roof of his mouth as slowly, inexorably, the figure turned to face him.

Twenty-One

T hough the hood concealed its upper half, seen from below the lower half of the face that turned to meet Vone's was undoubtedly the one that had been pushed through the sheet the day before. In addition to being unnaturally elongated, he now saw that it was grotesquely misproportioned; anencephalically flat-topped, as if lacking much of a brain pan. It was skull-like but in texture fleshy, as if made of gristle rather than bone; and the flesh, which was semi-translucent, had a quality Vone associated with something rotting in a plastic bag, a late-term abortion, a drowned puppy or a severed head. Or was it – no, he was certain it wasn't – some sort of mask? The eyes were hidden by the forward slump of the cowl and the lower jaw hung slackly open, exposing a ridged gum-line rather than teeth.

Seen up close, the robe was in its patterning and texture if anything scaly, the same leaden color as the face, and patchily rotted through. It trailed along the ground like the train of some undead queen or goul empress, or the detritus of a slaughterhouse or tannery. Like the face it had a translucency that made Vone think of the shed skins of tarantulas – or no; of the pale and softly swelling spider, hiding nearby.

Other than slowly turning to face him, the figure hadn't moved; nor did its expression change as he stood before it, the axe in his hands, his chest and muscles tight, not knowing what to do. As he watched, it rotated further, turning away from him, and looking up he saw that the top of the hood was tangled around a large branch. From the way the material hung – material more like rotting rubber or latex than fabric – it was, Vone realized, a costume without a tenant.

No, not a costume, a skin: a shed skin.

It turned a little further, releasing a stench like rotten meat, and Vone clamped a hand over his nose and mouth to stop himself vomiting. With the head of the axe, gingerly he reached out to poke at it.

The instant the blade touched the stinking thing the branch that held it up broke and, as if alive, the skin came tumbling down on top of him, making Vone shout aloud as the weight of it carried him backwards to the ground. It was like a huge roll of sodden carpet, and the flabby face, thrust against his own with stomach-turning intimacy, was clammy and reeking and had the particular unclean stickiness of old rubber. In panic he struggled, trying to shove the reeking thing off him, but the material tore like sheets of overcooked pasta that had turned putrid, and his fingers pushed through it, and each tear disgorged more stinking rottenness.

Kicking and elbowing a part of the flabby, twisted mass aside, Vone managed to roll onto his front, and in that position squirm out from under the rest of it. Gasping for breath and bracing himself up with the axe, he struggled to his feet. Then he spread his arms wide and gave a single loud, expulsive yell. It rang out almost metallically, and Vone realized immediately that, hearing it, Jay-Jay would be terrified: he wouldn't have been able to see anything once the figure had dropped down behind the fence on top of his father. Quickly he forced his way back to the gap, leant through and gave his son a cheery wave. Jay-Jay waved back tentatively. Vone signaled "five minutes, okay?" and gave a thumbs up.

Now he knew the thing wasn't alive, he could examine it dispassionately. He paced it out and found it was a disconcerting twenty-five feet long. Its tapered tail ended in a succession of partially-deflated globes. These were seven in number and resembled more than anything else the rattle of a freakishly large rattlesnake. The biggest, which was the most distant from the tip, was the size of an adult, if somewhat hydrocephalic human head, and had dimples in it that suggested a sheet of pastry draped over a skull. Its successors, which grew smaller in size towards the tip, like tsantsas or wizened apples, showed in addition a progression of a more disturbing sort, for each had the look of an increasingly enfleshed face. Not only that, but each face clearly belonged to someone in particular, and by their proportions – primarily their large foreheads – Vone saw that they were the faces of children. The penultimate globe, which was the size of a grapefruit, had more definite features than any of those preceding it, suggesting to Vone that there was a gradual dissolution or consumption of personality over time. He guessed, without evidence, that its features might have belonged to Tommy Dyer.

With a sense of dread he squatted on his haunches to study the final rattle-bone. It wasn't much bigger than a hen's egg, and that its face could have been Jay-Jay's – no more than "could have been," but still – didn't surprise him.

He straightened up. There could be no doubt that he was looking at the shed skin of an enormous snake, but what kind of snake? Only anacondas grew anywhere near this big, and then only in the depths of the Amazon. Anyway, this wasn't an anaconda: it had the tail of a rattler and the head of some kind of cobra, for what had looked like a hood from the front turned out, when the thing was lying face-down on the ground, to have ribbing running through it that grew out of the back of the head in a fan of presumably inflatable filaments.

With the blade of the axe Vone attempted to flip the cowl over to examine the face, but it tore and fell to pieces. The stink grew worse as it disintegrated: despite the coldness of the air, it seemed to be rotting fast.

Something rustled in the bushes nearby and Vone looked round sharply, his grip tightening on the haft of the axe. If the thing was there it would have to be at its most vulnerable, and the shed skin demonstrated that it was, despite the face thrust through the bedsheet that could have had no body behind it, a physical thing. Yet "most vulnerable" could still mean it had a hide too tough to be chopped into by an axe. And it was twenty-five feet long; presumably longer now it had shed. And Pepper's death proved it had a poisonous bite, and all living things are most vicious when most vulnerable.

On the other hand, whatever had rustled had sounded small, and surely, however adventitious it was, the creature couldn't have devoured *every* living thing of any size in the area. Or could it? He thought of cobras hypnotizing their prey, stories that must, after all, have come from somewhere, from something real; and of the chromatic pulsings of cuttlefish mesmerizing shrimp. The phrase came to his mind, *charming the birds from the trees*. And he thought of Medusa, whose glance turned you to stone. Still, some rabbit or whatever might have emerged from an early hibernation.

Keeping an eye on the spot the rustling had come from, Vone backed away through the bushes. He stepped backwards through the fence-gap too, so he couldn't be jumped at the last second by some darting thing with a lethal bite. Then he turned and jogged across the yard to the side door, fumblingly unlocked it, and went in. His skin prickled with relief at being in the warmth, and a shudder passed through him. The fabric of his hoodie was sodden under the arms with cold sweat.

Jay-Jay watched as Vone lent the axe by the door, locked it and slid the bolts across. "It was just some costume left over from Halloween," he said, "hung from a tree as a joke to scare people."

Jay-Jay said nothing, just looked at his daddy with a child's penetrant honesty. Then his nose wrinkled. Looking down at his stained hoodie, Vone realized he had brought the odor of putrefaction in with him. "Well, Daddy stinks," he said cheerily. "I'ma grab a quick shower, okay?" He thought a moment, and added, "Why don't you bring Dippy and play in the big bedroom while I wash up?"

Jay-Jay nodded and, picking up the toy, followed Vone into the kitchen passage. Vone peeled off his hoodie as he climbed the stairs.

Afterwards, sitting halfway up the stairs with his Macbook open on his knees and waiting for the burbling call tone to be answered, Vone felt the choking dread you feel when you know you have bad news to share. His thoughts looped like bats above his head. How to phrase what he had found? What words would sound not crazy? But there the thing was, stinking and scaly and real. Maybe before he made the call he should have –

"Bitch, so *now* you're calling me?" Rell was holding his laptop in one hand and moving about, looking stressed in black sequins. Behind him Vone could make out a brick-walled loft or industrial space, and there was the sound of hammering, thudding and a drill whining. Before Vone could say anything, Rell turned his head and said to someone out of sight, "No, that one needs to go over there by the stairs. The bigger one should – wait, I'll –"

Rell set the laptop down and moved out of view. Vone realized he'd forgotten all about his bestie's upcoming show. At once he was torn between the need, the duty to make Rell think that that was why he'd called him, and the nutcase-sees-monster-in-the-backyard reason he was really calling.

But I'm not mad. That's why I'm calling: it's real.

His chest was tight and he thought maybe he should have taken a clonazepam before calling, to help him present what he'd found more calmly. More sanely. Because here was the thing, the deep, profound thing: what he was about to tell Rell was going to crack both their realities open and turn their worlds upside down.

"I'm back," Rell said, redundantly.

Vone made himself ask how preparations were going.

"They're *all idiots*," Rell called over his shoulder, in a jokey tone that wasn't joking. "No, but seriously, girl, it's going okay. We're behind, of course, but I think it's gonna look really good. There'll be a virtual gallery too, for international buyers and galleries abroad. Pah-ree, darling. Mi-laahn." He stretched out the vowels luxuriantly. "The gallery takes 60% but what's a bitch gonna do?"

"Jack up the prices?"

"Exactly right." Rell opened a plastic clamshell container that Vone recognized was from Sweetgreen and forked some rocket into his mouth. "I'll send you the link when it's up."

Vone nodded. "Something's happened," he said.

Rell caught his tone and put his fork down. "Okay, what?"

"I found something in the woods."

"What something?"

Suddenly Vone couldn't face trying to put it into words. "I'll show you."

"Okay, bitch. Be mysterious."

"It *is* mysterious. Trust me."

Keeping the Macbook open, Vone carried it through to the kitchen. "This is our rustic yet cozy kitchen," he editorialized, glancing at the screen to see if Rell's face was still moving, which it was, meaning there was still a signal, and becoming self-conscious when he had to put the laptop down to pull back the bolts on the side-door. Hopefully city-dwelling Tar-rell wouldn't think their presence evidence of paranoia. Jay-Jay looked up from watching *Peppa Pig* on the iPad at the kitchen table.

Vone got two thirds of the way to the fence before he

realized Rell's image had frozen. Of course it had. He went back to the house, put the Macbook on the counter and went out again with his phone. He would take photos and a video and send them to Rell. Not to Jack though: he would ambush Jack with the real thing.

He hurried back across the yard and stepped through the gap in the fence. As he squeezed through the bushes he half-expected the skin to be gone, if for no more logical reason than mental torture by some higher – or lower – power, but no, there it lay. He took several photos, then a thirty-second video panning up and down its length, moving in to focus on the details, getting his foot into shot for scale. If he posted it on Tik-Tok maybe someone, some cryptozoologist if that was still a thing, might know what it was.

As he was recrossing the yard he glanced at the first of the photos and his heart sank: though the surrounding details were a billion (or however many) pixels sharp, where the skin lay there was only a hazy Gaussian blur. He thumbed through the rest of the pictures: all were the same. He imagined trying to reverse-engineer them to remove the distortion, but guessed the flaw arose out of some weird emanation from the source material, meaning there was no uncorrupted original to get back to. And even if he *did* somehow manage it, the results would inevitably look like shit Photoshop or some bogus A.I. confection.

Without hope he played the video. Rather than a blur there was a shiny pixelation, reminiscent of clusters of what people had believed for a while were spirit lights, before discovering they were in fact a byproduct of the lens design in those exciting new devices, smartphones: camera flare, not the idly loitering spirits of the dead. He could try again, but what would be the point? If it was a defect in the phone then the same thing would happen again. If not, he was fucked that way too.

Beaten, he re-entered the kitchen. The thought of calling Rell back was unbearable. No doubt he could make up some trivial thing he'd been going to show his friend and who cared that he couldn't. But then he'd be lying, shutting Rell out, preventing him from helping, supporting, believing.

Jack.

Jack would be his witness.

Okay, that's okay. The most important thing, actually.

But he should call Rell back, end their conversation on a sane note, otherwise he would be punishing his friend. *Just wish him luck. He got shit to do, don't have time for yo crazy ass, not today, Satan.* He carried the Macbook through to the front stairs.

Before he could call back, however, the doorbell rang, making him jump. The utter ordinariness of the sound turned his world schizophrenic. Out back was something monstrous and inexplicable; out front were postal workers, visiting neighbors, who knew, Jehovah's Witnesses.

Witnesses. Maybe he could beg one of them to come in and follow him out to the –

He put the Macbook aside. Jay-Jay appeared, curious to see who had come calling, but hung back in the passage doorway, watching as Vone pulled the bolts aside, took off the safety chain, unlocked and finally opened the front door. A cardboard box about a foot cubed sat on the porch; a delivery van was heading off in the direction of the covered bridge.

As usual there was no other sign of life on Cottonwood Way. A few pumpkins sat on porches, emptied of significance now and thus forlorn, and Vone fleetingly regretted depriving his son of Halloween, though Jay-Jay hadn't seemed to care. Perhaps because he was learning there were real horrors in the shadows, he had no desire to make a game of them. Vone found himself wondering whether the rarely glimpsed residents of Cottonwood Way were somehow in on it, whatever "it" was. Rory had talked about still being seen as an outsider, even after – how long had she said, a decade? – and marrying a local. She might be in on it, though: hadn't she lied about not knowing what had happened in their house?

Yet Ted had told. Ted, who wanted to teach a child to fire a rifle. Maybe it had been him in the woods that first day, hunting something that was smaller then. Something that he couldn't explain to anyone who didn't belong.

Vone picked up the box. It was very light, addressed to him neatly with a sharpie, and had no return address. After relocking and re-bolting the front door, he carried it through to the kitchen, followed by Jay-Jay, who watched seriously as he took a knife, slit the shiny brown parcel tape and levered up the flaps. Inside were Styrofoam peanuts. He scooped them out in handfuls and piled them on the table next to the box. Revealed was an ostrich egg. He lifted it out carefully. Underneath was a handwritten note from the seller: 'Thank you for your order, if you are satisfied, please rate us favorable, yours, Maisie and Cottonbud.' He looked the egg over. It was good-sized, without cracks, chips or discoloration, and its slightly nubbly surface was pleasingly even.

"What d'you reckon, Jackie-Jacks? Do you think anyone'll notice it's not the same?"

"It's smaller," Jay-Jay said with irritating candor, "and not so pointy."

He was right. On the other hand, who would ever come in the house who would care? Sarah hadn't wanted to set foot in the place, and who else was there, or would there ever be? Certainly the relative who had inherited it from Mamie Place seemed determined to remain distant. "Okay, well, let's see how it sits in the stand," he said.

They went through to the parlor. The stand waited on the glass-topped bamboo table. Vone sat the egg on it. The egg tilted over, a poor fit, the carving evidently tailored to the proportions of the original. "We can pad it underneath with something," he said. Jay-Jay looked unconvinced. Vone took a breath and asked as lightly as he could, "Do you remember what Mister Harris said to you when you were on your own with him?"

Jay-Jay nodded. "He said it's all the Owl Lady's fault. But he said she's our friend."

"Okay. Well, we tried our best. Let's leave it for now."

Vone ushered Jay-Jay out, closing the parlor door behind him. He would call Rell back later; right now he needed to speak to old man Harris. What was his address? It had been pinned to his lapel. Something like Log – no, Timber Road. One hundred something. He Googled Timber Road and found it branched off from the main western road a mile or so out past the Bounds, and ran north. Not far, then, though the houses might be miles apart, of course. He opened the route finder on his phone: from 13 Cottonwood Way to a median 150 Timber Road turned out to be a little over four miles – not walkable with Jay-Jay, and while Vone could cycle it, Jay-Jay wouldn't be able to. He didn't want Jay-Jay to have more contact with the old man anyway: every little thing Mr. Harris said seemed to worm its way into his son's brain and lodge there, and those "little things" were all disquieting. But Vone couldn't leave him home alone. *Perhaps Rory...*

By then it was noon. Vone put the hoodie and jeans he had been wearing when the skin fell on him into the wash and fixed himself and Jay-Jay sandwiches, ham and pickles on granary, though the stink was still in his nostrils and to eat felt like a chore. Afterwards he got Jay-Jay into his coat and a woolly hat and walked him round to Rory and Ted's. Rory's car was in the drive. Vone took a breath and pressed the buzzer. It rasped loudly. He waited, then pressed it again, imagining the sound tearing through the sad and silent rooms within.

As well as the buzzer there was a heavy pewter knocker in the shape of a hand. He banged it a couple of times, eventually adding a cautious, "Rory? You home?" – though as he called her name he looked round uneasily, in case some curtain-twitcher was marking him down as a potential robber or rapist. No answer came.

"Maybe she went for a walk," Jay-Jay said.

"Maybe."

They trailed back down the drive. Once back on the street Vone looked round. In an upper-floor window, a half-drawn curtain flickered.

Abruptly self-conscious – he was, after all, recklessly eye-balling a home with a fearful white woman inside – Vone took Jay-Jay back to Number 13. "Okay," he said, once they were safely back on their own front porch, "Daddy needs to go see Mister Harris. I was gonna leave you with Rory but she's not in. It's too far for you to cycle, so I'll sit you on my handlebars. It'll be a bit uncomfy, but we can take breaks if it starts to hurt you under your thighs and booty."

Jay-Jay nodded. Vone went and fetched his helmet and put it on him, carefully adjusting the chinstrap so it wouldn't slip.

"Why don't *you* have a helmet, Daddy?" Jay-Jay asked, with a child's sharp eye for inconsistency in rulemaking.

"I'll get ones for me and Dad when we go to Collingwood-Osprey tomorrow," Vone said. "I wasn't expecting to ride my bike before then, but this is a trip we need to make today."

They went around to the garage. Slipping the phone into the breast pocket of his coat so its directions would be audible, Vone wheeled out the less boneshaking of the adult pushbikes. Straddling it, he lifted Jay-Jay and positioned him so his knees, pressed together, hooked over the dip between the handlebars, and he could lean back between his daddy's arms and against his chest and not be too uncomfortable.

With Siri urging him to "head north" with what felt like symbolic insistence, Vone pushed off, realizing as he did so that he hadn't ridden a pedal cycle in over fifteen years. He thought he had pumped the tires rock-hard, but they felt wretchedly flabby under his and Jay-Jay's combined weight, and he wobbled badly to start with. The gears clunked and the chain slipped, then slipped again, but soon he had picked up enough speed to keep the bike upright and fairly stable – though they almost had a tumble bumping and slithering along the rutted, greasily leaf-strewn lane that led to the covered bridge, and Vone came close to straining his groin when he had hastily to throw a foot out sideways to stop them tipping over. But soon enough they were out the other side and rolling through the Vicinity.

Turning onto the main road, Vone found its edges, which were broken up like crumbled brownies in a pan, were jagged enough to wreck a bicycle wheel, and that as a result he was being forced out into the middle of the lane, where the danger of getting mown down by fast-moving vehicles coming up behind them was real. The threat was amplified by the curve of the road: a driver would have little or no time to notice Vone and pull farther out – and that was assuming no oncoming traffic: if there *was* any, the car or truck would have to slam on the brakes or swerve and have a head-on collision. On top of that, any logging lorry that passed the bike without keeping enough distance could all too easily suck it under its wheels.

Shoulda Googled cycle trails, Vone thought belatedly, though those would presumably mostly be for mountain bikes and holidaymakers in search of scenic views, rather than regular people just trying to get somewhere. He pedaled faster.

To his relief only two or three cars passed them, and no trucks, in the fifteen minutes before the satnav announced the turn-off he was looking for, which was in a small copse of pines at the bottom of a dip in the road.

Beyond that, Timber Road ran through a forest of oaks and, while straight and level, was narrower than the main east-west artery. That meant it wasn't a route logging trucks would tend to take, so Vone was able to relax a little. A breeze sprang up, sending the last of the autumn leaves whirling down around them. To be among the fluttering leaves was somehow magical. The air was clean, the sun bright, and the shed skin behind Number 13 began to seem like something from a nightmare, though the odor of it still clung faintly to Vone's nostrils.

The oaks gave way to pastureland in which piebald cows placidly chewed the cud. *Sarah would have said if she lived on a farm*, Vone thought. Still, he slowed to check the names on the mailboxes of every farmhouse they passed. Peletier, Thompson, Hall, Allen: names and no numbers.

After a while they came to another densely wooded stretch. The branches of the oaks arched above the road to create an architectonic roof tunnel, and the bike's tires crunched and bumped on fallen acorns. Just beyond the trees, to the right and in a pool of sunlight, he saw, flanked by hedgerows heavy with dead briars, a five-bar gate of rusty iron. A loop of orange nylon served as a catch, and next to the gate was a tin mailbox that had been freshly painted a bright, robin's egg blue.

His thighs aching from the unfamiliar exercise, needing a break, Vone wobbled to a stop in front of the gate and put his feet down. He lifted Jay-Jay from between the handlebars and set him down on the grassy verge. Despite the discomfort, his son seemed to be enjoying this unexpected adventure.

Propitiously the mailbox was labeled in neat black letters, "Anderson/Harris."

Twenty-Two

Beyond the gate was a freshly whitewashed, single-story clapboard house with a mono pitched shingle roof. Pink and white winter roses twined prettily around the columns along its porch. Right of it was a carport, currently unoccupied; and a close-clipped lawn ran around to the back. Set into this was a stepping-stone path like dinosaur footprints, and white plastic chairs stood around a table with a closed, multi-colored umbrella at its center. Back of that, beyond a low wire fence and flowerbeds bright with daisies and larkspur, was pastureland that sloped gently up to a distant rise of brown woods.

By way of contrast, to the left of the house was a dirty concrete yard with, along one side of it, a row of dilapidated sheds, and in its middle a small trailer with flat tires and grimy windows that were obscured by deteriorated mesh. Straw was scattered about the green-tinged concrete, and bits of rusty farm equipment and blown-out truck tires sat desolately about. Vone wondered if there would be a dog; if it would be properly chained up. Just then a cloud passed in front of the sun, sliding a shadow over the yard – or less a shadow, more a dreary desaturation.

"Wanna help me get this gate open?" he asked Jay-Jay, leaning the bike against a springy mass of briars dotted with shriveled green berries that had never ripened, and unhooking the loop of orange nylon rope. Jay-Jay nodded. Vone lifted the gate on its hinges and encouraged his son to join him in swinging it round. Once there was enough of a gap to wheel the bike through, he set it back down and did so: as a city-dweller he couldn't leave a bicycle, however janky, in plain sight for any passerby (though there were none) to make off with. Afterwards, out of some sense of something, he lifted the gate closed again.

With the sinking sensation he invariably felt at the prospect of meeting white strangers or near-strangers on their own ground, taking Jay-Jay's hand in his, Vone approached the trailer, the door of which was around the other side. As he came nearer, he saw that the "sheds" were in fact several old wardrobes and a droppings-spattered bookcase. There was also a low, rectangular chipboard box with a wire mesh front, through which the metal tube of a cable-tied water bottle was inserted. Inevitably Jay-Jay pulled him over to it, and as they approached, something stirred inside. Hoping to lure the inhabitant into view, Jay-Jay reached out. Vone smoothly drew his hand back before he could stick his fingers through the mesh. "Careful, Jackie-Jacks. It might bite."

Jay-Jay nodded, and father and son watched as, with quivering whiskers, a small animal came forward. It was long-backed, with sleek, dark brown fur, its ears were cuff-like and its eyes were black and bright.

"What species is it, daddy?" Jay-Jay asked, proud to use a new word correctly.

"A stoat or weasel, maybe," Vone said. "Or I guess it could be a mink." Seeing any animal caged depressed him, though its fur was glossy, and it didn't seem unhappy or manic. It cheeped endearingly. Jay-Jay laughed, and Vone thought how children, having such small spheres of freedom themselves, rarely feel the suffering of imprisoned things. His mind went to southern summers, collecting fireflies in mason jars: how none of them – himself, his cousins – had thought of the desperate longing in those abdominal lightshows they confined so casually behind glass walls.

As if the cheeping had been a signal, from the far side of the trailer came the clonking of pots and pans, followed by a splash as if a bowl of water – or something – had been flung onto the ground.

With a sigh Vone led Jay-Jay round to the trailer door and found it closed. A sagging laundry line ran between the trailer and the house, on which damp dishtowels hung. The pegs on the towels were wooden and mildewed. From somewhere under the trailer a frayed power cable ran along the ground to a junction box on the side of the house, and two blue butane cylinders stood in a rack next to the closed trailer door.

A rattling sound came from inside as Vone reached up and knocked. The noise stopped, but no one answered. "Mister Harris?" Vone called. Silence. "Um, you were at my house the other day. You spoke to my son." Beat. "I live at number 13,

Cottonwood Way. The house that belonged to Mamie Place. You said you knew her."

The door opened abruptly, swinging outwards so Vone had to step back. Mr. Harris was neatly dressed in chocolate-brown suit pants and a matching vest over a fresh white shirt. He was unshaven, but his hair was tidily brushed back. He looked past Vone suspiciously, then nodded sharply, as if the visit was expected. "You'd better come in," he said.

The trailer's interior was much as Vone had expected, cramped and hoarderishly piled with bills, books, magazines and newspapers, though it smelt dusty and stale, rather than cheesy or sodden with the urine and feces of mice or rats.

"Tea?" Mr. Harris asked, gesturing at a single-ring portable hotplate on the metal washboard of a small basin, its worn power cord nearer the faucet than was reassuring. Two mugs commemorating Las Vegas sat by it and, as they looked clean, Vone nodded.

The only seating was built into the front of the trailer, around three sides of a triangular folding table that like every other surface was piled with papers. Mr. Harris indicated for Vone and Jay-Jay to sit at it. The fronts of the cushions, formerly lemon and white, were now shiny and gray-brown, and Vone didn't think he could have sat on them in shorts. He helped Jay-Jay climb up and scoot round, then took the outer seat, placing himself between his son and the old man. Behind the window-mesh a sediment of dead crane flies lay heaped against the glass. Mr. Harris flicked a wall switch and set a kettle on the hotplate with a hollow clank, then turned to lift a stack of papers off a stool Vone hadn't noticed amidst the clutter.

"Um, I don't think you put any water in the –"

Mr. Harris looked round at the hotplate. "Oh, yeah." He lifted the kettle off the ring, filled it at the faucet and set it back on the now-orange coil. "I never let that house to families," he said, pulling the stool back so he could sit on it and fit his bony knees under the table. "Never did. 'Cept that one time. I'd had a watchumacallit –" He thumped his chest. "My business partner at the time, Joe Cook, he did it. I was in the I.C.U. in Collington-O, out of commission. He didn't tell me, though. Not even when they let me go home. I guess he thought I was a fool, saying no to money, and it's true I never gave him a proper reason. My eye was off the ball there. I only found out after the news come out about the, the – nineteen-eighty-something, that was."

"Eighty-six," Vone said.

"Ayup." The old man nodded. "So you knew Mamie, you said?"

"We're renting her house. Well, what used to be her house. Me and my husband. And you came by a couple of days ago, and you started to tell us stuff about it."

"I found the body, you know," Mr. Harris said, glancing round at the kettle. "A stroke, they said, though it turned out she had cancer too. A ball of whatnot the size of a grapefruit in her stomach. She knew, I reckon, or at least guessed, but she weren't keen on doctors, on account of the other thing, you know."

"Other thing?"

"Ayup." The old man stood up and brought down a tin caddy from a cupboard. Fumbling off the lid, he spooned too much loose tea into each mug. "She was what they used to call a he-she. There's a word for it, I mean a proper word, Abenaki, maybe. I forget. Feather, feather, wing, crow, eagle, bird – bird something – bulldagger?" Vone raised an eyebrow. "Naw, no. Something like that. Ah – berdakker, that was the word. What they call two-spirit, you know. Male and female in one. Or the one inside the other. They reckon – the tribes, I mean – they reckon if you're that way it means you got a gift."

"Gift?"

"You know: powers." The kettle began to rumble. The old man turned away and filled the mugs. "'Fraid I ain't got no milk," he said, adding to Jay-Jay, "I ain't got no juice neither," as he set the mugs down on the sun-faded Formica table. "Tea like this, it's too bitter for littleuns. It'd hurt your tummy."

With a sideways glance at his son, Vone said, "We, um, we found the room."

"You did? That's good, I reckon."

"Was she – did she keep someone a prisoner down there?"

"Why'd you say that?"

"The handcuff. The chain."

The old man shook his head. "No, no, you're wide of the

mark there, feller. She rigged all that up so she could sleep, do you see?"

"I don't –"

"The timer was so if she fell under *her* spell she couldn't go walking."

"Walking?"

"Sleepwalking, though she – Mamie, that is – said it weren't that, nawsuh, it was *her*. Calling from the woods, and she couldn't say no."

"Her?"

"Huh?"

"You said 'her'."

"Anyhow, she fixed it so she couldn't uncuff herself, not till morning come round and the clock wound down and the safe opened up. But she died in the end, of course, like everyone does. And I did what she asked, like I promised I would. A long time ago, it was."

"What *did* she ask?"

"I come 'round – there'd been complaints from the neighbors: trash piling up in the yard, that kind of thing. I thought, being young, I could gee her up some, help her clear it. Because we was friends, you know? Anyhow I knocked and got no reply and I went in and found her down in the cellar, in that room. Cold and stiff. I dragged the body up to the front hall, laid it out at the bottom of the stairs like she'd had a fall. That was a crime, I suppose, or at least a misdemeanor, but I don't think I was wrong to do it. I'd have rather put her in bed, that would've been more decent, but she was heavy by then: it was too much for one man to manage, even if you didn't mind getting close to a corpse. That was before I did my stint in the military, so I wasn't – you know, you toughen up. Anyhow, there was no one to ask. I locked the room up just as it was – she didn't want no one clearing it out, that was her particular wish – and I put the shelves across. Put the jars there – she'd just had 'em sat about on the floor – and left it like that. In case it was needed. The only thing I took was her diary. Lemme just –"

Mr. Harris bent over to rummage through one of the stacks of papers on the floor. This was all so much more than Vone had expected that he began to feel almost speedy. He stared at the old man's bent back, his wrinkled red, almost scaly neck.

The stack tipped over and spilled across the worn carpet tiles almost as far as the trailer door. Frowning, Mr. Harris looked round. "What're you doing in my trailer?" he asked sharply, and Vone was afraid he might have a pistol or even a shotgun somewhere to hand, though surely his granddaughter – great niece – wouldn't let him –

"I'm renting Mamie Place's house over on Cottonwood Way, Mister Harris," he said quickly. "You were telling me about how you knew her, how you helped her out, and about the room in the cellar. You said you were going to show me her diary."

The old man's expression softened. "Oh, yeah," he said. "Yeah." He gestured vaguely at the masses of paper. "I guess it's in here somewhere. I keep on meaning to..." He tailed off.

Vone rolled his eyes internally. "I'd really like to see it," he said.

"I'm sure I would too," Mr. Harris said. "If only I could..." Then, looking down at the papers on the floor, he added, "Well, looky here. Do you know, I think this is it."

Vone held his breath as, reaching with a large, knob-wristed hand, Mr. Harris picked up a small book, maybe five by eight inches in size, quite thick, and bound in –

Twenty-Three

Snakeskin.

Vone held his breath. He was sure that, however blandly he tried to act, Mr. Harris would detect his interest and become possessive of the diary, but the old man passed it to him indifferently. The binding was a colorful mosaic of reds, yellows and blacks, and had been skillfully done. With lips parted, Vone opened it. Glued lumpily to the inside front cover was a bookplate, its motif a scroll with gothic lettering that read "from the library of", under which was written in faded, blue-black ink in a neat, old-fashioned hand, *Margaret M. Place*. The paper was good quality manila, though the edges were discolored by damp, and it gave off a scent of dust and something else vaguely familiar that touched Vone's nostrils unpleasantly –

Looking round, he saw that Mr. Harris had set the now-empty kettle back on the red-hot ring of the hotplate, and the smell was its bottom burning. "Excuse me, sir," he said, standing up and stepping past the old man, taking the tea towel Mr. Harris had wrapped around its handle each time he moved it and lifting the kettle into the basin. Vone twitched off the lid, turned the faucet and ran cold water in. There was a hissing explosion of steam that quickly stopped. He switched the hotplate off at the wall.

Mr. Harris watched all this with a worried expression, as if Vone had authority over him: a social worker plotting to send him to an old folks' home, perhaps. Vone sat back down. "So can I borrow this?" he asked, picking up the diary again, taking shameful advantage of the old man's fear. "I promise I'll bring it back once I've read it." Mr. Harris shrugged a vague acquiescence. His eyes were no longer focused. "Thanks," Vone said, feeling dishonorable as he got to his feet. "C'mon, Jay-Jay. We should get home and fix Dad's dinner. Nice to see you, Mister Harris. I'll bring the book back once I've read it," he reiterated, and, after all, he wasn't lying.

Leading his son by the hand, Vone slipped round the old man, who had fallen silent, and, feeling like a thief, which he wasn't, and a con artist, which he kind of was, he exited the trailer, turning in the doorway to lift Jay-Jay down after him.

Once they were outside, in his eagerness to get away with his prize before the old man changed his mind, Vone found himself pulling Jay-Jay along. This made Jay-Jay drag his heels and start to whine. Vone yanked on his arm, then realized he was on the verge of hurting his son. Immediately he stopped, turned and squatted down to face him. "Sorry I did that," he said. "Daddy just wants to get back to the house." Jay-Jay nodded, and Vone gave him a hug that he knew was too intense but couldn't help himself. Hand in hand they went over to where he had left the bike.

It had subsided into the tangle of the hedge, and as Vone was wrenching it free, from the direction of the trailer came the voice of old man Harris, surprisingly loud and firm: "Hey! You! Hold up there! Hey!"

Vone groaned internally, suppressing a childish urge to run for it. Of course the old man would want the diary back before he had a chance to read it; of course there would be no answers. Forcing a smile, he turned to see Mr. Harris hobbling towards them, breathing hard and carrying a lidded wicker basket. This he thrust at Jay-Jay. When Jay-Jay was reluctant to take it, Mr. Harris wheezed, "For you, little'un. Go on, now. Take a peek."

Something moved inside the basket, and the face of the small animal they had seen before appeared at the mesh window at its front end.

"Aw, man," Vone began.

"It's not a gift," Mr Harris said quickly. "A gift is a burden, and a living thing can't be given anyhow. It's a loan."

"We really can't –"

"Just till you leave."

Vone's face stiffened. "We're not planning on leaving."

The old man didn't seem to register Vone's acid tone. "He's real friendly," he said to Jay-Jay encouragingly. "You can walk him on a leash just like a dog. I put it in there, along with his water bottle."

The little animal's nose and whiskers twitched and its black eyes glittered.

"Daddy, please can we keep him? *Please*?" Jay-Jay

implored.

Vone remembered the old hutch in the garage back at Number 13: it had looked sturdy enough. Maybe this gift – this loan – could offset the horribleness of what had happened to Pepper. "Okay," he said, though still reluctantly. His son's face brightened, and Vone thought how rarely Jay-Jay had smiled since they'd arrived. "What does it eat?" he asked, trying not to sound grudging.

"Worms, bugs, mostly. Fruit, even. Eggs when he can get 'em."

"What is it? Some kind of rat?"

"Mongoose."

"Does he have a name, Mr. Harris?" Jay-Jay asked.

"If he does, he never told me. Why don't you give him one?" the old man suggested. "You can tell me when you bring him back."

After thank yous and a stilted goodbye, Vone had the task of hauling Jay-Jay up in front of him while his son hugged the basket to him, and making sure he had a firm grip on it before they set off on their wobbly return journey.

As a result of the extra burden the cycle home was slower than the one to Timber Road had been, but, being familiar, felt shorter. At one point on the main road a logging lorry roared past them, veering alarmingly close, its wheels as high as Vone's shoulder, sending him wavering towards the broken verge, but that was their only scare, and a short while later he was pedaling his son and their new guest back through the Vicinity. The sun brushed the treetops ahead of them as Jay-Jay suggested increasingly random names for the animal. Vone had already vetoed 'Mong,' 'Mongie' and 'Goosie'. He suggested "Mink", which Jay-Jay misheard as "Mike", and somehow by the time they reached Number 13 it had been decided: Mike the mongoose. The poet in him was only slightly offended by the prosaic outcome so typical when you left things to a child's unbounded imagination.

After stowing the bike, Vone carried Mike's basket through to the kitchen. Then he went back out to the garage and struggled round with the hutch, which was solidly built and almost too heavy for him to lift. He felt his lower back muscles, not improved by the flabby mattress, start to tear as he lumbered the hutch along, but by setting it on his hips and leaning back he managed to stagger through to the kitchen and set it down without crippling himself. Down on his hands and knees, he slid it into a cozy corner near the stove.

After he and Jay-Jay had cleaned the hutch out – handily it was only dusty and dirty, rather than fouled – Vone went out and broke off some twigs from the overgrown herbaceous border in the front yard for Mike to nestle in. An old pillow-slip, folded up neatly in one corner for a bed, was a final homey touch. By chance the twigs were pleasantly aromatic: basil and thyme.

Then came the challenge of transferring Mike from basket to cage. Vone made sure the hall door was closed, and checked the baseboards. There were no obvious holes for him to escape down, though he could still dart under the stove or get behind the china hutch. Carefully Vone lifted the lid.

To his relief, Mike didn't immediately jump out and bolt for it. At first he kept crouched down; then, when he realized he wasn't being menaced, he stuck his head up, placed his front paws cutely on the basket's rim, and looked around, taking in his new environment. Vone knelt, close but not too close, encouraging Jay-Jay to do the same, and also to keep still and quiet. It was a joy to see the wonder in his son's eyes, especially after the nightmare with Pepper: Vone had been able to spare him nothing of that. His mind went back to the skin in the woods. Would critters be gnawing at it by now, dragging bits of it away? Or crows pecking?

But there were no beasts in the woods, and anyway why would they eat what had made him want to vomit? Gently Vone reached out to Mike, who pulled back, then grew curious, and with whiskers aquiver sniffed at his fingers.

Now he knew Mike didn't bite on reflex, Vone allowed Jay-Jay to do the same, and Jay-Jay giggled as Mike's warm snuffles tickled his fingertips.

"Okay," Vone said. "Let's see if we can –" Keeping his movements smooth, he reached into the basket and took hold of Mike carefully around the middle. The mongoose let itself be lifted and placed in the hutch, claws scrabbling at the chipboard as he set it down. He could feel its body warm and pulsing against his hands. Holding his breath, Vone released it, closed the mesh door and turned the wooden catch. Mike didn't at once fret to be let out; instead he began to explore his new home, sniffing and foraging around.

Relieved, Vone looked in the basket and took out the water bottle and the little leash and harness old man Harris had mentioned. He placed the leash on top of the hutch, filled the bottle at the faucet, running the water until it was lukewarm, and clipped it to the mesh so the drinking tube extended a decent length inside.

"Is Mike hungry, Daddy?" Jay-Jay asked.

"I guess he might be," Vone said, not relishing digging for worms in the backyard as dusk came on. Then he remembered: eggs. He went to the carton on top of the refrigerator and got one out, brown and speckled and heavy. He considered breaking it into a bowl, but then thought that surely a wild animal would recognize its own preferred food item. "Do you want to give it to him?" he asked his son.

Jay-Jay nodded. Vone placed the egg on his proffered palms, undid the catch and part-opened the door. Jay-Jay reached in and placed it carefully in front of Mike, who watched as the boy made his small obeisance. Vone shut the door and closed the catch, and he and Jay-Jay watched Mike sniff at the egg and paw at it, rotating it experimentally. After a short while he rolled onto his back and, holding the egg with all four paws, bit into the pointed end of it.

Vone noted Mike's incisors were very sharp, and realized he would have to put something down inside the cage to accommodate the little animal's inevitable pissing and shitting. Newspapers were what people used to use, but the only ones he had on hand were old, damp and rotten, and it didn't seem fair to Mike to choke him with their mold spores. He could take a couple of sheets from his son's scratch pad and shred them, he guessed: something to do later.

Jay-Jay brought his dinosaurs over to the hutch, to play parade facing his new pet's home. Vone fixed himself a mug of peppermint tea and sat at the table with Mamie Place's diary, contemplating but not at once opening it, as if the fact he could do so was what mattered, and in quantum anticipation of a probable dead end.

Dusk drew on. Soon he had to switch on the overhead

light.

"Can we let Mike run around?" Jay-Jay asked.

"Let's give him a day or two to get used to being here," Vone said. "We don't want him to vanish down a hole and have to tell Mr. Harris we lost him."

Jay-Jay nodded and went back to his game. Taking a sip of the tea, Vone opened the diary and once again contemplated the frontispiece. Then, to get an overall impression of what it contained, he leafed through the rest of it. The densely handwritten pages were at first fairly legible, but farther along were often partially or wholly stuck together, and the last third were badly damp-damaged.

The first entry was dated January 1, 1969, and began in a spidery hand, *Ordered shakes for the out house roof where its falling in. That hens not laying so good. Another prolapsed today so shes done. Off with her head. House v. cold. With the rumatism worse cutting kindlings hard but the cold makes it flare up more so I do it tho I'm weeping with the pain. No one to see me tho so it dont matter much.*

Vone scanned ahead. Most of the early entries were similarly commonplace, detailing a hard, fairly impoverished life. As with any diary not intended for other eyes it didn't give much context or explain names when mentioned. February 3 read, *Got a ready made cake from Larry's. Chocolate. Didn't let on it was my birthday. It was OK. Stomach ache after tho.* Vone wondered if that was an early symptom of the cancer that would go on to kill her. *Another shingles slipped, had to put out a bucket by the bed. Next to the comode. Irony.*

He turned more pages, depressed by Mamie Place's life, and discouraged by its being set down in a hand that was hard to read. His eye was caught by an entry that stood out because it had been more carefully written than those around it, the letters printed individually rather than scrawled. Undated, it followed on from a more usual-looking paragraph dated May 3, though was double-spaced to indicate a divide of some sort.

It must of come up from the well where they told me when I was a kid there was a village but the well water poisoned them and they all went mad and the children was put in homes and likely the adults too I dont recall. I found a story about it in that book from the library. It said not madness tho: mercury poisoning it said. But didn't say where the mercury come from because the writer didn't know much about it, or not what I know or guess.

Vone's mind went to the bright, metallic bead on Pepper's chest, and he read on more attentively. What followed was a series of mostly legible entries leading up to and through the Apollo moon landing of 1969, which took place on July 20.

July 3

To general store for kerosene. Then by Harrises. He was in and Sally F. werent and I was glad – no receptionist her, she wishes she was in a cocktail bar instead of behind a desk trying to block this crazy old lady, tell her how she smells, isnt welcome, too many weeds in her lawn et cetera. Sally F. thinks she is sophisticated but she is as shallow as any magazine and knows little of hard living and has never been to New York, not even once. She dont know I had adventures oncet, I wasn't always just here and nowhere else, even if that was years ago and I been here since, mostly quiet as a tree.

I went straight through to the back office and told Harris when I go, I mean kick the bucket, I can't just go, can I, I have that much responsibility, duty, I cant. When it is you who knows, it is all put on you. Especially things of this sort that most dont know and cant believe and if they did theyd be so sick with fear theyd run and not look back. Like I am now come nightfall and sometimes even in the day. I keep the shotgun by the door but own to the rumatism I dont know if I could pull a trigger now. Probably but breaking it open to load fresh cartridges I doubt, tho I keep plenty about, tho would it even be any use.

Okay so when I go this house it will likely go to some family aways off, they'll take property even if they can't stand to see me, never mind do nothing for me however hard up I am, on account of how I am and they dont approve. Its harsh and I don't especially forgive them for it. This house, if they don't sell it but rent it out, him being the only realtor in town Harris will get the bisness. I told him he is not to let to families with kids. And if he sells, the same, he must put them off. No kids, ever. I asked his word on it. He smiled and gived it too easy. I shall have to prove to him I know what I'm talking about or he won't stick by it. Your word dont mean much to the dead, I could tell he was thinking, and making money is more sacred than honor. He thinks its my Indian side, what I told him about why I am making the stipulation I am, didnt believe it of course. Hes partway right, about blood I mean, but not how he thinks he is. At church they look at Jesus up there on the cross and they think the Bible is old news and is the Beginning, the Word, alpha and then some time omega. They forget the things before alpha that are under the ground and older and will be there when the Bible is forgotten, Sheol and Hades for sure but creatures also that sleep and wake and then burrow up.

If I show him where I have to sleep at night maybe that will make all clear and he will believe. Because a family gets let in and I have not tried hard enough, it will be my fault. Also on account of what I had to do, had to even though I took it upon myself. My sacrifice, even if it was for others I don't even know. Future others. But do nothing and that is on you, we all know that. Also, anyone who does a thing, they are responsible for it.

I shall have to drive to C.-O. for medicine as what I am taking does not help much and ~~some~~ most is out of date. I am so much alone, always have been, but these days I am feeling it. Of course being how I am I do not care to be examined by doctors, they are never kind and sometimes downright cruel. They do not help.

Harris said he would come by the house. But maybe that was only to be rid of me and my b.o. He probly fucks S.F. or would like to.

July 7

TV talk is of a man going to be put on the Moon, all round here very excited like its the be all and end all. He must be American because otherwise we would look bad to the world and to ourselves. Beating the Reds to it because they beat us into space means money is no object, taxes I pay can all go on that not to the poor. Because America must do it or else. The men in the store were gathered round the radio when I went in for milk and flour discussing it like it means something to them personally, everyone had an opinion, if I went in the bars the same no doubt. The world of men I never understood even though they would say I was one once on account of things about my body, not that anyone round here remembers back to that, not now, the War dividing much, and kin keep well clear. If theyre still alive I would not know nor I suppose be told if they had passed away.

I been thinking and my thoughts is about the old Indian mound aways back in the woods, what some call The Breast, irony. Ive been thinking how if you dug into it you would find something you would likely regret. You would find how something put there had burrowed out sideways. Granite and buried stones the size of barns a great roof over all but in the cracks and under and around them mud or silt and small spaces could be made if a worm had patience and could swallow enough dirt and shit its way forward for decades.

Something about where I live makes people look past stuff mostly. Only not me.

Round here used to be called the Oziwaldam Trail, that was before houses and streets, and I believe that word means She Is Lonely, so all was known back then but then forgot about. Easier to go to church, or get drunk and forget that way I guess but I haven't drunk liquor for 20 years and I figured out some more. To start with I thought it was in my head but then I learnt it wasnt. Theres no one I can talk to about this, theyd put me away. I was put away for a spell oncet before, after New York, they said I werent right, needed fixing. I dont remember much of that but I dont trust doctors thats for sure.

Now I'm afraid all the time. And I aint mad. Weren't then, aint now.

July 10

Last night found myself wandering the back yard in the moonlight in just my night dress. My feet got cut up on the trash laying about I dont get round to clearing. Thats when

I knew for sure: Shes got her ways. They acted real funny at the hardware store this morning when I said did they have a chain and padlock. They know I dont have a dog. I said I was planning on getting one, for company I said, made some small talk about it, what breed was best, not needing fussing over &c, until they got bored and it was just more Mad Mamie stuff like when I asked for a big box of chalk. A normal person you wouldnt think why they might want chalk. With me its a topic, which is not fair. Starting a schoolhouse they asked, meaning stupid old bitch. And I am old, Im old and tired and no one gives two fucks about me. Only Harris is even a bit kind and of course thats pity, or most of it is, the rest is probably curiosity. Callous youth. Callow youth. Cotton candy freakshow youth.

Maybe I should get a dog. At least it would [illegible]

With the chain I can sleep and not rely overmuch on chanting words and drawing with chalk and lighting candles. She's not all magical, thats for sure maybe not even one bit, but She believes stuff just like we do. People, I mean. You believe in it then faith partway works, for Her like everyone. For her and against her is the thing. Like you can pray for your cancer to go and if it does thats Jesus but maybe it would have gone anyway, or maybe you thought it away, the power of that, brain power. Then when it comes back you get to praying again. Then you die.

Another thing I learned, it came in a dream: my totem is an owl.

July 15

Its gone wrong Im cursed it wont work. You bind and you get bound and you can even die and not get free of it. It goes two ways like duty. What binds her binds me. The way I am, this is what I am here to do. I never did find any meaning to my life when I was wandering but this is it, I guess. No one will know, ever, except I have to tell Harris, especially with the tumor. No one else, and thats hard because I have vanity like any woman. Or man, because what man goes to war if no one would ever know about it? I cry at night and I don't trust the grave will stop that.

July 16

Neighbors was pissed yesterday on account of I scolded the Jasper boys for target shooting back of my house. Why my house and not theirs is what I want to know. I heard the crack of air guns and went out mad. I shouldnt of took the hammer tho, that was my mistake, it made me look nuts. Then their old man was mad at me, told me theyre not my woods are they, anyone can go in them cant they, and all I could say was yeah but they might not come back out, and there I was holding a hammer and saying what he called threats. He went away saying he would call the cops on me, or the funny farm, get me taken away. Theyre only six and seven he said. Exactly, I said but he didnt get it, I mean of course he didnt. I'm not careful I could get put away again and then thered be no protection for any of them, much as I dont give a fuck. Its hard when theres no appreciation for what youre doing. I got dirty looks when I went in the store this morning so the news has got around of the latest by Mad Mamie.

July 17

She keeps her distance for now but I can feel Her pulling at me in dreams that maybe arent. If she comes in my mind do I see into Hers, I wonder. Maybe, or Im going mad on top of it all, for sure theres stress enough. I tested the clock work timer and it worked so that keeps me partway OK night times. It was hard to explain to Evan without going into what it was for but he took my money and my drawing of how it was to work and put it down to the usual Mamie Place weirdness. Evenings I have the radio, then downstairs theres no reception so I do my puzzles. Its no kind of a life and I dont much care about being dead except in relation to what Ive been going on about in these pages and my one chance to do right.

Of course theres things past being dead. Dead aint done. Never was. Ask Christ.

July 18

I guess I may as well put down what I did in this diary so

*others will have a clue if they come on this record of my
thoughts and doings. I took a piece of the old bundle my father left behind with the owl feathers on and the bits of he
said it was buckskin, wishing I could remember more of the
things his mother, that is my grandmother used to tell me as
a child. She told my father how what I was, or what I was
likely to become, was fine because it was a part of the old
ways, but Daddy didnt hear, or didnt listen, just got mad and
cursed her out and beat me for it. So I was close to her, I mean
in warm feelings, but I did not listen overmuch to her tales so
remember them only cloudily, and Daddy never told me any
tales at all, maybe on account of his not listening to her either, and for a time thinking he could go out into the white
man's world and make his mark, being half breed and not
visibly so to most white men.*

*He left only a few things behind him when he went for
good, maybe intending to come back, but didnt, and that
bundle was one. I wrapped a snakeskin round it, like for like,
so She would get the idea to keep off. She has ways of knowing a lot of what goes on inside my head. Then I got the twine
and I wound it round and round, and all the time I said over
and over*

> *Kita kita kita*
> *Bind and bind and bind*
> *This lady, this madahôdo*
> *To this hunting ground.*

July 19

*Harris saw enough last night. So many snakes, he said, all
come here. He understands why, or partly. He wont let to
families, not with little ones or where the woman is pregnant,
when Im gone. I didnt even need to ask his word this time.
We agreed what needed doing if I dont come through this,
he'll take care of the cellar and everything. Hes young and
has family here, a long line back to settler times so he wont
leave, and thats what I need, one whos tied by blood, enemy
oncet or not. The enemy of my enemy is my friend.*

*Did they ever burn a witch I asked, meaning: your kin.
Doing the burning or being burnt, he asked. Either I said.*

Probably he said, I never cared to try and find out, and he laughed, and thats good, because too much easy believing is a bad thing.

July 20

In the general store this morning all the talk was of the moon landing which is supposed to be happening tonight. Folks with big teevee sets are having parties, buying beer. Of course no one is inviting me. Since I started tying in the feathers and chicken bones theyve been more distant. Even Harris says why dont I try to look more normal. But theres a point where its too late for that, and Im at it or past it a long time ago. They call me ma'am, miss, missus and thats normal enough for me, thats my victory

I came home with the papers and sat and read em and thought how strange this great ball of rock came wandering across the sky and got caught, spinning round us like we spin round the sun. How come its the exact size to block the sun and make an eclipse? The odds of that. I dont believe in any big plan but its something anyhow.

As a child my uncle had an orrery of brass he liked to show me when we visited. You turned a handle and the planets went round the Sun and their moons went round them proportionate. He taught me about clockwork and was pleased to find I had an aptitude, or an interest anyway which is maybe the same thing. I earned a little that way for a while, till I was too much in the middle of my journey to be seen as one thing or the other so not acceptable even in a little room out the back. Why I went to New York. And come back as someone else. As myself. Started over. So many coming and going in wartime and many not coming back at all helped. Many links broken. Many changed.

Strange this split world of rockets and teevees and electricity: the future. And then theres the past, pushing up like old tree roots breaking through asphalt, wanting to become the future too and there's only room for one of the two. Both frighten me. There was a rape in one of the trailers last week. The world has always been divided up this way: predators and prey.

July 25

*Pain all night. Cant see how it wont be the hospital again. I
wont see no local croaker though, just the pharmacist to get
the scrip filled. Not be the subject of talk, even a doc will fail
to be close-mouthed when it comes to scandal like mine, Id go
to Bangor. Leave this. Dont know as its set up safe but who
would? Its not normal knowledge, and the only proof is
things dont happen or else they do, fuck up I mean, and you
got it wrong, and why should any of it work anyway. Hanging the skins and bones was my idea, but it's the chants and
chalk She cant get past, or not without it costs her a lot of
something. But Im old and sick and She comes in the house
now. I hear Her overhead at night, dragging around.*

*Long nights I think of New York a lot. Downtown, Time
Square, though I didnt have the confidence at first to do what
the pretty ones did there, for money. There was a riot in the
Village last month, June, and the news came even here. Days
it went on, I read. Homos and queens and drags throwing
bricks and bottles. Changing the world more I think than that
man putting a foot on the moon which what difference does
that make really. Folks here laughed about it of course, and
I didnt say anything but it took me back to my free days. I
remember the cops and their metal eyes and their disdainful
mouths, how you can be in a human body and not human to
others, but also I thought of the rest of us, sitting on stoops in
the Village in the baking hot sun, when for a short while I
belonged.*

I went in that bar once. Nothing special.

Maybe theres something can be done for me in Bangor.

Probably too late.

August 3

*Mostly this diary is for me but I think at times it could be of
use to others for the one specific thing, so I started putting
down the special words and marks and shapes, working
from the back cover inwards, though words without belief
probably do little, like it says in the Bible or is it the other way
round.*

My grandmother was a tale teller, and I used to go out and sit on the mound sometimes and think about her, when she was long gone and I first came back here and was mostly alone, D. being long gone too, him being a homo and wanting cock.

Sometimes I think my thinking woke the thing up though I suppose thats a vanity like the rest. I mean even the men who made the Atom Bomb did it a piece at a time with others all along the way, not like one day someone took a hammer and wham. The mound was a peaceful place for me back then, tho I dont dare go there now. It was hard for me to get there for a time because of my surgery didnt go so well at first, I shuffled and leaked, but then it was better. On summer days I would make my way out there, climb up it and I didnt care about polecats or bears because I would even sleep out there beneath the pines and dream.

I wonder if our dreams give her shape. I know she gets in our minds, or at least gets stuff out of our minds, because you cant inherit learning, I know that much, you have to come by it and take it in. My child wouldnt know a book I read unless I told em it, if I had a child. Which I dont.

Sometimes I guess I envy Her.

But this is about when I first knew there was something in the woods.

I woke from a dream. The moon was full and bright and I was on the mound. It was cold even tho it was June, like something was drawing off the warm. I looked down to the track that walks its way round the mound like underwiring on a bra. I couldnt see much because of the foliage being summer thick. Then through the leaves I saw what looked like a stream of mercury or molten lead, or water catching moonlight, and it rippled and moved along quick. It was strange but I wasnt afraid, not to start with. I went down and followed it, and part of me was choosing and part of me was drawn. The choosing part kept me hanging back, the other following. I saw it go down the old well, and then I came home. I caught the influenza or something that night because after that I was sick for a whole month. Vomiting, shitting. I would see wild things, hallucinations, and that was when She got in my head I guess. I heard her rattle and started to work things out. I suppose she couldnt go in my mind without leaving something of herself behind.

You have to give to get, I guess.

My stomach is swollen bad and Im in agony. The damp dont help.

My spirit animal is an owl, Vone thought. And: *They call me the Owl Lady on account of the feathers in my hair.*

The pages that followed were glued together by damp, and Vone's attempts to pry them apart were entirely unsuccessful. Remembering reading somewhere of a technique for saving a book if you dropped it in the tub, he put the book in the freezer compartment of the refrigerator, leaving it in there while he fixed supper. Distractedly he hummed "Gimme a Pigfoot and a Bottle of Beer" as he seasoned pork chops, lay them in a casserole dish on a bed of quinoa, then peeled sweet potatoes to roast in a tin along with red peppers, zucchinis and a thinly-sliced eggplant. That took about forty minutes, during which time he made a conscious effort not to think about anything; to feel instead the thingness of things. Then he retrieved the diary from the icebox.

Wiping down the knife, carefully he inserted the blade, and levering with patience, managed to split apart two pages that had seemed irrevocably fused together. What he saw there made him put his hand to his mouth.

Twenty-Four

Taking up a full page of the diary was a pen-and-ink drawing that was undoubtedly an attempt to depict the creature Vone had seen pressing its face through the sheets; the creature whose shed skin had been hung in the woods. The drawing was stylized rather than naturalistic: the thing's serpentine coils corkscrewed off into the background in a neat spiral and its front part rose up stiff and straight, the better to demonstrate its spread cobra hood. But it had the particular proportional accuracy that comes from observation rather than invention. Vone noted how in Mamie Place's representation the single central fang in the upper jaw was apparently the product of two incisors twisted round each other and fusing to make a single point, like a narwhal's tusk, perhaps allowing simultaneously both injection and extraction.

Above the drawing was printed, in letters gone over several times for emphasis but producing a blotted effect, *Skog Madahôdo, Mother of Serpents*. Below was written: *a childs soul for each egg she hatches.*

Vone's hackles stiffened, though it was only the confirmation of what he had already guessed. Or more than guessed: known. For it seemed from the beginning a knowledge bone-deep in him, or perhaps soul-deep was more accurate – something he had access to that Jack did not. Had his psychotic episode opened a door into other worlds, other minds? He had always considered any such notion the worst kind of new age bullshit, but now he wondered if there might not be something to it after all. And he thought of the phrase "poet as shaman," and of the – surely true – idea that there were other sorts of knowing than the merely analytic, taxonomic and quotidian.

Yet what could he do with this other knowledge, which was of a particularly deniable sort? The drawing had horrified him only because he had seen its source. Others – Jack for sure – would dismiss it as a proto-*Dungeons & Dragons* doodle, pitifully unscary and unconvincing. And Jack had seen Vone rave at invisible things suspended outrageously in the empty air; had had to commit his husband to a locked ward in a mental hospital and – and here was the kicker – had been right to do so. And he had seen Vone emerge two weeks later, a worn tire with a new tread, as Sylvia Plath put it, and slowly recover, and recovering meant returning to the world of normal perceptions: to what was understood by society as lucidity. How could Jack see all this, now, as anything other than backsliding into madness, Mamie Place's diary the record of another mind swallowed up by obsession and delusion. He would be frustrated. He would be frightened. He might even leave, and take Jay-Jay with him, and not Vone.

But there's the skin, remember. Proof.

Maybe he should have tried to drag it back to the house, get it in range of the WiFi, but the texture was too repulsive to handle even with gloves on, and anyway anything he pulled at tore and fell to bits. *Jack'll be home soon.*

Almost nothing in the rest of the diary was legible. On the inside back cover was a pentagram around which was drawn a circle. Sigils had been drawn in its sections, but over a third of them were lost to damp. Maybe he could cross-check the surviving ones against the partially-erased circle on the basement floor, fill in a few of the blanks.

Because that's not crazy at all.

He tried to think through what he'd learnt from the diary. *Treat it as a story: what's the logic, what's the narrative?* Witches summoned demons. Was that what Mamie Place had been trying to do? Clearly she was afraid of this creature, Skog Madahôdo, and the point of a chalk circle was to protect you from what you summoned up, or so all the spooky movies said. But Mamie had Native blood in her too, and that seemed more significant: she had mentioned a spirit animal, not a familiar; and despite the pentagram, what she wrote about seemed closer to the cosmology of the First Nations than Cotton Mather's witchery. What else? Something that had at some point been "'put'" in the old burial mound had burrowed its way along to the well-bottom and got out that way. Did Mamie Place mean there was a tunnel down there that ran all the way from the well to the burial mound? Vone briefly pictured himself being lowered into the dank dark. Whatever hid down there would have night vision, no doubt; or other senses, like the heat pits of spitting cobras.

A childs soul for each egg she hatches. Could digging into the mound help, striking at the creature's lair? *Make a shaft,* he thought. *Pour drain-cleaner in*. But excavating the mound was far too big a job for one man, in the context insane, and beyond that probably illegal. And the thing was already twenty-five feet long, and hadn't it shed its skin so it could grow larger still? If he poured anything into the mound – pre-supposing he could get gallons and gallons of Drano from somewhere and cart it all the way out there unremarked on – the creature would come out fast and pissed. And all of that was assuming it kept what had been its prison as its lair. Maybe it just slept curled up in the bottom of the well, or maybe somewhere else entirely.

A thump at the front door brought Vone back to reality. It was followed by a rattle at the letterbox and Jack's voice, shouting crossly, "Vone! What's going on with the door? I can't get it open."

"Hang on!" Vone called. He closed the diary and hurried through to the hall. Unbolting and unlocking the door, he opened it to his flush-faced husband, bags of groceries cradled awkwardly in both arms. They exchanged a brief kiss as Vone took one of the bags from him and set it down on the window seat. After Jack came in, Vone immediately closed, re-locked and re-bolted the door. Jack watched him, not saying any-thing, then headed for the kitchen. Vone called after him, "Watch out for the mongoose!"

"Jesus, Vone," Jack said when he saw the hutch, which now seemed uglier, bulkier and dirtier, but his annoyance was forestalled by their son's eagerness to have Dad squat down and meet his new pet, and by Mike's bright-eyed whisker-quivering.

Mike cheeped cutely. "Okay, okay." Jack threw up his hands. "But" – to Vone – "don't we discuss stuff like this any-more? I know I'm working all the time right now, and I'm sorry the weekend was a bust: that was a one-off because of the conference. It'll get easier soon, I promise. And we get the car tomorrow."

"Something's happened," Vone said.

Jack took in his expression. "What?" He glanced over at Jay-Jay, who was brushing his fingers along the mesh of the hutch to get Mike's attention. "Don't pester him, Jackie-Jacks."

"I'll show you," Vone said. "It's not far." To their son he said, "I'm going to show Dad where the fence is falling down. When we get the car tomorrow, we can go get some new pickets and fix it."

Jay-Jay didn't say anything, but looked worried when Vone picked up the axe from where it leant by the side door.

"Do I need to put on boots?" Jack still had on his work suit and office shoes.

"You'll be okay," Vone said, pulling back the bolts on the kitchen door.

Jack followed him out. Vone said nothing: he wanted him to see without preamble or interpretation. Afterwards he would show him the diary and the drawing.

Dusk had arrived by then, swallowing the last of the blue-gray air, and the temperature was sinking fast. Wordlessly the two men stepped through the gap in the fence. Jack followed close behind Vone as he forced his way through the bushes, screening his eyes from the twigs that sprang back in his face.

"Here it is," Vone said, working to keep the emotion out of his voice, indicating with the axe head what lay stretched out on the ground, not looking at it directly. *No observer effect, no Schrödinger's Cat.* All was in shadow now.

Jack squatted down to examine the gray length. He reached out towards it but didn't touch it. After a while he looked up at Vone, and his eye sockets were shadowed. "It's – I don't know what this is, Vone. Fungus, maybe. I dunno. Don't some kinds of insects spin webs like this? Autumn moths or something?"

All Vone's attention had been on his husband's response. Now he looked down and saw the thing through Jack's eyes and his heart sank. In the few short hours since it had fallen from the tree it had rotted into an indeterminate gray mess. No structure remained at all, the scales had dissolved into a textureless blancmange, and the face as he tried to turn the hood over with the axe-blade fell apart entirely. Even the stink of it had dwindled to no worse than an acrid tang. He made his way along to the tail, to point out the terrible rattle of faces, but found only a series of gray blobs like the decaying fruiting bodies of some large fungus, puffballs or earthballs.

Jack stood up. His expression was hard to read. "Let's go back in," he said. "Junior'll be getting worried."

"Shit," Vone said abruptly. "We didn't lock the back door."

"Vone, we're right —"

But Vone was already pushing past his husband and hurrying back to the gap in the fence. From there he saw light spilling from the side door, meaning it was open, and he knew he had closed it. His chest tightened, but as he crossed the yard he saw Jay-Jay lean out, wondering where his daddies were. Setting the axe down as he reached him, Vone swept his son up in a hug. He barely noticed Jack stoop behind him and slide the axe out of harm's way, under the steps.

They went inside. Vone locked and bolted the kitchen door; Jack went through to the front of the house, noisily unbolted and unlocked the front door and went out to the station wagon for the rest of his stuff. Vone started to unpack the groceries, pausing to listen as Jack came back in. Would he relock the door? He did, and after a silent moment shot the bolts across too. Then he came through to the kitchen with his briefcase, laptop bag and a stack of files, which he dumped down on the breakfast table. He noticed Mamie Place's diary with its snakeskin cover but didn't touch it. "I'm gonna shower," he said, and went upstairs.

Vone's mind was blank. Once again he was powerless. He had been brought face to face with what amounted to a crack in the world, a crack in what is called reality, one through which his life – all their lives – were in sudden terrible danger of tumbling; a world in which there were revealed to be monstrous forces beyond nature, at least earthly nature; forces, entities that could terrorize and destroy, and here he was, confounded by evidence that melted away like frost, or a dream. Alone.

What about that girl from the eighties who had ended up in a mental hospital and had apparently spent the rest of her life there? She knew, didn't she? He could seek her out. But was she even still alive? Then again, for all he knew her "lifelong incarceration" was just a tall tale. She might have been released three months later and be living a totally normal life, running one of the stores in Gaugeville – maybe the Crab Pot diner, and the chubby waitress was her daughter by a second, happy marriage. Or maybe, just maybe, she too had confronted the shattering of human vanity; had seen the carapace of family, community and faith, of streets and automobiles and railroads, telephone wires and radio waves, disintegrate and fall away, and what lies beneath rise up strange and predatory and above all real. And she had killed her boyfriend with an axe, which had been a real, a concrete act. What had led him to kill their son? Or had it been him?

Poisoned by mercury, Ted had said.

A child's soul for each egg she hatches.

Vone's thinking started to accelerate, becoming garbled, and panic rose up in him. He focused on putting the groceries away. Butter here, milk there... If he tried to take Jay-Jay away – and they would have to go right now, while Jack was in the shower, because for sure Jack wouldn't believe anything he said from here on in; would try to stop him – he and his son could get away. Jack would follow, puzzled, angry, threatening, but all that mattered was to get Jay-Jay beyond Skog Madoo's range, this ophidian horror that squirmed with a terrible hunger back and forth between the well and the mound, and surely Number 13 was its triangulation point as it hunted for children to carry away. *For our child.*

But what was its range? Gaugeville? Surely Collington-Osprey would be safe. Briefly he imagined state-wide conspiracies of covens, worshippers, enablers. And then he remembered there had been birdsong in the Vicinity: in the Vicinity, but not on Cottonwood Way. Cottonwood Way, also known as the Bounds. Perhaps it had always been a boundary of sorts.

And if Vone wondered then, and he did, whether he was mad, or deluded, wasn't there always, behind everything, horror? Slavery, genocide of the Indians, the Holocaust, the Rwandan genocide, Hitler, Stalin, Mao, Pol Pot, Leopold of Belgium, AIDS; the gaudy, bloody march of European imperialism; the tantalum in every cell phone that was mined by child slaves in Congo, and everyone had a cell phone and everyone didn't think about the tantalum. And though those phones didn't, as it turned out, cause brain tumors to grow, wasn't the metastasizing group mind of social media causing a cancer of madness, a near-schizophrenic assault of endlessly blatting, hate-filled voices telling you that you didn't deserve to exist, telling you to kill yourself? Wasn't the shadow more consuming than the light? And wouldn't the Earth itself, with humanity long ago in ashes, end as a cold and lifeless rock orbiting an extinguished sun? And if all that was true, and it was, then what was it to believe in this one uncanny creature? Why couldn't he get Jack to –

Standing at the counter, he began to hit himself in the face with the heel of his hand. He got to a count of eight before Jay-Jay grabbed at his waist, crying, "Daddy! Daddy! Stop! You're hurting yourself!"

Blinking back tears, Vone slid down onto the kitchen floor, his back against one of the storage units. He let Jay-Jay hug him around the neck, and hugged him back, and couldn't reply when his son said, "Please don't hurt yourself, Daddy. I love you," because he was too choked.

They hugged for what felt like a long time, and Vone thanked god that Jack chose to take a long shower, because by the time he came back down, though Vone was still sitting on the floor, and his eyes were visibly swollen and red, he was amiably playing dinosaurs with their son.

Jack didn't comment on Vone's tear-bruised eyes in Jay-Jay's presence, and there followed several hours of quietly performative normality, during which he did admin and Vone finished fixing dinner and laid the table. Then Jack put his laptop and papers away and the three of them ate together.

Vone pushed from his mind thoughts of fleeing the house, and tried to attend to his husband's monologue about having to stretch the budget to near breaking point; how the Black woman he'd originally liked was turning out to have a problem for every solution, and how he'd had to struggle to ensure trans issues were included in the information pack in the face of transphobic political pushback. There was also some sort of zoning problem that Vone couldn't follow. Jack risked a joke. "Did you know that in Abenaki, that's a tribe, k'wawidokawa means 'you are being warned?' So Kwawidokawa County literally means 'you're being warned county' and they got *that* right when it comes to b.s. about business regulations, and how if you're part state-funded are you wheelchair accessible but of course there's zero money for you to pay to have a ramp or elevator installed if you aren't."

"'You're being warned'?"

"There's another one, I forget. Oh yeah: the hills north of the house. Oz something. Ozwildam. It means, 'She is lonesome'." Then, realizing he was pushing the conversation towards the sinister, Jack changed the subject to a wrangle with a local proudly "Christian" printer. "It'll be the wedding cake war all over again," he said. "And I don't wanna have to go all the way to the Supreme Court just to get some workbooks printed. Especially not *this* Supreme Court."

"You could use another printer."

"Yeah. And they don't deserve the business anyway, with their shitty can't-do attitude. But they don't deserve to be let off the hook either."

She is lonesome, Vone thought.

The Abenaki knew.

They knew, but what good did it do them?

Twenty-Five

J ack put Jay-Jay to bed a little after eight p.m. Vone washed the dishes, anxiety surging through him uselessly. *Where is it what's it doing what's it planning? The well then the woods then the backyard then –*

Thinking an extra clonazepam might help, he went upstairs. By chance or intention he moved quietly, and reaching the landing heard his husband's voice coming from Jay-Jay's room, its tone low and serious. Though he knew he shouldn't, Vone couldn't resist sneaking along to eavesdrop.

Through the hinge gap he could see Jack sitting on the pirate chest. Turning Dippy in his hands, he was looking down at the plastic toy. "You know how Daddy was ill before?" he said.

Jay-Jay was out of Vone's sightline, but Vone heard him say, "Uh-huh."

"I'm worried –" Jack choked, then went on: "I think Daddy's getting ill again. He'll get better," he added quickly. "He'll be alright. But we need to help him by not mentioning anything strange or spooky."

"You mean the Owl Lady," Jay-Jay said.

"Talking about anything like that'll only make him sicker."

"But, Dad, she's –"

"*Please*, Jackie-Jacks. It's really important. We both love Daddy very much, don't we?"

"Uh-huh."

"And he was upset earlier, wasn't he?"

"When?"

"When I came down and you were both sitting on the floor." Evidently Jay-Jay nodded. "So will you promise?" Silence. "Okay, good."

As Jack bent forward to give their son an out-of-shot kiss, Vone slipped away to the main bedroom and got a pill. He made sure to click the bottle fully closed afterwards, then splashed water on his face. Everything around him was mundane. *The thingness of things*, he thought. The fluorescent light had no magic. A small black beetle lay dead in a corner, its legs in the air. It had no greater meaning. He was an ordinary man in an ordinary bathroom in an ordinary world, and the enamel of the basin was smooth and cool against the hot palms of his hands.

When he went back down to the kitchen he found Jack fixing a fresh pot of coffee. "Robusta," he said, sounding pleased. "And organic. Who says Collington-Osprey's stuck in the '70s?"

"It's *The Twilight Zone* episode Rod Sterling forgot to write," Vone said, taking a seat at the breakfast table. Jack didn't seem ready to sic the men in white coats on him quite yet.

"Oh, I got these too." Jack produced a box of almond biscotti, the same brand they used to have back in Brooklyn. "First thing tomorrow we pick up the rental car," he went on, coming over and sitting by Vone and filling their mugs. "Then you won't be marooned here. You can meet me after work in C.O. some days, and we can all go for dinner together. Next weekend I promise I'll be home and we can do family stuff, moose trails, maybe a boat trip or something."

Vone nodded. He had meant to say, *You think I'm going crazy again. You think I can't even be at home minding our son for one week without going off the rails. You see me in terms of medication and looming institutionalization. I need you to not lose sight of me; to not let me vanish under the diagnosis. I need you to see me as the man you proposed to on one knee on that terrace on the edge of Brooklyn, with Manhattan as the backdrop, plighting your troth as the Hasidim passed indifferently by, one muggy August afternoon in the dappled shade of a willow tree, and I said yes, and you cried. I need that and I'm afraid.* Instead he said, "We're not safe here."

"We're perfectly safe here," Jack said. "Just because there's some weird storeroom in the basement that's been made into –"

"We should sleep down there," Vone said. "You, me and Junior."

Jack sighed. "That's just – I'm sorry, Vone, we're not gonna do that. We're not gonna give in to this." The mongoose chirruped in its cage. "And that thing goes back to where it came from, okay, first thing in the morning. What were you thinking?"

"But Jay-Jay –"

"Yeah, well, sometimes you have to be a parent and disappoint him."

"Fuck you."

"No, fuck *you*." Jack got up, stalked from the room and clomped upstairs. A minute later he returned with Vone's pill bottle. "I know you haven't been taking them," he said, tipping the pills out onto the table. Vone watched balefully as Jack counted them, and observed his husband's righteous anger turn to embarrassment: there were in fact, as Vone knew would be the case, several fewer than there were supposed to be.

"I didn't know you secretly counted my pills," Vone said bitterly. "I guess you really don't trust me."

Jack's face flushed as he carefully swept the pills back into the bottle. "I'm sorry," he said, screwing the cap until it clicked. "And I'm sorry I worry. I can't help it. What am I supposed to do?"

Vone twitched an angry shrug and they turned to each other and hugged awkwardly. Though it resolved nothing, the contact made him feel more anchored in the world of people and daylight. "We'll get through this," Jack said.

Again, rather than what he had meant to say – something in humble gratitude for that "we" – Vone found himself saying thickly, "Something is going on in this house."

Jack released him. "It's not the house, Vone, it's –"

"What? What is it?"

Jack avoided his eyes. "I was thinking of having Mom to stay," he said. "Just for a couple of days. I know she's a pain, but she offered, and you know she wants to make up for having been such a shit parent by being an all-star Nanna. And Jackie's really fond of her."

"Yeah, because she gives him stuff we say she shouldn't because it costs too much."

"She'd be some grown-up company for you."

Vone, who found Jack's garrulous, evangelically twelve-stepped mother exhausting and hard not to argue with, was about to reply tactlessly when the doorbell rasped, making them both look round. "Rory," he sighed.

"I'll go," Jack said, getting up from the table.

Vone managed a "Thanks, man." He listened to Jack unlock, unbolt and open the door. Then cringed as Jack said, "Yes, officer?"

"Is everything alright, sir?"

Vone reckoned the voice belonged to one of the cops who had stopped him and Jay-Jay in the Vicinity.

"Yes, why wouldn't it be?"

"Neighbors reported a disturbance," the voice said blandly.

"There's no disturbance," Jack said.

"Can we come in, sir?"

"Why?"

Vone held his breath as the cop said, "Your – friend – was seen earlier, acting in a way that made people uneasy." *That bitch*, Vone thought. *I fucking knew it.* "And there were reports of raised voices. And with a young boy in the house..."

"My husband, not my friend," Jack said, his tone bland, and Vone knew all too well the cost of maintaining such blandness. "And that boy is our son."

Vone could picture the smirks on the cops' faces. "Neighbors said an axe was being used."

"My husband was using our axe on our property earlier, to break up some old crates for firewood," Jack said.

"There are clean air ordinances in this county, sir."

"There's smoke coming out of both those chimneys over there," Jack said.

The other cop, who hadn't spoken before, but who Vone had known would be there, said, "And the raised voices?"

The whole thing was naked dog-whistle bullshit, but Jack said, "We had a row. Just like you probably do, if you're married. Are either of you married?" – an edge of defiance creeping in. Vone felt the smothered rage he always felt when whiteness meant you could get away with shit that if you were Black could get you Tasered or shot. Even though this particular white man was his husband, defending him and their home and their child, still it stung.

"We're just doing our job, sir," Cop #2 said. "This is a decent neighborhood. We take child endangerment seriously."

There was a long moment during which some threat was implied, or at least the cops wouldn't let shit go, because Jack called in a tight-throated voice, "Vone, could you fetch Junior down, please?"

With a feeling of strangled resentment, Vone got up from the table and went through to the front hall. Jack was blocking the doorway against the two officers. As he'd expected, they were the same pair as the other day. "He'll be asleep," he said flatly. The cops said nothing, just stared at him with bovine hostility. "He'll be scared. He's scared of the police."

It had no more impact than addressing a complaint to a pair of cinder blocks, so he went upstairs. He found Jay-Jay awake and indeed, he was afraid.

"C'mon, Jackie-Jacks," Vone said, turning back the duvet and getting him out of bed. "We got to prove to the po-po we treat you right, okay?" His tense attempt at a smile didn't elicit one in return, though Jay-Jay let himself be lifted out of bed, clinging to his Daddy's neck as, with building reluctance, Vone carried him down, as demeaned as what – a maid? A junkie mom confronted by The Welfare? His own mom?

Jack moved back slightly as Vone approached, not enough for the cops to step over the threshold, but so Vone had room to stand alongside him. Vone found himself unable to not stare at the cops with undisguised dislike. But then, what advantage came from concealing it? Playing nice got you maced, beaten, choked and shot too. What was that Zora Neale Hurston line? *If you are silent about your pain, they'll kill you and say you enjoyed it.*

"This is Jack Junior," Jack said, lifting Jay-Jay from Vone's arms, and Vone hated this: their child being presented to the contemptuous agents of white power for them to look upon as they chose, when they chose and for as long as they chose, their indifferent gaze in and of itself a violation. Did his white husband feel this way, he wondered. Surely he did, even as he said in a forced, light register a notch off a crack, "Jackie, these are the police, checking that we're all okay."

Jay-Jay kept his face buried in his dad's neck, but he was obviously clean and well-fed, and had after all been pulled from his bed at a responsibly early hour. The cops dragged the moment out. Then the first one who had spoken said, "Thank you for your assistance, sir."

Jack said with careful neutrality, "Thank you for your concern, officer." He and Vone watched the cops saunter back to their cruiser, take their time getting in, sit there a while before starting up the engine, do a leisurely three-point turn and drive away.

Up and down the street, for the first time since their arrival, lights were on behind most of the drapes and shutters; and for the first time also Vone saw, standing on the porch of the house diagonally across from theirs, one of their neighbors, an older white woman with lank, shoulder-length brown hair. She wore a full-length pink padded silk housecoat, and seeing him staring at her, threw down a cigarette and went back inside.

While Jack took Jay-Jay back upstairs, Vone closed and locked the door, pushed the bolts across and hooked on the safety chain.

Back in the trap.

Twenty-Six

They didn't return to the argument they had been having earlier: after the encounter with the cops it would have been too draining and futile, and they needed to pull together. Instead they sat in Jay-Jay's room and made up a silly story to distract him, Vone providing the narrative (he was good at improvising situations) and Jack, who was good at voices, the dialogue. And if Oscar the Ocelot sounded suspiciously like Porky Pig, keeping the story going took their minds off what had just happened, at least for the duration of the tale.

Once Jay-Jay was settled, Vone and Jack went back down to the kitchen. There Vone pressed the diary on his husband. With a sigh, Jack opened it, reading bits near the start, then flicking through the rest. Vone watched for his reaction as he came to the drawing of Skog Madahôdo, but Jack passed over it in search of some revelation he didn't find.

I'm alone in this, Vone thought, sitting with hunched shoulders as Jack closed the book. It was the breakdown all over again: the sense you possessed insights and knowledge no one else could understand, insights that you didn't understand yourself, and so could not explain.

"I don't know what you want me to see," Jack said.

"The drawing," Vone said, though he knew it was futile. "It's Jay-Jay's Skog Madoo. And Mamie Place literally calls herself the Owl Lady. Or she says other people do. And that was back in 1969."

Jack's face stiffened. Wordlessly, he got to his feet. Vone watched as he crossed to the counter, picked up the electric drill and headed down to the cellar. Shortly afterwards there came the sound of planks being dragged about, then the whirr of the drill.

Suddenly realizing what Jack must be doing, Vone got up and hurried down after him. He found his husband reinstating the shelving in front of the secret door. Grabbing at his wrists, Vone tried to wrestle the drill off him. Startled, Jack resisted, and they struggled round the dusty, low-ceilinged room, each trying to push the other off-balance, the drill the prize, the light swinging crazily overhead. In all the years of their relationship they had never fought physically. Now they were staring into each other's eyes as they staggered about, their hips banging painfully against the corner of the washing machine, battling for mastery until eventually the drill went flying. It hit the concrete floor, its housing shattered and internal parts went skittering brightly away.

The destruction broke the moment. Vone stepped back from Jack and put up his hands. Jack's chest was heaving and he looked scared, and Vone knew he was afraid not of occult horrors but of himself, of this man who was a crucial few inches taller than him, stronger than him, and right now crazier than him.

"I'm sorry," Vone said, then again, "I'm sorry." He opened his arms, hoping for a hug, aware as if he were someone else looking on of the bulk of his biceps and chest. *Like some monster crab, chitinous carapace, cold from the sea. No: a big Black man. Just that. Even so, see me. Hug me. Please.*

Jack did hug him, but warily, patting him on the back as perhaps a colleague might: that disavowal of genuine intimacy you see among straight men afraid to go too far. Vone enfolded Jack as if he were something delicate, something precious, and Jack allowed him to. Encouraged, he hugged Jack tighter. Jack hugged him back, and the heat of their bodies was healing. "We should go to bed," Jack said quietly, and Vone nodded.

Jack had managed to put three of the planks back up, at neck, hip and knee height, spaced strategically to make clambering through them to the inner door, though it opened inwards, extremely difficult. He went up first, a gesture of trust. Making no attempt to clear up the broken drill parts, Vone followed him.

Once they were both back in the kitchen, Jack locked and bolted the basement door. Together they passed through the house, turning the lights off as they went, and to Vone it was as if each room ceased to exist as the darkness swallowed it. And after all, wasn't life like that, a series of exits? And then you came to a final door and passed through that.

*

He brushed his teeth until he was spitting blood in the basin. He couldn't take any more anti-anxiety meds for another eighteen hours or he'd overdose. Instead he scrubbed his face with a soapy facecloth, rinsed it off, then studied his features in the mirror. His expression was haunted but not crazy, and he knew crazy when he saw it. No: this was different.

Different because real. Abstractly he moisturized. The aroma of rosemary and bergamot was something from another world, another life.

Jack was reading in bed, frowning over some report or other, asserting the primacy of the everyday world and being an anchor and exemplar for his troubled husband – or no, Vone was overthinking, like always: Jack was just getting on with the things he had to, to earn a living and pay the bills, like everyone does who has never had to face the truly uncanny. Contemplating him from the bathroom doorway, Vone felt as if he were watching someone in a small rowboat being born away on a riptide, and the riptide was his, Vone's, mind, and he himself was treading water frantically, the heels of his bare feet thudding against the cold but living backs of cruising sharks or snapping turtles or who knew what else, all the while doing his best to appear calm and normal on the surface. "I'll go check on Jackie," he said.

"Don't frighten him," Jack said, shooting him a warning glance.

"I won't. I promise."

Vone found Jay-Jay awake and sucking his thumb for comfort, which he didn't usually do nowadays. *At least he doesn't seem afraid of me*, he thought as he sat on the toy chest, though Jay-Jay was watchful in a way a child shouldn't have to be. Vone was about to ask if he was okay, then didn't. He had always disliked that sort of question as a child: simultaneously too open and too insincere, it invited only the "correct" response "Yes," to save the other person worry or trouble. Instead he said, "I think the Owl Lady is our friend."

"I don't think she can help us, though," Jay-Jay said.

"Why not?"

"Because Dad doesn't want her to. He wants her to stay in her room."

"Well, if she does show up, or if anyone else does, come

get me or Dad right away, okay? Or if you can't come, then yell. I know it's all – I don't know what it is, actually. But if we stick together it's gonna work out, because your daddies love you very much. Okay?"

Jay-Jay nodded. Again Vone thought of snatching his son up and fleeing the house with him. But no: Jack would call the cops on him if he did that, and with one wild, unjustifiable act their relationship, their family, would be permanently destroyed. He would be in jail, then a mental hospital, and the cops, meanwhile, would return Jay-Jay to Jack and to this house. *I have to stay*. He bent over his son and kissed his forehead. "Do you want the door open?"

"Yes please."

Leaving the nightlight on and the door ajar, Vone returned to the main bedroom.

"Is he okay?"

"He's still awake, but yeah, I think so. Hopefully the b.s. with the cops didn't freak him out too much."

"Yeah," Jack said. Then, avoiding bringing up the other things that might be freaking their son out, he added, "Come to bed."

"I'm just gonna –" Vone said, and without even trying to come up with an excuse he went downstairs again, and, leaving the lights off, checked all locks were locked, all bolts bolted, all window catches fastened. Returning upstairs, he looked in briefly on the two unused bedrooms and checked their window catches too.

Jack set aside the report he was working on as Vone got into bed. "All tight?"

"Yeah."

Jack put off the light and they lay side by side in the dark, their shoulders not quite touching. "Would you at least read her diary?" Vone asked. "I mean properly read it."

"Tomorrow, okay?" Jack said.

"Okay."

"I promise."

"I love you."

"I love you too." Jack kissed Vone on the cheek but didn't snuggle into him as he usually did.

Twenty-Seven

Though he was sure that without more drugs he wouldn't be able to sleep, at some point Vone must have drifted off, because he was awakened by a faint scratching sound, like mice behind the baseboards. He stared up at the blank gray ceiling, listening, unable to tell where the sound was coming from, but certain it wasn't only inside his head. Carefully turning back his side of the quilt, he sat up, pulled on a tee and went out into the passage and along to the landing. From there he could tell the sound was coming from downstairs. It was somehow insistent, and wove itself through the tick of the grandmother clock. Barefoot, Vone silently descended the staircase.

As he passed the clock, with a clunk it stopped – chance, surely, but obscurely ominous. The moon dial, he noticed, had rotated to the full.

Scritch scritch scritch.

Vone found Mike fretting at the wiring of his hutch. The animal quieted at his approach, reassured perhaps that its noise had summoned someone it knew to be kind. He brushed his fingers across the mesh, reluctant to open the door in case he ended up having to play monster hunt for real, however small and cute the monster. He noticed Mike's water bottle was nearly empty, refilled it and clipped it back in place. How much did mongooses eat? He got some bacon from the refrigerator, cut off a rind, and offered one end to Mike through the wire. Mike snuffed, then began to gnaw it.

Vone put the bacon back in the refrigerator. In the dim light its interior dazzled, the logos of the foodstuffs that crowded its shelves garish and brash – intended, he thought then, to reduce citizens to consumers and distract them from the choices that mattered: who to love; what to fight; what to fight for. He closed the refrigerator, went over to the window and looked out across the backyard. Lit by the moon, which was at that hour riding high, it had an artificial quality, the woods beyond the fence as black and depthless as a backdrop. As he watched, a cloud passed over the moon's face and the yard sank into darkness, like the prelude to a play.

Leaving Mike he hoped contentedly gnawing the rind, Vone went upstairs. For no particular reason he decided to check on Jay-Jay. As he made his way to his son's room he told himself not to peek through the hinge-gap, but did so anyway. He saw only the room as it should be. He went in. It was cozily warm and Jay-Jay was deeply asleep. Vone was at first relieved, then vaguely troubled. He fought a desire to shake his son awake, to reassure himself that the sleep was normal, not – what? Drugged? But none of his pills were missing: Jack had counted them. He settled on a vague "unnaturally influenced."

His mind went to the question that had been displaced by the intrusion of the police: how had his pills ended up on Jay-Jay's windowsill? They had been put there, and surely with malicious intent, but by who, and why? He thought of Rory or Ted, but that made no sense. Sarah and old man Harris didn't seem plausible secret intruders. Everett? No. Jay-Jay, sleepwalking? No: he couldn't reach the medicine cabinet. Himself, in some sort of trance? But he was sure he had experienced no time lapses; no unexplained apparent leapings forward of the clock.

That left the Owl Lady, long-dead Mamie Place. *She wants to be let out*, Jay-Jay had said. Was Mamie Place trying to make trouble, torment him, drive him and his family from the house? Or was it Skog Madoo, the Mother of Serpents, reaching out telepathically or telekinetically from the woods, attempting harm by remote control?

He looked down at his sleeping son. "He'll be a heartbreaker," women would say, when Vone wheeled him in his stroller through the parks of Fort Greene, or took him visiting around Bed-Stuy. Jay-Jay was dark enough to establish his pappy's woman wasn't white, and so the Black women he encountered would look at Vone a certain way: with approval, that was; some with a certain hunger. Yet the brown boy they fussed over only existed because Vone hadn't gone their way. And sure, if he'd been heterosexual then some other child would have likely come to be, somewhere else, with someone else. But not *this* child, even if you believed it was somehow the same soul, waiting for whichever vessel came along, as women who have had a termination sometimes do, feeling they will have "the baby" later. Not this unique, special boy, bright and shy and full of life and promise, good at drawing but good at sums too. Vone touched Jay-Jay's caramel cheek with his knuckles: so soft, so smooth. He wondered if his own father had ever looked on him with that same sense of wonder. It was hard to believe, but he hoped so anyway.

A sound at the window made him look round, a clattering and then a thud, as if a bird had thrown itself against the glass from outside and then somehow, impossibly, fallen to the floor inside the room; and now lay concealed, possibly stunned, behind the drapes. Without giving himself time to think, Vone went over and pulled them open.

There was no bird. What met his eyes appeared at first simultaneously, then sequentially in three optical layers, two ordinary, one extremely odd. First there was the black mass of the woods, the treetops moon-silvered and somehow sensate: the outside world made fairytale. Then his own reflection, its features underlit macabrely by the night light, behind which were also reflected the ordinary details of the room.

Into that reflection, as if a stage set were being spun on a revolve, Mamie Place's secret room slid into place; and as it did so, as disconcertingly as a wardrobe door being thrown open, the Owl Lady was revealed, her thin lips moving silently, her big black saucer eyes inhuman, and she was crying and he guessed imploring, because she put her bony hands together as if in supplication. The feathers in her steel-gray plait rose, her greasy greatcoat flared, and somehow she was both floating outside the window looking desperately in and down in the cellar; and also, Vone realized with a thrill of horror, in Jay-Jay's bedroom, behind him and drifting closer. He could smell the dankness of her coat, the moldy plaster of the cellar, licorice and the rancid rosewater she used for perfume; and her breath was sour and cold. She herself was silent as a shadow and perhaps as weightless, but from somewhere there was the panicked beating of wings, and their thrumming compressed the air.

With crawling dread, he turned to face his madness, or to face a manifestation that, proven, would turn the whole world mad, but met only his son's bedroom, peaceful, orderly, and with no alarming, airborne tenant. The flapping sound had

ceased, the air was warm and still, and there was only the faint
scent of cedarwood mingled with sleeper's breath.

Jay-Jay hadn't stirred: what had happened had been for
Vone's eyes and ears only. He turned back to the window. Outside was the night and nothing else. He closed the drapes, and
there came to him the certainty that it was the Owl Lady who
had moved his pills; who had placed them in Jay-Jay's room,
putting his son in harm's way.

What might she try next?

Unable to leave Jay-Jay on his own in a house where he
felt increasingly sure malign forces were converging, Vone
turned his duvet back and, doing his best not to wake him,
carried him through to the main bedroom. He could tell Jack
Jay-Jay had had a nightmare if he asked. *Get through tonight*,
he thought, as he set Jay-Jay down between them. *Drive to
Collington-Osprey in the morning, get the rental car.* Away
from the house, away from the Bounds, things might come
clearer. And if Jack read Mamie Place's diary, he might... But
Vone's hope it would convince his husband of anything was
thin, the more so since the fiasco with the skin.

Jay-Jay stirred but didn't wake. Vone got back into bed
and lifted the quilt and throw and undersheet over him, then
over himself. He lay on his side in the dark, facing his son and
husband. Something was missing, but he wasn't sure what. He
realized it was the ticking of the clock downstairs. Funny how
quickly he had become used to it. He closed his eyes, and at
some point sleep came over him.

Amplified by the medication he had taken earlier, which
was still metabolizing inside him, Vone's dreams were, inevitably, troubled: a confused jumble of birdwings and talons,
ophidian coils, a hinge-jawed mouth and a vibrating bone rattle on which children's faces wailed zoetropically. In his
dreaming mind's eye the crying faces resembled more than
anything else those old, now mostly suppressed, coonshow-
inflected cartoons of skeletons pulsing to swing jazz syncopa-
tions and the louche blaring of trumpets. Cartoons like that
had always scared him as a child. And then a line of bright silver darted out of the dark like a snake's tongue –

Vone's eyes snapped open. He was lying on his side, facing

the door to the passage. It was half open, though he knew he had been careful to close it when he brought Jay-Jay through. Moonlight spilled along the passage, and he wondered what had woken him. Then he heard a small skittering sound, approaching quickly, and a moment later Mike the mongoose came into view. At first it seemed he would scamper straight past, but instead he stopped and looked in, sniffing at the threshold. Smoothly Vone turned over in bed, intending to try and wake Jack without waking Jay-Jay, but Jay-Jay wasn't there.

Vone shook Jack's shoulder. As on other nights, his husband's sleep had a drugged quality to it. "What is it?" he asked groggily.

"Jay-Jay's gone."

"What do you mean, 'gone'?"

Jack had been asleep when Vone brought their son through; hadn't known he was ever there.

"Look." Vone pointed at the mongoose. It chirruped, and once it was sure it had their attention, it scampered back the way it had come. As one, Vone and Jack got out of bed and followed it, in their haste going barefoot and wearing only shorts. Rather than heading towards Jay-Jay's room as Vone had expected, Mike stopped at the top of the stairs and looked back. *Follow me.*

Unable to descend the steep flight headfirst, the little creature tumbled its way down, a furry Slinky eventually landing sprawling but unharmed on the polished floorboards of the hall two flights below, then darted off towards the kitchen. Vone and Jack hurried down. Comical though the sight of Mike was, he was undoubtedly a part of what was going on in the house that night, and Jack finally seemed to be aware of the nearness of strange things, even if consciously he would have refused to name them.

Even before they entered the kitchen they heard the sound: a rhythmic thudding at the side door, like a basketball being bounced against it from outside, but heavier; a medicine ball maybe; or a swung loop of tarred rope, nautical and old, or a tawse, with its sadistic implications.

Mike darted under his hutch, the door of which was open. Twigs were scattered in front of it, and the catch was broken:

he had forced his way out. Meanwhile, at the side door, Jay-Jay stood on a kitchen chair he must have pushed across the room from the breakfast table, rucking up the rug along the way. On wobbly tiptoes he was struggling with the topmost of the pair of bolts that kept the door closed; the lower was already drawn back.

What was outside thumped metronomically against the door, each blow visibly warping the wood, animate yet somehow dead. Then came a hissing that was if anything like the result of some vast pressure differential, like oxygen from a tear in an astronaut's spacesuit rushing out into the frozen, lethal vacuum of space.

"Junior!" Vone called. "Boy, don't do that!"

Jay-Jay turned his head in his fathers' direction. His eyes were glassy, his expression was blank and somehow formless. Almost defiantly, he pulled the top bolt back.

As he did so, a blow from outside split the door from top to bottom. Vone and Jack watched paralyzed as their son reached down and turned the key – *strength from elsewhere, projected through those small fingers* – and opened the door to what was banging to be let in.

Twenty-Eight

F orced by the mass and weight of what was outside, the door began at once to open, pushing Jay-Jay and the chair he was standing on backwards into the room. With a cry of alarm he grabbed hold of the chair back, though as yet the door shielded him from viewing what writhed beyond. But Vone and Jack could see.

And there she was, revealed at last, filling the frame and radiating cold. Lead-colored, skull-faced, venom-fanged, anencephalic Skog Madoo, the Mother of Serpents, come to claim their son's life force to fertilize her egg. Ribbed filaments flared out from her pickled head, fluid or internal gaseous pressure inflating the great cobra hood, and a coruscating iridescence radiated out across it in pulsing waves, the colors unplaceable, like gasoline on a puddle, but somehow other. Behind the floating head a mass of great gray coils blocked out the night, and she was larger, far larger than Vone had thought from the discarded skin; and he thought that she could pour herself into the house and entirely fill it.

Now he could see there was really nothing human about her face, its apparent similarity to a shrieking skull no more than a chance convergence of forms, the matte black holes that vaguely resembled eye sockets and a nasal pit in reality housing receptors for who knew what alien senses. Nor did she really resemble an earthly serpent, for rather than twin fangs, her venom was channeled through a single prehensile needle – an insectile proboscis evolved from the corkscrew intertwining of rigid twin labia, and at its fused, quill-like point quicksilver beaded.

As one, Vone and Jack darted across the room in the direction of the side door, knocking the chair aside and sending Jay-Jay tumbling as they threw their weight against the split panels in a desperate attempt to shove it closed.

Perhaps the Mother had expected no resistance; perhaps she believed that just the sight of her would paralyze them, or make them flee in fear and abandon their child to her. Either way, she had barely begun to enter the room, and their

combined weight and momentum forced her back just enough
to allow the latch to catch – though how fragile a barrier it
was: symbolic more than physical, and Vone doubted her
mind was really controlled by symbols; doubted she would be
unable to cross a threshold because not invited in, and anyway
the door was already cracked from top to bottom.

"Junior! Run!" Jack shouted, dropping to the floor and
bracing his back against the door as a coil thudded against it
from outside, the impact visibly jolting through him.

Jay-Jay scrambled to his feet and bolted from the room as
Vone, now on his knees next to Jack, tried to turn the key in
the lock, hoping to buy them a few more seconds before the
door was wholly broken down. He couldn't: the shoving from
outside forced the strike plate out of alignment. "Where's the
axe?" he shouted above the thumping and hissing.

"I put it under the back steps," Jack shouted back.

"Why the fuck you –"

"I thought you were losing it."

At that moment the picture window blew inwards along
its entire length, as if a heavy firehose had been swung against
it from outside, showering both near-naked men with broken
glass, and they shielded their eyes but could not look away as
Skog Madoo's great rattle flicked up into view. It waved about,
grotesquely beguiling, the chitinous segments vibrating blurrily, in appearance a macabre totem pole; and the skulls and
the heads of the other children and Jay-Jay, his face now swollen to near life-size at the top of the stack, at the tip of the tail,
screamed dry cicada screams. Was she drawing off his life-
force remotely, Vone wondered; was it already too late? But
no: he had been able to run away; he could be jolted free of
her extractive control. *Not fully hers yet.* A whirring filled the
air that stabbed through Vone's head like ballooning cabin
pressure, and, he didn't doubt, through Jack's head too. "The
safe room!" he yelled, his voice mushy and flattened in his own
ears.

"We're not going in the cellar," Jack yelled back. "We'd be
trapped down there. Anyway, where's Junior?"

A further crashing thud burst the kitchen door open, splitting it entirely in two, twisting it off its hinges and thrusting
both men aside. Where they landed, flung onto all fours, their

bare knees, splaying toes and the palms of their hands were pressed into broken glass, though with their adrenalin surging, at that moment they felt no pain.

Keeping on all fours, they scurried across the room and into the hall passageway, Vone first, then Jack. Behind them, Skog Madoo's great gray coils poured into the kitchen, and Vone noticed she inclined her head to pass beneath the lintel and didn't raise it again. It was as if, he thought briefly, she were making a ritual obeisance; as if she were some strange, intimidating lady-in-waiting – though more likely she was smelling about for, or otherwise sensing, the prey she sought, as electric eels, being purblind, sense the current within the living things around them. As she did so, the mongoose, forgotten in the chaos, jumped first on top of the hutch, then the windowsill, then sprang at the Mother's face just as Jack kicked the passage door shut.

The latch caught. Jack sprang forward, grabbed the handle and forced it up hard. The door opened away from him, into the kitchen passage, meaning it could only be broken down from that side by what was in there forcing the frame out of the surrounding brickwork. Keeping hold of the handle, Jack leant back, arms stretched out like a rower's, hoping to be a counterweight if the thing came tugging at the door – though, being limbless, it was surely more likely to barrel straight though, carrying the frame with it; and there was then no need, and in any case no time, for Jack to say that Vone had been right all along.

"Jay-Jay?" Vone called. "Boy, where you at?"

From within the kitchen there came the sound of thrashing and furniture and crockery being thrown about, and in the midst of it a screech like nothing Vone had ever heard. Could Skog Madoo somehow fear the mongoose? Vone remembered something to that effect – the story of Rikki-Tikki-Tavi came to him later; and later still he would wonder whether those buried childhood memories of the mongoose devouring the cobras' eggs had somehow fed fear into the mind of the Mother, a creature that drew so much from other minds; that was herself an aching lack. *Perhaps I put the fear into her*. But just then there was only chaos and great danger.

Abruptly, the noise in the kitchen ceased. Vone and Jack

looked at each other, their chests heaving, mouths partly open, pupils dilated; bare skin sheening, speckled with blood and glittering, as if they were revelers at some carnival of violence, sparkling slivers of glass held glued in place by sweat.

Whatever moment of grace this was, they had to make the most of it.

Jack let the handle go. It sprang up with a clack. Beyond the door was silence. *Okay*. But they hadn't heard the creature leave: might it be waiting, and this quietness, this stillness be a lure? Jack reached for the handle. "Should we –?" he began.

"First go find Junior," Vone said.

"What about you?"

"I'ma go out the front, go round, get the axe."

Because hadn't the girl in the '80s had an axe? Hadn't she believed an axe could damage the thing? Jack looked like he was about to say something, but didn't. The blacks of his pupils had almost entirely swallowed the sea-green of his irises. *Celtic-ass motherfucker*. Vone had never loved him more.

Quickly they went through to the front hall. Jack looked in on the dining room while Vone sneaked back the bolts on the front door, calling softly, "Jay-Jay? Are you in there?" He wasn't. Jack checked the front parlor as Vone slowly turned the door key, his chest tightening as the mechanism clicked back, a sound as loud it seemed to him then as a gunshot in church. *She would hear. She would rush round.*

He opened the door. The hall's heat evaporated as if sucked out into space, and the icy air bit into his bare skin. There was a cindery smell that made him think snow was on its way, and the sky above was clouding over fast. As he descended the porch steps the varnished planks were salt-rough beneath his naked feet, and cold as metal.

Through the gaps between the pines that fronted Number 13 he looked along the street. The frosted asphalt sparkled under the streetlights, but no lights were on in any of the houses. Even had there been, this was no time to rush over in his underwear, hammer on doors and rave about monsters; to try and not get himself shot while attempting to convince strangers that he wasn't mad; that his child and husband were somewhere inside the blighted house behind him, and in mortal danger.

And indeed, though this too was a puzzle for later, why hadn't those absent neighbors, otherwise so quick to call 911, heard the smashing in of the door, the demolition of the kitchen, and run to their phones? Were they somehow a part of this? Old families, living here for generations, falling under a creeping influence – something barely perceptible, like the slow downward flow of glass in old windows. Or was it the other way about? Had Vone and his uprooted family, human beings of the now, been cursed for moving, however ignorantly, onto poisoned land, and thus become caught in some bubble beyond the bounds of which indifference reigned forever? So long as the sacrifice was made, the ghastly deity appeased, their own children spared, what else mattered to the other residents of the Bounds? And face it: wasn't that true of everyone, everywhere?

He hurried to the right front corner of the house, the frosty leaves night-damp beneath the cringing soles of his feet. His skin prickled so hard it was as if it were crusting over: the temperature was falling fast. He shuddered and wondered if it was Her draining the heat, her skin cold, maybe, as the distance between stars, and thought fleetingly of the patch of frost in the dip on top of the mound; how it remained even after the sun should have melted it. *She must have been in there.* Hadn't he in some way sensed it? Hadn't Jay-Jay? A breeze caressed him unpleasantly, and he shuddered again.

Peering round the corner of the house he saw the woodshed, laundry lines, a black slice of the backyard, the swallowing woods and nothing else. *She can move impossibly fast*, he reminded himself. He came forward quickly, peck-walking on the rough concrete, and the glass-cuts in the balls of his feet began to throb warmly despite the cold. He came to the sidesteps, groped about under them and found the axe. Straightening up, he hefted it so the flat side of the blade rested on his clavicle.

Before going back, he took a moment to look in on the kitchen. The halves of the shattered door had been flung across the room, and table, china hutch, cupboards, bench and chairs had all been piled up in front of the door to the basement. Pots and pans had been torn down from beam-hooks, glassware and crockery smashed, and amidst the litter lay the rigid body of the mongoose, crushed and grotesquely elongated, its eyeballs ruptured.

Vone stepped back down. *Check the backyard, see if She's gone that way.*

Just then, close behind him and from the direction of the front of the house, he heard a stealthy sound. Turning fast, brandishing the axe as he did so, Vone, wild-eyed, speckled with blood and almost naked, found himself facing a figure silhouetted by the streetlights of Cottonwood Way; a heavyset white man, and he was leveling a double-barreled shotgun at Vone's chest.

Twenty-Nine

I t seemed to Vone then that this was the ending his life –
a sudden synecdoche for all Black men's lives – was des-
tined to come to: despite every important thing he
needed to do, for his son, for his family, here was the inevitable interruption: a white man's finger nervy on the trigger.
The burly backlit figure was, Vone would realize moments
later, Rory's husband Ted, but in the extremity of the moment
its silhouetted face had no more individuality or indeed humanity than an executioner's hood, and Vone swung his axe
at it wildly.

Ted pulled the trigger just as the axe blade knocked the
barrels of his gun sideways, sending both simultaneously-dis-
charged blasts wide of their target, though close enough to
Vone's head to set his right ear ringing.

The momentum of Vone's swing spun him round so his
back was to Ted, and he turned that to his advantage by letting
it carry him up the steps and send him stumbling into the
kitchen, thereby getting out of Ted's line of fire before the
white man had a chance to reload – if he had spare ammo on
him, that was. But didn't gun nuts always have spare ammo?
Vone had never fired a shotgun himself, or any gun, though he
had handled his father's pistol a couple of times, nominally
concealed but easily accessible to his prying offspring in a bedside drawer. From outside there came a pneumatic hissing
and a whirring rattle, followed by a second double blast – Ted
had had more ammo – and then a yell, abruptly cut off.

Vone now knew what he had to do, in this house of horror
patrolled perhaps by residents who had been tasked with
keeping the victims inside, much as they had once ensured
that those accused of witchcraft could not free themselves
from the stake as the bonfire blazed up around them. Setting
the axe aside but within ready reach, he went over to the furniture piled in front of the basement door and began rapidly
to pull it aside, while he did so calling, "Jack! Jack, where are
you? You got Jay-Jay? Bring him to the kitchen!"

"We're through here!" Jack called back, but in a strange,

tense voice that made Vone break off from what he was doing. Picking up the axe, he stalked through to the front hall.

There he found Jack and Jay-Jay, hand in hand, facing the open front door, and in the doorway stood Rory. She was wild-eyed and wild-haired, in a loose man's shirt, barelegged with moccasined feet, and for a moment Vone thought that some-how it had been her all along, barren, lonely, needy, lighting candles and chanting spells in some attic or cellar. As she opened her mouth, either in shock, if she was, in fact, human, or to say something occult and inconceivable, perhaps com-mand Skog Madoo to come forth and do her bidding, Jack reached for one of the walking sticks in the elephant's foot stand, and Vone, joining him, swung back the axe baseball-batter style. Rory's pale eyes were blank, and her hands hung loose at her sides. Behind her, what Vone could see of Cotton-wood Way was in darkness: either the streetlights had gone out, or a wall of shadow had interposed itself between their property and the street, a cyclorama in reverse.

Rory screamed.

Almost instantaneously her cry was cut off, as the Mother struck at her from the side, with such ferocity and velocity that both Rory and the spring-coiled gray monstrosity were in-stantly and entirely carried from view.

Not even wasting the fraction of a second it would take to slam the front door, Vone, Jack and Jay-Jay fled in the direc-tion of the kitchen, Vone carrying with him a near-subliminal image of the jaw hinged back, the monstrous prehensile pro-boscis sliding base-deep into Rory's neck. He led Jack and Jay-Jay over to the basement door. Jack, trusting him now, and oh, the mercy of that was everything, helped him drag the last of the piled-up furniture aside, glancing repeatedly in the direction of the hall as he did so. Would She, Vone wondered distractedly, swallow Rory? How long would that take? *Food, not a sacrifice.* But no –

"Key!" Vone called as he yanked the bolt on the cellar door back, pinching and cutting one of his fingers painfully on the keep, and cursing.

Jack looked over at the counter. "It's not there," he said, sounding panicked. Had She taken it? It seemed unlikely her mind worked that way; that it was concerned with such minor physical barriers. Dropping to his knees, he fossicked among the shards of china and pottery, the strewn dried herbs.

Vone watched anxiously as Jack searched, noticing then the many small cuts and abrasions latticing his skin. It was hard for Vone not to feel that this was all somehow his fault: *Shoulda run when I could, who cares if I spent the rest of my life in a –*

Jack swore in frustration; Vone turned to the basement door. To shoulder it in, as he knew from getting locked out of his college room one time, would be harder than it looked – he had broken his collarbone trying and failing to do so; and even if he did manage it, it would be hard not to go tumbling down the stairs on the other side.

Then Jack had the key and was hurrying over. As he inserted it into the lock Vone noticed Jay-Jay's eyes going to the horribly squeezed body of the mongoose, and small thing though it was amidst the larger horror, he wished he had thought to cover the little corpse with something, to spare his son that trauma.

Jack yanked the door open and, clicking on the light, led the way down, his bare heels thudding on the dusty wood. At the bottom he turned for Vone to lift Jay-Jay down to him. Vone did so, then picked up the axe and followed his husband, pulling the door closed behind him, buying them a few seconds, maybe – though a few seconds to do what?

Now they were faced by the shelves Jack had reinstated to block off Mamie Place's saferoom. Vone hacked into them with the axe, sending splinters flying; Jack turned Jay-Jay towards him to shield his eyes and face from harm. Half Vone's blows bounced off the planks uselessly, and each blow jarred his shoulders painfully. Finally he was able to get the axe head in between one of the planks and the wall, lever it toward him and twist it out of the way; then after a couple more blows the second came loose from the moldy plaster and he dropped the axe, got a hold of it and dragged it aside.

From overhead there came a sound like heavy sacks being dragged along. Vone stopped what he was doing and they all looked up. Plaster dust sifted down onto their sweaty faces, stinging their eyes, though Jack quickly positioned his hand above Jay-Jay's brow to shield him from the worst of it.

Fear surging, Vone tore away the last and lowest shelf with his hands, splitting a thumb nail to the quick as he did so, a sharp pain that seconds later bloomed into a hot, ugly throbbing; and side by side he and Jack began to shoulder in the flimsy door. Three panicky and ill-coördinated attempts later it flew open and they staggered into the darkness beyond. Jack found and yanked on the light cord as Vone took Jay-Jay's hand and drew him into the room after them. Then he heaved the damaged door as nearly closed as he could, though with no lock, no bolts, and hinges half torn from the frame, as a barrier it was almost entirely worthless.

He looked round to see Jay-Jay step kid-careful over the chalk circle on the floor – don't break yo momma's back! – and clamber up onto Mamie Place's narrow, lumpy bed. Jack followed suit and Vone joined him, stepping carefully too. Like Jay-Jay both men drew in their feet, as if that would somehow keep them safe. *Jay-Jay's mind; Her mind.* What was that game? Pirates. Huddling together they looked up as, overhead, the thing made its ponderous way to the basement door. Thud, thud, the great coils struck. Crack. The door broke open. Clatter, clatter, it fell down the stairs.

Shit fuck shoulda run out the back while we had the chance. In the woods maybe we could've –

The thing was now audibly slithering down the basement steps. *Too late it's too late.* Vone's hand found Jack's and gripped it, and his husband's blood pulsed against his fingertips. He and Vone moved round so they were shielding Jay-Jay from what was on its way, and in that moment they became warriors of a sort, braves, maybe; those who will die for their family, for their tribe. *This tribe of warriors and outlaws*, as Elder Essex put it.

The snake skeletons began to turn above their heads, rotating as if there were an oncoming wind, though there was no wind, nor anywhere for it to have come from; and the snakeskins rustled like the silk dresses of courtiers, anticipating Her arrival. Maybe they and the dry bones longed for a biblical vengeance upon whoever held the axe that had been used against them over fifty years before, as punishment for daring to bring their forked tongues around Mamie Place's plot.

Due to some distortion of the light, or possibly it was

happening only within his mind, it seemed to Vone that a darkness was gathering round the bed, isolating him and his family from everything that was sane and normal – how rarely he yoked those two words together; and the discolored plaster walls with their pitchy sigils sank away into the gloom.

With a gothically protracted creak, the broken door swung open. Radiating a cold so intense it both stiffened the goose-bumping skins of the three human beings who crouched cowering on the bed and drained their cores, Skog Madoo filled the doorway. Her gelid skull face was as expressionless as a pewter pharaoh's mask, her glistening fang flexed ecstatically, and there was nowhere to run, nowhere to hide.

Yet suddenly, Vone felt less afraid. *This* was his destiny, not a blast from a white man's shotgun. It was in its grotesque way a near-magical escape from the poison and prison of race. Almost without volition, he found himself putting his feet on the floor and standing to face Her. In his right hand was the axe; with the left he reached back to keep a hold of Jack's hand, and there was in doing that a defiance even when facing a foe who could not conceivably care about transgressions of sex and race and genital interaction among human beings. The tips of his toes brushed but did not break the ghost curve of the chalk circle, and daring now to look her full in the face, Vone saw there was a gouge in Skog Madoo's cartilaginous right cheek: Mike the mongoose's teeth had left a mark.

Not indestructible.

Riding on her coils, the Mother surged slowly into the room. There was no need for her to hurry now: her prey was cornered and, axe or no axe, she had other powers with which to daunt them, and she was close to the child, which was all that mattered to her. And Mamie Place was fifty years dead, a heap of bones and hair in an unremarked-upon grave from which no living mind could draw power, her small, weak store of magic buried with her.

Yet when her frontmost coil touched the chalk circle Mamie Place drew all those years before, the Mother drew back sharply, and Vone smiled inside, because it meant that, whatever came next, he hadn't lost his gamble: the dead woman's beliefs, and his own belief in her, energized as it was by some connection latent within him to systems of spirit long sundered by the Middle Passage, had power. And so he stood before her, bloody and all but naked, a warrior, defiant, and love was both a shield and a spear – his for Jack, for Jay-Jay; theirs for him. He felt it vibrating in the air between them, and he felt Her lack.

And then he felt the terrible pressure of her mind. She tilted her head and the great hood flared. A pattern began to radiate across it, and her tail-tip flicked up and began to whirr with an intensity that compressed the air and made Vone dizzy; and to his horror he saw that the final face, the last bone on the rattle, was now fully and exactly that of his son: a living severed head trapped in a gray plastic bag pulled tight, its features filled with fear, a vision of what hell might be; and a glance showed him that in a nightmare of soul transference Jay-Jay's actual face now looked waxy, mask-like and oddly lacking in detail, his eyes – pupils and whites alike – dulled to a leaden opacity. *Petrified.*

As she pulled at Jay-Jay, the Mother pushed at Vone, attempting to expel his mind into the white dark; and he realized that this power of hers, this power of possession, keyed into traces within himself that she could draw up from the bottom of his mind, and, though consciously he would have disavowed them, she could use them against him. *What's known in the bone.* The ability to control his limbs passed from him, and with a clonk he let the axe head hit the floor, probably much as that girl had done back in the eighties. *And hadn't She risen up columnarly and looked down.* The haft tipped away from his slackened grip, its length violating the chalk circle, a possible bridgehead for Her to cross over by.

The Mother swayed but did not advance. *Had* the axe handle broken the circle? Yet what would it matter, if Jack and Jay-Jay were also mesmerized and thus commandable? Vone tried to turn his head to see but couldn't: She would not permit it. All he could do was try not to shuffle forward; try not to break the circle with his living body, because then he would be dead, and Jack and Jay-Jay in their turn would shuffle forward like penitents, like zombies, and die.

No, not Jay-Jay: him she would take back to her lair under the mound. Feed him to –

With an effort, Vone managed to close his eyes. The

pressure inside his head lessened slightly, and he found himself able to look down before lifting his eyelids again, in that way escaping for a few more seconds Her mesmeric radiance. Silvery patterns slid over his sweaty skin, over his heaving chest, kaleidoscopic, almost beautiful. He focused on his right leg, commanding it to lift, but to no effect. Futility overwhelmed him.

Yet at the same time as all that a wind was building fast behind him, though he knew there was nothing beyond the bedhead but the wall – no flues, no vents, no chinks or cracks or tunnels to the outside. He risked looking up, not at but past the Mother, and saw the mysterious wind was sending the snakeskins flaring up floatingly, and the skeletons spiraled faster and faster on their threads. It rushed on, accelerating rapidly and noisily, and then the walls of the room fell wholly away, like a rotor ride at a carnival, and he, Jack and Jay-Jay were at once both trapped in a small underground room and floating in an empty, inky, vastness. Amongst the skins and bones feathers began to whirl – owl feathers, soft as snowflakes at that tipping point where the air is just cold enough for them to hold their shape. A moment later, Vone, Jack and Jay-Jay were enveloped in a choking blizzard of feathers, white and black and brown.

Through that smothering vortex Vone could still see the Mother, and he thought she flinched as the feathers struck her, fixing themselves to her skin in some gothic tarring-and-feathering, but still her hood flickered with the cold, beguiling light of remote stars, some of them a thousand million years dead, yet somehow caught within her. *We are all starlight.*

Despite the adherence of the feathers – *ruined Quetzelcoatl* – she was refusing to relinquish control of Vone's mind, and his reckless glance, oblique though it had been, had once more put him under her spell, as to look at Medusa in anything other than a mirror would turn a man to stone. And perhaps the myth of the Gorgons began in Her, or in her progeny, three thousand years ago or more: the children of a successful spawning, before the bounds were set by the spells of the long-perished Red Paint people – a transatlantic migration easily enough undertaken, for whatever could survive the frozen vacuum of space could surely live underwater. *How many children?* There had been three Gorgons, hadn't there? Medusa, Megara and –

With an effort of will that was aided considerably by the interposing curtain of feathers, Vone wrenched his head round and focused his eyes on Jack and Jay-Jay. Jack looked uncertain and afraid, Jay-Jay inexpressive, and Vone knew that more than anything Skog Madoo wanted him, Vone, to take Jay-Jay from his husband and set him down outside the circle: to give his child to her; to make an offering as he didn't doubt others had done across the centuries, the millennia, in a futile attempt to placate this implacable thing that was not a god, not even a spirit, but an animal, and one less predatory than parasitical, and in some curious way mindless, using as its vessel the minds of others.

Yet her radiance overwhelmed him. He would have to make the offering, he could see that now. His mind was silver-bright, ringing and singing, and She was inside him, terrible and wonderful and dazzling. Only a sacrifice would end this; would bring peace.

"What are you *doing*?" a paralyzed Jack asked through clenched teeth, somehow sensing Vone's intent as, robotically, Vone began to clamber along the bed towards their son. Jay-Jay, his terror breaking through her hold – a hold now focused it seemed entirely on Vone – squirmed away from his daddy until his back was pressed up hard against the bedhead. And Vone knew from his son's expression that at that moment his own face was no longer human; that he was feral then, naturally on all fours, a degraded beast coming for his son at Her behest.

Beyond the bedhead was no longer a wall but a plunging darkness in which a vortex of feathers spun. It was as though the bed was suspended in the eye of a cyclone. Vone grabbed hold of Jay-Jay and Jay-Jay screamed.

At that moment a vast shadowy form passed overhead, hurtling towards the Mother of Serpents, a screeching bird form, the details of which were obscured by the choking feathers. Vone had a glimpse of rusty iron talons the size of digger scoops, and then the lightbulb that somehow still floated just above their heads exploded. Abruptly the room was plunged into darkness, and it was as if the bed, like a sycamore seed, was spinning on an unseen swell, though those upon it were buffeted not by the heaving ocean but by a frenzy of flapping wings. There was a hissing and a screeching, and a surge that made Vone fear they were being borne up on a great wave and lifted into the violence of a lowering electrical storm.

And then, abruptly, it was over. The bed ceased floating and as it were sunk down. The beating wings, the hissing, the shrieking, all stopped. The sense of a vast space evaporated, though the darkness remained absolute. Vone, Jack and Jay-Jay huddled together, too frightened to move. The hissing began again, but now it had a punctured, labored quality. They listened as something bulky dragged itself slowly from the room, heaved itself up the cellar stairs, and moved effortfully across the kitchen floor, pulling with it shards of broken crockery that scraped against the polished boards. And then there was silence.

Vone realized he was shivering. So were Jack and Jay-Jay, though the room was less cold now than it had been before, which meant the thing really had gone: that, at least, it could not control or counterfeit. He remembered there had been a candle stub and matches on the side table, and reached over and felt about for them, though without much hope, for surely everything had been turned upside down in the maelstrom. But his fingers found both candle and matchbook where he would have expected. The matches were damp: their cardboard sticks bent ineffectually as he dragged the head of one, then another, across the sandpaper strip, but he managed to get the third of the six to strike, and brought the flame tremulously to the candle's wick. Mercifully it caught, and he held up the stub to view the room.

Other than the broken-in door, at first glance all was as it had been: four plain walls, a low, slightly bowed ceiling – and Vone and Jack and Jay-Jay, sitting on the bed with their feet drawn up, looking at each other, shocked, in the small sphere of the candle flame. Impulsively Vone hugged Jack and Jay-Jay to him, and neither flinched at his touch. Their bare skins were toad-clammy, as no doubt was his, but the contact was a mercy.

It was only then that Vone noticed that the snakeskins and skeletons were gone, as were the sigils on the walls. So this was an ending.

An ending, but She was still alive. Where was she, and where was she going? Back to her hole. Her lair. Her nest. And in that nest – "We've got to end this properly," he said thickly.

"Properly?"

"We've got to finish what the Owl Lady tried to do."

Jack looked at him. "How?"

"With the axe. There's kerosene in the garage. We have to go to the well."

"That's crazy, Vone. No fucking way. That's –"

"It's not her, Jack. It's the egg."

"What egg?"

"It's in the diary. 'A child's soul for every egg she hatches.' Jay-Jay's not safe yet. He'll never be safe, not for sure, not unless we –" He and Jack looked in the direction of the kitchen stairs. A trail of the dark gray fluid that served Her for blood led that way.

Wounded, badly. It would be possible. Maybe.

"Yes," Jack said tonelessly. Yet though even a second's delay was surely a mistake, still he and Vone were reluctant to climb down off the bed that had served them as a life raft; and only with hesitation did they step over the scuffed circle of chalk that had protected it. Picking up the axe, Vone went ahead of Jack and Jay-Jay, holding up the candle to check the way was clear. He made sure not to allow his bare feet to touch the gray fluid, tales of Medusa's blood being poison somewhere in his mind, and indicated to Jack, who was carrying Jay-Jay, that he should do the same.

They went up to the wrecked kitchen, passed through it and climbed the stairs to their bedroom. There, wordlessly, Vone and Jack dressed. The quiet, everyday orderliness of the room made them feel like interlopers.

Looking down as he pulled on a boot, Vone noticed, half-protruding from under the bed, a large, dark brown wing-feather: a pinion. He picked it up and, without thinking, slid its quill into his hair at the back. It stayed there upright, and he could be a tracker now, maybe.

Then came what was in its way the hardest part. Vone sat Jay-Jay on the edge of the bed, and he and Jack squatted down in front of him, their serious son, for whom they hoped so many things, not least, a normal lifespan.

"Daddy and Dad have to go out now," he said. "We have to stop that thing from hurting anyone else. To do that, we need you to stay here, okay?" Jay-Jay nodded. "If you get scared, you can go hide in the safe room. She can't get you in there." Jay-Jay nodded again. Vone hugged him, and his son held on with an intensity that was unbearable. "You gotta be brave," Vone said in a cracking voice. "Be a brave little man, okay?" And he was crying, and Jack was crying, and Jay-Jay began to cry too, and time was bleeding away fast, and tears were no use.

They left their son sitting on the edge of their bed with his feet dangling, and feeling like traitors, like bad fathers, went down to the hall. Should one stay, then; be the comforter? But what if both were needed for the task ahead? What if the impulse to comfort and care led to failure, to death?

Before they left, Vone made a brief detour to the kitchen to get a flashlight he had noticed in a drawer. He clicked it on. It worked. He clicked it off again and rejoined Jack, and together they went out through the front door. The streetlamps were on now: the dark screen had been withdrawn. Yet no lights were on in any of the houses, and no curtain twitched when with a hollow, reverberant clang Vone wrenched up the garage door. It seemed some power was still isolating them from the rest of the world, but whether it belonged to the Owl Lady or Skog Madoo, Vone had no way of guessing; nor whether it would help or hinder his and Jack's mission.

At the back of the garage three rusty gallon cans of kerosene waited. One was mostly empty, but judging from their weight when he lifted them the other two were pretty much full. Jack took the light can and one of the heavy ones, Vone the other. Awkwardly holding the axe and the light in his free hand, he led the way back along the path.

They passed the steps up to the front door and went on. At the corner of the house Vone stumbled over something: a pair of bare, pale legs, sticking out pornographically from the dark tangle of the herbaceous border. A glance confirmed that it was Rory, lying on her back among the bushes. Her features were fixed in a horrified rictus, and her mouth was choked with foam. On her neck was a puncture wound so viciously inflicted that he could see inside the hole, the interior a red mush.

Ted lay on his side by the kitchen steps, a matching wound in his thick neck within which quicksilver pooled. Putting down his cans, Jack bent over and picked up Ted's shotgun. Vone kept watch as, making a face, Jack reluctantly frisked the pockets of Ted's hunting vest. Finding a handful of cartridges, he reloaded the gun, snicked on the safety and pocketed the spares. Usefully it had a strap, so he slung it across his back. Then he picked up the cans again.

There's no way out of this, Vone thought. *We'll be jailed for killing our neighbors. At best we'll be written off as drug-fucked nut jobs. They'll find my psychiatric record. Jay-Jay will –*

At least do this. Then it's for something. Even if no-one knows.

Just then the moon broke through the clouds, revealing a smudgy black track that led straight to the gap in the fence, and there was a smell like old pennies.

Cans clonking, Vone and Jack crossed the yard, ducked under the wire and passed through the gap. Ahead was the trail, running straight in the moonlight.

Thirty

Soon the house was lost behind them, the reassuring lights in its windows swallowed by the night, like fire-flies caught then sunk in tar – gone, along with any proof of human existence but the trail; and that, after all, would have been the same five thousand years ago, before iron was mined and cast, and all the battling and birthing of nations and empires that followed on from that.

The woods felt different that night, not only because Vone had never been in them after dark, but also because before he had been an outsider, a city boy with senses that slept. Now he was as certain in his movements as some Abenaki hunter of long ago; as some Red Paint tracker, seeking spoor. It was as if their sensibilities had been gifted or at least lent him, perhaps by Mamie Place, because tonight he was vividly aware of secret signals in the dark, of scents and sounds, of the things that slept and the things that were awake. And Jack, silent at his side and purposive too, had hunted as a teen, knew how to handle a rifle and so, presumably, a shotgun, and god knew, as did any cop or kindergarten kid, the principle was simple enough: safety off, point, pull the trigger.

Tonight, as on that first morning, the path ran straight, without forks or turnings: a summons, perhaps, in which the pacing, padding beasts of the woods had colluded before being devoured, and maybe the huntsmen too, mesmerized by Her even while she slumbered – men and animals alike tasked with trampling brush and bracken down to make a path impossible to miss; assisted in the task thereafter, as Vone had come to guess, by the secretly dominated citizens on the periphery of the spellbound territory, men and women compelled to walk in their sleep and so, by and large, too tired to leave their homes, or even their beds, by day. Had Rory and Ted unknowingly tramped the night-paths too?

The trail narrowed and he and Jack went on in single file, Vone leading the way, and they went fast, not caring much about making noise because just then speed seemed more important than stealth. Moving fast also helped keep Vone's wobbling courage firm. This was just as well, because with every step he took he asked himself if he was right in this; if She, injured though she unquestionably was by the Owl Lady's talons, would really be vulnerable to the things of this world: an axe and kerosene, three matches and a handful of shotgun shells. He didn't doubt that Jack was on the verge of catching his arm and saying, "Let's leave it, let's go back, get Jay-Jay, get in the car, drive and keep driving. She came to the house because she's tied to it and can't leave."

"But boundary fences rot in time," Vone argued back inside his head. "Boundaries are forgotten and transgressed." The Owl Lady's powers of containment would fail as those of the Red Paint people had done. Skog Madoo would be free again – maybe only when he and Jack and Jay-Jay were all long dead, but she would spawn and steal other children's souls, raise more young, and they too would spawn, exponentially perhaps: apex predators that would in time become the dominant species on the planet, and humanity would go the way of the dodo. And Jack would ask, did that fever-dream justify risking their lives now? Risking their son's life?

But Ted and Rory lay dead outside their house: there was no easy escape; no opting out of what had been begun by other powers except by trying to end it, and hope that in doing so they might be permitted an exoneration, though there was no sense in worrying about that now. Mike the mongoose had torn Her flesh: hold onto that.

And so they trudged on. Vone had no sense of how much time had passed, just a growing awareness of the ache in his shoulder from lugging the kerosene and the throb of the glass-cuts that were all over his body but especially on the soles of his feet – there had been no time to pick the splinters out earlier: he had had to tug his boots on over them regardless. A stitch began to burn in his side, and his and Jack's stumbling progress was further impeded by great lengths of briar clawing at them across the trail, as if nature was siding with Her. Surely the well was near now?

He adjusted Mamie Place's diary where he had shoved it into the front pocket of his hoodie – one corner now gouged his stomach painfully – along with the flashlight, as yet unused, since to switch it on would be less to see anything than be seen by it. In his pants' pocket was the basement matchbook.

Abruptly he halted, sure he had heard a sound close by. Jack blundered into him, swinging one of his kerosene cans into Vone's with a noisy clonk and a sound of internal sloshing. "Fuck, what?" he said.

"Ssh."

Tensely the two men stood listening. A breeze stirred the upper branches of the trees, and maybe that was what Vone had heard. He could sense no movement in the surrounding darkness, and though Skog Madoo could move fast she was large and wounded and surely couldn't be silent. *A thing. A beast. Not magical.* His mind went to Jay-Jay, sitting on the edge of their bed, alone in a house he had lived in for all of ten days, a house with two dead bodies in the front yard, the dead the only neighbors he knew by name. Trying to believe that his daddies would return despite the truth their eyes had disclosed as their lips spoke certitudes to quiet him.

And what if the cops came in the house while Vone and Jack were out in the voracious woods? What if they didn't return? Nothing spectacular. Another police report to be filed away and forgotten. A story on the local news, made briefly memorable by an abandoned child's fancies; by the parents' homosexuality. A cursed or haunted house yarn to spread online. A promise by social services to do better.

They went on more warily, trying to be quiet now that the thing they were pursuing was likely close by, though Vone had no sense of how near the well was, with its weak edges, its precipitate black mouth.

With one last ripping stagger forward they escaped the clutching briars and, quite suddenly, there they were on the edge of the clearing. As if theatrically, the clouds parted to reveal the well waiting in the bright moonlight. Vone could see that something leaving a stain had recently dragged itself to the edge and gone down.

"What do we do?" Jack asked in a husky whisper.

Faking definiteness, though as he gave voice to it his plan seemed to him then simply bad, Vone said, "Pour the kerosene in. Light it. Force her to come up. When she does, I put the axe in her head and you blast her with the shotgun."

"D'you think it'll work?"

Vone shrugged. He had nothing better. The two men set the fuel cans down by the well and knelt to unscrew their lids. The weight of the can Vone had been hauling had almost wrenched his arm from its socket, leaving his left bicep strained and trembling, and no doubt it was the same for Jack. *Weak before we begin.* Unscrewing the rusty lids was cruel to their cold-pinched fingers, but, grunting, they managed it. Side by side they tipped the cans so the kerosene went splashing down into the well, its particular sharp, headache-inducing smell filling their nostrils. *Us getting high as kids,* Vone thought, as if he and Jack had grown up together. *The tin for the motor mower at Uncle Fred's, out in the 'burbs.* The liquid seemed to take forever to glug out, something to do with why you cut two holes in a juice container, he forgot the reason. Pressure or a vacuum or something. Why you had to bleed radiators. Why injecting a bubble of air could stop your heart.

Once it was empty, Jack let his can tumble down the well, and Vone followed suit. They clonked hollowly and there was no splash. Was that the bottom they hit or Her? Maybe she had grown that crucial bit too big to squeeze into the tunnel Vone believed led to the mound; maybe she was stuck down there. If so, good.

A cloud passed in front of the moon, sinking the clearing into darkness; and as if the lunar were solar, the temperature sank by several degrees. Vone took the matchbook from his pants' pocket. Only three of the soft, old paper matches remained. He had had to use three in the cellar before he could get one to light, and that was in air that was, if not particularly dry, at least motionless. Ripping out the first match, fumbling in the dark, forgetting the flashlight and relying on touch alone, he cursed himself for not having thought to pick up the cook's box from the kitchen floor, though to do so might have taken up vital time as he searched for it among the debris.

Luck was with him: the match flared brightly. But even as it did so, there came from alarmingly close by a loud hiss. Jumping up, Vone turned to face its source, twisting oddly as he did so to keep the match still, as if it were fixed in position and he its satellite. The tremulous globe of yellow light revealed Skog Madoo's skull-face level with his own, and she radiated cold like flames of black ice, and her breath stank.

That close, he could study the gougings inflicted by the Owl Lady's talons. The flesh gaped to reveal a meaty mass of structures like kidney tubules, but gray. Like cut brake-cables they dripped dulled quicksilver; and the dark sail of Skog Madoo's hood, rent like a slashed umbrella, was no longer beguilingly iridescent.

Still she was formidable. Vone stared into the black, unseeing but sensate pits of her eyes, if they were, if they had ever been, eyes; and that terrible corkscrew fang flexed like some double-jointed limb, semi-translucent like a bird's quill or a squid's pen, suggestive at that proximity less of a serpent's tooth than some sort of complex insect mouthpart, and he thought of flies and spiders sucking up the flesh their toxins had dissolved.

All that, Vone took in in a heartbeat. With a sour, cold, hissing exhalation the Mother blew out the match, plunging the clearing into darkness, and Vone and Jack yelled aloud in fear and dread. Her icy breath smelt like old brass, and in the blind dark Vone knew it was all hopeless: he was dead, Jack was dead, this was Her terrain, not theirs. Naïve, stupid trespassers; feckless rabbit prey.

The clouds withdrew from the face of the moon and in the sudden silver blaze Vone saw the great serpent form rear back to strike at him. The well mouth was at his back, and to attempt to dart right or left felt futile: she was too fast-moving. Nothing passed before his eyes; there was no time to remember anything, only to gaze up as She rose above him, a muscular gray-black column. And wasn't she the serpent in the Garden of Eden, Satan and Lilith combined, primordial avatar of whatever long-forgotten myths preceded the Babylonian, Assyrian and Sumerian, that birthed the book of Genesis? She came from the Moon, he thought, and it was as if he had caught something that had slipped out unbidden from Her alien mind. *Satellite; bridgehead.* Long ago it had wandered here and was caught by the Earth's gravitational field, and when, in the ellipse of its orbit, it came close, came closest, She
Descended.

Two shotgun blasts, discharged simultaneously, burst the night and broke the moment, and Her mortality was confirmed as chunks of her hood were blown away. And she couldn't, it seemed, see far enough into Jack's mind to understand a shotgun must be reloaded, because she changed the direction of her strike away from Vone and with alarming speed darted towards his husband. Jack was looking down, breaking the breech open, when the flabby, torn hood fell heavily upon his chest, and though Vone couldn't see it, surely She meant to drive her single tooth into Jack's heart.

Jack collapsed like a puppet with cut strings. All Vone could think then was, if they were defeated, if they were dead, maybe he could still burn the egg, her egg, assuming it had been dragged out of Her burrow and lay waiting at the bottom of the well.

Turning away from the serpent and his husband and dropping to his knees, with nerveless fingers he fumbled one of the two remaining matches along the sandpaper strip. It didn't ignite, but the small sound brought the Mother's attention back to him, and she turned whip-fast, hefty and heavy though she was. Glancing round, he saw in the moonlight that she was now more than thirty feet long, and had the strength to lift almost half that length from the ground. Gathering her coils she faced him but didn't strike. Maybe her poison sacs were depleted. Instead she sent chromatic patterns pulsing across what was left of her hood, aiming to control his mind or at least to dazzle him. But the rents in the webbing weakened her power and even as he stared into the face that had never been a face, he managed to drag the match along the sandpaper strip a second time.

It flared into life.

In a moment the flame had burnt the tip of his forefinger and, though it was a small thing, the pain jolted his mind and allowed him to turn away from Her. Quickly he set the match to the tangy wet tongue of kerosene. It caught and the flame streaked off into the darkness. The mouth of the well lit up, a sudden bowl of orange in the blue-black night, a defiant assertion of warmth beneath the frozen stars, and sparks rushed up from it as from a bonfire.

Amazed he hadn't had a fang driven into the back of his neck, Vone crawled quickly round the lip of the well on all fours, wanting to have the blaze between the Mother and himself, and now she was frontlit in flickering amber.

If he had expected some moment of dramatic climax, it didn't come. Weaving her hooded head from side to side she watched him, the firelight dimming her bewitching radiations to faint shimmers. Yet though she no longer had power over his mind, Vone knew it would be futile to try and run: she could dart her head quicker than he could sprint, and if she tossed a muscular loop of her length around him, he was dead. *Eyeballs bursting...*

The flames died down almost at once, birthing slanting spirals of black smoke. At the same time sparks were caught and carried upwards by the breeze, an almost magical effect. They passed among the tree trunks as if in a processional. Some continued to rise and, starved of fuel, winked out among the upper branches; others drifted down to the forest floor. Here and there they connected with the tinder of dry bracken and brightened.

As this was happening, there spread out from the well-mouth a widening web of creeping orange threads, and Vone doubted the rain of a few days ago would be enough to prevent a forest fire beginning. Indeed, blue-gray twists of smoke were already starting to rise up here and there around the clearing as, hesitantly, the Mother moved forward. Axe in hand, Vone moved back, trying to circle round to where Jack lay, though he doubted he could do anything to protect him, and Jack was likely – unbearable thought, pushed away – already dead. But could it be that this cold thing from a cold place was afraid of fire? This creature that had traveled through the vacuum of space, that had then somehow skimmed its way down through the searing friction of the upper atmosphere? She couldn't be harmed by or really fear this little blaze, could she? – though perhaps she had come shielded or in another form – as an egg, maybe, or in a mineral or metal chrysalis.

Making Vone jump back with a yell and fall on his ass, the Mother darted forward and slithered headfirst into the well, plummeting down with the weight and rapidity of a collapsing firehose.

The instant she was out of sight Vone dropped the axe, stumbled over to where Jack lay and knelt beside him. He was staring up at the sky, his breathing was ragged, but he was alive. Vone wriggled his fingers into the rip in Jack's hoodie where the Mother had struck and used both hands to tear it and the tee-shirt beneath it open, baring Jack's chest to the moonlight. Blood spotted black on his pale skin but there was no sign of any mercury, no web of lethal black lines: apparently the creature had used up its supply of venom on Ted and Rory.

"Thank god thank god thank god." Tears of relief stinging his eyes, Vone gathered Jack into his arms. Jack grunted wheezily, and Vone at once laid him back down. Briskly he explored the area around Jack's wound with his fingertips. It was on – or in, or through – his right pectoral.

"I think the fang punctured a lung," he said, trying to sound matter of fact. By chance, a similar thing had happened to a friend of his when they were teenagers – a stabbing following an argument at a house party: literally different worlds, but the same damage, the same danger. Luckily someone had known first aid and his friend had survived. "You've got what they call a sucking wound," Vone went on. "It sounds scary but it doesn't have to be that big of a deal. If you can hold the wound closed and keep the hole blocked by pressing your hands on it you'll be okay till we can get help. Your other lung's still working fine so you can still breathe."

Assuming, that was, that no trace of the Mother's venom was working its way through Jack's body with paralyzing intent. Wasn't that how neurotoxins worked? *The tiniest amount.*

Jack nodded weakly, looking both scared and dazed, and his breathing was shallow: panic, Vone hoped, rather than incipient cardiac arrest. He placed Jack's hands over the wound, pressed down on them gently, then reluctantly let them go. Jack had enough strength to keep them in place. *Good.*

Getting to his feet, Vone went and collected the axe. Leaving Jack alone and defenceless in the woods while he ran back to the house to call an ambulance seemed a potentially deadly blunder with Skog Madoo still in the area, but it was obvious his husband couldn't walk even if supported, and Jack was too heavy for Vone to carry. And with every passing second Vone reckoned She would be rallying in her hole, needing, as he had strongly come to believe, to make a final attempt to seize Jay-

Jay that night. Because she had her cycles, didn't she? Moon-linked cycles of ovulation and fertilization, and so he guessed she couldn't hole up and wait. And tonight was the full moon, and when she came up and found Jack helpless, she would certainly kill him.

Briefly Vone wondered if it would be better to wait for her to re-emerge: to attempt to ambush her and strike the killer blow as he had originally intended. But if he had to wait too long, then Jack would die.

The embers that drifted up from the tiny fires now dotting the forest floor made him think of votive candles; the smoke, of incense. Torn by indecision, he wandered over to the mouth of the well and looked down.

And saw what he hadn't been close enough, or observant enough, to see before: a couple of feet down, bolted into the curving brick, was the top of a narrow iron ladder.

Thirty-One

For better or worse, this was his destiny: to descend into the underworld and battle the monster; return a hero or be bested and die, for his husband, for his son.

Lying flat and facedown, he pulled himself forwards to the edge of the well, trusting that the weight of his legs and hips would counterbalance the upper half of his body as he leaned over, reached down into the dark and felt around for the top of the ladder. The sourness of soil and the sweetness of bruised bracken was in his nostrils. When his fingers found the topmost rung it was rough with rust and clammy. He pulled on it, gently at first, then as hard as he could, half expecting – half hoping – the entire ladder would come away in his hand and drop down into the dark, liberating him from his quest, but it held firm. A few pebbles skittered down around him but triggered no response below, and there was no emanation of unnatural cold. Mamie Place had been right: Skog Madoo had burrowed her way to the well from the mound and now, badly injured, had squirmed her way back there, to lick her wounds, recover her strength and re-emerge.

But why burrow *along* though, and not straight up? Yet that was what she had done. Another puzzle for later.

He wished he had some dynamite to throw down the well, to seal it and with any luck trap her in her lair for years, if not decades or possibly even centuries. But even if he could have done that, the egg would still be waiting, and if not for Jay-Jay, if not for his little boy, then for some other equally undeserving child. And living, Skog Madoo would surely produce more eggs and come hunting for more children. He couldn't turn away, not when there was the possibility, however small, of doing something.

Jamming the axe down the front of his hoodie so its blade hooked over the neckline and the base of its handle jutted into his scrotum, like a gymnast swiveling on a pommel horse, he rotated his body so his legs were sticking out over the void. Slowly he backed out farther, then panicked as his hips slipped over the edge, grabbing at bracken and briars and kicking around to find the topmost rung before his weight pulled him down into the dark. One foot found its purchase, then the other; and he clung there for a long moment, fistfuls of dead undergrowth in both hands, breathing hard, the axe blade shoved up under his jaw, its flat side cold against his larynx, and he had inconveniently to straddle its haft.

Next he had to lean back, let both feet slip down a couple of rungs and, while clutching the thorny stem of a wild rose in one hand, with the other hurriedly feel around for the top rung, knowing as he caught hold of it that he was counting on the ladder not wrenching out of the wall when he put his full weight on it, jerking him off and sending him plunging down.

The roots of the rose tore from the soil like a strip of Velcro. Vone slipped down three more rungs than he had meant to and, holding on with his right hand, swung out over the drop, wrist and ankle pivoting like hinges. With his left leg he kicked out; in his left hand was the rose. He let it fall as with agonizing slowness he swung back into place, allowing him finally to get both hands and both feet on the ladder. It bore his weight solidly. The rungs were narrow, about twelve inches wide, and slick.

There was nothing to do but begin his descent.

He went slowly. The dank air was tainted with the strange, sour animal/non-animal smell of her. At one point he looked up at the moonlit disc of sky. As he did so, the clouds closed like an eyelid and the moonglow was gone and he was sunk in darkness.

His feet reached the lowest rung, which wasn't, to his alarm, the bottom of the well, though the brickwork ended where the ladder did: below it, his toe caps met rough stone: some sort of naturally-occurring fissure. How deep did it go, he wondered, as reluctantly he lowered himself past the ladder's end. His questing toes found cracks and protrusions, but he could tell they were too small to be much help climbing back up. Which meant that if the drop to the bottom was more than his own height with arms outstretched, he would be trapped down there.

He doubted if it came to it that he would have the courage to drop into the dark with no idea of how far he had to fall. Even if it wasn't much of a distance, it would be impossible not to land badly, and he could easily wreck one or both ankles. His arms began to tremble. However, to his relief his feet touched base before he was hanging at full stretch. That meant hauling himself up would be possible, if by no means easy for someone whose arms were already strained. *Afterwards.*

The ground underfoot was dry, granular and impacted. To one side of the space was a heap of grit and gravel. On top of the heap he could just make out two angular objects like large shelf-Ls, and he squatted down to examine them. They were shotguns, and the barrels had been bent upwards, to nearly 45°. Vone thought of the unseen hunters that first time he and Jay-Jay went walking in the woods, and how he hadn't heard shooting on any subsequent day despite it being, as Ted had told them, hunting season.

He felt around for the entrance to the Mother's burrow, expecting it to be where the rock face met the ground. When he didn't find it, he felt his way round again. Still nothing. He felt the beginnings of panic. *Well bottom*, he thought. *Well water.* If she had tunneled through where he'd been feeling around, all the water would have instantly drained into her burrow, flooding it and leaving the well permanently dry. But people had drunk from it, and kept drinking from it over a substantial period of time, and gone mad.

He straightened up and with his hands explored the rock face more generally. Directly above the pile of dirt, logically enough, he found what he was looking for: a way in. Only now did he think to get out the flashlight. If it had stopped working, he couldn't go on: squirming headfirst into the dark in pursuit of something that could see, or at least sense, without light would be suicide. And if her poison sacs were empty for now, her coils could still crush; and even emptied of poison a six-inch fang was as lethal as a six-inch blade, and he would be going face first and entirely unprotected.

The light worked, though its beam was wan, indicating the battery was already failing. He shone it into the waiting hole. The mouth wasn't much wider than his shoulders, and what extended beyond appeared to be a slightly flattened cylinder. It smelled of soil and airlessness. Did the Mother breathe oxygen? He doubted it. A horror of suffocation came over him then. Once he had entered the tunnel it would be hard to back up if he needed to, and what if it got narrower farther along? What if he got stuck, elbows pinned to his sides, face thrust forward, eyes and tongue tempting fleshy morsels? Or what if the tunnel caved in on him, smothering him with a mouthful, then a lungful of choking earth?

But he couldn't abandon the attempt without trying. Like Mamie Place, this task was his to do. Feeling around inside the opening to gauge how firm the soil was, he touched something that was wet and cold in a curious, burning way, like drain un-blocker. Shining the light on his hand, he saw gray-black slime on his fingertips: Her blood; and that gave him heart, because if she was still bleeding the wounds must be deep, rather than ugly but superficial. Assuming, that was, that she had an arterial system like that of animals on Earth. The lights within her cowl had a pulse to them, a rhythm. Some kind of heart, then, pumping within her strangely metallic, mineral body. *Silicon*, he thought suddenly, thinking of the fleshy heaviness of out-size sex toys, and that episode of Star Trek, 'Killer in the Dark'. *A silicon-based life form.* He wiped his hand briskly on his pants.

Just do it.

He shone the light into the opening: the tunnel ran away into the dark, going straight and descending gently. Holding the light in his mouth, hauling the axe out from his hoodie and pushing it in ahead of him, Vone pulled himself headfirst into the tunnel on his elbows. *Okay. We doin' this.* There was just enough room for him to move forward on his hands and knees, though his shoulder blades and spine rubbed against the roof.

To his alarm, just ten feet in, the tunnel began to run down more steeply, tipping him forwards, and he had to fight panic as the axe threatened to slither away from him and vanish be-yond the reach of the light. He was horribly aware that revers-ing up such an incline would be all but impossible even if conditions were favorable. But they weren't: his body took up most of the tunnel's circumference, and what air there was ahead of him was stale and depleted.

To his relief, a little way along the tunnel planed off. *How deep am I now?* He squirmed forward determinedly. The rub-ber handle of the light was already making his lips and jaws ache, and he struggled to swallow around it. He became aware of holes in the rocky soil beneath him, numerous small fissures running who knew how far down, and there rose in him the fear he might come to a pit he would be unable to haul himself across, over which the wormlike Mother could glide with ease. He might find himself unable to go either forward or back. *Lie there and dehydrate to death. Or she swallows me headfirst, gets past me by stretching her mouth, her gut around me, carries me up backwards, crushed narrow inside her. Suffocation inside suffocation. Then she shits me out and goes on her way.*

How far was it between the well-mouth and the mound? Half a mile, he had reckoned the day they climbed it, though perhaps She had had to take a more circuitous route, which would add considerably to the tunnel's length. He'd read in a moment of fleeting preparation for the move that upstate Maine was composed primarily of granite, and that Kwawidokawa County was a plateau shaped like a shallow stone dish. Maybe She had had to struggle along beneath that dish, pushing herself through whatever grit-filled gaps she could find between the buried slabs and boulders, perpetually seeking and never finding a fissure leading upwards. Turning this way and that in the stone-dense mud, dead-ending repeatedly and having to double back again and again during her long years of burrowing in the airless dark before finally chancing on the bottom of the well, and liberation. In which case Vone was as much in danger of becoming lost as an archaeologist who finds himself in some labyrinth of unknown size and design, and then the light goes out.

He wondered how long he could keep going. His lungs already felt seared, as if he'd gone out in a polar vortex with nothing covering his mouth, his face was stiffening and his fingers and toes were painfully numb. He thought of documentaries he had seen about frostbite: the blood thickening, the circulation failing in your extremities; blackening then putrefying fingers and toes – though at the same time as that, he was sweating heavily from the work of heaving himself along. He shifted his aching jaw to keep the light beam angled down, though surely she wouldn't expect this: the battle brought to her. He longed to spit out the light and yell aloud, to dispel a little of the tension building so wildly within him; to shrink his lungs and ribcage and thereby marginally ease his passage. And he thought of Jack and his punctured lung and sunken chest, unable to do anything but lie there and be afraid, for Vone, for himself, for their son, and hauled himself forward with renewed determination.

As he did so, however, Vone had to face a new fact. Though the tunnel now ran fairly much straight and level, even if there was somehow nothing to do at the end of it, and She just lay there bled out and dead, he had come too far and was too exhausted to even attempt to shove himself backwards all the way back to the now-distant well-bottom. His only hope was that there would be some space under the mound where he could turn, and not just a tube-shaped coffin of whatever size She had been when the Red Paint people buried her.

Though the soil above his head was impacted to rocklike hardness, it was also granular, and particles of it speckled in his eyes, making him blink and wince, and got into his mouth, coating his parched tongue; and the feeling of suffocation intensified as, going ever more slowly, he dragged himself laboriously along.

The tunnel widened, but, ominously, grew flatter, as if he were now passing beneath the underside of the granite dish, and its roof pressed down on him with an oppressiveness all its own. After he couldn't tell how long, maybe fifty or a hundred feet, it began to rise again, but though that felt hopeful, the upward curve was steep enough to force him to arch his back, stretch out his spine, and with arms and legs splayed like a face-down newborn, claw with his fingers, hook with his elbows and push with his outspread knees and toes, all the while craning his neck painfully with the flashlight in his mouth and shoving the axe ahead of him. He wondered if he had somehow taken a wrong turn, though he was sure he hadn't passed any holes bigger than a man's arm. But perhaps She could compress herself bonelessly, or pour through small openings: he recalled the finger of mercury he had glimpsed withdrawing itself under their bedroom chimney-guard, and what Mamie Place had seen that night from the mound: a stream of quicksilver. What, after all, was Her true form? Yet there had been the skin in the woods. The crushed and then regurgitated possums. The undoubted physicality of her single, puncturing fang. The rents in her flesh and her sour gray blood.

His jaws too tired to keep the flashlight angled upwards, Vone let its light pool uselessly on his forearms. As a consequence, he became aware of a gray pallor up ahead that at first he thought an optical illusion. He fumbled off the flashlight, closed his eyes for a count of ten, then opened them again. It was still there: somehow there was a light source up ahead. *Journey's end.* He made more of an effort to control his breathing, to not grunt aloud with each forward heave of his body. *She won't be expecting this: don't blow it now.*

Thirty feet farther on, he found himself nearing the end of the tunnel, a palely glowing oval that seemed to pulse slightly. Warily and wearily he pulled himself forward the last few feet, lifting his heaving chest and trembling stomach over the length of the axe, so it wouldn't protrude into the space in front of him and potentially catch the eye of what waited there, and lose him his small advantage.

His weapon now pinned beneath him, in that strange moment he was the inversion of an effigy of a medieval knight on a tomb.

Shifting about, with his left hand he managed to jam the flashlight into a pants' pocket. This worsened his position overall, however, because it meant his left arm was now pressed against the side of his body while the right was folded and pinned under his chest, the spread fingers of his right hand trapped beneath his breastbone. No way of using the axe, no way of shielding his face from attack, no way back. Anything would have been smarter than this. Like an ossifying caterpillar, he eased himself up to the mouth at the tunnel's end.

He found himself looking into an egg-shaped chamber roughly thirty feet across, and maybe forty long, and the tunnel mouth came out where you would prick an egg for boiling, eight feet or so above the curving floor. The walls and ceiling – not that there was any structural differentiation – were plastered in ocherous clay, and dense with pictograms in pitch and whitewash – illustrations that told, perhaps, the tale of the Red Paint People and the coming of the Mother of Serpents;

of the battle that brought her to this prison. Amongst the pictograms were bands of incised patterns that looked like hieroglyphs, and were, maybe, the words of the spells that had bound her, in which the Red Paint People had believed, and so She had believed them too.

Or rather, the spells that used to bind her. But three thousand years had passed, the Red Paint People were gone to the happy hunting grounds, and she had escaped, *Good God almighty, free at last*, and thought herself unbounded.

And then, by chance or fate, She had encountered a distant descendant of one of those who knew about her, once upon a time. And though Mamie Place could not properly remember the spells and words; could not return Her to the mound, she could confine her within a range, and attempt to keep the others on which she needed to feed outside it.

And if Mamie had failed, now he, DuVone Mapley-Stevenson, husband and father and forgotten descendant of shamans, was here, to make the ending the tumor in her stomach had prevented her from making, and he was spirit kin and kind, and yes, it might be possible.

The belly of the chamber was strewn with the regurgitated, cylindrically crushed skeletons of many animals: several deer, perhaps a young bear, a small moose, wildcats and of course every sort of smaller mammal; many birds; and what were surely the narrow remains of two human beings. Vone thought again of the rifles at the bottom of the well with their bent barrels. A sour tang like bile hung in the breathless air.

Vone could see what he saw because the chamber was lit by a pale effulgence, the source of which sat upright at its center, in a nest of heaped bones: a silver-gray egg. Six feet high and four across, it was without texture, and the light that came from within it rendered it translucent. Around that light, the light perhaps of distant suns or long-dead, mirroring moons, a serpent embryo squirmed. It was quicksilver bright and its skull-face was visibly a copy of its mother's. At that stage of its development it was just a little smaller than a human being's; and through the pellucid shell Vone thought he saw a fang flex. When it emerged it would be between six and eight feet long, he reckoned: large enough to be extremely dangerous.

Coiled loosely and lumpily around the radiant egg was the

Mother. Her back was to Vone and her raised head moved slightly from side to side, a dance to soothe a child, maybe. Her tattered hood flared out dully. As Vone watched, she began to hiss, softly at first, modulating the sound as it grew louder to produce a sibilant melody, a maternal crooning remote as the stars, eerie and almost beautiful.

What was she planning to do, he wondered. Would she try, when she had recovered enough, to drag the egg down the tunnel, through the woods and to their house, the one house within her permitted territory? Whatever the mechanism of psychic transference was, the victim needed to be close by for it to work or else it would already have happened: Jay-Jay's face would be on her rattle forever, his real head reduced to little more than a featureless bud of flesh, retaining only, perhaps a brainless, sucking mouth.

But the egg was large and the shell appeared rigid: it wouldn't, he thought, fit down the tunnel. Perhaps She would let it hatch out and shepherd the bright silver newborn along in the dark, like the stream of mercury Mamie Place saw after falling asleep on the mound that midsummer night, making its way purposefully through the woods. Hurrying. Because if it didn't get a soul to feed on in time, it would die. *She can't do nothing, then. Can't just leave it and sneak on back to kill.*

Vone looked around for a way to get down from the tunnel-mouth. Pulling himself out of it headfirst only to fall on his face amidst a tangle of bones would be suicide, but there wasn't enough room for him to turn and lead with his feet. Jay-Jay had almost been a breech birth, he remembered. Forceps in Ellie's womb had managed to turn him while Vone and Jack waited outside, helpless, fearful, chivvied away by the nurse. *You don't want to see this*, she said.

Looking up, he saw that there was in the center of the chamber's curving roof a protuberance like a stalactite: a blunt stone cone pointing downwards. Its surface was decorated with many brown and red markings, and Vone thought *spike, plug, volcanic plug, decanter* and then: *oubliette*. The Red Paint people had, it seemed, found a hole in the granite saucer that underlay Kwawidokawa County. They had dug out a chamber beneath it, sealed its walls with spells, dropped the captured creature in, and afterwards sealed the one physical way out with a great stone spike. This spike, chanted over, enchanted. *Why she had to go out sideways.*

Much later he would reflect on a detail he had noticed but at the time not understood: though much of it had dropped out over the years, around the spike dull orange clay had filled the join where it met the ceiling. That could only mean that someone, or several someones, had been buried alive with the creature, to seal and complete the prison. Presumably it had been tied up, allowing them to carry out their final task. And presumably their bones lay brown and brittle beneath the other, more recent skeletons.

Despite the care they had taken, Vone saw that over the millennia small roots had managed to force their way down through the join and spread out weblike across the roof, belonging perhaps to the predecessors of the ancient pines atop the mound. Their incursion had been in some way cauterized, but had left a tangled mesh of dead growth like partially-burnt hair at some delinquent beauty parlor.

Keeping his eyes on the Mother's gently weaving, solicitously inclined head, Vone managed – with considerable difficulty, and a painful wrenching about of his left shoulder – to get his left arm free from where it had been pinned alongside his body, twisting it round under him and pushing it forwards so it stuck out in front of him, jutting into the space of the chamber like the handle of a broomstick. His right arm remained pinned under his chest.

Vone reached up with his left hand, groping around awkwardly, and with an effort caught at the hanging root mesh. A little soil slipped down as he took hold of it, falling close to, but not on, one of the Mother's great leaden coils. Several rootlets tore out as he pulled on them, but as a mass the mesh held firm, at least firm enough for him to be able to –

Vone let go of the roots and, using knees and toes, pushed himself farther out into the chamber. Now, as well as his extended left arm, his head, shoulders and chest were clear of the mouth of the burrow. *Like being born.* Arching his back, he managed to wriggle his right arm free from under him and thrust it out next to the left. Awkwardly he reached up and with both hands took hold of as large a clump of roots as he could. The clumps held, and with a barely suppressed grunt he hauled himself forward so half his body was free of the tunnel. His biceps and the small of his back burned as he hung suspended facedown like a human hammock, so far unnoticed.

It would all have to be done together, he could see: he would have to pull himself forward and let the axe fall to the floor as he did so. Holding onto the roots, he would have to drag his legs free of the tunnel mouth and in one move drop down, land without wrecking one or both ankles, snatch up the axe and strike.

All his hope – his small hope – lay in speed.

Nothing in his life had in any way prepared him for this. He hadn't even thrown a punch since he was fifteen. He had done a couple of self-defense classes after a spate of queer-bashings in Brooklyn, but that was over a decade ago, he didn't remember much of it, and it wouldn't be any use here anyway. He had used an axe on firewood, but to the disdain of his country cousins had never killed a chicken: the harshness of life in the big city had shown itself in other, mostly psychological ways. But fuck it, didn't that make him tough? Didn't surviving shit make you tough?

With a growling grunt he hauled himself out of the tunnel mouth, fast.

Thirty-Two

T he axe slid forward with him, tumbling down onto the carpet of bones with a clatter as Vone heaved himself out of the tunnel mouth. For a long moment he hung there, the web of roots he clutched with cold-numbed fingers tearing away from the roof, but he needed to drop at once anyway, not hang there like a target for bayonet practice. He landed clumsily – buried beneath the litter of bones, the floor of the chamber was more curved than he had realized – and sank into an off-balance crouch amidst heaped femurs, cracked pelvises and grotesquely compressed ribcages. Grabbing the axe, he raised it, and with a yell and a ferocity he would have believed himself incapable of before that night, stepped forward and up onto one of her great coils, and drove the blade deep into the back of the Mother's head.

She jerked forward, wrenching the embedded axe from Vone's grip, tearing his shoulder muscles painfully, almost dislocating his arms, and flailed and twisted wildly in panic, her rattle vibrating frenziedly. Vone threw himself back to try and avoid her thrashing coils, though there was nowhere in that confined space that was away from her. All he could do was turn sideways like an illustration from an Egyptian papyrus, crouch down, press himself against the curving wall and watch as dull mercury gouted steaming from the gaping gash in the back of Her cartilaginous head, welling up around the axe blade, which she tried, but was unable to flick loose.

And then, quite suddenly, it was over: she collapsed and lay still. The hissing and rattling ceased. Unable to believe that she was really dead, and dreading some final subterfuge *like in every horror movie ever* he waited for what seemed a long time, watching warily until he was sure the coils really were as immobile as if they had been cast in lead. Still doubting, though he knew she had breathed, or at least respired, with the tips of his fingers he pushed at the scaly gray skin of the nearest coil. It was unyielding, solid as a fossil. Already it was hard for him to believe that she had ever moved.

He could only see all this, of course, because the room was

still lit. Untouched by the Mother's thrashings, protected by her even in her dying, the egg stood on its dais of bones, coldly effulgent, correctly upright. Its tenant was unmoving now, sensing that something disastrous to its future wellbeing had happened in the as-yet unknown world beyond the shell.

Vone knew that some animals emerge into our world instantly venomous – the tiny but lethal blue-ringed octopus sprung into his mind, legacy of an aunt's collection of *National Geographic*s – and he didn't doubt this thing was like that. But he wasn't afraid of it now. Almost with a swagger he approached the face-down head of the Mother of Serpents, placed a foot at the base of her skull and with a grunt wrenched the blade free. Coolly he approached the egg.

Silvery stria began to radiate across its surface: an infant attempt at mesmerism that, undeveloped though it was, already had the power to pull at Vone's mind – a defense mechanism, evolved to render a threatening presence passive. Squinting to mute the effect, Vone hacked into the shell. His first blow bounced off the leathery surface, but the second cut into it, and after a third and fourth blow some inner membrane must have torn, because a clear, steaming liquid with a toxic reek began to pour out through the gashes, and the shell started to collapse in on itself. The serpent within, seven feet long and muscular, tiny only in comparison to its mother, was caught by the partially stoved-in casing, pinned and unable to get itself free. Vone began to hack into it too, randomly along its squirming length, not stopping until he had chopped it into four separate pieces within the wreckage of the now split-open shell. Using the axe blade he levered the pieces free from the egg casing, then kicked the lifeless, silver-gray lumps of flesh this way and that among the distorted skeletons that littered the chamber floor, yelling, "Done! Done! Done!"

Even as he did this, he felt his vision dimming: the moment he cut into the egg the light in the burial chamber had begun to die. Evidently the product of some sort of bioluminescence, it failed when the life animating it failed, and the chamber was now sinking rapidly into darkness. Vone pulled out his light and clicked it on, but the bulb had broken when he fell. Escape would be impossible without light, he knew: he would struggle to find the mouth of the tunnel, never mind pull himself up into it and crawl away wholly blind. *I don't wanna die down here.*

He picked up the axe and once more hacked at Skog Madoo, amputating a small part of her to be his trophy, his proof. Then he hurried over to the curve of wall directly below the entrance to the tunnel. As he did so, he noticed fleetingly that the painted symbols had at that point been entirely worn away – by time or condensation or the rubbing round and round of Her restless coils – and later came to believe that that might have been why she had been able to burrow out of her prison at that particular point.

There was very little light now. He lobbed his trophy up into the tunnel mouth, threw the axe down, and on a tiptoe so extreme it compressed his calves painfully, reached up with aching, outstretched arms. He found himself able to grip the lip of the tunnel and tried to haul himself up, but it crumbled and he fell back among the bones. In rising panic he tried again and fell again, knowing as he did so that each attempt used up more of his little remaining strength. The tendons in his wrists and fingers were increasingly weak and strained, and the last of the light was almost gone.

Looking round for something he could stand on, he saw the axe. Snatching it up, he hacked the blade sideways into the curving wall two feet or so from the floor. It dug in and stayed there: a step, a rung. Maybe.

He moved as far back as the Mother's great leaden coils permitted, ran forward, bouncing erratically among the bones, set his right foot on the flat of the partially-embedded blade, and managed to propel himself upwards in a leap that enabled him to get both his arms into the hole-mouth past the elbow, at the same time thrusting his head forward so the top of his skull didn't hit the roof, concuss him and send him tumbling back.

He hung there a moment, arms extended, shoulders wrenched, elbows jarred, hips and legs hanging limp, still in danger of backsliding, his chest heaving. Then, triceps and lats burning, he hauled first his ribcage, then his gut, then his hips and bruised and aching balls onto the ledge.

Behind him, the light died entirely.

There was nothing for him to do but crawl forward in the

now-total darkness, praying as he did so that there were no divisions ahead; no misleading forks or side-tunnels. He remembered none crawling in, or none of enough size to deceive him, but trusted neither the environment nor his own senses. After a while he closed his eyes against the oppressive dark, grunting or shouting aloud with every forward heave: there was no longer any need for quiet. And ahead of him he shoved the thing he had cut from Skog Madoo.

On and on he squirmed, for how long he had no idea. And then, unexpectedly, his fingers touched what seemed a sort of fin of stone in the middle of the tunnel. Perplexed, he felt about on either side of it. It was what he had dreaded: there *was* a substantial division in the tunnel. *Shit shit shit.* Panic surged through him, and it took him several long minutes to regain control of both his breathing and his thoughts.

I came down this tunnel. Are both branches wide enough for me to go back up? If one's too narrow, then that's not the way out. Simple.

He felt about. Each was just wide enough for him to squeeze along.

Air – stale air. If one's a dead end the air'll be no good.

He inhaled as deeply as he could, to the right then to the left, but could detect no difference. The lefthand fork ran slightly upwards, the right slightly down. Wasn't up good? But wouldn't She always have been trying to go up? How many dead ends had she pursued in her random breathless tunnelings before she happened upon the well? He felt about some more, for what he didn't know, inspiration perhaps, and his fingertips touched something small and soft. He recalled then that he had one match left. He struck it, and it caught.

The thing was a feather, the pinion feather of an owl, and it lay in the entrance to the descending fork. He reached up and touched the back of his head: no feather: it must have tugged itself out as he crawled along on his way in. For the first time allowing himself to think of Jack and Jay-Jay, he took the descending fork, worming his way forwards as fast as he could, scraping elbows and forearms, bruising chest and knees and belly.

To his relief he came to no other forks, and after what seemed like hours or days or nights was hauling himself out of the end of the tunnel and tumbling down onto the heap of grit beneath it at the bottom of the well.

He drew the cold night air into his lungs, and as he did so he looked up at the charcoal-gray disc of moonless sky and felt both empty and more alive than he had ever been. Something cold and soft landed on his upturned face, then another something, and he realized it was snowing. He stuck out his aching tongue and thought of tales of time lost in fairy mounds and wondered how long he had been gone.

He sat for a while at the bottom of the well, resting his aching limbs, then, damp-assed and feeling his muscles start to seize up, got to his feet. The lowest rung of the ladder was within reach when he stretched up his arms, and, after the difficult initial business of hauling himself onto it, which took most of his remaining strength, the rest of the climb was easy – though getting from the top of the ladder onto the ground surrounding the well was as alarming as climbing down had been, requiring a surging leap and wild clutching at stalks and stems that came perilously close to dropping him back into the neck-breaking dark. But he managed to grab hold of a knot of dried bracken that was solidly rooted, haul one knee up and round, then quickly squirm enough of his bodyweight round after it to be safe from sliding down again. He rolled over so he was safely away from the well mouth and lay on his back, heaving for breath, and the snowflakes kissed his face like ghost butterflies.

The snow began to fall more thickly, and the air had the sour tang of woodsmoke. Turning his head, Vone saw that the small fires the floating cinders had started earlier had grown into quite a widespread blaze while he'd been underground – though with a scattered handful of winking orange exceptions, tamped down by the snow, these no longer burned but smoldered, sending up columns of smoke that showed gray against the darker gray of the snow-clouded sky.

Now Vone looked around for Jack. He was lying on his back exactly where Vone had left him, and not moving. Weary and dreading, Vone rolled onto his front, and on his hands and knees crawled over to his husband. Mercifully, none of the little trails of fire had reached him before the snow smothered them, and though Jack's eyes were closed, Vone saw him swallow. His chest was rising and falling, and, though limp, his hands still covered the wound in his chest.

Vone hauled himself alongside Jack and snuggled into him, kissing his cold cheek and saying, "It's done. We're safe. Jay-Jay's safe." Jack didn't respond in words, but Vone took his sudden, racking cough as an acknowledgment. He kept his trophy bundled up under his hoodie, bulky as two partly deflated basketballs or a monstrously metastasized tumor. Time hung gauzily and the falling snow was wholly silent.

Then nearby there came the sound of something crashing around clumsily. With a groan Vone rolled onto his back, too exhausted to do anything more than watch what was coming – bear, cougar, whatever it turned out She hadn't got around to eating after all. Instead, through the drifting curtain of snow, he saw powerful beams of light stabbing about among the tree trunks. "Here," he called weakly, making a feeble gesture. "Help."

The beams turned towards his voice, converging on him and Jack dazzlingly, and as the men came forward, running heavily, Vone saw the fluorescently banded tabards of fire fighters.

And Vone and Jack were wrapped in silver blankets and a paramedic attended to Jack's wound, a light-skinned young brother, and in that surely there was the hope of safety. Vone nodded to him weakly but found himself unable to speak, poisoned perhaps by his exposure to the mercury or other extraterrestrial elements in the Mother's smoking blood, or maybe simply sickened by the woodsmoke. Stretcher bearers arrived, and as they lifted Jack onto one Vone tried to stand, wanting to walk alongside him as he was carried, but couldn't. So they strapped him onto a stretcher too, looking grossly pregnant with his trophy shoved up inside his hoodie, and the two of them were jolted through the damp, dark woods, back to the house. Along the way, the snow ceased to fall.

As they were brought around the side of the house, Vone saw that the bodies of Ted and Rory had been removed – placed, he supposed, in one of a pair of ambulances that waited in the street, the one with its doors closed and its flashing lights turned off. Pulled up alongside it was the police cruiser. Vone felt nothing: what would be would be.

And finally the neighbors were out: all of them, it seemed; men, women and children, watching in silence from every house in Cottonwood Way but one, some on their porches, some on their front steps, others gathered on the perfect, snow-covered asphalt, in robes or pajamas, dazed witnesses to this longed-for and unexpected release, their faces more than anything simply tired.

Fumbling at his straps and waving off the paramedic's attempt to assist him, Vone struggled up from his stretcher and got to his feet, and Jack watched as Vone drew out from under his hoodie the thing he had hacked from the Mother of Serpents at the last. It was the tip of her rattle, the last two spheres. He raised the gristly thing aloft and all who saw it agreed yes, the final bone *did* look like the two men's son; and those who remembered swore later that the globe adjoining it was the spit of Tommy Dyer, who died so queerly back in '86.

Once he was sure all had seen, and suddenly so dizzy he doubted he could continue to stand, Vone shouted, "It's done!" and dropped the rattle. Then, looking about him wildly, he called, "Jay-Jay? Son?" and Jay-Jay, breaking free from a uniformed policewoman nearby, came running over to him. Vone sank to his knees on the snowy front lawn and hugged Jay-Jay and wept, and Jack smiled weakly and reached out, and the stretcher bearers brought him close enough so he could take hold of his son's hand.

"Safe," Vone said, smiling through his tears. "We're safe."

And he straightened up, and hand in hand, he and Jay-Jay watched as the paramedics carried Jack to the ambulance and lifted him in, and the white, clinical light of its interior projected him back into the modern, earthly world as the blue-gloved paramedic deftly inserted an IV, connected a saline drip and attached adhesive monitor pads to Jack's chest. Vone heard a murmured question about insurance, and was thankful Jack's new job provided it, sparing him – all of them – a grotesquely ironic coda; and he and Jay-Jay stood by quietly, waiting for the invitation to accompany Jack on the ride to the emergency room in Collington-Osprey.

And it seemed that somehow all was known, because the cops who'd threatened him and Jay-Jay, and then him and

Jack, and who stood there now with their hands on their hips, looking on as ever impassively, didn't bustle forward to arrest Vone, or cuff his husband to the gurney, for the slaying of Ted and Rory Cutler.

That night they became locals.

Epilogue

That night they became locals, though for DuVone the price he and his family paid was grotesquely emblematic of the price Black people must always pay to be permitted to live in a world that claims to be white. Because this was what it took to earn a forefinger touched to the brim of the cap of the white cop patrolling the neighborhood; to have the neighbors drop by to introduce themselves and bring gifts of home-baked cakes and cookies, and produce and cuttings from their gardens.

Still the white women joggers of the Vicinity blanked him. But now the white women of Cottonwood Way shook their heads collusively, keen to show how modern they were – how more truly modern than the incomers, the trippers: how woke; how awakened. And it wasn't fair, and it was what it was.

And he and Jack and Jay-Jay did make a home there. They made an offer on Number 13 the following spring, and it was accepted.

Mamie Place's things were packed away carefully and stored in crates in the attic, and the front parlor became a family room, scattered with a boy's toys, and they had the chimney swept and lit fires on days when it was cold. The secret basement room was left as it was, but the door was boarded up and plastered over and the shelves were reinstated. Vone and Jack put their own pictures on the parlor walls. Ted and Rory's home was sold, and those who remembered, remembered them kindly, for it was they who had been the sacrifice.

The following midsummer's day, Vone, Jack and Jay-Jay picnicked on top of the old burial mound. The sky was blue and cloudless, the short grass bright with daisies, and the branches of the pines creaked gently above them in a welcome breeze. There was no patch of frost among their roots, and their boughs were heavy with new, bright green cones. And if Vone was the guardian of this place, he was not compelled to be, and knew he could leave when he chose. Jack and Jay-Jay watched as he poured a splash of beer on the ground for Mamie Place. Then Vone and Jack clinked bottles, and there was a rise of birdsong.

The End

About the Author

John R Gordon lives and works in London, England. He is a screenwriter, playwright and the author of nine novels, *Black Butterflies*, (GMP 1993), for which he won a New London Writers' Award; *Skin Deep*, (GMP 1997) and *Warriors & Outlaws* (Millivres 2001), both of which have been taught on graduate and post-graduate courses on Race & Sexuality in Literature in the USA; *Faggamuffin* (Team Angelica 2012); *Colour Scheme* (Team Angelica 2013); *Souljah* (Team Angelica 2015). His historical epic of same-sex love in slavery times, *Drapetomania* (Team Angelica 2018) won the prestigious Ferro-Grumley Award for Best LGBTQ Fiction. His eighth novel was the Young Adult interracial romance *Hark*.

John script-edits, executive produces and writes for the world's first Black gay television show, Patrik-Ian Polk's *Noah's Arc* (Logo/Viacom, 2005-6 and ongoingly). In 2007 he wrote the autobiography of America's most famous Black gay pornstar from taped interviews he conducted, *My Life in Porn: the Bobby Blake Story* (Perseus 2008). In 2008 he co-wrote the screenplay for the *Noah's Arc* feature-film, *Jumping the Broom* (Logo/Viacom) for which he received an NAACP Image Award nomination; the film won the GLAAD Best (Limited Release) Feature Award. That same year his short film *Souljah* (directed by Rikki Beadle-Blair) won the Soho Rushes Award for Best Film, among others. He is also the creator of the *Yemi & Femi* comic, for adult readers, and their theatrical spin-offs.

As well as mentoring, dramaturging and otherwise encouraging young LGBTQ+ and racially diverse writers, John paints, cartoons and does film and theatre design.

www.johnrgordon.com

Also available from Team Angelica Publishing

Prose

'Reasons to Live' by Rikki Beadle-Blair
'What I Learned Today' by Rikki Beadle-Blair
'Faggamuffin' by John R Gordon
'Colour Scheme' by John R Gordon
'Souljah' by John R Gordon
'Drapetomania' by John R Gordon
'Hark' by John R Gordon
'Fairytales for Lost Children' by Diriye Osman
'Cuentos Para Niños Perdidos' – Spanish language edition of 'Fairytales For
            Lost Children', trans. Héctor F. Santiago
'The Butterfly Jungle' by Diriye Osman
'Black & Gay in the UK' ed. John R Gordon & Rikki Beadle-Blair
'Sista!' ed. Phyll Opoku-Gyimah, John R Gordon & Rikki Beadle-Blair
'More Than – the Person Behind the Label' ed. Gemma Van Praagh
'Tiny Pieces of Skull' by Roz Kaveney
'Fimí sílẹ̀ Forever' by Nnanna Ikpo
'Lives of Great Men' by Chike Frankie Edozien
'Lord of the Senses' by Vikram Kolmannskog
'Movies That Made Me Gay' by Larry Duplechan

Playtexts

'Slap' by Alexis Gregory
'Custody' by Tom Wainwright
'#Hashtag Lightie' by Lynette Linton
'Summer in London' by Rikki Beadle-Blair
'I AM [NOT] KANYE WEST' by Natasha Brown
'Fierce' – a monologue anthology ed. Rikki Beadle-Blair
'Common' – a monologue anthology ed. Rikki Beadle-Blair
'Lit' – a monologue anthology ed. Rikki Beadle-Blair
'BI-TOPIA' by Sam Danson

Poetry

'Charred' by Andreena Leeanne

'Saturn Returns' by Sonny Nwachukwu

'Selected Poems 2009-2021' by Roz Kaveney

'The Great Good Time' by Roz Kaveney

'Perfect.Scar' by Robert Chevara

Milton Keynes UK
Ingram Content Group UK Ltd.
UKHW030623250924
448780UK00004B/59